# SCARECROW

## A Crow's Row Love Story

Julie Hockley

iUniverse LLC
Bloomington

**Scare Crow**
A Crow's Row Love Story

*Copyright © 2014 Julie Hockley.*

*All rights reserved. No part of this book may be used or reproduced by any means, graphic, electronic, or mechanical, including photocopying, recording, taping or by any information storage retrieval system without the written permission of the publisher except in the case of brief quotations embodied in critical articles and reviews.*

*iUniverse books may be ordered through booksellers or by contacting:*

*iUniverse*
*1663 Liberty Drive*
*Bloomington, IN 47403*
*www.iuniverse.com*
*1-800-Authors (1-800-288-4677)*

*Because of the dynamic nature of the Internet, any web addresses or links contained in this book may have changed since publication and may no longer be valid. The views expressed in this work are solely those of the author and do not necessarily reflect the views of the publisher, and the publisher hereby disclaims any responsibility for them.*

*Any people depicted in stock imagery provided by Thinkstock are models, and such images are being used for illustrative purposes only. Certain stock imagery © Thinkstock.*

*ISBN: 978-1-4917-2615-0 (sc)*
*ISBN: 978-1-4917-2655-6 (hc)*
*ISBN: 978-1-4917-2616-7 (e)*

*Printed in the United States of America.*

*iUniverse rev. date: 3/24/2014*

*To my two smart, strong, beautiful babies, G and M.
Remember, broken hearts will heal.
And to anyone who breaks my babies' hearts, run.*

And these children that you spit on
As they try to change their worlds
Are immune to your consultations
They're quite aware of what they're going through.

—"Changes," song by David Bowie

# Prologue

*Watch the whales from your backyard!*

Emmy—my Emmy—was in a tiny bikini, lying on the sand with a book leaning against her knee.

*A spectacular opportunity to own this pristine piece of heaven. Enjoy this quaint little island of just over five acres of unexplored terrain surrounded by sandy shoreline.*

There was a mountain of greenery behind her that looked like an elephant's rump. Our shack was somewhere in the depths of our jungle. But only we knew it was there. It had a tin roof. Emmy loved to hear the clack of the rain against the metal. So did I.

*This island offers a serene and remote setting, where you can be at one with nature and forget about the rest of the world.*

I was standing in the water, hip deep in the ocean, facing the shore. The waves crashed against my backside, and I watched her, wishing this moment would last forever, noticing that the ocean water was almost touching her toes, resisting the urge to disturb her.

*Just a twenty-minute helicopter ride from Bora Bora International Airport ...*

Then again, life was short. I fought the current and found my rightful place on top of her. Bathing suits were for the rest of the free world. Not for us.

# Chapter One: Emily

## Omen

When the strap of my bra snapped, fanned out like a goose taking flight, and took a bend in the road just so it could whack me in the face, I knew it was a bad omen. Getting dressed had seemed like a necessary step. Not a step forward or a step backward. Just a step. At least it was something. Better than just sitting there. Better than waiting for something to happen.

But I had to admit—the sting of the strap against my cheek had felt almost enlivening.

I stared at my face in the plate-sized mirror of my bedroom wall, floating my fingers over the strap-length redness on my cheek. And I decided, to a 99 percent certainty, that the pleasure of physical pain didn't mean that I had been reduced to masochism. After weeks of having the emotional quotient of a rock, feeling something, feeling anything, was better than the numbness that had engulfed me.

Though I did wish that my human need to feel hadn't left yet another blemish on my cheek.

The other bruises and cuts, the ones that Victor had left behind, were just a pale pink now—easily concealed with a touch of foundation. I supposed that the newest addition to the facial collection was a reminder that, no matter what I tried, big or small—even getting dressed—I would never be quite the same again.

I realized how bad of an omen the breaking of my bra strap was when I remembered that this was my one and only bra. The other one had already been eaten by the demonically possessed washing machine at the Laundromat.

I sighed, pulled myself away from the reflection in the mirror, and tied a knot to hold what was left together.

Meatball was hiding under my bed, where I longed to be. He had adjusted pretty quickly to our new existence—like moving in with me was just a vacation, a change of scenery. Within minutes of Carly dropping him off, he strolled around the place like he was renting it—sniffing everything, leaving his scent in creative places, like my roommate's bedpost. He wagged his tail, he jumped around, he begged to go out to run and play. To him, nothing was different other than the setting. It was as if nothing were wrong, as if Cameron were coming back. There were days when I envied him for his ability to forget so quickly. But sometimes I felt like he was a traitor. Cameron was something we had once shared, but only I was left with the pain of his memory.

I couldn't even think of Cameron's name without my breath being cut short, feeling like I was going to throw up. Cameron's face colored my every thought, like everything I was seeing and feeling was through the veil of his beautiful face—like I was looking out through a window, and Cameron was my windowpane. It was excruciating.

If it hadn't been for Meatball, I would have never left the house or the couch. I would have never gone to the supermarket to buy dog and people food; Meatball refused to eat anything unless I joined him. If it weren't for him, I would have never gone to the supermarket to buy food, only to be stopped at the cash register because my card rang insufficient funds. Meatball's needs, Meatball's life, Meatball had kept me alive for the last few weeks.

I was officially broke.

I hadn't been to work since May, since I had been taken from my lackluster life and thrust into the underworld—Cameron's world. This was the world where I had longed to be so that I could stay with Cameron. Now I belonged nowhere.

After missing work for over three months, I had lost my job, though my salary had stopped coming into my bank account only a few weeks ago. The fact that it took so long for the school to figure out that Emily Sheppard, a once-dedicated student employee, wasn't showing up for work every day would have normally hurt my feelings. Nowadays I was indifferent to this.

While I was getting dressed, my dog—it was still hard for me to call him "my" dog—remained sulking under the bed. My bed was still the same. Still stilted on top of the milk crates I had stolen last year from the darkened parking lot of the corner store. After Meatball had spent his first night in his new house endlessly pacing around me, I had pulled my stuff out from under my bed so that he would have a space of his own, one that was—and would forever be—within my space.

And the burrow under my stilted bed was where Meatball had plastered himself ever since my roommates had started filtering back a few days ago. He had grown too comfortable with our seclusion. Now we were being interrupted, overwhelmed.

I had expected Spider's and Victor's minions to burst through the door, realizing what a liability I was. While Cameron had never shared too many details with me, I knew enough about them and their criminal enterprise to cause major problems.

But Meatball and I had been left alone for weeks. And before we knew it, my roommates had started coming back, like everything was normal. Normal had never been my thing, and I wasn't about to start now. Everything had changed. I had changed. Maybe Spider and Victor didn't see me as a threat. I was just a girl, right? Little Emily Sheppard, nineteen years old, sheltered by the Fortune 500 Sheppard family, could never be a threat to the underworld.

If only they knew how much I despised them.

If only they knew how much my hate fueled me.

Meatball's big head was the only thing that was sticking out from under the bed. When I leaned down to pat that big head of his, he flattened his ears and closed his eyes. Apparently he was still mad at me for having ordered him to not bite anyone's head off as my roommates came back, one by one, carrying baskets of the clean clothes their mothers had carefully packed for them. They came back from summer break with tans and absolutely no money saved.

I came back from my so-called break completely lifeless.

Meatball and I mostly kept to ourselves, staying hidden in my room, leaving only to go outside or make a quick meal. We avoided run-ins with the others as much as possible. Avoiding others had basically been my life before Cameron. So, as far as I knew, no one noticed a difference in me. Other than the fact that I now had a very hairy roomie living under my bed.

I rubbed Meatball's ears while he pretended that he didn't care, though the low rumble betrayed him.

I was about to switch my pajama bottoms for jeans when I noticed my curtain door flutter.

"Just a minute," I called out, pulling my bottoms back up, knowing full well that I wouldn't have a minute. Hunter had already poked his head through the curtain door.

"That wasn't a minute," I snapped, letting the elastic of my pants snap back to my waist.

He folded his arms and leaned into the doorframe. "It's nothing I haven't seen before."

I knew he was trying to be cute. But I had no smiles left in me.

I sat on the floor and dug my flip-flops out from under the bed. They were a little wet and had canine-sized punctures along the toe line.

Hunter stood waiting and cleared his throat.

"What do you want, Hunter?" I wiped my chewed-up sandal against my shirt and narrowed my eyes at Meatball, who was looking a bit sheepish.

"I need all of your rent checks for the year. The landlord insists that everyone needs to provide checks for the whole year upfront so that he doesn't have to worry about the kids who'll quit school midyear and take off without paying the rest of their rent."

*Oh, crap.* It wasn't just money for food that I needed. I would need money for rent too.

By default, because he was most likely to return to school—he had been coming back to school every year for the last eight years ... still no degree to show for it—Hunter was the house "manager." The landlord gave him a discount on his rent just for collecting checks and doing the chores that he was supposed to do but never did.

"Is that it?" I tried to mask the mass of panic that was growing in my throat.

Hunter hesitated, put off either by my irritability or by the guard dog whose head had popped up at the change in my tone of voice.

"And your bins are blocking the hallway. It's a fire hazard," he added. "It's my job to keep this place from burning to the ground, ya know."

"The power cords that snake between our rooms are fire hazards. The microwave that you found in the garbage, fixed with duct tape, and plugged in your room is a fire hazard. My bins are the least of our problems." I knew full well that my bins were not the issue.

When Hunter began fidgeting, scratching his goatee, I took a calming breath. "I need the extra room under my bed. Now that Meatball sleeps there. But I'm happy to send him to your room to sleep."

He eyed my mammoth-sized pet. "My room already smells like urine thanks to him. And I'm pretty sure it's not Joseph's doing."

Hunter had to share a room with Joseph, who spent almost all his time in their room in front of his computer screen. Since moving in a year ago, I'd only spoken maybe twenty words to him. We got along famously. And Meatball's scent was definitely an improvement to the smell of their room.

I had brought up the subject of Meatball on purpose—to give Hunter the window he was obviously looking for to warn me about having a dog in a no-pet-allowed zone. I faced the fact that I might have to move out, though finding a place that was so cheap, in September, at the beginning of the school year—when students still had hopes that they would make it, that they wouldn't be dropping out three months later—would have been nearly impossible. I didn't know what I was going to do, but whatever happened, Meatball and I were going together. And the faster Hunter and I dealt with it, the faster he was out of my room.

But Hunter continued to tiptoe around the issue. "Why did you name him Meatball?"

"I didn't." I passed him and stopped outside my curtained doorway, where my blue bins were neatly stacked, one on top of the other, in a non-fire-hazard type of way. I pulled the lid off the top bin and pretended to be looking for my checkbook.

"I thought you said you found him on the street."

"I did," I answered, eyes trained on my task.

I lifted one sock at a time, as if my checkbook might magically be hidden in the rolls. I felt more eyes on my back. I knew that Cassie was behind me and that I wasn't going to be left alone. Once I was out of my room, I was easy prey to my roommates.

I poked my head out of the Rubbermaid bin and confirmed the apparition. There was Cassie, drenched in black clothes, black hair, and enough eyeliner to supply three Vegas showgirls for a year.

It was hard for me to understand why Cassie felt the need to look like a zombie quarterback.

Last year, someone (who we suspected to be Hunter) left dirty socks on the radiator. When the socks started smoking in the early morning hours, the fire alarm went off, and all seven of us crashed into each other as we charged down the stairs and out the front door. Cassie didn't have any makeup on, and it turned out that she was really pretty, with full pink lips and blonde—blonde!—eyebrows.

That was the first and last time that I had seen Cassie without makeup. After that, she slept with her game face on.

While Cassie stood expressionless, waiting, Hunter did something that he rarely ever did—he stuck around. He and Cassie were as similar as a monkey and a cobra. And they got along similarly. They were rarely within the same breathing space.

Cassie didn't look like she was trying to do me any favors by interrupting the inevitable revelation that I was bankrupt. Rather, she had continued to stand staring, straight-faced, holding up a piece of paper. I was shocked when I recognized the name at the top of the form.

"Is that *my* class schedule?" I accused.

"Looks like we're in the same ethics class," she told me.

All of a sudden, an image flashed through my head. I was back at the Farm in the study, my favorite room apart from Cameron's bedroom. Cameron watched me while my fingers floated over book spines. There was a whole shelf dedicated to ancient philosophy.

Then I was on one of the chairs, Plato book in hand, sitting across from Rocco while he ate cheesies and wouldn't give me any quiet time.

I closed my eyes for a mere moment and steadied myself on my Rubbermaid bins.

Then I snatched the piece of paper from Cassie. "Where did you find it?"

"It came in the mail." She said this like opening someone else's mail was a perfectly normal thing to do and not at all a felony.

"You *read* my mail?"

She grabbed my schedule back and pointed to the first rows. "You've already missed four classes."

Meatball had kept his station under my bed, his eyes following the tug-of-war with my mail. I snatched the paper from Cassie's grasp, again. But this time I quickly folded it and stuck it in the waistband of my pajamas. It wasn't until more roommates popped their nosy heads out of doorways that I realized this discussion wasn't a coincidence. It was an intervention.

But I stood my ground. "That's right. I missed *my* classes. And?"

"I thought you were on a scholarship?"

I was. It was a microscopic, merit-based scholarship that barely covered my tuition and books. And at one point, a few months ago, this was my only saving grace, the only way I could be on my own without having to take my parents' money.

"The school will pull your scholarship if you miss too many classes," Cassie pointed out while everyone else watched. "Our ethics class is in a few minutes. We can walk together."

****

I stood outside in a T-shirt and my pajama bottoms while Cassie ran back into the house, probably to put on another layer of vampire makeup. The great thing about college was that going to class in flip-flops and pajama bottoms was a completely normal thing to do.

I had agreed to walk to class with Cassie. Ethics, a branch of philosophy, was my favorite subject. In my first year at Callister University, I had never missed any of my classes, no matter how boring they were, but philosophy was the sole class that I actually looked forward to.

Though now, agreeing to go to class with Cassie was just better than trying to explain to her and all of the other doorway assessors why I had no plans to go back to school, why that part of my life was over now.

For the first time since he had come to live with me, I had to leave Meatball. My dog. He had followed me out of our room to the front door, where I was forced to order him to stay before I closed the door behind me.

While I waited for Cassie, I started kicking at the loose pebbles on our small crosswalk, trying to block out the sound of

Meatball's whine through the door. My chew toy of a flip-flop brushed against something soggy, and I looked down to see a humidified piece of cardboard. It was a business card. It took me a minute to realize it was the one that had fallen when Carly had tried to hand me a piece of paper with Cameron's bank account numbers. Before I had thrown it back at her. That had only happened a couple of weeks before, and yet, it felt like another life ago. Cruelly, the sun had been shining, brightly, happily ever since then. No stormy weather. No thunder or lightning. Not even one damn drop of rain to loyally commemorate Cameron's death.

I bent down and pried the card off the cement, being careful not to rip it. It was made of thick, indented paper. The really expensive stuff. Most of what had once been an accountant's contact information had been washed away. Just a few letters and numbers remained.

I pulled my notebook out of my bag and pressed the card under the hardcover. This sodden piece of cardboard was the sole connection I had left to the underworld.

Cassie finally opened the front door, but she never had a chance—Meatball charged right through her, knocking her into the doorframe. While I was prepared to grab his collar, my arms extended, he darted around me and ran to the house across the street. He made his way up the wooden side steps to the second-floor apartment.

I didn't know who lived there. In fact, apart from my own roommates, I didn't know and had never talked to anyone on our street. This wasn't a mingling type of neighborhood, and I wasn't a mingling type of gal.

Whoever lived there, I knew they wouldn't appreciate having a beast of a dog barking at their door.

As I ran across the street, shouting at Meatball, my eyes did a quick once-over above to the second-floor front windows.

I could have sworn—

I stopped in the middle of the street, my breath cut short. It wasn't possible. I knew that I was imagining it.

Cameron's face had flashed by the window. Hadn't it?
But that wasn't possible.
I *knew* that wasn't possible.

The week before, I had interrupted Meatball's private business, pulling him leg up behind me while I ran after Cameron as he exited a coffee shop. The perfect stranger I grabbed by the shirt thought I was completely nuts. And he hadn't even remotely looked like Cameron. The day before, I had caught myself yelling after a bus driver. He had also turned out to be not-Cameron.

I was slowly losing my sanity. Yet as I ran up the steps and grabbed Meatball's collar, I gazed ahead, debated, then peeked through the small window. Inside, it was completely empty, devoid of any furniture, of any Cameron.

I was unequivocally nuts.

"The landlord's never going to let you keep the dog," Cassie said to me as we headed to school, after I had dragged Meatball away from the empty flat. I practically had to shove him inside and quickly close the door before he could charge back out. I could still hear him barking as we rounded the corner.

"I could always try to hide him."

"Yeah, good luck with that," she said with a smirk.

More walking. More silence. But I could feel her watching me with her peripheral vision.

It wasn't until we were stopped at a light, waiting for the walk signal, that she confronted me again. "You're doing a really shitty job trying to hide that big scab on your lip."

I kept my eyes ahead, feeling nauseous all of a sudden.

"I can give you a hand with the makeup stuff, if you want," she offered to my muteness.

"The light changed," I answered and crossed the street. We made our way to school without speaking of what she really wanted to know: *what the hell happened to you? What the hell is wrong with you?*

Last night, I dreamed of Rocco. Again. Almost every night, I dreamed of Rocco—in the same way that as a child I used to dream of my brother, Bill, for almost two years after he had passed away. Sometimes screaming in my sleep, sometimes waking up to a puddle on my pillow. Waking up and not really remembering what I had dreamed about, but having that lingering, aching feeling that it was about Bill. And now Rocco.

But I never dreamed of Cameron. Not once.

I needed to see him. To see his face.

Just one more time, feel him next to me—breathing, even if it were only in my dreams.

Waking up with a broken heart, it feels like being stabbed a million times by a jackhammer. I would wake up when all I wanted to do is sleep and never wake up again.

Being forced to go to class, with Cassie on my tail, was another living-second strike of the jackhammer. And then Cassie and I actually got to this damn class, only to see my ex-boyfriend Jeremy chatting with another student outside the heavy classroom doors. This day was getting better and better. Jeremy darted in, obviously hoping that I hadn't spotted him. We had dated for a short while last year. Now one year seemed like an eternity ago.

We followed the herd as the students ascended the steps into the auditorium. The classroom was encased in cement blocks, painted pee yellow, with no air circulating through. The plastic chairs matched the beige linoleum. Whoever decorated the university's classrooms was clearly color-blind.

The lack of air and the buzz of student chatter made my head pound, so I took the first available seat, even if it was at the very front of the class. Cassie shook her head at my teacher's-pet choice of seating and made me scoot over so she could sit next to me. There was an old guy at the front of the class, leaning cross-legged against the desk. This was the professor. I had seen his picture hanging in the philosophy department. Then there was another guy swaying in front of him and holding a clipboard, hands slightly shaking. Picture-day gelled hair, abused Nike runners, Green Lantern T-shirt. Definitely a grad student.

"Sophia Jane Ackermen," stuttered out the superhero T-shirt guy while students were still filtering in.

The professor had his grad student do the roll call, the cattle call, while he chopsticked his way through something that looked like tofu but smelled like rotten fish. I instantly regretted my choice of a seat in one of the front rows.

I bent my head, pretending to be digging in my bag for a pen and willing the gag reflex to get under control. The attempt was frustrated when my bionic fingers kept getting caught in the spirals of my notebook. I had injured them after I had managed to pry myself from Spider's minions and punch Spider in his ugly face. Now my fingers were stuck in wedges that looked like metal banana peels, and it made everything I did clumsy. Clumsier.

Cassie was observing this struggle to surface a pen.

"How *exactly* did you break your fingers?"

"They're not broken."

"Eugena Cassidy Goldblath," the grad student called out.

Cassie rolled her eyes at him. "Yep," she answered, then turned back to me. "I suppose the splint is just a fashion statement?"

I sighed. The grad student wasn't even halfway through the alphabet. It would have been an extremely uncomfortable few minutes if I didn't give her at least some sort of response.

"One of the fingers *was* broken. But it's probably fine now. I haven't had it checked in a while." This reminded me that I needed to drop into the school's medical clinic for a follow-up and get the stupid thing off my hand.

"Cameron James Hillard," the grad student called out.

My blood pressure dropped to the pee-colored floor.

I had heard wrong. Just like I was seeing Cameron everywhere, I was hearing his name.

"Cameron. James. Hillard," he called out again, practically spelling it out.

I hadn't imagined it. I shot up from my seat and turned around to face the rest of the class.

"Do you go by Cameron or James?" Green Lantern asked me.

I heard a few students chuckle.

"Emily, what on earth are you doing?" I heard Cassie hiss. She was tugging at my T-shirt.

I looked, waiting for him to speak up, to stand. I searched from row to row, searching for the face that I would be able to recognize in a stadium in the middle of a rock concert.

The room was spinning. Blurred faces I didn't know.

I finally gazed down at Cassie, who looked horrified.

"Emily?" she asked.

My mouth was covered with one hand.

I stepped over Cassie, tripping over her legs. I used her shoulder to push myself out into the aisle and kept running, slamming my body into the push bar of the double doors. Just as the doors drew to a close, I threw up. Right in front of the doors to the classroom.

****

I sat on the floor of the girls' second-floor washroom, holding my head in my hands.

*He would have been in the same class*, I thought to myself.

Cameron had once admitted to me that he would check up on me after Bill died. But to what extent, I hadn't known. There was so much I hadn't known.

*He would have been in the same room as me.*

Would I have ever even noticed him if Meatball hadn't introduced us?

*He would have been in the same breathing space as me.*

Last year, in my first year at Callister University, ancient philosophy had been held in the same oversized auditorium. And there had been a whole shelf dedicated to ancient philosophers in Cameron's study, with books that had clearly been read before. Had Cameron been in that class with me?

Had he been enrolled in any of my other classes just so that he could "check" on me?

I could have had more time with Cameron, but I was too blind, too self-absorbed to notice anyone.

I realized how very little I knew about his secret life.

Professors did roll calls at the beginning of every semester to see who had made it out of summer break alive. Cameron hadn't.

And no one but me cared that he wasn't coming back.

When my mind and stomach had cleared, I went down to the front desk. Someone would have to clean up the mess I had left in front of the auditorium. Hopefully before class finished and students started slipping and sliding out the door.

There was another student in front of me, talking to a clerk who was hiding behind bulletproof glass, typing on her desktop. Why did everything always have to be bulletproof? We were in the philosophy department. They of all people should be able to talk the crazies away from their guns.

When my turn came up, the lady behind the desk never looked away from her screen.

"Student ID card," she commanded, cupping her hand like a catcher's mitt up to the half-moon hole at the bottom of the glass. We were all just another student number.

A thought occurred to me as she entered my number into the system. But while the plan was still forming in my head, the administrator waited for my student problem.

She was actually forced to look up at me, her eyes bugging out. "Can I help you?"

"One of my," I hesitated, "classmates, forgot his," I stammered again, "book at my house," this was the most drawn-out sentence ever, "and I wanted to give it back to him, but I don't have his address so …"

"So, you need me to look him up in the system and give you his address?" she finished for me, a sweet smile on her face.

"Right," I said, taking a small jump forward as I said this.

She pushed my student card back through the hole and rested her hands on her lap.

"I'm sure you can understand, Miss—" she glimpsed at her

screen and turned back to me, "Miss Sheppard, the university has a policy of not sharing the personal information of its students. Perhaps you could simply tell the boy that you like him instead of lurking around his house?"

I pasted a smile on my face and took my student card back.

I wished I would have put a little more thought and conviction into my plan. I expected that the primrose behind the glass would be putting a note on my file, in red letters and twenty-point Times New Roman font: stalker.

I spun on my heels and yelled over my shoulder, "You might want to send someone with a mop to Auditorium B. One of the students made a real mess in front of the doors."

\*\*\*\*

From the row of chairs that were in the hall screwed into the wall, I watched the janitor come and go. He had kept his headphones on and had the floor mopped up in less than two minutes. He must have been through the puke drill multiple times during frosh week.

When the ethics class finally finished, Cassie was one of the first ones out the doors.

"Did the peanut butter bagel you ate this morning come back to haunt you?" she asked me as she approached.

Peanut butter was Meatball's favorite. So I ate it every morning ... I *used to* eat it every morning. Just the thought of it ...

Cassie handed me my bag. "I was going to go look for you, but unlike some people, I didn't want to make a scene."

I kept my eyes trained on the doors and got up as soon as I saw Jeremy walking through.

"Be right back," I told Cassie as I had already started sprinting.

"Don't worry about me. I'll be waiting. For you. Right here," she shouted, sarcasm heavy.

Jeremy was my plan B. Hopefully plan B was a better plan.

"Jeremy," I called out as I ran up to him and stopped, blocking his escape. "How are you?"

"Hi," Jeremy said carefully. "I'm fine."

He had been walking out with another guy, and I had interrupted their conversation. His friend slapped Jeremy's back and bowed out.

We stood for a moment, while students herded out the doors, sidestepping me.

"That was quite an exit you made earlier," he said, clearly happy with my misery. "I could hear you upchuck from the back row."

I cleared my throat. "So, you had … a good summer?"

I remembered why I tended to avoid conversations generally and with ex-boyfriends. Wholeheartedly awkward.

"Better than yours, I guess," he said, bitterness coloring his tone. "Your ears seem to be back to normal."

I wrinkled my nose, trying to grasp Jeremy's meaning. Then it hit me, again. That gash in my heart that would never heal, intent on torturing me. Once upon a time, Cameron and Rocco had played a joke on Jeremy, telling him that I was in the hospital with some unknown disease so that he would stop calling me. Memories that would never be anything more.

Jeremy had no idea how much his comment had wounded me. I took a breath and regrouped.

"Yeah, sorry about that. I lost my phone for a couple days. Someone answered my calls as a joke."

"Whatever. It wasn't important. I just wanted to tell you about the computer thing so you wouldn't have to show up at work for nothing."

"What computer thing?"

"The computer program. At the library." When a blank look came over my face, he arched his eyebrows. "The program. That the library was using. To catalogue the book scans." Still nothing from me, even if he was spelling it out. So he continued. "It got hacked, and the library lost all the data we had inputted. We all lost our jobs when the library decided to abandon the electronic library project and bring the books back. Where have you been?"

Jeremy's father was a professor in the political science department. When we had been dating, he had used his connections to get me a job in the library archives.

I thought I had lost this job because I hadn't showed up. Turned out the job didn't even exist anymore.

My plan had been to ask for help getting my job back so that I could find a way to get into the system. But it was pretty hard to get my job back when the job didn't even exist anymore.

Plan B was sucking already.

"I need a job," I blurted.

"Good for you. What does this have to do with me?"

"Jeremy," I said slowly, almost pleading, "I wouldn't ask unless I was desperate. I'm broke. I'm going to get kicked out of my house if I don't come up with rent soon."

He sighed. "I suppose I could get you in where I work. At the campus store. Selling sweatshirts and bumper stickers. Think you could handle that?"

I could, but that wasn't what I had in mind.

"How about working front desk in one of the departments?"

"Yeah, that's not going to happen. They only hire grad students to do that stuff."

Cassie had come to my side, apparently tired of waiting patiently for me. Jeremy eyed her for a second. Maybe, by the grace of whoever ruled the Graceland, he wouldn't remember her or how mean she and the rest of my roommates had been to him when we'd dated.

"Please, Jeremy," I full-out begged.

"Yeah, I'm late for my next class. I really can't help you."

Jeremy left Cassie and me standing in front of the classroom doors, where the floor was still moist from the janitor's mop.

Seemingly, he had remembered her and still hated my guts. Plan B was a bust.

When Cassie and I stepped outside, she grabbed me by the

shoulders. "He's not the one who did that to your face and your hand, is he?"

I shook my head and gave her her hands back.

I should have taken Jeremy up on his offer for a job in the campus store when he had offered it. Now I had no money coming in and no way of finding out more about Cameron. Not a great day.

\*\*\*\*

The next morning, I ran out before anyone else could accost me outside my bedroom. I needed to get to the clinic, get the splint off my fingers, and get the attention off me. My day started off with waiting. Waiting to get checked in. Waiting in the big waiting room while I waited to get invited past the receptionist into a smaller waiting room. They called that last waiting room a consult room, where patients got to wait for the doctor. It took a couple hours, but I finally made it to the consult room. It was either the same room or identical to the room I had been in when I had come in with my broken fingers a few weeks ago. They had obviously cleaned out the trash bin after I had thrown up in it. But the room was mostly unchanged. There were the quintessential germ-infested *Reader's Digests* lying around. A few scattered boxes of free samples for students and faculty. None of the good stuff, though. Mostly just sunscreen and dental sticks that no one ever uses.

There was a dusty cardboard box of yellow rubber balls. To squeeze and relieve stress, or something like that. It had a happy face painted on it. I grabbed one for Meatball. He might like to chase after it. Then I took a second ball. Meatball might want to play with this second ball after he devoured the first one. I also snagged the box of Kleenex on the doctor's desk because we were running low on toilet paper at home.

I was pondering the box of Band-Aids when the doctor on duty appeared. He looked at my chart, and refused to take the cast off until he was sure that the fingers had healed properly. I had waited all morning for that five-minute denial.

"I'll sign a release form. It'll be our little secret. I promise not to sue you."

The doctor was already out of the room. He was like a waterspout. You'd never know he'd been there unless you had actually witnessed it.

I stole the box of Band-Aids before being sent to another door down the hall, where I was to meet yet another medical authority for an X-ray. As I came to open the door to Callister University's X-ray room, I happened to read the warning sign hanging on the door, and I paused.

Insignificant details of the past few weeks started trickling through my head.

Insignificant details became momentous signs. Life-altering.

I headed back down the hall. When I got back to the clinic, I found and flagged down the first medical staff I could find. A young nurse, in training. There were a lot of those here. I pulled her aside, came close to this stranger's ear, and whispered.

When I was done, she took a breath, arched her head up, and smiled, obviously struggling to control the inexpert fit of giggles that were climbing inside of her. She went to the cabinet of free stuff for students, where college medical essentials were stocked. Barf bags. Medication in samples, the better stuff (whatever the staff hadn't already looted). A shelf just for condoms, and in the corner, long white boxes that reminded me of the jewelry boxes—diamond necklaces, diamond bracelets, diamond watches—my mother would get as gifts from my father. Usually as an apology or bribery.

The nurse handed me a white box, and I took it into the washroom.

I sat in a stall and waited for the umpteenth time that day, even though I already knew. My world was spinning out of control. The signs had been ignored, by me, but they had been there. The theatrical nausea, the throwing up in trash bins, in front of the doors to the philosophy class. Even before the full five minutes was up and the two lines on the complimentary pregnancy test had revealed themselves, I knew I was pregnant.

While I held the evidence—the pee stick—in one hand, my free hand had found itself to my belly. When I noticed, I whipped it off like I'd been burned. Then I threw the pregnancy test on the ground and used both my feet to systematically stomp it to pieces.

Revenge is a strange thing. It tests you. It changes you. It makes you do things that you would have never thought yourself capable of doing.

Revenge feels a lot like survival. The need to hurt, the need to kill consumes you. Except that when revenge turns to survival, hate is replaced by total desperation.

## Chapter Two: Cameron

## Erased

I had spent so much of my time designing the Farm. Every board, every rock, every shrub, I had placed there with Emmy flooding my brain—her likes, her dislikes, the color of her eyes, her smile, her laugh. Though I would often daydream and see her flowing through its rooms, I never thought she would actually ever see it, let alone live in it. Still, the Farm had always been meant for her.

Now all I wanted to do was burn it to the fucking ground.

Maybe someday I would be so lucky, but for now I was forced to let our guards erase all of us from it. Once we had finished packing, wiping it down, scraping the blood out, we would board it up and vacate.

Spider and I were outside leaning against the rail, watching through the glass doors as our cleaning crew pulled the floorboards up. This was where my brother was murdered, his blood left to soak through the floor, his ghost left to forever haunt me and this place.

Carly walked through the living room, keeping her eyes ahead and making an extra-wide circle around the cleaners. She came to join us on the deck and wiped her blackened hands on her jeans.

"I hate moving," she grumbled.

She watched the guards carry out her millions of boxes from the pool house.

"Maybe moving wouldn't be so bad if you didn't have so much crap," I told her.

Spider sneered, until Carly shot him the look of death.

"It's not like we don't move every other month, Carly. You think you would have figured this out by now," I added.

This comment would have normally gotten me my very own look of death, but Carly had been very careful around me lately. Like I was holding a gun to my head. I hated that she was doing this, so I provoked her whenever possible. And Spider let me get away with it. This too irked me.

It had taken a while for us to feel safe enough to return to the Farm after Victor's men had stormed it and started the war against us. We could not return until we were sure that the echo of shots being fired hadn't attracted unwanted attention from the distant neighbors or local police.

We had just a few hours to pack up and go back into hiding.

We had over a hundred hideaways throughout the United States, Canada, and Europe. Not counting my cabin, which Spider and Carly didn't know about. We moved every other month. Sometimes we moved, only to pack up the next day. No one was as good at disappearing from civilization, so often, so quickly, as us.

My mom and I moved around all the time when I was a kid; I had learned to travel light from birth. I didn't get attached to anything, and Spider had the same philosophy. Carly, on the other hand, had so much junk that she was running out of room for it in the pool house. She was constantly picking up stuff at flea markets, garage sales, curbside garbage. She was attached to all her junk and everybody else's.

It had been a while since all three of us had been together for longer than a few minutes at a time. I had created a mile-high pile of shit in the underworld, and the captains were incensed. It hadn't helped that I had brought up the subject of retaliation against

Shield. I couldn't explain to them why we needed to risk notice by taking out the union leader of the United States police force. I had no proof that he had been the one to storm the Farm and kill off my men. The only person who had witnessed the crime, and was still alive, was Emmy. As far as they were concerned, Emily Sheppard did not exist. As far as they were concerned, Rocco had never been related to me. As far as they were concerned, I was insulated—I had no lovers, family, or friends who could be used to distract me from making them money.

Because of my negligence, we had lost two drug shipments to Somalian pirates, our Canadian allies were in a state of chaos, and the Mexican drug cartel had broken the southern turf treaty. Just a couple months of Emmy, and I had lost control over the underworld.

And Shield had used all of this to start campaigning against me with the captains and helping some of them out by messing with the justice system, pulling favors. While he may have denied involvement in any of this, we both knew that he was the cause of my grief. He would have to pay for that, eventually.

I had never made so many dumbass moves in my life. I needed to refocus on the one thing I was good at—making money for the lords of the underworld. But this was easier said than done because I missed Emmy so badly that at times I felt like doing exactly what Carly expected me to do: shoot my brains out. Having had Emmy by my side—immediately addicting—nothing would ever be as good again.

I missed how her lips tasted. I missed the softness of her skin and how her hand fit so securely into mine. I missed the smell of her hair and the puffiness of her face when she was tired. I wanted to wake up next to her and have her all to myself every day, forever.

I missed all of her, and I needed more. But all I could get nowadays were glimpses into her life—something that used to be enough for me. Now, just seeing her walking down the street made me ache even more.

All of a sudden, I found myself walking through the glass doors and getting held back by Carly's hand on my shoulder.

"Did you hear what I said?" she asked me.

I hadn't heard a word. All I could hear was the echo of Emmy's voice bouncing around my head, pulling me back to her with the force of a magnetic field.

Carly kept her hand on me. "Where are you going?"

"I've got stuff to do before we head to California."

"Like?" Spider was keeping his spot against the rail, his arms permanently crossed over his chest. He still had traces of a black eye after Emmy had broken his nose with her tiny hand.

He thought he knew everything about the business—what I did, who I talked to, who I killed. And that used to be true, but things had changed. He wasn't involved in everything I did anymore. He had been distracted himself over the last few weeks—disappearing, bowing out of meetings. And I had made decisions that I had wanted to keep from him and Carly.

While I tried to figure out how to get out the door without further inquisition, Carly looked to the heavens in exasperation.

"Oh, for Christ's sake, Cameron. We know where you're going."

I shut the glass door in her face, stopped at the landing, and changed course to the library at the end of the hall. A couple of guards were packing up the books into cardboard boxes.

"Get out," I ordered.

They sprung up and left, keeping their eyes ahead, as if I were never really there.

Most of the books had already been pulled off the shelves and packed. The packed boxes were spread across the room, with a few tossed over the piano I had bought for Emmy. This whole room had been for Emmy—the floor-to-ceiling shelves filled with books, the stone fireplace, the windows overlooking the forest. Out of every room in the house, this one I had made especially for her, imagining her lounged on the couch, reading in front of a fire.

When Emmy had entered this room the first time, I had been

nervous—and I *never* get nervous. But to see her fingers stroke the back of the books, to see her face light up, I wanted to kiss her. I wanted to pull her off her feet and dance around the room with her in my arms.

As realization set in that I would never dance with Emmy in this room or any other room, I wanted to take an ax to it.

I shoved the boxes off Emmy's piano and started tearing open the boxes on the floor. When the door slammed behind me, I kept going, hoping I would quickly find what I was looking for so that I could escape the cross-examination.

Spider and Carly sat on the couch in the middle of the room and watched me for a little while. But Carly is the most impatient person I've ever met.

"How was Emmy when you saw her?"

There was an immediate squeeze to my heart.

I had been watching over Emmy from the apartment across the street. Sitting by the front window for hours, hoping that I would be able to see her, even if it was just to see her come and go. But she didn't come out very much, just to take Meatball out for walks.

I had never seen Emmy look so … despondent, as if the life had been sucked out of her. She was frail, like a gust of wind would be enough to break her in half. She didn't look like herself. She didn't look like my beautiful, strong Emmy. As happy as I was to see her, seeing her in this way made my heart recoil.

Carly had been analyzing my countenance.

"Cameron," she pleaded, "enough already. Go get her. You can't let her fall apart like this. There's still time to make it better."

I kicked the recently emptied box across the room and tore into the next one that was closest to me. "Go get her, and do what? Have her stay here as a sitting target? Wait 'til someone else has it in for us and takes it out on her? She's not meant for this shit life."

Carly locked eyes with me. "You don't give her enough credit. She's a lot tougher than you give her credit for. Than we all gave her credit for."

"She deserves better than this," I said, my tone severe. Emmy had the luck of being born into privilege and could have had anything she wanted. She should have been happy. Someday, she would forget; someday, she would be happy and safe and alive. I had convinced myself of this. "We're stuck living in this kind of shit. There's no room for family or friends here."

I watched as Carly and Spider shifted in their seats as I said this. And I saw Carly draw back.

But Spider wasn't about to back down.

"If you keep spying on that chick, she'll eventually see you. For all we know, she could have already seen you."

I kicked yet another emptied box across the room, and then kicked the loose crap that I'd strewn on the floor so that I could clear a path to the last unopened box that was next to the piano. "She *didn't* see me. She *won't* see me. I've been able to hide from her all these years. I know her too well. She had no idea I was even there."

This hadn't been exactly true. Meatball had spotted me watching from the apartment and had almost given me away to Emmy. I had to hide in the bathroom when Emmy came to drag him back into the house. How could a dumb dog be so goddamn smart?

"Except that it's not just her, Cameron," Carly continued. "You know that Victor probably has people watching her too. After everything we went through to make her believe that you were—"

Carly took a breath and stopped herself from reminding me of the most painful day in my life.

"We've worked hard to get them to think that you left her and that you don't give a shit about her," Spider continued. "If they find you, they'll know that we've been playing them. And then we're all in fucking trouble, including Emily."

I ripped open the last box and immediately found the books I had been searching for. I got up and took the box with me.

"You can't keep living in between." Carly's face was drawn in concern. "If you're adamant that you're not going to go get her, if you really want her to move on, then let her grieve and give her a chance to live on."

"We have to get back to business," Spider added. "The constant interruptions are not going to get us back into the good books."

I knew they were both right, but I wasn't about to admit it. And staying away from Emmy … forever … I didn't think I would ever be able to, even if I knew in my heart that it was in Emmy's best interest.

"You have to stay as far away from her as possible," Spider said.

While I stood, ready to leave, heavy goddamn box in arms, Spider and Carly watched me and waited.

"Did you forget the promise I made Bill?" I asked to Carly specifically. "I told him I would always watch over Emmy. Keep her safe."

As expected, this made Spider irate. "Bill's dead. Who cares if you break your promise to that idiot? Besides, I don't think he expected you to watch her so closely that you'd be naked on her."

My fingers dug into the cardboard while Spider smirked. As much as I knew how to get a rise out of him, he knew how to get a rise out of me.

Carly put up a white flag. "If you just want to make sure she's safe, I can make that happen. That way, you can still keep your promise to Bill without risking being around her."

This caught both Spider's and my interest. "How?" I wondered.

"Do you trust me?" she asked me.

"Mostly."

"Do you trust me to do everything possible to keep Emmy and the rest of us safe?"

"Yes," I said without hesitation.

"And do you promise to stay away from Emmy?"

I hesitated there. "You're not going to tell me what you're planning, are you?"

She shook her head. "It's better if you remove yourself completely and let me take care of Emmy."

When I eyed Spider, looking for elaboration, he just raised his shoulders. This was all Carly.

"Cameron, you know it's for the best. If you don't go get her, then you have to let her go," she said.

My heart tightened and my teeth clenched, because I knew that Carly was right. "I'll stay away from her."

The words coming out of my mouth felt like knives on my tongue.

When I got to my car, Tiny, one of the few men I ever trusted with my life, was waiting for me. I was carrying the box of wordy and dense philosophy books from the class Emmy and I had once secretly shared. An amphitheater-sized class where I could keep an eye on her and easily keep myself hidden. We should have been attending another class together this school year. But I wasn't going to be there.

I placed the box on the backseat, and we drove off.

I didn't know if I'd be able to keep my promise to Carly. Keeping away from Emmy, letting someone else look after her ... just the thought of it made me want to slit someone's throat.

****

We drove into a tidy neighborhood in New Jersey. Tiny dropped me off on the corner and drove away. It was already dark. Through brightly lit windows, I could see families sitting down eating their dinner in front of the TV, oblivious to the fact that I was stalking through their backyards. When I got to the neat backyard of a little bungalow, I swiftly peered through the backdoor window and chuckled at the sight of the red eye of a motion detector.

Alarm systems aren't just a joke; they're dangerous. Their purpose is to make you think you're safe. Make you feel like you can relax and let your guard down. But anything that one human created, another can destroy.

Nothing man-made is foolproof. Death is the only untouchable, and a false sense of security could get someone killed.

I put some gloves on, quickly disarmed the system, and let myself in. I hadn't had to get my hands this dirty since I was a kid. Breaking and entering, stealing, was a method of survival where I came from.

As I prowled through the house, I remembered the rush I used to have at taking things from people who had too much and selling them just so we'd have money to pay to get the heat turned back on.

But this house was no average Joe's house. This was a cop's house. A place where, even when I was a stupid kid, I would have never ventured. By the plaques on the wall and the medals, you'd think this was the house of a fine member of the police force. But this police officer was no hero. If you looked hard enough, if you knew where to look, you would find the dirt, like a black light in a motel room.

The fifty-year-old bottle of Glenfiddich in the liquor cabinet, the over-the-top entertainment center, the Rolex watches, and the cocaine stuffed in the couch. I had learned a long time ago that there were no real heroes left—just good actors. And this guy wasn't just crooked; he was flamboyant.

I quickly got on his computer and linked into a few sunny destination sites on the Internet. The intricate firewall caught my interest, and out of sheer curiosity, I started searching through files, finding his extensive Internet porn collection. I had come across a lot of sick people; but this guy was really messed up.

After bringing his firewall down and turning off the computer, I rearmed the cop's false sense of security and found a dark corner to wait, away from the motion detector.

When he came home, the fat cop disarmed the system, threw his gun holster on the front bench, and sat down at his computer desk. I watched from the shadows as he went straight for his favored collection, already panting from excitement or from having to walk his fat ass around.

Before he could get too comfortable, I strolled up behind him and placed the butt of my gun against the back of his head. I leaned in to his ear, smelling the sweat stained into his shirt.

"Officer Breland," I murmured, "let's go have a seat in the kitchen."

"Boy," he said as we made our way down the hall, "you don't know what shitstorm you just walked into. You ain't gonna walk out of here alive."

I bade him to sit at the table, and I sat on the opposite side, placing my gun on the table's smooth surface, the barrel pointing at the police officer.

"Do you know who I am?" I asked him. I knew he had no idea who I was; nobody did. As far as he was concerned, I was just a twenty-something kid who was getting caught up in something he couldn't manage.

"I don't give a shit *who* you are," Officer Breland howled.

"A couple months ago, you stormed into my compound and killed some of my guards."

He scowled and folded his arms over his chest. "I don't know what you're talking about."

I smiled. "I lost a lot of men that night."

I took a piece of metal out of my pocket and took care to screw it onto my gun. His complexion blanched a little.

"One of the guards who was shot was unarmed. One of your colleagues ratted you out as the trigger guy."

"It wasn't me." Sweat started to seep through the blubber on his face.

"Come on, now. We both know that's not true."

I put the gun back on the table, with the silenced barrel facing the policeman, and kicked my feet up on one of the chairs, lacing my fingers behind my head.

"I was just following orders," he confessed. "If I wouldn't have done it, someone else would have, and I would have been killed myself."

"You and your chumps cost me a lot of money that night."

"I can pay," he immediately offered, as I had expected. "I have a lot of money socked away."

"Oh, I doubt you can afford my price. I'm going to need a lot more than whatever shit nest egg you've saved up. Someone has to pay for this."

While Officer Breland gave this some thought, I watched as his chunky hands started to shake. He knew what I was asking for, and he knew that this could mean his death now or his death later. When he looked at the clock clicking over the refrigerator, I knew he had made his decision.

"I know where you can get more money. A whole lot more money."

"Boy," I said, mimicking his voice, "that's the best news I've heard all day."

Officer Breland and I got in his Chevy, and I made him drive us so that I could keep holding the gun on him.

"They're moving the money tonight," he explained. "Shield has them move it around every two weeks until he can use it."

By use it, Officer Breland meant launder it.

"How many guys does he have guarding the money?"

"No more than two."

"Just two?" That would have left his money a little too vulnerable.

"Shield doesn't trust anyone with his money," he told me. "I only know about it because for the last two weeks, he has been keeping the stash at my folks' old farm. I inherited it after they died but never did anything with the property."

I watched every move he made as he said this. He kept his eyes on the road, his hands firmly upon the wheel, his breath steady. He was telling the truth.

"If you get me that money, I'll let you keep a chunk of it," I vowed. "You can use your share to disappear before Shield comes after you."

He took a breath, nodded, and relaxed his grip on the wheel.

We drove to a farmhouse outside Jersey. Up the driveway,

there was a cube truck with its headlights on. As we neared the truck and the house, I could tell by the white fumes rising against the dark night that the truck's engine was still on, but we still hadn't seen a soul. I bade Officer Breland to park in front of the truck, and we waited there.

There were no lights on inside the house, but I could see flashlights shining through the windows every few seconds. Two distinct beams of lights—two flashlights. This, so far, corroborated Breland's story that there were only two men guarding Shield's money.

We watched as the flashlights flew around the house, from window to window. The officer looked at the clock on the radio. "They should have been done loading up the money by now."

Breland's inherited farmhouse was tall and slim, like a box of Kleenex that had been turned on its side. It had a façade of old bricks that were the size of a speed limit sign and bulged out. The bricks on the house reminded me of a bulletproof vest under a too-tight T-shirt. A few feet ahead, at the end of the pebble driveway, there was what was left of a barn. The roof had already caved in, and the structure hung on its side as though it had had too much to drink and was close to being cut off by the bartender.

"Nice place," I sneered.

"My parents were assholes. I'm taking pleasure in watching their place fall apart one piece at a time." His glare was stuck to the barn in the back. A glare that I recognized all too well. A glare that echoed that of a boy who had been beaten up more times than he dared to recount.

When the lights were focused on the side door and grew, Breland and I stepped out of the car.

A dark-haired gangly man came out, rump first, with a flashlight tucked in the back pocket of his jeans. He was bent over a red can of gas that he was pouring in zigzags. A second man followed him out. He was bigger and older, and he was carrying a wooden crate while holding his flashlight between his teeth, lighting his arsonist buddy's way out.

"What the hell are you doing?" Breland shouted. I let him go a little as he marched toward the men who were planning to torch his childhood house of horrors.

The firebugs stopped short, crowded on the small cement stoop in front of the side door.

"What the hell are we doing? What the hell are *you* doing? Here?" demanded the older of the two men.

"Shield sent us over here to see what was taking so long," I answered calmly.

While his young friend held on to the gas can and hadn't moved an inch since we'd been spotted, the big guy put the crate on the ground.

"Who the hell are you?" he asked and kept his eyes on me as he reached to the gun holster looped against his chest.

I stretched my arms over my head and yawned. "Where are the other guys?"

"What other guys?" the kid wondered, his brows furrowed.

He'd confirmed that there were indeed only two of them. I shot them both in the head before the old guy ever got a chance to pull his gun out.

Breland and I went to the bodies. I ordered him to pull the bodies inside the house while I opened the crate. It was loaded with cash. A couple hundred thousand dollars worth of it. Then I walked to the back of the truck, where the men had left the door up. There were at least another fifty more crates in there. Whatever Shield was planning to do with ten million dollars, it was big money for him. And while it was probably not his only stash of cash, he was definitely going to miss this.

From the glow of the headlights, we could still see the boots of the dead bodies that were inside the entrance. Breland was still winded from having dragged the two men.

"Do you smoke?" I asked him with a smirk.

He glanced at me, glanced at his childhood home, chuckled, and pulled out a gold-plated Zippo lighter. He lit it, and without hesitation, threw it onto the trail of gas. The house was engulfed in seconds.

I told him to load the last crate into the back of the truck and followed him. He reached up to pull the doors closed, and I fired two shots—one for each of his knees. He screeched, falling face-first into the back of the truck. I shut the door and locked him inside with the money.

I drove away with Breland and the cash, leaving behind two of Shield's men dead and Breland's car, fingering him as the escaped culprit. When Shield went searching for Breland in his tidy bungalow, he would find that his man's last Internet search was for flight destinations in South America.

I could still hear Breland howling in the back when I pulled up to the junkyard. Tiny was standing next to my car, waiting for me. He opened the back and pulled out Breland, dragging him to a pit in the sand. He threw Breland in the pit and moved to the side.

I watched Breland coil in pain and smiled.

"You have your money," he yelled. "What else do you want?"

"That unarmed guard you shot," I explained. "He was fourteen years old. He was harmless. Just a kid."

"I was just following orders. I didn't know he was a kid."

Tiny handed me a box, and I took a breath. That kid wasn't just any kid. "He was my brother. His name was Rocco."

I lit the match and threw it into the pit, lighting up the gasoline that Tiny had already poured in there. I walked to the truck, pulled out a couple money crates, and threw them in with Breland. He would die a rich man.

I got in my Audi and left Tiny to clean up.

Like the man who had ratted him out, Officer Breland had paid for what he had done to my kid brother. While my spree of payback was far from over, this one small kill had refueled me. But I wanted, *needed* more.

Breland was the fourteenth man to die at my hands—fourteen, which was how old Rocco was when he was murdered. Every time you take a human life, something—a darkness—grows inside of you, pushing you out, until eventually there's nothing but that darkness left. The only time I had felt the darkness recede and make room for me again was when I was with Emmy. Without her, the darkness was creeping back like the venom that it was.

\*\*\*\*

When I drove up to our plane, I was an hour early, and Spider and Carly weren't there yet. I got on the plane and ordered the pilot to take off. Then I called Carly.

"I need you to liquefy my personal funds," I told her after she had answered a groggy hello.

"Why?"

"Just do it, Carly."

Once upon a time, she would have been taken aback by the harshness in my voice. But this harshness was all I had to offer these days.

"When do you need it by?"

"Yesterday."

"Fine," she answered abruptly. "How much?"

"As much as you can get me on short notice."

She paused as the plane's engines roared and pulled us into the air. "Where are you?"

"Plane."

"Is Spider there too?"

"The two of you will have to catch the next flight out. I don't have time to wait."

"I'm not going. Spider was on his way to meet you. A couple more minutes wouldn't have hurt," she snapped.

"Call me back when the money's ready." I hung up on her and turned my phone off.

I looked through the window as daylight brought the New York landscape back to life. Pastures looked like tiny soccer fields below … and I immediately thought of Emmy.

The first time I saw Emily Sheppard, Bill had just passed away, and she was just a kid. She was on a soccer field in the middle of a game—this gangly, whitewashed, redheaded kid. I sat in my car, amazed. I had never seen a worse soccer player in my life. She was fast but tripped so many times over the ball or her own feet that her teammates practically burned a hole through their lungs to try to outrun her so that she would be nowhere near the game ball.

And then it had started raining. The field became a sodden mud pit. The girls were sliding everywhere, the coaches had their coats pulled over their heads, and the refs were trying to keep steady on their feet. But Emily was unaffected and seemed more determined than ever. The muddier the field got, the steadier she became on her feet. She found the ball, kicked, and scored just as the ref blew his whistle to stop the rained-out game. While the crowd ran for cover inside the school, Bill's sister stayed behind to help one of the assistants gather up all the balls and lug the nets back into the school.

On that rainy afternoon, I drove out of the parking lot shaking my head, with a smile on my face. Bill's sister was not the rich snot I had expected her to be.

Soaring daylight followed me into San Francisco. When I got to the apartment, I sent one of my guards to take word to Shield that I was in California, ready to meet.

I didn't have much time before Spider would be in town too, so I threw my stuff in a room and headed back out. I drove across the bridge into Oakland. I turned into the employee parking lot for the Port of Oakland and inched my way through the lanes, searching for the right Burgundy minivan. When I found it, I parked the car a few spots away, checked my watch, and waited.

I had done my research, knew everything about him on paper, but I needed to see him for myself. See from my own eyes what kind of man he was.

I watched the cargo be lifted from the ships to the docks and wondered what Emmy was doing.

## Chapter Three: Emily

## Fish Tales

I found myself staring at the glow in the dark stars that were stuck to my ceiling, left behind by the student who used to occupy my broom closet. I counted them, as I usually did whenever I couldn't sleep. The stars had started peeling off, and once in a while I'd find one on the floor. One was missing since I'd last counted.

Funny, I hadn't found any on the floor lately.

I imagined Meatball would be glowing in the dark soon too if he kept eating the plastic stars.

The house was darkened and quiet except for Meatball's snoring. The last thing I lucidly remembered was flushing the shards of a pregnancy test down the toilet, but the rest—petting Meatball, brushing my teeth, drinking a glass of milk after brushing my teeth—I could only remember as though I had been watching the automated me from a distance.

When I had left the clinic, it was early afternoon, and now it was almost dawn the next day. How did it get so late? I wasn't even sure if I'd slept at all or if I had been blankly staring at the plastic stars all day and night.

As soon as a bit of light from those rooms in the house that had the luxury of windows started poking through my curtain door, I couldn't wait to get outside and take Meatball for a walk. But the minute my feet hit the floor, I ran to the toilet.

When I was good and empty, I resurfaced to find Meatball sitting, quietly, by the bathroom door. He didn't even go totally nuts and spin around in circles when I asked him if he wanted to go for a walk.

The nausea had disappeared just as quickly as it had come. Yet I still needed to climb out of the cloud of lethargy that had taken my brain hostage. For the first time in many weeks, I grabbed my running shoes at the door.

But instead of taking *me* for a walk as he usually did, Meatball stayed to my side, so closely that his fur rubbed into my pant leg. This made it very difficult for me to run. So we slowed down and took an extra-long walk, one that took us out of the slums and into the suburbs.

We came to a park outside an elementary school, where houses and patio sets backed onto the green space. I could tell that the houses were new builds by the lack of weeds and the wisps of trees that were planted on every third lot. Exactly the same tree in exactly the same spot over and over again. I felt like I was in Legoland. The leaves had already started to change color, and the air smelled full, like the final give-it-everything-you've-got round of explosions at a fireworks show before everything goes dead silent.

While we snaked the pathway, I was humming some nonsensical tune under my breath and cramming my brain with as much useless detail as possible. Like the number of houses that had a birdhouse in their backyard. There were five. Like the number of picnic tables in the park. There were seventeen.

It must have been still quite early in the morning because the park was empty, except for a toddler who was playing in the sand by the climbers, while a woman who I assumed to be his nanny watched him from a park bench. Meatball had a leg up, so I stopped by the chain link fence, watching the little boy. He went up the climber, ran around, and went back down the slide. But when he reached the bottom, he tumbled off.

He started to cry.

The nanny ran to him, wiping his tears and hugging him while he dug his face into her shoulder. They held on to each other so tight, so naturally.

She was his mom, not his nanny, I realized. And something inside of me triggered.

I took Meatball back home.

As soon as we walked through the door, Meatball fled to the kitchen before I could fly to my room. I poured dog chow into what used to be a salad bowl, and he sat next to it, waiting.

I sighed. My nausea was creeping back, and the last thing I wanted to do was put anything in my mouth. But we had a ritual: if I didn't eat, then Meatball would sit there all day until I did. I opened my designated cupboard. There was a ketchup bottle, a pouch of Lipton soup, and a deflated bag of bread. I pulled out the last piece of bread and forced myself to chew. Meatball scarfed down his meal.

"Hey, puke breath," Hunter said as he strolled in. "Heard you made a scene in class yesterday. Puking on command to get out of school. That takes serious dedication."

I quickly closed my empty cupboard while he was busy riffling through his own overflowing cupboard. His mom regularly sent him totes stuffed with food and underwear.

I waited for Meatball and wondered whether dog food was fit for human consumption—though the half empty bag wouldn't last much longer either.

Hunter was shifting his weight from foot to foot and finally turned to face me. "I hate to bug you with this," he started, "but the landlord's coming by soon to pick up all the rent checks. Yours are the only ones that I'm missing."

I was having difficulty breathing but still stuck a smile on my face and called Meatball over. "I'll go get them right now."

Meatball and I went back to my room, and I fell onto my bed.

*Spider. Victor.*
*Spider. Victor.*

Every night I would rhyme off the names of the ones who had murdered Cameron and Rocco. Every night I had imagined myself ruining them, killing them, even if it killed me. But now, even this thought wasn't enough to calm the panic that was rising inside me.

I was broke and soon to be homeless. I was alone.

And I was pregnant.

*I can't even take care of my dog or myself,* I thought. *How can I take care of a child? How can I be a mother when I've never really had one? How can I protect a child against a whole other world?*

I had never heard my mother say, "I love you."

Apart from my brother, Bill, Cameron was the only person who had ever said those three massive words to me. There was one time when my mother had mentioned in passing that she liked the way the nanny had styled my hair that morning. I refused to wash my hair for five days, until my mother told the nanny that I looked *tres sale*, which was her French way of saying that I needed a bath.

I grew up loving nannies who were not allowed to (or paid to) love me back. My mother forbade them from ever showing affection, as this would not have been proper. For good measure, to ensure that none of them ever got too attached, she would change nannies every two years. Our maid, Maria, was the only constant in my life—she was the one who would fill in when we were between nannies. She was promoted to head maid when I got too old for nannies, but I still considered her as my nanny.

My mind wandered back to the park, where the mother was soothing, hugging, loving her child. And I wished I knew what that felt like.

I stuffed my face into my pillow and started to sob.

I cried so much that it felt like the fear, the pain, the loneliness were getting rung out of my heart and escaping through my tears.

I cried my heart out, and Meatball never left my side.

When I was a kid, my mother made me go to the Canadian Muskokas for a couple of summers. My so-called vacations were always impeccably timed with the nanny *du jour*'s vacation. It was kind of a summer camp—if summer camps had executive chefs and a butler for every bunker. Most kids arrived in their driver-driven Bentleys or limousines. My mother made me go in the Sheppard helicopter, even though I was terrified of heights. The helipad was conveniently floating in the middle of the lake, for all to see. The Sheppards always needed to put on a good show.

There was a dock where none of the well-to-do kids ever wanted to go swim because a fish kept nipping at their toes as soon as they would get in the water. Every summer, a mother fish would lay her eggs under the dock and attack anything that came close. One year, one of the boys had the bright idea of putting a fishnet near the fish's eggs. The mother fish immediately started attacking the net, and the boy scooped her out of the water. One of the counselors stopped the boy from killing it and ordered him to put the fish back in the water.

"She's only protecting her babies," the counselor explained.

The next summer, the fish was gone, and so was the dare-to-chastise counselor. I was left wondering why the fish valued the life of eggs more than its own when it had never even met the babies.

For a split second, I thought about going to my parents for support. After all, they had more money than they knew what to do with, though they never parted with it unless they got something in return. In the Sheppard family, charity rhymes with "what's in it for me?"

But a daughter coming home pregnant ... this would be worse than having a son who was a troublemaker and a drug addict. Of course, my mother had gotten pregnant with me after she'd had an affair with my then-married father. But this was different. Cameron could not bring my father's company a highly sought-after international merger as my mother's well-to-do family had. The ultimate shame for the Sheppard family wasn't getting pregnant; it was getting pregnant *for no reason*, without any financial gain to the family. The child growing inside me was worthless to them.

The thought of anyone thinking, let alone saying, my child to be worthless made me immediately stop crying. I clenched my fists and eventually flipped onto my back, lacing my hands behind my head and watching the stars on my ceiling again.

Victor and Spider would come, eventually. Before dropping me off at home, Spider had put forward that they couldn't touch me because of who I was—because sooner or later, someone would notice that the heir to the Sheppard empire was missing, and this would be big news, something the underworld would avoid at all cost. But this didn't change the fact that I would always be a threat to them. I knew too much; I had seen too much. I was a loose end, and loose ends did not exist in the underworld. Victor and Spider were just waiting for an opportunity. Timing was everything with these people. Like my parents, they were only out for themselves.

My child belonged nowhere. Not in my parents' world and certainly not in the underworld. But there was still my world, wherever that was. I brought my hands to my belly and whispered, "I love you." Because I did, more than anyone, anything, and everything else in the world.

Cameron's voice suddenly echoed in my head. "Sometimes the person you love is killed just because you love them." I shot up as though a tarantula had crept onto my pillow.

My child, Cameron's child, might not have had any value in my parents' world, but in the underworld, this child was priceless. If they wanted to shut me up—quietly—my child would be their leverage. If they couldn't come for me, they would come for the former drug lord's child. Of this, I was certain.

Everyone in my life would sooner or later leave me. Even Cameron had given up. I would do what Cameron didn't. What he wouldn't.

I would stay and fight.

All the money in the world could not have made my own mother love me or even give me a second thought. I had no idea how to be a mother, but I would try; I would do everything in my power to be a good one. Like the mother fish, I would fight for both of our survival, until my last breath.

I went from counting stars to counting fingers. According to my calculation, I was about two months pregnant. Killing Spider and Victor *was still* an absolute. But I had to kill them before they figured out my little secret. Time was running wild.

I fell asleep with one hand on my belly and the other on my chest. My index finger was entwined in the chain that Bill had given me before he died.

****

I was awoken in the afternoon by my cell phone ringing. The caller ID warned me who was calling.

"Jeremy?" I answered, half asleep, half incredulous.

"You owe me big-time," Jeremy said. "I found you a job in the admissions office. You have a meet and greet with the admissions director on Monday. It's not in one of the departments, but at least it'll look good on your resume."

If Jeremy had been in front of me, I would have kissed him.

"I don't know what to say."

"Don't get too excited. You're mostly going to be stuffing envelopes and carting mail back and forth. And the pay sucks. Just a couple of cents above minimum wage."

This was even better news. I had been making minimum wage in my previous job.

I must have thanked him at least twenty times in a row before Jeremy finally stopped me.

"No big deal, Em. I saw on a bulletin board that they were looking for a scholarship student. I called them and gave them your name. You'll just need to keep your grade point average up."

I had no idea how I was going to keep my grade point average up or how long it would take for the school to notice that I had stopped attending classes, but I was thankful nonetheless. I had really underestimated Jeremy.

"Are you sure you wouldn't rather come and work in the store? With me?" He paused for a second. "We'd be able to hang out again."

I knew that nothing came without a price. While I was grateful, I did not want to lead Jeremy on. He was better off without me; he just didn't know this yet.

"I don't think that's a good idea, Jeremy."

"Sure thing," he quickly responded. "I was just saying that because the pay's better at the store."

After we hung up, I realized that I would have to be more careful whom I sought favors from.

When everyone had finally trickled out of the house, it was past lunchtime. I left an exhausted Meatball snoozing under my bed and took a bus downtown.

The bus stopped outside my bank. There was a huge lineup leading up to the cashiers. While I waited in line, I fished a pen and a bubble-gum wrapper out of my purse and pulled my pendant off my neck.

Before he died, Bill had given me a silver chain with an angel pendant. It was a humble present, by Sheppard standards, but I never took it off. For years, I had assumed the pendant was a thoughtful gift, but Cameron had advised me otherwise. What I had once thought were product codes under the pedestal on which the angel sat were in actuality numbers for a bank account that Bill had put in place for me. I had no idea how much money was in the account, but from what Cameron had said, it was substantial. Enough for me to make plans; enough for the baby and me to survive Spider and Victor.

While I waited in line, I quickly transcribed the sequence on the bottom of the pendant, keeping an eye out to ensure no one noticed what I was doing.

"I'd like to access the money that's in this account," I

announced as I got to the next available cashier. I handed her the bubble-gum wrapper.

The cashier looked about as old as I was. Her dark hair came down to her chest and ended at a point, like arrows to her abundant cleavage. She picked up the wrapper by the corner as if it were diseased and stared for a minute.

She gazed up, doe-eyed. "I'm not sure I understand."

"I need to get the money that is in this account out of this account and into my hands," I rephrased for her, like she was a five-year-old.

"But this isn't an account number."

"It isn't an account number *here*. The account is offshore."

When we finally understood each other, the clerk directed me to the second floor, where I sat on the chairs by the elevator.

Cameron had told me that the account was in a Cayman Islands bank. I had assumed getting money out of the account wouldn't be as simple as going to a cashier and asking for it. I just didn't have any idea how to go about it. So I sat waiting for the personal banking manager, hoping he would know.

Another kitten walked up to me. She had a little bit less cleavage showing, but still left little to the imagination. Her blouse was so tight it looked like the buttons were torpedoes in waiting.

"Ms. Sheppard?" she asked. I nodded, and she led me to an office.

When she sat down, I realized she was the banking manager. The multiple degrees on her wall still gave me some hope that she might be able to help me.

I handed her the bubble-gum wrapper. "The bank account is in the Cayman Islands."

She took a look at the paper and wrinkled her forehead. "Are you sure you wrote the numbers down correctly?"

She handed me the piece of paper back. I knew I had copied them exactly as they were on my pendant.

"They're the numbers that were given to me."

"Well, your numbers don't add up," she told me. "They're not bank account numbers anywhere."

She turned her computer screen and showed me what she meant. "All banks follow a certain code in setting up bank accounts. The codes may not be the same in all countries, but each country has its own identifier so that there is no repetition in bank account numbers across the world."

She showed me what the numbers for a Cayman Islands bank account should look like. It was obvious that the sequence on my pendant was far too long and complicated to be a bank account number.

I thanked the account manager for explaining something that she had probably learned on her first day of training and left the bank empty-handed.

I knew that Bill would not have made a mistake. And I knew that Cameron would not have lied about the money that Bill had left me. Cameron had once showed me something Carly had devised to avoid detection by the authorities—an encryption system.

I sat on the bank's steps and unfolded the bubble-gum wrapper. Now that I took the time to really look at the sequence, it looked a lot like their encryption system. And I realized that I would not be able to access Bill's inheritance unless I could crack Carly's code.

"*Merde*," I muttered. I never swear in English.

I stuffed the wrapper back into my bag and stomped away.

People like Spider and Carly did not exist in the normal world. They only existed in Cameron's world. So finding Spider was going to be tricky, especially since I didn't even know his pre-underworld name. But I had an idea where to find Shield, also known as Victor Orozo, my brother, Bill's uncle. He trekked between worlds.

When I got to the police headquarters, it was almost dark; the days were already getting shorter. There were so many steps leading up to the edifice doors that I almost did a Rocky dance at the top, but I was way too winded and tired.

I pulled the hood of my jacket over my bright red hair before walking in.

Past the doors of the Callister City Police Department, it was total mayhem. People getting lugged around in handcuffs. Two women screaming at each other by the water fountain. Some guy in pajamas walking around with a sign that he had written in blue crayon on the back of a cereal box. According to his sign, only God could make him pee in a cup.

Luckily, the line up to the desk was fairly short and moving quickly. It wasn't until I got to the front of the line that I realized that this was a lineup just to get a number, and the number that the little red printer spit out told me that there were at least fifty people ahead of me. And there was only one clerk serving clients. Seemed like the whole city was ahead of me today.

I took a number and looked for a seat. The only one available was between someone who looked like she was possibly a hooker and an old man who was doubled over and seemed like he might have already peed himself. I was exhausted but stood and waited my turn. I found free wall space and leaned against it.

It wasn't hard to eavesdrop on the reasons why people were there because all of them were bellowing their issues at the police clerk. And everyone was there to complain about something. A noisy neighbor. Police brutality. Stolen wallet. Police brutality. Bailout. Police brutality.

I, too, was there to complain, in some measure. The difference was that I would be asking for the sheriff and my complaint would rock law enforcement and the underworld.

Victor was a police officer, who longed to rule the underworld. He had abused his status to steal me from Cameron with the hopes of using Cameron's love for me to control him and the underworld. Victor was a bloodsucker, but Cameron could not touch him because he was a police officer; killing a police officer, like killing a rich man's daughter, brought too much unwanted attention to the underworld.

I, on the other hand, was not bound to the underworld and had no aversions to killing Victor. I also had no way of making this happen quickly, before the baby came. The only way I could protect the baby from him was to get him off the streets and put a spotlight on him. After that, anything Victor did or planned would be watched, including putting a hit on me. One day, when I was ready, when he wasn't looking, I would come find him and seek justice for what he had done to Rocco.

I imagined myself going into the police protection program. But I knew there would never be a safe place for me once I ousted Victor and his enterprise. Luckily, Victor's reign over the underworld had petered out after Bill and Cameron had taken over. If I could figure out how to get hold of Bill's inheritance, then I could hide us, better than the cops would.

When the water fountain ladies' argument turned to fisticuffs and hairpulling, two police officers came to pull them apart. It took me a little while to recall where I had seen them before. It was the third officer who came to help them that refreshed my memory. He was a tall baldheaded guy with sunken eyes and puffy cheeks that reminded me of beanbags from a summer-camp toss game. I had once whispered to this man through a locked door. I had once stolen his gun and held it to his head. The baldheaded officer was named Mickey. And his fellow law enforcers were also Victor's minions.

I was an out-and-out moron. How could I have not assumed that at least some of the men under Shield's reign would have also been police officers? One dirty cop will attract more dirty cops. Street thugs, dirty cops—all bad guys are genetically created to gravitate toward each other.

Callister's police department was the most dangerous place for me to be, and yet there I was, idiotically defenseless. I turtled inside my hood and slid down the closest hallway.

I could hear the women scuffling in the short hallway while

Shield's men tried to pull them apart. The hallway had only one door, metal, and it was locked with a card scan. At the end of it were two glass cases that stood side by side. I used the reflection in the glass to watch what was going on behind me and find an opportunity to escape.

When pajama guy chimed into the chaos and started screaming his legal woes behind Shield's officers, more officers started pouring through the metal door. I stood as close to the glass as I could, trying to stay out of their way and field of vision. The hallway was a really bad place to be stuck. Moron. Out-and-out.

While I was observing the show, something in one of the glass cases caught my eye. The first one was a trophy case, containing mostly baseball and football trophies and a few Little League thank-you plaques.

It was the second case that made my breath feel as though it were turning to fire.

It started with a picture of Victor receiving some kind of medal of honor, shaking hands with Callister's city sheriff, who looked giddy, like he was rubbing elbows with a rock star.

Then there were newspaper articles. "Victor Orozo Cracks Down on Organized Crime." "Orozo Biggest Drug Bust in History of USA." The last one read "Callister's Victor Orozo— Elected President of the National Police Association."

And then there was a picture of Victor at the White House, standing next to the president of the United States of America. All smiles. All sham.

Newspaper articles, pictures, certificates, plaques, and trophies, all in admiration of Victor Orozo, Callister's hometown hero. There were even a few letters from children depicting how Victor's charity work had changed their lives. Could the whole world be so blind to this psychopath? Or perhaps everybody was in on it.

I quickly came to the realization that Victor was not just another dirty cop. He was the top cop. The leader of their union. He was much smarter than I ever wanted to give him credit for.

His grasp, the underworld's grasp, ran deep in everyday life. Children, families, the good people of Callister City believed he was one of the good ones, believed that the police officers who walked their streets were there for them. But they were there for themselves. And their sociopath union leader.

While the entire corrupt Callister police force was breathing down my neck, or at least it seemed like it, I had no other choice but to wait, keep myself hidden in the corner, and pray. I was a turtle wedged in a corner while the hammerhead sharks sifted through the seaweed for easy prey.

Eventually, the women were cuffed and dragged away kicking.

Then pajama man was thrown out of the building.

The traitorous officers disappeared behind the armed door once again.

And I didn't wait for something else to draw the sharks again. I calmly walked out of the station, keeping my hood over my flaming red hair.

I had to climb through the back doors of the bus, stealing a ride home, because I didn't have any money left. I hadn't stopped running from the time I left the Victor worship wall until I took a seat on the bus.

Victor shaking hands with the president.

Victor union leader, leading all police organizations in the USA.

I didn't know what all this meant, but I was acutely aware that if Victor's minions were all police officers and that if Victor was their union leader, there was no safe place for me to be.

While I was walking home from the bus stop, I spotted our landlord down the street. He owned at least five other houses on our street and was making his rounds to collect rent checks for the year. It was dinnertime—he had the same good sense as a telemarketer. I ran the rest of the way home and called Meatball over as soon as I got my foot in the door.

Meatball trotted outside with me, and we headed to the

back of the house, where a piece of crap car was parked. It was periwinkle blue, dented, rusted, and all mine.

I pulled my keys out of my purse. We got in my car, and I hoped to hell that it would start. When it did, I checked the gas gauge. It had plenty of gas, so I backed out of the driveway and drove away, in the direction opposite from where I had seen the landlord. I didn't know how long it would take me to make enough money to pay for rent, but I knew that I would have to dodge the landlord until I could. And I would have to figure out a way to keep Meatball hidden from him when he made his spot visits.

Meatball and I had nowhere to go, so we drove around in circles for a while. Meatball took over the passenger seat and watched the world go by while he licked the window clean. I was becoming a little more adventurous and started widening our circles as the evening became the black night. Eventually, we left the city lights and were driving on county roads. I knew where I was going. I suppose I always knew I was going to go there. Eventually.

If I closed my eyes, I could see myself being back there. The long road. The pebbled path. The rickety porch. My favorite place in the world. I wasn't sure if I would be able to recognize the driveway. Even in bright daylight, it was so well hidden in the trees that it was hard to spot. It was Meatball who convinced me I was on the right track. He had woken up as soon as I had turned on the road and started wagging his behind and barking when I slowed to the driveway.

When we drove up to Cameron's cottage, it was early in the morning.

When Cameron and I left the cottage on the day of Rocco's funeral, we left Meatball behind. This cottage was supposed to have been Cameron's little secret, but when Carly brought Meatball to me, it crossed my mind that perhaps they had known about this place the whole time. I couldn't be sure, because Cameron could have gotten Meatball before he rescued me from Victor, but there was always a chance that Carly and Spider knew about this place. I knew it was a dangerous place for me to be; then again, with Victor at the helm of all police organizations and Spider by now likely at the helm of the underworld, so was every other place in the world.

After taking in a bit of bliss watching Meatball run off to smell his favorite spots in the surrounding woods and grabbing the key that was hidden in the shed's eaves, there I was, standing inside the place that would always be home to me. I swear that as soon as I closed the door behind me, I could smell Cameron. It was as if he were still there. Everything in the cottage was exactly the same as I had remembered it, except that there was no Cameron.

And that was when I realized that I would never stop feeling this way. That there would never be another day, another second when I wouldn't miss him.

****

Maria had a small garden in her room. She would keep as many flowered plants as she could fit in her small windowsill. My mother didn't allow for live plants in the house because they were—according to her—dirty and could leave fallen leaves on the floor that could be too easily dismissed by the house staff. The only live plants she would allow were cut-off flowers that needed to come in the morning and be gone by bedtime. Maria would explain to me that she kept her plants because life brings life, that caring for another life meant caring for your own. Though secretly, I knew she kept them because it was a place where we could both escape the coldness, the lifelessness of the mansion.

There was one early morning when she came to drag me out of bed. Today was the day that the walking iris was blooming. I could smell it as soon as I walked into Maria's room. We had been waiting, caring for it for months. And there it was, finally with its white and violet petals. It reminded me of a starfish wearing purple shoes. The most beautiful and sweet-smelling flower I had encountered. And then, at the end of the day, the bloom was gone.

****

I should have hugged him. That first day in the park, when Meatball knocked me over. The first day I set eyes on Cameron. I should have known that he would change my life so much. I should have known that he was too much for me, that we were too perfect to last. Like the walking iris, he was too much of a good thing, something nature can't allow for too long. If I could have just realized that my time with him would be cut so short, I would have held him in my arms and never let him go.

Being in Cameron's cottage, in this place where we were perfect, just made me want to start crying again. I had been alone pretty much my whole life. Only since I had lost Cameron had I really felt my loneliness.

I waited for Meatball to finish his round of the property, let him in, and went up the shaky stairs to the loft. I climbed into our bed, brought Cameron's blanket to my nose, and fell asleep to the hum of the refrigerator.

Rocco's face came back to haunt my dreams. I woke up, but there were no tears or cold sweats this time—just a great sense of loss. The room was almost completely dark, with the only light coming from the moonlight that shone through the small cottage windows. Cameron was next to me, but he wasn't really sleeping. He never really slept.

"I love you," I heard him murmur, and I turned around.

Cameron found my lips in the dark. He kissed me, softly but with purpose, like he was taking a bite out of a peach for the first time. His tongue tasted every inch. His hand climbed up my thigh to my breast, and he moved on top of me, pulling my T-shirt over my head. I wrapped my legs around his waist, taking the full weight of him on me as he took me whole.

We were one skin once again.

This was the first dream of Cameron I'd had since his death. But it wasn't like any other dream I'd ever had. This dream was vivid, to the point that I could still feel Cameron's breath tingling against my skin even though I was awake now.

If something actually happened the same way you remembered it while in slumber, was it still a dream? Or was it something else? Perhaps a memory. Or wishful thinking, as they say. When does dream become memory, and when does memory become dream?

This dream was not just a dream. It was exact. It was a few months ago. The night had started right here, in this bed, with a nightmare about Rocco just a few days after his death, and had ended with Cameron and me making love for the first time.

Dream. Memory. Who cared? I went back to sleep, hoping to find Cameron there.

\*\*\*\*

I took Meatball to the dock when I woke up again. He couldn't wait to jump in the pond even if the water was freezing. I lay on my back and watched the sky through the trees, as I had done with Cameron. Even though I knew I was taking a risk by staying at the cottage for so long, I felt safe here.

Spider was well hidden within the underworld, but Victor was everywhere, on purpose. He didn't want to just rule the underworld; he wanted to control *everything*. He had made a good name for himself, even though it was all a lie.

I had gone to the police station. I had thought about tarnishing his reputation—spreading the word on Victor's deceit—and hopefully get him arrested, but what good would that do? Who would take my word against that of a hero? What evidence did I have, other than my own observation?

And then there was Spider—as if Victor didn't give me enough to worry about.

I hoped that by finding out more about Cameron, I would find Spider. Cameron had told me that he and Spider had been so-called friends since they'd been in juvie together. They had been partners in crime when Cameron was in high school. Cameron's hidden life would surely lead me to Spider, or at least give me clues as to how to find the bastard.

All this would take time, and time was not on my side.

All these questions were floating around in my head; yet I was unusually calm. The rippling of the water against the dock, the sloshing of Meatball's paws, the sway of trees—all made it easy for me to forget about everything else and focus on the biggest issue: how to survive.

\*\*\*\*

After finding dog and human food in the pantry of Cameron's cottage, Meatball and I spent another night. But at the end of the weekend, I knew we couldn't stay any longer. Eventually we would run out of food here too, and there weren't many job prospects in the middle of the woods. I packed up whatever food was left and dragged Meatball into the car. I knew how he felt. I didn't want to leave either.

Meatball's head was low the whole drive home. It was weird and extremely lonely to know that my only friend, the only one who knew who I was and where I had been, was a dog.

It wasn't until I got out of the car and into the chilly night that I realized I'd left my jacket hanging on the kitchen chair at the cottage.

All the streetlights were on, and so was the porch light. I didn't even know we had a porch light, let alone one with a working lightbulb. Between Meatball's leash and the bag of stolen groceries, I struggled to turn the front door handle. It didn't matter. The door flew open, and I got dragged inside. Even Meatball had been taken by surprise.

He had me in his arms so quickly that I didn't have time to take a breath and validate who it was.

"Bloody hell, where have you been?" he demanded. "I've been pacing this shithole for the last twenty-four hours."

I pulled myself off his chest and out of his grasp.

I shook my head, certain I was imagining things again.

His blue eyes were creased with worry, but his trademark grin was slowly spreading, softening his features again.

I was still shaking my head in disbelief. "Griff? Is it really you?"

He arched his brows. I dropped my groceries and jumped in his arms.

He pulled me in, and I felt as though I'd been encased in cement for years and suddenly set free. As if the circle of Griff's arms had taken us to another world, to our own realm, where money didn't matter, where people like Spider and Victor did not exist. Where everything would be okay. Where just for a moment, I could be weightless.

# Chapter Four: Cameron

## Paying the Price

I figured I would have some explaining to do. After I had deliberately left Spider in Jersey and flown to San Francisco without his knowledge, Spider started asking questions. When we finally met up in Los Angeles, we had barely spoken ten words to each other. Then again, we were both busy planning for the biggest drug shipment of our careers. We both knew this was going to be our redemption ... *my* redemption for the captains. If we could pull this shipment off, it would bring more money to the captains than they had made in the last three years.

Now we were on a plane heading to Montreal. A few hours together with no escape.

Spider kept his eyes pinned on a drop of water that was slowly making its way across the window. Wherever he was, he wasn't sitting on a plane with me. Suddenly I realized that while I had been avoiding Spider, he had been avoiding me. And this concerned me.

"Carly not coming?"

Spider jumped a little at the sound of my voice. "She's not feeling well."

"Seems like she's been sick a lot lately. We have a business to run. Do I need to find someone to replace her?"

Spider was back in his head, looking out the window.

He was usually on top of everything. I had never had to ask anything of him twice or have him do anything over. But in the last few days, mistakes had been made, by both him and Carly. Numbers were coming back incorrect, messages were being fuddled, everything was coming in just a bit late. I normally wouldn't call him on it, especially with the mistakes I'd been making myself lately, but there was something in his demeanor that now had me *very* concerned.

"You know you screwed up the order coming in from the Colombians," I told him. "That was the third time in a row. I had to call and fix it myself."

Spider's hand twitched, so I knew he was listening to me.

"Do I need to find someone to replace you too?"

He turned his head. "I'd love to see you try."

"Everyone's replaceable."

Spider stared back at me. "Carly's pregnant again."

I coughed up my club soda. I wasn't sure what part had made me more surprised: the fact that Carly was pregnant ... or that she was pregnant *again*.

"Jesus," was all I could muster.

Spider was staring off into space, shaking his head.

"What the hell are you two thinking?" I finally managed.

"You think this was *my* plan?"

"You obviously had *some* part in it."

Spider shut his eyes.

I already knew the answer to his conundrum. When it came to Carly, when Carly had something on her brain, Spider and the rest of the world were defenseless.

As far as I was concerned, there never was a Spider without a Carly. When Spider and I met, Carly wasn't just in the picture; she was the picture.

We were cellmates in juvie. I was a fourteen-year-old wisp of a kid, and Spider was the kid no one dared to mess with. Rumor was that he had gotten nabbed beating up a man twice his size to the brink of death. Spider traded me all my telephone privileges in exchange for protection. It was an easy trade; I had no one to call.

He called this chick named Carly frequently, obsessively, first in line for the phones every time. I suppose I was a little surprised when he confessed to me that the man he beat up was the chick's father. And that she was still taking his calls.

As weeks of quiet nights passed, our friendship grew, our trust grew, and while Spider and I weren't very chatty, I had heard enough bits and pieces of information to put the whole story together.

Carly's father was a drunk, who beat up his wife, spent any money he managed to make on booze and women, and had a preference for younger girls, like his own five daughters. Because Carly's mother didn't speak English, any work she managed to find had to be at night and under the table. She still barely made ends meet. Spider was Carly's next-door neighbor. He had spent most of his childhood creeping through her window in the evening and sleeping on the floor next to her bed, keeping Carly's father away, usually with a baseball bat or a broom, like one would an alley rat.

One night, as a luckily not-quite adult, Spider had accosted Carly's father after he had gone on a drunken rampage of the house, breaking everything in sight, including Carly's mother's jaw. Spider ended up in juvie, and Carly's father ended up in jail after he was released from the hospital.

Time was running out until her father was done paying his debt to society and ready to take his revenge on the six women in his life.

Kids like Spider and me belonged in juvie. It prepared us—people like us—for things to come. First comes juvie, then comes prison. That's just the way it is for people who come from the same shitholes as us. There's no sense hoping for anything different. A kid like me should have never been enrolled in Saint Emmanuel, the most prestigious and expensive private school in the eastern

Unites States. Hell, a kid like me should have never been enrolled in any kind of school. We were lucky if we finished grade eight.

And yet I was enrolled in Saint Emmanuel's Academy. Not because of any kind of Daddy Warbucks selfless rich benefactor. I just happened to be the kid of a con man who needed to put on a show, who found a way to pay Saint Emmanuel's ridiculous tuition because he knew that it would pay off ten times over if he played his cards right. With an outlandish foreign accent, a sports car, and a kid in prep school, my father was irresistible to any rich old lady.

When I'd told Spider about Saint Emmanuel, he didn't believe me at first, until I told him about my con-artist father. Fraud, scams—using innocent people to our advantage—these things were second nature to us. So we started talking about using my so-called good fortune to prey on the rich and reckless. The plan he and I concocted to sell drugs at my private school wasn't just a way for him and Carly to get out of the slums; it was a way for them to pay her dad enough money to stay away from her mom and sisters forever. Carly's father left town with a wad of cash and never looked back.

Now, once in a while, Spider showed up with cash in whatever hole Carly's father had been lying in. He woke her father up long enough to sign a letter of apology to Carly's mom and throw money his way. Carly sent the letter to her mother, along with a hefty sum of money. Having it come from her useless husband was the only way Carly's mom would accept the handout.

Carly and Spider chose this life so that Carly's mom and sisters could live a better life.

Now we were on a plane, heading into another pile of trouble. And Spider was expecting a child with the girl he'd devoted his life to.

"You know we can't have this, right?" I told him.

"I know."

"There's no room for a kid. Especially with all the shit that's been going on."

"I know!" he barked. "I'll figure something out."

Spider went back to the raindrop on the window, and I poured us both a stiff drink.

We landed at a small airport in Quebec, and a driver took us to downtown Montreal.

Canada was loaded with ports, with two of the biggest ports in the world located in Montreal and Vancouver. We had established them as our main conduits for everything from guns to drugs to stolen cars to anything else that could put money in our pockets. It had been a profitable relationship. And yet, over the past few months, infighting among the four factions was causing delays in shipments and one major loss in drug cargo. Blood had started spilling into small towns, reporters were starting to dramatize, and the people were looking to the government to stop the violence. Once the government started to turn its limited funds to the issue and got too involved, shipments started to slow down, and we had to spend more money funding temporary measures.

Unlike the cooperative we had created in America, the Canadian factions still operated independently. This meant that whenever I needed something brought in through Canada, I had to deal with five different groups: the bikers, the First Nations gangs, the three street gangs, the Italian Mafia, and the Asian triad.

This was inefficient, and it was all about to change. As I had put forward to the American captains a few months before, there was opportunity for us to move in and "help" our Canadian brethren get organized and get richer and safer in the process. By working as one coalition, the Canadians could benefit from the American Coalition's and each other's resources and contacts and be better protected from police authorities by working as one unit. After all, a lion is stronger in a pack than he is solitary.

Of course, once the Canadians were organized, we would be collecting our commission while keeping total control over everything.

In the end, an American takeover was inevitable, and the

Canadian underworld had, with my firmness, finally come to terms with this.

Word had already spread among the factions that we were now ready to establish a single leader for the Canadian underworld. And they were all chomping at the bit, ready to pounce on the top job. After deliberations from the American captains, only the triad and Mafia bosses remained in the running. I was in Montreal to make the final decision and promote an underling. Spider was there to make sure I didn't get murdered in the process.

Montreal was Italian Mafia territory and had been since the 1920s. They controlled its ports, unions, and anything deemed entertainment—booze, drugs, guns, gambling, girls. Two years ago, Ignazio had taken the reins of the Mafia after the former boss had been shot down in his driveway while he was in his pajamas taking out the garbage.

Our driver stopped in front of a janitorial services building, and we were ushered in by a couple of Ignazio's men. We were taken through corridors and into a janitor's closet. Apparently even a janitorial services company needed janitorial services. A shelf was pushed aside, revealing a dummy hidden passage. We made our way down through a tunnel and then another until we reached double metal doors. When the doors were opened from inside, a waft of air stifled with the smell of cognac and cigars hit my nose.

Ignazio was ready to greet Spider and me with a fervent handshake as soon as we walked in. He was dressed humbly in jeans and a sports jacket but still well-manicured, perfectly tailored. The room was meant as a restaurant for Ignazio's elite. A shark tank behind a bar adorned one wall, while a twenty-foot-high wine rack adorned the other. Two tables had been set up in the middle of the room: one for the bosses and one for their seconds-in-command.

It seemed we were the last ones to arrive and all had been waiting for Spider and me to show, though based on the ridiculous grins spread across the faces, they hadn't been bored.

I felt as though I had walked into a New Year's Eve bash. There were more girls in small sparkly dresses than there were men in overpriced suits. The music was louder than my own thoughts.

As soon as Spider and I were shown to our respective heads of table, the music subsided, the beautiful girls disappeared, and Ignazio called for a toast as Italian waiters refilled glasses.

"There is a time for business and a time for play. *A travola non si invecchia*. At the table with good friends and family, you do not become old. Tonight you are my guests. Tonight we play. Salud!"

Ignazio raised his glass to me, and everyone at our table and the second table followed suit.

We had expected to be wooed, but the lavishness Ignazio showered was unprecedented.

He personally went around refilling glasses with whatever booze of choice, clapping men on the back, making small talk, making jokes. Ensuring that no one was left wanting. Plates were brought out at Ignazio's click of fingers, exotic foods were served, and a brick of cocaine was thrown in front of every patron. There were smiles all around, except on the faces of Seetoo and Zhongshu, triad boss and his underboss. Which was exactly why Ignazio insisted on having them there.

Unlike Ignazio's recent rise to leadership, Seetoo had been triad boss for almost twenty years. His ascension had been steady but slow, as had been his gang's fortunes. The Mafia had been making more money than the triad, but this had come with the price of constant struggles for power and messy, high-profile killings.

Seetoo was on enemy territory, and by the glower of his face, he wasn't happy about it. I had decided that the bosses should all suffer together, given that they had a lifetime—some shorter than others—to work together. Besides, his turn to woo would come soon enough, but for now, he was forced to watch Ignazio make his pitch to me.

With his attention to needs and details, Ignazio obviously knew what we were looking for in a leader—someone who knew how to make money; someone who knew how to bring all these gangs together to form one collective.

I grabbed my steak knife and slit the cocaine package. I stuck my finger in the powder and licked it. It was perfect, pure. Bolivian cocaine. As the rest of the table tested the merchandise, a sense of awe spread around the tables. Seetoo leaned back in his chair and watched me. We both knew I had made my decision.

It wasn't the first time I had come across such purity, but the stuff was definitely hard to come by. Ignazio wasn't just a great host ... he had great connections.

I turned to Spider's table and noticed that he had already checked the merchandise and was deep in conversation with Feleti, Ignazio's second-in-command.

Seetoo and Zhongshu left before the flaming desserts were served.

When the plates were practically licked clean and the girls came back, I pushed my chair back and met Spider at the door.

Ignazio was midsentence with the biker boss when he spotted us leaving. He left the bar to come say good-bye. He and I looked each other in the eyes as we shook hands and parted.

****

"I need you to arrange meetings," I told Spider after we were dropped off in downtown Montreal.

"I know," he grumbled, and we parted ways without another word.

While Spider got people together, I had someone to see.

Gabrielle—my Montreal girl. She was a dark-haired beauty I'd met some time ago. I was at a meeting, and she was the eye candy. She now had an apartment in the entertainment district. It was a small place but expensive, and at least it wasn't the shithole she lived in when we met.

I used my key to open the door and prayed she was out or

asleep. I stepped through the door and listened in the dark. All was quiet.

As I made my way around her oversized furniture, the room lit solely by the glow of streetlights through the window, I noticed for the first time some of her pictures spread across her tiny little living room. They could have been pictures of her family, her friends, her world. Who knew? We had never done much talking.

"Keith," I heard Gabrielle call out from her bedroom. She had heard me come in. Shit.

Gabrielle knew me as Keith because that was what I was drinking the night we had hooked up.

I placed an envelope on her kitchen counter and left. The elevator doors closed just as she was opening her apartment door. She depended on the money I left her every time, but I couldn't stay.

I couldn't just go back to the way things were, to the man I had once been.

All I could think about was how every time Emmy fell asleep on me, she would dig her fist into my stomach and clench my shirt so tight that it stretched the material. As if she were afraid of waking up alone.

Someday, it would be someone else's T-shirt that she would ruin. She wouldn't wake up alone forever.

But I would.

A taste of Emmy, and everything else tasted like sand.

I left Gabrielle enough money so that she would leave her crappy apartment, disappear, and never have to depend on guys like me again.

****

By the time all the bosses were gathered together again, it was the next night, and we were well outside the city. They were all seated around a table, while the underbosses waited in another room. Spider sat by the wall, a few feet behind me. He had been able to find us an empty windshield factory to stage our meeting. It was common ground for all tonight.

Ignazio and Seetoo flanked me as the room quietly awaited my decision.

Ignazio grinned, while Seetoo gazed ahead stone-faced.

"Everyone around this table is going to make more money this year than you have in your whole lifetime. But the only way that will happen is if you all work together. From this day on, everyone is now a captain in this Coalition except for one of you, who will lead and report directly to me. My decision is final and is upheld by the American captains."

I got up and stood behind Ignazio, placing my hands on his shoulders.

I slid my hand to my waistband, grabbed the steak knife from his restaurant, and plunged it into his neck, severing his carotid artery. Spider held Ignazio down while he bled out, and I took my seat.

"All profit must be handed to the leader of the Coalition for distribution," I continued, my hands splayed over the table.

Seetoo threw a brick of cocaine—the party favor from Ignazio's merrymaking—on the table. Pure, perfect cocaine.

Bolivian cocaine was indeed difficult to obtain, and I had specifically ordered this shipment from Peru before it had apparently gone missing on its way to the Port of Montreal. Ignazio had reported that Somalian pirates had captured the missing ship, seizing the pure, perfect cocaine.

Bolivian cocaine had been Ignazio's mistake. I would have recognized that purity anywhere, as would Spider and Seetoo. Seetoo knew he had captured leadership before Ignazio had even ordered the desserts to be brought out.

Ignazio slumped to the floor, and Spider moved him over. I took my time, looking each captain in the eye. No one moved.

"If you steal, if you take *anything* from the Coalition, you *will* be replaced. If you lie, you will be replaced. If you fall out of line, you will be replaced."

I nodded at Spider, and he opened the door. Feleti, Ignazio's underboss, walked in, looking ahead as he stepped over Ignazio's body and calmly took his place at the table. After Feleti had willingly shared Ignazio's betrayal following Spider's prodding, it had been decided that he would live to take Ignazio's place as captain.

Seetoo's underboss then came through the door, carrying a couple of clear plastic garbage bags with almost as many heads as there were men around the table. At this sight, there was a slight gasp from the captains. All of their underbosses—they each had one—had been shot through the head and beheaded. The bags were thrown on the table.

"Your leader is Seetoo. How you do business, how you make money, who you're allied to, this will all change from now on." I pointed to the bags on the table. "Seetoo has made his first decision as leader. I will leave him to tell you how he will help you become richer than you could imagine."

Spider and I left behind a dead, silent room and left Seetoo to take the reins as leader of the Canadian underworld. We walked through the factory as headless bodies were being fed to the giant glass ovens by Seetoo's men.

"You think Seetoo can do it?" Spider asked me as we were on our way to dinner.

I shrugged. "If he doesn't, it's his head."

Ignazio was the fifteenth man I killed.

\*\*\*\*

I flew back to Callister, leaving Spider to iron out the details with Seetoo and get my drug shipment back from the Mafia.

The last place I wanted to be was Callister because I knew that being so close to Emmy and not being able to see her would be more painful than getting my fingernails yanked out one by one. But Carly was now refusing to fly or travel anywhere, and I had to talk to her about the money.

By the time I drove up to our Callister hideout, I was fuming. It wasn't the fact that Carly didn't want to travel when she was barely pregnant or the fact that I'd had to reschedule a meeting because I had to make an extra stop in Callister; it was the fact that she was making me come back to Callister, forcing me to be so close to Emmy, dangling a damn carrot in front of my face—and it was the fact that she was doing this to me because she was pregnant, because she wanted to be pregnant, because she thought it was okay for us to act like we were normal people who could have families and love and be loved unconditionally.

By the time I raced into our private parking lot, punched the elevator button, and stomped down our carpeted hallway, I could feel every clenched muscle in my body.

Tiny was sitting on the couch watching TV.

"Where's Carly?" I asked him.

"Lying down." He thumbed toward Carly's bedroom.

Of course she was. Because that was what normal pregnant people did. They lay down in the middle of the day.

I stormed into my room and felt like flinging my bag against the wall. But I didn't. I set it down calmly, rationally, like the leader of the underworld ought to behave.

And then I saw the bed where Emmy had woken up after Rocco had hit her over the head in the cemetery. And then I saw the chair in the corner from where I had watched her sleep, worried over her, worried about how I was going to handle everything. Carly was torturing me, practically pushing me to the brink of my emotions.

I slumped on the chair and sank my head into my hands. I turned my head and watched over the city, my eyes making their way toward the direction of Emily's slum of a neighborhood.

I didn't know how long I'd been staring out the window when I heard the door open.

"I'm sorry I made you come here to meet me." She was blanched and struggled to make it to the bed to sit. I thought pregnant women were supposed to glow.

"I didn't tell Spider about the money you asked me to get," she told me.

"Thanks."

"It's not like Spider and I talk much these days," she said. "I was able to get a good amount of your money released."

I turned my eyes back to the city.

"Are you going to tell me what you're planning to do with all that money?" Carly asked.

I didn't answer her.

The only sound came from whatever show Tiny was watching on TV.

But Carly finally ripped through the silence. "It feels like we're falling apart, Cam. You and Spider. You and me. Spider and me. We hardly speak anymore. And you've been so secretive. It's like you're trying to shut us out of everything, and I don't know why."

"I don't need to report on what I do with my personal funds."

"I was hoping you were going to tell me that you had found a way to go get Emily back."

I flipped my eyes to her. "That's not going to happen."

"Why not?"

"Because Emmy is better off without me." I knew that Carly had never approved of my plan to fake my death and release Emmy from me. But the fact that Carly was bringing this back up again made me angry.

"Emily isn't the porcelain doll I thought she was," Carly continued, unscathed by my determination. "I'll admit that she's innocent, even a little naïve. But there's something about her, about how we all change when she's here. It's like she's a light at the end of a dark road."

Carly was an alien to me now. The lovely words coming out of her mouth were not those of the sarcastic, angry, bitter Carly I knew and loved. Yet despite all the borderline bullshit religious crap she was insinuating, I knew what she was trying to say. Emmy brought us—brought me—love.

But I could only bring her pain.

"Having Emily here, it was like everything felt right for us. Like things would finally get better somehow. Like maybe we would find a way out of all this blackness," Carly persisted.

Why was Carly so intent on rehashing this? She was losing it, losing her grip on reality.

"There's no way out, Carly. I figured that out a long time ago. Emmy wouldn't change that for us. She would just get jammed, like we are. This is our life. Live with it. Emily isn't coming back. The day you get that in your head is the day we move on."

All of a sudden, Carly winced, from the outside in. She held her breath and clenched her teeth. Then she shut her eyes.

Redness seeped through her beige pants.

When she opened her eyes, she shot up from the bed. I could see her start melting as she put her hand to her soaked pant leg, touched it, pulled it away, and stared at the blood on her doll-sized hand. She started shaking her head, her eyes filling with every shake. When she looked up at me, she was already unconscious. I caught her before she slumped to the ground.

****

Doctor Lorne was used to getting woken up in a panic, even if it was in the middle of the day. Everything for us was always a matter of life and death.

Tiny helped me carry Carly to my car, and he called Doctor Lorne as we sped out of the city. Doctor Lorne was sobered when we got to his farmhouse. Carly was starting to wake up as I carried her into Doctor Lorne's fully operating emergency room.

"You'll be okay," I whispered to her, though I hardly believed it myself.

She stared at the ceiling as Doctor Lorne bent over her, and a nurse directed me out of the room.

Doctor Lorne's farm had been built in a conclave on his property. While I felt like a gofer every time I came here, at least it was buried and away from prying eyes as we dragged bloodied bodies out for Doctor Lorne to fix.

The pastures came down the hill in front of the house where a handful of horses neighed and walked around. Meatball used to love tormenting them.

A few times when we had been here early in the morning, I had seen Lorne walking out to tend to his horses, always with a stiff drink in his hand. I guess that made him a functional drunk. I wasn't used to that kind of drunk.

Tiny and I were pacing about on the porch for a while before the doctor came back out. When he appeared through the doorway, Tiny disappeared. He knew his place, and he knew what was none of his business.

"It was inevitable," Doctor Lorne told me as he dried his hands on his smock. "There wasn't much I could do. Her body never let the fetus develop. I just made her more comfortable."

I stared ahead. "Thank you."

"She's awake, if you want to go see her." He went back inside.

Carly was no longer pregnant. Carly was no longer going to be bringing a child into our monstrous lives. This was what I had wanted, wasn't it?

I went back into the house and into Carly's room. There was a nurse busying herself by Carly's bedside, checking Carly's temperature, checking her IV. When she was done, she left us.

Carly was awake, eyes still on the ceiling. Except for the pillows plumped under her head and the change of clothes, it was as if she hadn't moved at all.

I felt like all the air had been sucked out of the room.

What was I supposed to say to her? That I ought to be shot for telling Spider that he needed to make sure this baby never came to be?

I stood over her. "Carly," I started to say as the fist in my throat expanded.

Carly turned her eyes and looked through me. "It's for the

best. It's like you said, there's no way out for us. This is the life we made. This is the life we'll die in."

I came to grab her hand, but she pulled away and pulled the covers up to her chin, turning her head away.

I stayed for a minute, searching for something to say. I came up incompetent. I wasn't built for this kind of stuff.

When Spider finally got there, we had been there just a few hours. He sent a cloud of dust storming through the air as his car came to a halt. He ran past me on the porch without ever noticing me, his eyes straight ahead, desperate to see Carly.

After a while he came to join me on the porch and sat, staring at his shadow on the floorboards.

"Will she be okay?" I asked him through the sounds of crickets in the darkness.

"Physically? She'll be fine. She just needs to rest," he said. "But every time she miscarries, she changes. She gets a little darker. None of this is her fault. It's a medical thing. Her body just keeps fighting against any pregnancy. There's nothing the doctors can do to change that. She'll probably never be able to have kids. But Carly sees more into this than that. To her, the miscarriages are a form of punishment. She says it's God's way of retaliating against us for what we do, what we've done."

"How many have there been? How many times has she miscarried?"

"This is her fourth miscarriage," he told me.

"So why does she keep—"

"Why does she keep getting pregnant knowing that she'll probably never be able to have children?" He shook his head. "She has this idea of what her life *should* look like. She misses her family and wants what her sisters have. A bunch of kids running around. A normal family life."

"This won't happen again," he promised.

I was about to apologize for what I had said on the plane, but then I realized that Spider was talking to himself.

"I can't let her do this to herself anymore," he breathed, his head in his hands.

I left Spider and Carly alone so that they could grieve and regroup; I sent Tiny on an errand before I drove off.

I should have been off to travel for business. Especially with Spider out of commission for however long it took. But Doctor Lorne's farm was too close to my favorite place in the world for me to pass up the opportunity to stop by. It felt like a lifetime ago since I'd last been. In some ways, it had been in another life.

Besides, it was already night.

When I turned onto the gravel mile-long road to the cottage, I missed Meatball. This was usually the point when he'd start to go nuts in the car, forcing his meaty head through the small opening I'd leave for him when we drove. He always had to be the first to smell the cottage air. Then he'd pummel over me as soon as I opened my car door so that he could be first to the porch, first to the pond, first to get everything in the cottage soaking wet and smelling of waterlogged dog.

Meatball had led a charmed life with me as far as a dog's life was concerned.

But that hadn't always been the case.

The first day I laid eyes on him, Meatball was in a cage that was barely big enough for him to stand in. I had business dealings with a creep of a distributor who ran dogfights on the side as a pastime. We were walking past the two dozen cages of barking, raging dogs. That was how I noticed Meatball. He was the only one that wasn't acting up. He sat and watched us go by without a sound.

When the meeting ended and I was walking back to my car alone, Meatball was there, waiting for me by the car. I had no idea how he had gotten there. I hesitated at first—he was, after all, a huge ball of meat that was trained to fight to the death. Though the dog didn't growl, he wasn't moving either. I opened the door; he got in and took possession of the front seat, staring straight ahead. I glanced around, shrugged, and followed him in. We never looked back.

It took a while before he would even let me give him a bath. I had to coax him with hotdogs. He had a big gash that went from one ear down to the side of his jaw and multiple lacerations on his thick neck and paws. I cleaned him up and decided to keep him. Or he decided to keep me. I wasn't really sure how it had really happened.

Before I knew it, I had a dog named Meatball.

As soon as I opened the door to the cottage, I knew Emmy had been there. It was the way the dust had shifted, and it was the jacket she had left on the back of one of the kitchen chairs. My heart bounced. I didn't know which was worse—the thought that she might still be there and see me, or the thought that she was gone.

I kept the light off and crept upstairs.

The bed was empty.

I stared at it for a while, as though it were unfamiliar. The only way I remembered it was with Emmy in it. Now it was just sheets and a mattress. Foreign.

I climbed in and turned my face into the pillow. I could still smell her shampoo. Or I dreamed of the smell of her shampoo.

I dreamed that my face was in her hair. I could hear her soft breaths over the song of the crickets outside.

I honestly tried to resist at first. Hearing her breathing, so close, was a piece of my heaven.

But my fingers crept up the side of her body, following her curves, over skin and T-shirt while she squirmed in her sleep. By the time my fingers made it up her neck, she was awake and had flipped over, her face flush and plump from sleep. Her sweet, teasing smile made my darkness crumble.

With my fingertips over her eyelids, I bade her to close her eyes before putting my lips to hers, drinking in their smoothness. It was like silk falling over an apple.

I worked my way down to her neck. What I really wanted to

do was bite off a piece of it, to keep. Instead, I nuzzled in hard, on purpose. She twisted, trying not to laugh.

I kept going to the top of her chest, jealous of the collar of her T-shirt that bordered her clavicle. I glanced up, catching Emmy's emerald eyes peeking through thick eyelashes. She never listened to me, not even at play … but God, did I love to see those eyes.

I kept our eyes locked as my chin ran over her cotton T-shirt while my fingers crept up to pull her shirt up, revealing her delicious stomach and tiny belly button. I growled, took the skin between my teeth, and gently tugged. She laughed, finally.

I loved to hear her laugh.

I loved that I could make her laugh.

I wished she would laugh always.

I kissed her stomach, and she resisted, twisting again, taking a slight jump back. Gasping. I chuckled and kissed it again. She screamed, in horror. I looked up to find her pushing herself up to the wall, away from me. I tendered my hand to her, trying to calm her, but she screamed again. Her hands were covered in blood.

I looked down at the beautiful milky skin of her belly to find it oozing red, a gash in place of where my lips had been. I tasted her blood in my mouth. It was thick and luscious.

My eyes shot open like a bullet had gone off in the dead of night. I sat up in bed and took a couple breaths to shake it off.

I jumped out of bed and went to the fridge to get a drink. It was totally empty. Not even a ketchup bottle.

I flipped the switch on and checked the cupboards and the pantry. They had also been cleared out. I grit my teeth and grasped the back of the kitchen chair. I closed my eyes and took a few more calming breaths, resisting the urge to fling the chair across the room.

I sighed and pushed the kitchen table over. There was a loose board where I usually hid a stack of cash for emergencies. One of my many spots around the property.

I took the stash out and poorly hid it under the pillow of our—her—bed. So that the next time Emmy was desperate for money and couldn't afford damn groceries, she would miraculously come across this hidden stash of cash. I only hoped that she wouldn't be too stubborn to take it.

Before closing the cottage door, I put everything back the way it was, as though I had never been there. I sat in my car for a while and looked at my little cottage, the place that I loved, the place where I loved. It was her place now—hers and Meatball's.

I was drumming my fingers against the steering wheel, debating ... then ran back inside to get the jacket that Emmy had forgotten. I put the key in the ignition and vowed to never return.

# Chapter Five: Emmy

## Unhinged

Griff, with the smile that could melt an ice rink and the arms that could crush a car. Griff, with the shot of enflamed hair that could only be overtaken by mine. It was hard to not let his effortless joy spread through when I was around him. Before I knew it, I was smiling, with such force that I could feel it in my teeth.

"What are you doing here?" I asked him as I pulled out of his grizzly arms and bent down to reassure Meatball that this was a friendly attack.

"I could say the same for you." His gaze jumped from the peeling wallpaper to the secondhand furniture to the disgusting stains that covered every possible surface of the house. "Is this how the other half lives?"

I heard a cackle to the side, where Hunter was fidgeting by the archway into the living room.

"Is this how the other half lives?" he repeated to himself, giggling, shaking his head in utter amazement. And he continued to stand there, impervious to the fact that he was surplus.

"How did you find me here?" I whispered to Griff.

"Is there somewhere we can talk?" He eyed Hunter from the corner of his eye. "Alone."

"My room is at the top of the stairs. Behind the curtain."

He sighed. "Sounds glamorous."

I went to the kitchen to put the stolen food away. Meatball and Hunter were on my tail; only one of them was welcome.

"Do you know *who* that is?" Hunter was so excited he was vibrating.

I stood on my toes to put a box of cereal up on the top shelf. "No. I have absolutely no idea who that man I called Griff and hugged is."

"That's Griffin the Grappler Connan. *The* Grappler."

I was sure that if I'd turned around, I would have found that Hunter had tears in his eyes.

"He's the best fighter known to man! His technique, his persistence, his dedication to the sport ... I cried when he retired. I have his poster in my room."

When Hunter's voice turned to that of a tween girl, I threw whatever was left of the groceries into the cupboard and stepped back.

"Oh my god!" he peeped. "You think he'd sign my poster if I asked him?"

"I don't know, Hunter," I said as I got out of the kitchen as quickly as I could. I had so many questions lighting up my brain that I couldn't afford to focus on anything else.

"Can you ask him?" he called out from the kitchen as I ran up the stairs.

It took me a little while to come to terms with the fact that Griff, *my* Griff, was under the same roof as me. This was the same Griff who had been at the Farm, entrenched in the underworld with me. This was the same Griff who had loved Rocco as a brother, as much as I had. This was the same Griff who had known, though hated, Cameron. It wasn't until I saw Griff lounged on my bed that realization really set in. I hadn't imagined it all. Cameron, Rocco, Carly—they had really existed. Which meant that Spider also existed; he still lived.

Having Griff there was like having characters in your favorite horror novel come to life.

"I've been waiting here since last night," he told me in his colossal English accent. "Interesting mates you have. Seems no one knows anything about where you go or what you do around here."

I stood by the doorway, trying to find something to do with my arms.

He pointed to the ceiling. "Looks like the roof's about to cave in."

The roof had been leaking into my room since I had moved in. I mostly ignored it. I didn't have a window, so at least I knew when it was raining out, and Meatball would enjoy the water bucket that would fill up once it started raining again.

When I had finally settled on coolly stuffing my hands in my pockets, Griff sat up and smiled. The sleeves of his button-down shirt hid the tattooed skin that I knew was somewhere under there.

"You gonna sit or what?"

"I'm fine standing." I attempted to lean against the wall, but I misjudged how far from it I was and staggered a few steps back instead.

This made him laugh his deep belly laugh. He was on me before I could find the edge of the wall. He grabbed me in a tackle and carried me to my bed, where he sat me down and kept me in his clinch. I had forgotten how much warmth exuded from Griff. He didn't hold back anything.

Meatball had taken a seat in front of the door, watching every move I made. I didn't know much about canine behavior, but I could swear he was mad at me for some reason. I assumed he was still upset at having to leave Cameron's cottage.

"You don't know how glad I am to see you," Griff said, his voice low and solemn. "Can't say I ever expected to see you again. But when I got here, got so close, and you weren't here …" He caught his breath. "Well, I thought I was going to go mental."

"Yeah, Hunter has that effect on people." Honestly, I had never expected to see him either. The last time I had seen Griff, he was working for drug barons in the middle of a cornfield somewhere in the eastern United States. I had no way of ever being able to find him again.

"I'm just glad you're here, safe."

I pulled away so that I could look him in the eyes. "How on earth did you find me ... here, of all places?"

"I've got a guardian angel."

He got up, searched through the red duffel bag that he had flung on my bedroom floor, and threw a grocery-sized paper bag onto the bed.

"Go ahead," he insisted when I hesitated. "Take a look."

When I opened the bag, I found money. Stacks and stacks of hundred-dollar bills. I couldn't hide my surprise when my head popped up. Griff mirrored my astonishment.

"A few days ago, a couple of guards came up to me, told me that I was done guarding the shed, and blindfolded me," he explained and turned his eyes to the sky. "I thought for sure that I was a goner, Em. We drove for hours, or at least it felt like it. No one talked the whole way. Then the car stopped. They pulled me out, handed me the bag, and gave me a sealed envelope that had this in it."

Griff took a piece of paper out of his pocket and handed it to me.

I unfolded it delicately, like I was disarming a bomb.

Emily. 1777 Riverside Road, Callister, NY.

My first name. My address. Neatly typed.

"I don't understand," I said as I held on to the piece of paper. My hands were shaking, and I didn't know why.

"Neither do I," he admitted, taking my hands, steadying them. "The guards told me to walk south and took off. When I took the blindfold off, I was alone on the side of a logging road with a bag of money, my stuff, and the only key I had to find you. I walked for two hours before I found a town and a convenience store, which was also their bus station.

"The weird thing is that I'd been planning my escape from

hell for weeks, and I was about to run when they gave me my leave. I was going to come find you, rescue you from that asshole. That hellhole he was keeping you in." A drop of water fell from my ceiling into the bucket on the floor. His mouth stretched thin. "What new level of hell have you gotten yourself into this time?"

I couldn't really disagree with Griff. The house made a pigsty look like a palace. But it was the only thing I could count on. At least when I woke up in the morning, I knew where I was. With the rest of my life completely in turmoil, I needed this stability. This place was like the bully you befriended just so you could get a little peace.

"It's really not that bad of a place," I said. "It grows on you after a while."

"If you say so. Doesn't really matter, though. It's not like we're staying."

"It's not?"

He patted the paper bag. "There won't be much left after I pay off my loan sharks, but I'm sure we can afford to live somewhere better than this shanty."

We? It had suddenly dawned on me that Griff meant to live ... with me. It had also struck me that I didn't want Griff to leave. That I *wanted* to him to stay ... with me. But I couldn't leave this fleapit, either.

"I can't leave, Griff," I confessed, my heart racing just a little bit.

His head jerked back. "You can't?"

"I go to school here. The school year has already started. We're never going to be able to find a place that's close to school and affordable."

Though this was not the real reason I couldn't leave, this was all true.

Griff was unshaven and dusty. He had let his short-cropped Mohawk grow out, and now his hair went helter-skelter. While he looked like he had been through a third-world car wash, his green eyes still managed to outshine the grime. I wished I had a hot shower to offer him, but our showerhead had been streaming out lukewarm water lately.

With the way he was looking, with what he had been through, telling him the truth now seemed like it would have been more information than he could have handled.

He assessed me for a few seconds, then he sighed. "You don't want me around, do you?"

"No, that's not it at all. I just meant ... What if you moved in *here*?"

"Here?"

"Here."

Though he seemed to be a little less crushed, the idea wasn't fully winning him over.

"How many roommates do you have?"

"Just a few," I embellished. I had six roommates, in a four-bedroom house, if I counted my broom closet as a room—nobody did. There were two new students who had moved into the other bedroom. I hadn't met them yet, but that meant that the house was full.

"Where would I stay?"

My curtain door flew to the side, covering Meatball's head.

"You can stay in my room," Hunter offered in a squeak. I wondered how much he had overheard.

Griff closed his eyes and rubbed his temples with one hand.

"The lack of any privacy in this place is reason alone to want to stay," he said, his tone heavy with sarcasm.

He opened his eyes and scanned my face. I waited and hoped, though probably not as much as Hunter hoped. When I saw the twinkle in Griff's eyes, I remembered how his joyfulness was almost addictive.

"Well," he exhaled, "can't be all bad if you're here."

Hunter stood by grinning, as though Griff and I weren't in the middle of an extremely personal moment.

Despite my reluctance, Griff didn't seem to be deterred by Hunter's presence. He held me in a long hug, as though years had passed since we had last seen each other, and yet as though no time had passed. As though this were the last time he would ever see me.

My head had started spinning, and the tiredness had made my nausea creep back.

It was all a little too overwhelming.

Griff must have sensed that I was running on fumes. He held me at arm's length, worry creasing his own weary eyes. He brought his lips to my ear.

"Get some sleep," he ordered in a whisper.

He went to examine his living quarters, with Hunter trailing him.

\*\*\*\*

I didn't see much of Griff over the next few days. He once told me that he had been a martial arts fighter but had to go into hiding after his gambling debts had overtaken his life. Now he had to go back in time and use the money to settle the score. I'd hear him come in very early in the mornings. He would poke his head through the curtain. But I was so exhausted I couldn't even lift my head from the pillow to see him.

By the time I woke up in the morning, he was already gone.

I had assumed that catching up on my schoolwork would be easy. School was one of those things that I was good at. But I hadn't counted on the waves of sheer exhaustion that would take my mind and body hostage throughout the day. Cassie had had to not-so-gently nudge me awake during our ethics class.

At least I was puking on a schedule now. No more running out in the middle of a class.

But every time I walked into class, I searched for him. Like Cameron would just magically appear out of unventilated air. When he didn't appear, it was like a fresh nail being plunged into my heart. I didn't know why I was so hell-bent on torturing myself like that.

I hadn't given up hope of finding out more about Cameron. I wanted to know how many classes he had taken with me last year. And finding Cameron meant finding Spider. Of course, one day I would have to explain to Cameron's child who his or her father was. But it was more than all that. Cameron had known everything about me, and I realized that I had barely scratched the surface of who this man that I loved really was.

Who was Cameron James Hillard?

All I knew was that he had been discarded since birth by an alcoholic mother and a delinquent father. The streets had raised him, and these same streets had raised his little brother Rocco and the rest of his half-siblings. Products of their mother's womb—kids who were destined to stay on the streets and repeat their deadened parents' cycle of misery. But Cameron had been the exception. He was exceptional in every way. He had used his adversities, learned from them, and created a position for himself as the leader of the underworld. He became the worst kind of man. Deceitful. Manipulative. Premeditated in his every action. His con-artist father, his cold and abusive mother, the knowledge he gained on the streets and in juvie—these misfortunes had created the most dangerous criminal in the United States.

These were the things that Cameron had divulged to me.

Except that this wasn't who Cameron had been. It had just been his smokescreen, his survival mode. The Cameron I knew, the real Cameron, had been gracious and fair. He had been warm. Tender. When you saw him—when he let you see him—Cameron was exquisite. He was all my love and my joy. My paradise.

My paradise lost.

If I were being honest with myself, what I was really looking for was someone to talk to, someone to share my pain. When Bill died, I had Maria. She loved Bill, and we had memories to share as we grieved and healed. But except for Meatball, who never answered me, I had no such channel to grieve Cameron. As far as the world was concerned, Cameron was a nameless thug. Nobody knew the truth.

The truth. The truth has so many layers, so many versions.

My deep-down truth was that I was afraid of forgetting him. His face, but most of all, his voice. How can you remember a voice after it disappears? With Bill, I had pictures and stories to fill my memories. But the day I realized that I couldn't remember what his voice sounded like anymore, it was like getting crushed by a boulder, like I was losing him all over again. Forgetting his voice was the hardest part about Bill's death.

A face at least can stay imprinted on your mind. Right now, if I closed my eyes, I could still see Cameron, hear his voice. But I had no pictures of him. All I had was my mind's version of him. How long did I have before my mind started forgetting details? I was afraid that if I stopped thinking about him, even for a second, all those parts that made him would disappear, that he would disappear because I was the only one who remembered him.

Someone else had to have loved this beautiful man. Someone else must have seen what I saw in him.

For now, the most basic information I needed was locked away in the school informatics system. At least I hoped it was.

****

The admissions office was the hub of Callister University. It looked a lot like a bank, which was appropriate considering the amount of money they stole from students every year. While the admissions director's assistant showed me around the office, I watched as student after student came up to the counter begging for more time to pay his or her tuition. I suppose it was preparation for what would come later in life when they couldn't pay their mortgage either.

Jeremy wasn't kidding when he had said that there wouldn't be much to my new job. I would spend the few hours I was there every weekday shuffling incoming mail from one desk to the other, stacking it neatly on people's desks and grabbing the outgoing mail. Turn around. Repeat. Mindless was good when my mind was already too crowded.

From the minute I walked into the admissions office, I analyzed everything and everyone I came into contact with. I was changing. I could feel myself changing inside. It was as if I were growing claws. Like I had grown a second set of teeth, and I was prowling underwater, hunting bait until I was ready to attack and pull them under. Roll until I drowned them. I needed information, and I needed it quickly.

While I shook hands with the people I was introduced to, I decided who would be my easiest target. I found her in the form of an overly friendly woman in her fifties. I had first spotted her working the front desk, smiling compassionately at the begging students while she tapped at her keyboard. We hadn't been introduced yet because she was too busy trying to help the helpless.

As soon as the assistant released me from orientation, I headed into the staff room, where I had seen my target head earlier. The staff room had a few tables in the center and a small kitchenette for the staff to use during mealtimes. Around the edges were benches and doorless lockers. Each locker was preassigned by management. I knew this because the assistant had just told me this a few seconds before, and because each locker had its owner's name clearly stuck to the first shelf. I also knew that my preassigned locker was in the corner. I realized now as I spotted my mark at her locker in the front that this was just too far. So I went to the locker that was next to the lady and hung my backpack on the hook inside.

The lady had an extra-large coffee sitting atop her locker, and she was bent over, recounting her change from her coffee purchase as she put it away in her wallet, one bill, one coin at a time. She was wearing an obviously self-knitted orange and green sweater, with a brooch pinned at the breast. The brooch looked like a hangman Mr. Pumpkin Head. I guessed it was meant as a conversation starter, a need for attention.

"I like your brooch," I said, keeping my tone shy.

She glanced up and immediately smiled. "You must be our new recruit."

"Emily."

I tendered my hand over, and she grasped it between both of hers. "Welcome, dear. I am Betty Devinport."

"I've been looking everywhere for a sweater like that. Where did you buy it?"

She stood a little straighter, almost on her tiptoes. "Thank you so much. You might not believe me, but I actually made this myself."

I was about to guffaw when I was knocked forward.

"Is this your bag?"

I turned around to see a man in desperate need of a haircut who was holding my backpack by the top loop as though it were filled with dirty diapers.

"She's new, Dave. She didn't know."

Dave gave Betty the stink eye and let my bag fall to the ground. "My name is on my locker. It's not hard to see that." He hung his lumberjack coat, kicked his saddlebag onto the bottom shelf, and left.

Betty placed a consoling hand on my shoulder. "Dave is our IT guy. He's not very good with people."

"I don't think he likes me," I said as I picked up my bag and turned around.

"Don't take it personally. He doesn't like anyone. And no one likes him." Betty's cheeks had all of a sudden colored. I had picked up on this.

I gave her another shy smile before walking away to put my bag in my designated locker.

****

My first shift ended shortly before lunchtime. I headed back to the staff room, straight for Betty's locker. I quickly grabbed her wallet from her purse, glanced over the cat photos, and took the ten-dollar bill she had so neatly placed there earlier and stuffed it in Dave's saddlebag, letting a small corner of the bill stick out. Then I left for the day.

The next morning, I was back in for day two of my mechanical shift. I arrived a bit early, hoping to catch Betty before work. I was glad to catch her reading alone at one of the staff-room tables, with another extra-large coffee cup in front of her. I dropped my bag in my designated locker and went to sit with her.

"Hi, Betty," I said softly, enough to rouse her from her severely used Harry Potter book.

"How was your first day yesterday?"

"Okay," I started, slumping my shoulders. "Most people have been really nice to me."

"Most people?"

"The IT guy. Dave, I think you said his name was? He definitely doesn't like me."

"Oh? Why do you say that?"

"When I came back to the staff room yesterday to fetch my bag, he bolted as soon as I came in the room. Almost ran me over trying to leave."

Her eyes veered to her locker, then to Dave's. She glanced down to the bottom shelf, where Dave's bag would have been, where she would have seen her ten-dollar bill sticking out after she found it missing from her wallet yesterday. When she returned her attention to me, she forced a smile. "I'm sure it's nothing, dear."

With a common enemy, Betty and I became fast friends, magically finding each other in the staff room at her every break. She told me about her three cats and her hopes for grand-kittens someday; I made up stories about my endearing parents. This wasn't much of a stretch for me—I had been making up stories about my parents my whole life, though I usually reserved these for myself. As far as Betty was concerned, I was an all-American homesick schoolgirl just looking for a surrogate mom while I was away from home.

After graduating from Callister University some thirty years earlier, Betty had never left, turning a part-time gig as an admissions clerk into a full-time prison sentence. This was when I manufactured an interest in following in her footsteps one day and becoming an admissions clerk. This made her gleefully happy, as happy as my mother was whenever someone commented on her timeless beauty (usually after one of her nip-tuck vacations).

With so many years under her belt, Betty had built solid contacts. On my third shift, I happened to mention to her that my fabricated cat, Mr. Voldermort, had a cold, but I couldn't afford to take him to the vet until I got paid. By the end of the day, the admissions director's assistant came over to let me know that the director had approved an advance on my paycheck and that I would be getting it by Friday.

On my fourth shift, Dave walked into the staff room as Betty and I were sitting together during our break. He dumped his bag, gave his overgrown hair a toss back, and left without the slightest glance in our direction.

"Late as usual," Betty whispered to me.

I leaned in, feeling opportunity knock. "You know what he said to me yesterday?"

"No. What?"

"When I told him that I couldn't wait to graduate and become an admissions clerk, he said that the admissions clerks were useless. He said that his computer system does everything nowadays and that Callister University doesn't even need frontline staff anymore. Actually, I think he used the term *archaic*."

I shook my head as I remembered my imaginary conversation with Dave, the meanie IT guy. Betty's kitten demeanor turned tigress.

Before I knew it, she was showing me how the system worked, how valuable her job was, and how Dave's computer system badly buried student information. From this, I learned two things. One, I needed a student's ID card to get into the system. I had initially assumed that the university was attempting to protect its students' personal information, but Betty clarified that the university had changed the system when clerks were caught using it to search porn on the Internet.

Now, the system would shut down as soon as the inquiring student left and wouldn't turn back on until a new card was handed over. This meant no more porn for the faculty, but it also meant that I needed to get someone's card to get any information from the system. If I used my own card, I risked getting caught, because Betty told me that management kept track of all the ID numbers that were entered into the system—a good way to know which students came begging and which suffered in silence.

The second thing I learned was that I absolutely needed access to Betty's computer because she was a stickler for rules. I knew there was no way I could sway her to search the system for Cameron. And even risking asking for something like this would have lost me my all-American-girl title.

I had to be sneaky and quick.

On Friday morning, the day of my fifth shift, I slipped a couple of laxatives in Betty's extra-large morning coffee when her head was bent down to grab and show off her latest knitting piece.

When our shift started, I stuck close to my adopted mother. This was a big day. After weeks of dodging the landlord and Hunter's not-so-subtle inquiries, I had just cashed my advance on my paycheck so that I could finally pay for my rent and buy decent groceries. And now I was about to break into the system to get what I needed.

After an hour or so, I was starting to lose confidence that my plan would work. But all of a sudden, I noticed Betty start to fidget on her stool. She was in the midst of a conversation with a student, crossing and uncrossing her legs, swaying from one cheek to the other. Then a look of sheer panic came across her face. Her skin started blotching, her hands clenched the edge of the counter, and her lips disappeared inside her mouth.

The student she was supposed to be helping had kept on talking as if nothing were wrong.

I ran to Betty's rescue.

"Can you take over for me, dear?" she hissed and ran away before I could even answer.

I gave the boy over the counter my most comforting smile. "Can I help you?"

"I was just telling the other lady that my name isn't appearing on any of the class rosters. Some of the professors won't even let me come into their class until they see that I really did sign up."

"Hm," I said, pushing my eyebrows together. "That's very weird." There was nothing weird about it. I had given his account a quick once-over, and he hadn't paid last year's tuition. Based on the red lettering at the top, he wasn't even a student anymore, and the length of his dirty dreadlocks told me that he probably wouldn't be paying the establishment for this year's tuition either.

I winked at the boy in the dreadlocks. "Let's see what we can do."

I was already out of his account. And while I clicked away furiously, he stood by and watched with an expectant grin. As if we were both about to screw the establishment together.

As I typed *Cameron James Hillard* and saw it appear on the screen, I bit my lip, and my hands quieted over the keyboard.

"Everything okay?" Dreadlocks inquired.

"A bit dizzy," I managed to mumble back as I pressed enter.

"It's the air in here. They're trying to poison us with this recycled crap they call air. They want to keep us down. Subdued."

While he carried on about the government machine, I was staring at Cameron's file. He had been enrolled as a part-time student this year and last. His tuition had, of course, been paid in full.

He had been enrolled in two classes last year and would have been enrolled in two more classes this semester. I recognized those classes—all ones I had taken and was currently taking. The classes he had picked were the ones that were being held in the biggest auditoriums, where he could have easily gotten lost in the crowd.

I didn't know which was worse: the fact that he would have

been sitting in class with me now, or the fact that he had been there the whole time and I had been completely oblivious to this.

I hadn't realized that I'd stopped typing and held on to my stomach. The boy was too engrossed in his discussion of political immorality to notice. But a hand fell upon my shoulder, and I turned to see Betty.

"You're ill too," she said to me with concern on her motherly face. "It must be the flu. I'll finish up here. You go home and get some rest."

I used my body to hide the screen from her and took my time getting off her seat, enough time to click my way back into Dreadlocks' file and cover my tracks. And enough time to memorize an address.

I left without saying good-bye to Betty. Now that I had gotten what I needed, I would probably never speak to her again. People were just that disposable to me now.

I did go home as Betty ordered, but as soon as I got there, I grabbed Meatball and got in my car.

I hadn't known what I was going to find in Cameron's file, but when I saw the address, I had immediately recognized it. It was in the other slummy part of Callister, where, with a little more money, you could rent a place that looked like a box of cereal, with a door and two windows. I suppose the people who lived in this part probably thought of themselves as better off than the folks in my neighborhood. At least they had a front yard.

I turned into the row-housing district and eventually found the right street, where Cameron's mother lived. I had thought about coming here many times, but I knew that, unless I went door-to-door, there was no way I would ever find the right place among these concrete multiples.

There were kids everywhere, like the neighborhood was overrun with them. Most of them were just walking the streets, goofing around. Kids pushing babies and toddlers around in rickety strollers. Kids sitting on the sidewalk, smoking cigarettes.

It was hard for me to imagine Cameron here, walking these

streets. And yet, this was the world that he had come from. This was part of who he had been.

I vividly remembered coming here with Cameron. I remembered how embarrassed he had been. I remembered Cameron calling me his girlfriend. And I remembered how devastated his mother had been after hearing of Rocco's death.

I was there to do the same—tell Cameron's mother that she had lost another son. I assumed that Spider and Carly, the only other people who would have known about Cameron's mother, wouldn't have come running to tell her that they had murdered her son. But I wasn't doing this for his mom; I was doing this for him. Because he deserved to be missed. I wanted his mother to miss him, mourn him like she had Rocco. I wanted Cameron to have the love of his mother, even if it was only in the end.

When I stopped in front of number 65, Meatball simply sat back and growled, letting the hairs on his back spike up. There was a group of men in the yard next to number 65. They were loitering, beers in hand. But this seemed to bother the hell out of Meatball, so I left him in the car. I didn't want him running away on me again.

I knocked on Cameron's mother's front door and could hear Meatball barking at me. Surely he would pay me back for this later.

As was the case when Cameron and I had last been there, no one answered the door. I tested the handle and let myself in. Not much had changed since I had last been there. The smell of wet clothes and cigarettes was still first to greet you at the door. The television was still on in the living room, and Cameron's three half siblings were still sitting there sockless, staring blankly at the television.

I cleared my throat to announce my arrival. Only one of them, the boy, glanced my way. I would have recognized those eyes anywhere. Dark brown, almost black. Cameron's eyes. I temporarily lost my breath in the smoke-filled room.

"Hi, um, do you remember me?" I asked the kid.

But Cameron's stepbrother had already lost interest and was back to watching television.

I walked in and made my way to the kitchen—the last place I had seen her. The kitchen was still a disaster, with the lipsticked cigarettes still overflowing in the ashtray on the table. Cameron's mother, however, wasn't there.

But when I heard thumps coming from upstairs and then tandem cackles, I figured out where she was and that she wasn't alone.

Slightly grossed out, I went back to the living room and decided to wait for the grown-ups to be done. There were boxes and bags everywhere, as though someone had just moved in. My guess was that Cameron's mom had a new boyfriend again.

I found a box and pushed a few bags of clothing aside and sat.

In any other place, it would have been weird for a strange girl to invite herself in, sit, and stare at the kids. But I couldn't help myself. I found a little bit of Cameron and Rocco in all of them. The crazy brown hair. The slight curl in the right ear. And these kids already had that blank expression, that look of defeat that Cameron had when he had decided to end it, end us.

I had to look away and find something else to keep my mind busy.

I noticed the overturned pop bottles and ripped bags of chips. It was like raccoons had been through looking for any last morsel of food, however small. This family, these kids, depended on the money that Cameron would give to his mother. With him gone, there was no one to look after all of them. What would happen to them?

All of a sudden, the noise upstairs ceased and the house went quiet, with the only noise coming from the television. And I realized that I did not want to face Cameron's mother. I didn't want to tell her what had happened to Cameron. Not now. Not after ... what she had just been doing.

I grabbed at my jacket and pulled the money that I had cashed from my first paycheck. I separated the money into roughly three piles and went up to the kids. I had their full attention now.

"Don't tell your mother," I told them in a rush.

Without a word, they grabbed the money and ran out the door.

I hurried behind them, running to the car before Cameron's mother found me.

On the way home, I couldn't get their faces out of my head. And it wasn't just because they reminded me so much of Cameron and Rocco.

The only mistake they had ever made was being born to that woman, being born into poverty, being born at all. I wanted to judge Cameron's mother. I desperately wanted to hate her. Yet I couldn't. Because I wasn't that different from her.

I had just given away all my rent and grocery money. The kids needed it, but so did I, so did the child I was carrying. Like Cameron's mother, I was bringing into this world a child that I wouldn't be able to take care of. I would love this child. But love wouldn't put food in its stomach, wouldn't protect it from the world that wanted it dead.

I couldn't remember the last time I had seen Griff, and as I parked my car in the back, I realized how much I wanted him to be there. And this scared me.

I had spent a lifetime shutting people out, telling myself that I was better off on my own. And when I had met Cameron, I hadn't just let my guard down; I had given him my trust and my heart … despite knowing so little about him. I still hadn't figured out how this could have happened. Why had I let myself fall so utterly in love with a man I hardly knew when, in the end, this man had ended it all and taken my heart and the rest of me with him?

Now I had Griff. I needed his friendship and his support so badly that just the thought of losing him again would have been enough to put me over the edge.

But I hardly knew him.

All I knew was that he had shown up on my doorstep with a

bag of cash and a note with my name and address written on it. Deep down, I thought I could trust him. But deep down, I had also once thought that Cameron would never hurt me. And he had found a way to hurt me so badly that I had been turned inside out, like a beach washed away in a hurricane.

Obviously, my judgment was lacking.

There were things that I needed to do before the baby came, things that I would need Griff's help with. But at what expense? It wasn't just about me getting hurt anymore. I had two people to worry about now.

Griff had been sent to me for a reason, and whether or not he knew that reason, I needed to put my guard up—and keep it there.

\*\*\*\*

It seemed like the whole city was in our house when Meatball and I came through the door. I'd forgotten it was Friday, which meant that the house was party central. The last thing I needed was more people around. Maybe moving out with Griff wasn't such a bad idea after all.

I found myself having to weave through a crowd as I went looking for Griff. The smell of beer, the loud music, the strangers trying to make small talk with me as I walked by, Meatball baring his teeth at anyone who tried to get too close, and still no Griff. It was just too much. Three people offered me a drink, one guy actually put a drink to my lips, and a girl spilled her drink on the bottom of my pants.

I was about to go hide in my bedroom when some guy accosted me in the upstairs hallway. I'd never seen him before, but he seemed to know who I was.

He practically shoved a piece of red rubber in my face, which made an already jumpy Meatball ready to pounce. I grabbed his collar before he could jump on the kid.

"Your dog ate one of my boxing gloves," the guy barked.

*Scare Crow*

I sighed as I realized that he was one of the new roommates and that the piece of rubber he had shoved in my face was the remainder of his boxing glove. Perfect. Great way to start the school year.

I glared at Meatball, who had gone very quiet all of a sudden. A *whole* boxing glove? Really, Meatball?

I could feel myself flush. "I'm sorry. I'll buy you a new one."

But the guy wasn't done. "He ate my brother's bike helmet too."

A boy who looked like his duplicate, but wearing a different shirt, came up behind, carrying a black half-chewed strap, which I surmised was all that was left of the helmet.

So the new roommates were twins—identical twins—and apparently, I needed to feed Meatball more than four times a day.

"I got it for my birthday," the new twin whined. "What am I supposed to wear on my head in the meantime?"

By this point, everyone upstairs had stopped chattering and had started staring at us. Even Cassie was standing in her doorway, staring with the rest of them. Meatball cowered into my room, leaving me to fend off the accusers. I was mortified. I was tired. I was afraid they were going to make me get rid of Meatball. So many emotions were whirling through me that I just couldn't handle this. I shook my head and started pacing back toward my room.

Hunter came out of his room with a girl, oblivious to what was happening in the hall.

"Oh, hey, Emily," he said, "I need—"

"I don't have your damn rent money, Hunter. Can't you just give me a goddamn break!"

And Hunter stopped in his tracks, his eyes rounded and his mouth slack-jawed.

I stormed into my room, wishing I had a door to lock myself in.

But after a few seconds, Hunter knocked on the doorframe before coming through the curtain.

"I was just going to tell you that I got your mail and left it on the table downstairs. And Griffin already paid your rent for the year. He even paid for half of mine and half of Joseph's since he's crashing in our room. I thought you knew that already."

I didn't, and I wished Griff hadn't paid my rent because I wanted to leave.

"Is everything okay?"

I grabbed Meatball's leash and marched past him. "I'm fine."

I kept my head down as I made my way out of the house and took my bottomless-stomach monster for a long walk. Getting my mail would have to wait until I didn't have an audience of drunkards.

Meatball's ears stayed flat against his head the whole time. Eventually, after the twentieth time he nudged my hand, I gave in and rubbed his sweet spot under his chin. His little tail wagged jubilantly as I forgave him, though I had no idea what I was going to do when we got kicked out.

By the time we got back, the party had left for the school pub. I put my pajamas on and crawled under the covers, thankful for the peace and quiet.

When I heard the front door open, I knew it was Griff just by the heaviness of his steps. I got out of bed and pulled my curtain open as he was heading into his shared accommodations.

"Griff?"

He paused at the door before turning around.

I gasped.

His face was bloody and swollen. He had a gash on his chin and over his eye. His bottom lip was puffy.

Griff smiled, revealing bloodstained teeth.

I put my hand to my mouth, and he put the palms of his hands out between us as a white flag.

"Don't freak out, Em. I'm fine. It's not as bad as it looks."

"Not as bad as it looks?" I exclaimed, trying not to yell and wake up the whole house.

He pushed me back into my room and forced me to sit down on my bed.

"Nothing comes without a price. Not all my loan sharks were content with just getting paid back with cash."

"So? What? They put you in a cage and made you fight a lion?"

To my astonishment, he nodded. "Maybe not a lion, but yeah, some of them wanted their interest paid in blood."

"*Your* blood? Griff, this is nuts."

"If I didn't do this, I wouldn't be able to walk the street without having to look over my shoulder every two seconds. And you wouldn't be safe with me."

I got up, made him sit on the bed, and went downstairs. I grabbed ice out of one of the beer coolers, stuffed it in a Ziploc bag, and grabbed a washcloth.

"There has to be another way," I said as I walked back into my room, still stunned at the state of his face.

"There wasn't. But don't worry. It's all taken care of now. I'm free and clear and don't owe anyone anything else."

"That's a small relief."

I sat next to him, examining his face, unsure of where to start. Griff was doing the same with my face. I wiped the blood under his nose, which sent a new stream of red flowing down.

"Put your head back," I ordered him and started tugging him down with a little more force than needed. He laid his head on my legs, and I brought the bag of ice to his fat lip. He stared at me while I held the ice with one hand and cleaned the blood out of his scruffy beard with the other. His hands were laced over his chest. I noticed that his knuckles were also bloodied and raw.

"For a guy who's in such bad shape, you don't seem too upset about it," I remarked.

He smiled from one side of his face to the other. "I'm free, Em. I haven't felt like this in a really long time. I feel as though I'm starting with a brand-new life."

I wiped the rest of the blood away, focused on my task. I had to scrub pretty hard to get the dry blood out of his hair.

"You're worried," he surmised. "What are you worried about?"

I chuckled. That was a loaded question. What wasn't I worried about? "You come back with your face beaten to a pulp, and you wonder why I'm worried?"

He shrugged. "I've been beat up far worse than this."

"That's really comforting. I suppose we'll have to keep a bucket of ice around if you're going to live here."

"Fighting used to be my life. But not anymore. I'm starting over, starting right now. I'll never go back to that life again."

I stopped and held on to the blood-soaked washcloth.

And he looked at me. "What?"

That wasn't what I wanted to hear. Griff wanted out of the underworld. And I wanted back in.

I sighed. "Never ever say never."

He grabbed my hand and steadied it over his face, so that I was forced to look at him.

"I'm serious," he said. "I won't ruin this chance that I've been given. I won't hurt you like that."

*Yeah. Like I'd never heard that before.*

"You don't believe me?" he asked.

"Close your eyes," I grumbled. I put the wet cloth over his eyes, partly because his right eye was starting to swell shut, partly because I couldn't stand him examining me like that anymore. It was like he was trying to get to me, to the Emily who was hiding behind the armor. It made me want to cry. And I was done crying.

It didn't take long for Griff to fall asleep. I would have loved to follow suit, but he was taking up most of my bed. He emitted so much heat that it was like sleeping with roast beef. I finally gave up and left Meatball and Griff to fight each other with their snores.

I grabbed a spoon and jar of peanut butter from the kitchen and went to find my mail. The "dining room" was the place where we had a table, one that someone had put on the side of the road with his or her garbage and that my roommates had rolled back to the house, balancing it on two grocery carts. There were no chairs around it, but it made a great surface for gathering everyone's junk and for storing empty beer cases.

I pulled a stack of boxes from under the table and sat on the stack, cuddling my jar. I was beyond starving. It was as though my stomach had grown a hole and everything I had ever eaten in my life had totally disappeared.

The carpet was sticky and crunchy. Someone from the party must have spilled something on the floor and used newspaper to soak it up or try to hide it.

*And they criticize Meatball for being an animal*, I sneered to myself.

While I was digging into the peanut butter jar, I was kicking at the newspapered floor. A picture on the front page of the paper diverted my attention. With the spoon still in my mouth, I bent over and pulled the paper off the floor.

I slid my fingers along its edges and got a paper cut. At least I knew I wasn't dreaming.

There were allegations of corruption, of embezzlement, of fraud. Millions of dollars had been misappropriated ... allegedly. Someone had been arrested and set free on bail. And in the middle of all this was a picture of a gray-haired man in an Armani suit—my father, in handcuffs, being led out of his office building. He was smiling, and so was his lawyer at his side.

I could probably count on my fingers the number of times I had seen my father growing up. He was more of a mythic figure in our household. On par with the Easter bunny, I supposed. But I always knew he wasn't a figment of my imagination, because the father I had made up as a girl was a dentist who came home every night to make sure that I brushed my teeth.

Whether my father was at the office or he decided to stay home one odd day, there was always a reason. All reasons always lead to business. If he was home, that meant that someone important was coming over and I had to ensure to appear and disappear on command. Apart from the fact that he had been to a fancy law school—something that my mother would never let me forget—and had taken over the family empire, I knew very little of what my father did for a living. The newspaper article enlightened me on what he actually did, or at least how he was making so much money, allegedly.

From the smile on my father's face, it seemed as though this had all been one major misunderstanding, one that the government would be paying dearly for. I wished I knew my father well enough to know if he were guilty or not. If he were guilty, the newspaper reporter surmised that the Sheppard empire could implode.

The paper was dated a few days earlier. How was it that I hadn't heard of this until now?

While I was engrossed in my father's smile, a glass of milk had come around my shoulder and been placed on the table in front of me.

"Milk might help that peanut butter go down even faster, if that's possible," Griff whispered.

I stashed the paper between my legs and yanked the spoon out of my mouth while Griff pulled a stack of beer boxes from under the table.

"Can't sleep?" he asked.

I shook my head and took a big gulp of milk.

"I've been told more times than I can remember that I'm a blanket hog. Sorry. Should have warned you."

I cracked a smile and arched a brow. "So, you've stolen a lot of other girls' blankets, huh?"

He laughed. "Yeah. That'd be a better story." Then he cleared his throat. "Nah. I used to have to share a bed with my two older brothers. They used to beat me up in the middle of the night when they got cold. That is, until I got bigger than them."

Griff's face was swollen, scratched, and bruised in spots. His hair went every which way. And he was completely relaxed. I could see the boy that he had once been, that he was becoming again. I couldn't help myself from staring at him.

While I had been studying Griff, he had been studying me.

Under the light of the kitchen, in the quiet darkness of the house, with nothing else to do but look at each other, I had all of a sudden become a little shy. By the ruddiness of Griff's cheeks, I wasn't the only one.

I smiled, and he smiled back. And we both chuckled a bit at our awkwardness.

Eventually, the smile left his lips, and he really assessed me.

"You've changed in the past couple months," he told me.

"Have I?" I remarked, while I took up my love affair again with the peanut butter.

I could feel his eyes on my face. "You seem older. And a little sadder, I guess."

"And here I thought the dim lighting was doing me a favor," I said.

But Griff remained serious.

I had about a million questions for Griff. And I knew he had a million questions for me too, none of which I was prepared to answer. Where was I supposed to start? How much could I tell him?

"I'm sorry," he said, interrupting my thoughts.

I cocked my head. "Whatever for?"

"I wasn't there for you. I didn't keep my promise of getting you out. Before it was too late."

"I'm still here, aren't I? I'm alive."

He searched my face. "Are you?"

I gave him a blank look when I really wanted to stick out my tongue.

"Your roommates are worried about you," he said.

I had a hard time believing this. "When did you have time to talk to my roommates? I've hardly seen you in the last week."

"That Hunter kid won't shut up. If he doesn't let me sleep soon, I may have to choke him to sleep."

I couldn't tell if Griff was kidding. "Was this before or after you paid my rent?"

He only shrugged in answer to my question. "Do you really think no one notices you?"

Meatball came up and laid his head on my lap. I gave him a spoonful of peanut butter, which had him smacking his lips and tongue loudly.

"I'm not exactly tight with my roommates."

"You come back, bruised up, with a dog. You hide in your room. You don't eat—"

"Is that what they told you?" A demand more than a question.

"I can see for myself, Em. I see how skinny you're getting. I look at you, and I'm afraid you're going to turn into a ghost soon. What happened over the summer ... you can't keep that stuff inside. Do any of your roommates know what happened to you this summer?"

"Did you tell them?" I hissed.

"Tell them what?" Griff was trying to keep his voice low. "*I don't even know what happened.* One day I'm guarding some sleazeball's house, thinking that my life is basically over. I'm in the darkest place I've ever been, and all of a sudden, this beautiful girl shows up. She's this amazing person, and she makes me want to stay there forever. Then I realize that she's not there of her own free will and I'm ready to put my life on the line to save her. Just as I'm planning to escape with her, to set us free, I get shipped off to a barn in the middle of nowhere where I have nothing to do but worry about my girl. I imagine the worst, and there's nothing I can do because I'm being watched all day and all night. Until a couple weeks later when that beautiful girl walks in with the sleazeball, the worst person in the world. She smiles at me. Even though she shouldn't be smiling. I smile back because I can't help myself and she's clearly delusional."

"He wasn't the worst person in the world," I whispered, the blood rushing to my head.

"I start thinking of another escape plan and ways of trying to find my beautiful girl. Ways to try to save both of us again. Before

I know it, I'm sent to be with her in this shithole, and I still have no idea who she is. And yet …"

Griff stopped to catch his breath.

"And yet?" I started for him once he had regained his composure.

"And yet," he said, shaking his head, "I'm exactly where I want to be."

Griff took my glass and finished my milk for me. Then he gently put the glass in front of him and waited … for me to speak? I felt dizzy. I had to lean over the table and rest my forehead on my hands. I didn't know what to think, let alone say.

"Why are you here, Em?" he wondered, his voice serene.

"Because I go to school here," I told him. That was the simple answer anyway.

"You know that's not what I meant," he said. "Why are you still here? On this earth? Alive?"

I froze and looked at him. He was so wound up, but I could tell that he was trying hard to keep calm for me.

"Do you really think no one notices these?" he whispered. He reached over and passed his thumb over the scar Victor had left on my cheek. I flinched, expecting pain. But the scars were healing, and the physical pain was gone. Only the heat of Griff's thumb against my skin was left.

I managed a smile. "Are we comparing scars now? Because I fell off my bike when I was nine and got a really good gash on my knee."

Griff's lips spread thin. "Whatever happened, whoever did that to you, they deserve to die."

I suppose that this was what I had been hoping for. A partner in revenge. But the dark look on Griff's face made me miss the new Griff, the one who was free, the one who was never going back.

"Do you even want me here?" he asked me. I could see the despair in his eyes.

And my heart was already screaming the answer to this. I nodded and held his eyes, trying very hard to keep my tears at bay.

Then I pulled the newspaper from between my legs, held it for a few seconds, and handed it over to him.

I cleared my throat. "This is me."

I waited as Griff scanned the article and the picture. He glanced back up and waited patiently for me to explain.

I took a breath. "My name is Emily Sheppard. And this man is my father. I'm still alive because of my family."

Griff nodded. "So you're still alive because your family paid your ransom."

A nervous laugh escaped my lips. I doubted my parents would ever pay my ransom, especially now. "No, I'm alive because my parents are rich, and eventually, people would have figured out that I was missing. My face would have been plastered all over the news, and finding out what happened to me would have become a popular subject for every news agency around the world. Drug lords don't need that kind of publicity."

A wrinkle formed between Griff's eyes. I could see him trying to understand this, as Spider had made me understand.

"Okay," he said slowly. "You're Emily Sheppard. Rich Emily Sheppard."

"My parents are rich," I corrected.

"Your parents are rich," he said, trying to keep himself from looking too amused. "And you can't afford to pay your rent in this crappy place?"

I was happy for the change in mood, even if it was at my expense. "I was going to pay my rent. I just needed a bit more time."

He rolled his eyes. "That's not the point—"

"You told me earlier that everything comes at a price. The same applies to my parents. Their money, their rules." I pointed to the newspaper article. "You can see what kind of rules they live by. Money isn't everything."

"Says the girl who's never had to share a bed with her siblings," he joked.

But this had really hurt my feelings.

He leaned over and squeezed my shoulder so that I would look at him. Then he extended his hand, and I took it.

"It's nice to meet you, Emily Sheppard."

As Griff shook my hand, my heart tugged and squeezed. The blood rushed to my head again. All I could see was Cameron walking in the rain after I had crashed the car. We had shaken hands, in truce, in this same way.

"Hey," Griff bellowed, "where'd you go?"

I forced myself to start breathing again.

"Did you really mean what you said earlier? About never going back into that world?"

Griff's eyes darkened. "Why?"

"Do you remember the kid?" I asked, trying to keep myself composed.

He nodded somberly. "Of course I remember him. He was a great kid. I liked him a lot."

"His name was Rocco." Saying Rocco's name aloud had felt like someone had just lit a match against my lips. "The night that Rocco died ... I was there. He got killed trying to protect me. I saw everything ... "

I had started shaking. Griff grabbed me by the shoulders and steadied me. "I knew that the kid got somehow caught up ... but I had no idea you were there. Jesus!"

I could see it in his eyes. The compassion. But that wasn't what I was going for. I pulled his hands down and used my own hands to steady him.

"The people who are responsible for Rocco's death are the same people who are responsible for what happened to me."

Griff stared back at me, his eyes falling on the marks that Victor had left on my face.

"Em—" he started, his voice low-slung.

My face twisted. "I'm not looking for pity, Griff."

"What are you getting at?"

I knew this was a pivotal moment. I had to decide whether I could trust him and tell him about my plans.

"I'm trying to tell you that I agree with you. That the people who are responsible for this need to die."

He frowned. "Yes, I do feel that way. What happened to you, someone needs to pay for this. But if I'm understanding you correctly, I don't think we're on the same page as to *who* should make them pay for it."

I bit my lip. I knew I'd have a hard time convincing Griff that this was what needed to be done. I had to try harder.

"Did you know that Rocco was only fourteen? They shot him down when he wasn't even armed."

Griff considered this and sighed. "How many people are we talking about?"

"Just two."

"Just two," he repeated in a mumble. "Let me guess. The creep who walks around like he's a god. The big boss man. The one you followed into the barn?"

I could feel my throat closing. "No. He's long gone. I'm talking about the guy who used to work for him. The one with the spider tattoo on his neck."

"Sheesh. Okay, so that's psycho number one. Who's psycho number two?"

"His name is Shield. His men killed Rocco, and he personally left his impression on my face."

Griff took a moment to let all this sink in, his finger nervously tapping the table in front of him.

"Em, I'm sorry all this happened to you—"

"I already told you, Griff, I'm not looking for pity," I said, my voice cold and steady. "I'm looking for your help."

"What you're asking is ridiculous," he exclaimed. "What exactly is your plan? To march in with a gun and shoot these scumbags while their millions of armed minions look the other way?"

"That's why I need your help."

Griff got up, and I watched and waited as he paced the dining room.

He stopped and kneeled before me. "No," he said, keeping my eyes.

"No?" I repeated, incredulous.

"No, I won't help you. And no, I won't let you do this."

Heat rose to my cheeks. "You won't *let* me?"

"I won't let you put yourself in that kind of danger. These men you're after, they eat girls like you with their afternoon tea. You're safe now, and that's how I'm going to keep it."

"No, I'm not safe. They'll eventually come after me."

He squinted. "Why would they do that? Why would they have let you go just to come back to take you again?"

My hand had made its way to my stomach, but I pulled it away before he could notice.

Griff scowled. "Emily, are you telling me everything?"

I grabbed my stack of mail and pushed away from the table. I got up, and he followed my lead.

"I'm going to do this with or without your help," I told him, holding his glare.

He pushed a strand of hair away from my face. "Then I won't leave your side. Ever. I need you to stay safe, Emily. The fact that you're still alive, the fact that you're still in one piece, is a miracle. I'm not going to throw that away."

I turned my eyes ahead and called for Meatball.

\*\*\*\*

When I got into my bedroom, I yanked my curtain shut and sank to my floor.

*What just happened?* This was the question that was circling my brain as I stroked Meatball's meaty head. His normal horrid dog breath now had a bouquet of peanut butter added to it.

I hadn't expected Griff's reaction. To me, it was crystal clear.

Victor and Spider had to die. Though I suppose I couldn't really fault Griff for refusing to help me, especially when he didn't have all the information. The fact that I was pregnant, I knew that I couldn't divulge this. But I was still unclear on whether I was keeping this secret because I didn't trust him or because I was afraid that he would leave. The best of humans were only equipped to handle a certain degree of mess. I was a walking disaster. A calamity.

When Griff had insisted on keeping me safe, Cameron's face had popped into my head because he had said the same thing to me. I had always suspected that Griff had feelings for me. How deep those feelings ran, I wasn't sure. To me, he was more than a friend. His arrival had brought me the air that I needed. Was there something in between friendship and love?

One thing was clear: when it came to Spider and Victor, I was on my own. If Griff held his promise of never leaving my side, my decision to try to enlist Griff's help had just made my life a living hell.

I just wished Griff had had enough faith in me to help me, or at least, let me be. Even if he didn't know *everything*.

Even though it was the middle of the night, I grabbed my phone and dialed my mother's number.

"It's urgent," I told the maid who picked up my mother's line.

\*\*\*\*

"Emily, why on earth are you calling me this late?" she asked me, her voice groggy and irritated.

Most mothers would have been worried if they had received a call in the middle of the night from their daughters. But Isabelle Sheppard wasn't like most mothers.

"Why didn't you tell me?" I demanded. "Dad gets arrested, and I have to find this out from the newspaper. Why didn't anyone call me to tell me what was happening?"

My mother tittered. "Oh, dear. It's nothing to worry about at all. These things happen all the time. It will all blow over soon."

I took a moment and sighed. "Okay. Can you just call me if something else like this happens? I really don't want to have to read the paper to find out what's going on with my father."

"Yes, of course," she agreed, her voice a little tighter. "Now let me get some sleep."

I hung up. My mother was being overly nice. And she had actually laughed. I knew that this wasn't about to blow over. And I knew that my father was guilty.

I heard Griff walk up the stairs and stop in front of my door. Then he kept going into his room, leaving the door open.

I laid my head on my pillow and closed my eyes, only to open them again. There was no way I was going to be able to sleep.

I grabbed my stack of mail and started shuffling through.

It wasn't until I got to an envelope the size of a greeting card that I realized that today had been my birthday. Happy birthday to me.

## Chapter Six: Cameron

## Sixteen Candles

Today was Emmy's birthday.
    Today she got to reach the age of twenty. This was the best gift I could have ever offered her.
    It was four years ago to the day that I realized I was in love with Emmy.
    I would always find a way to check on her as often as possible, but especially on holidays and her birthday. Initially, because I had promised this to Bill. But eventually, this became more of a ritual, something that I needed. It made those days seem a little less lonely to me.
    When I drove by her parents' East Hampton mansion that evening on Emmy's birthday, cars were lined up for miles down the adjoining streets, parked neatly by the hired help. It was Emmy's sweet sixteen party, and it was the social event of the year. I was a little surprised by this—Emmy had never seemed like the type, though I supposed I didn't know her that well after all, even if I thought I did.
    I didn't have an invitation, but luckily I was driving a Maserati. No one ever questioned that I didn't belong there when I drove up to the valets and tossed my keys over to them.
    I had always watched Emmy from the outside, at school

mostly, because it was easier—I could do it without attracting too much attention. Actually getting onto the Sheppard acres, this was a definite first. The drive through the iron gates and the parklike grounds had been impressive enough. But inside, it was excessive. The foyer itself was bigger than my high school gym, with a marble staircase that split in two halfway before leading to a mezzanine. It reminded me of a two-headed snake.

Everyone was dressed like they were going to an over-the-hill prom. I was wearing a T-shirt and jeans, but that didn't scare me off. I grabbed a glass of champagne from the first paid penguin I could find and immediately blended in, searching for Bill's little sister.

That year, we had finally established the Canadian pipeline, and I hadn't had time to check on Emmy. But I would never dream of missing seeing her on her birthday.

I hiked through the crowds, walking through rooms with ceilings as high as a movie theater and the ugliest paintings I had ever seen. The orchestra was so loud I could barely hear myself drink. The expensive perfume, the cigars, the feigning of interest in someone else's topic of conversation ... When I finally found the outdoors, I barely had time to breathe a sigh of relief before I realized there was another damn orchestra playing outside. These people were obsessed with violins.

I was looking for an escape route out of this luxurious madness when the inside and the outside orchestras finally stopped playing and a voice over a microphone directed the crowd poolside.

"The *outside* pool," the voice specified after a few seconds of chaos.

I managed to politely nudge my way through the crowd to the edge of the outside water. And as the last of the gray heads parted, I saw her, and something inside me shifted.

Emmy.

She was standing on the other side of the lake-sized pool, hidden only by her mother's shadow. She was wearing a white eyelet lace dress that went down to her knees. Her red hair fell over her shoulders in long thick locks. The white of her dress made every freckle, every strand of red stand out and made the green of her eyes entirely magnetic. White immediately became my new favorite color. I could just stand there and watch her forever.

Emmy kept her eyes on the back of her mother's head and tucked her hair behind her ear. Then she waited for her mother to pick up the microphone before tucking the other side behind her other ear.

Emmy's mother was a beautiful woman, and on any other day, I would not have been able to take my eyes off of her. Her dress alone was obviously meant to be a showstopper—a silver spaghetti-strap number that hugged all of her tight curves. Her red hair pulled up with strands falling perfectly around her face. But even she was no match for her daughter's beauty.

Emmy's mother took center stage, but my eyes stayed on Emmy. She was no longer just a cute kid; she had blossomed into an entirely different species.

Emmy's mother said her words of welcome, as well as a bunch of other stuff rich people say to each other when they're forced to be nice. During her mother's speech, I watched as Emmy's eyes momentarily veered to her left to a gray-haired man who was deep in business talk with some other joke in a tux. Burt Sheppard—Emmy's father.

A birthday cake that looked like it could hide at least two strippers was brought out. Emmy stood by her cake while the crowd sang "Happy Birthday," led by the damn orchestra. As Emmy blew out the sixteen candles, her mother looked onto the crowd, a smile pasted on her face. And Emmy's father never broke away from his conversation.

As soon as the candles were blown out and the orchestra changed its tune, Emmy was off the stage and disappeared into the crowd.

I immediately started pushing through people so that I could have her in my sight again, trying to get around the pool as quickly as I could.

I searched the grounds, then went back inside and searched for her there. The partygoers were getting drunker by the second, making it difficult for me to weave around them. When some frisky old lady grabbed my ass as I walked by, I left the hub of the party and stuck to the sides, my eyes continuously scanning faces, hoping Emmy's would pop up again.

But once I stood on the outskirts of the party, I was exposed. It didn't take long for my tux-less self to get spotted by one of the Sheppard guards. An older fellow who, by the extra-crisp and extra-white short-sleeved shirt, seemed like he was running security on the property.

I ducked back into the crowd before he had taken one step in my direction and headed out back, sticking close to the house so that I wouldn't get lost in the Sheppard parklands on my way to my car. I got to the help quarters unscathed and ran into a bunch of waiters who were smoking pot outside the kitchen. When they spotted me, they stood still, took one look at my T-shirt and jeans, and offered me a smoke. I civilly refused, not having the heart to tell these poor slobs that what they were smoking was rolled-up shit.

Then I heard it—Emmy's laugh. It had echoed out of the kitchen through the screen door. I inched over a step and immediately saw Emmy. She was sitting on a bar stool, with two other women at her side. From the uniforms, I gathered that one was a maid, and the other was a cook. They were congregated around the stainless steel countertop, eating cake, while the rest of the help bustled around them. Emmy's hair was back into a ponytail, and her sandals were kicked off under her. She had her legs crossed up on her seat.

The maid kept adding more and more whipped cream to Emmy's plate until the piece of cake disappeared under the whipped mountain. Every time Emmy took a bite, more whipped cream was sprayed on, and this made my Emmy laugh from her core. And I found myself standing outside, chuckling with her. I had never heard her laugh before. To be honest, I never saw her smile much either. She was serious most of the time; the rest, she would find a way to put on a fake smile when the occasion called for it.

I didn't know what love was until the moment when I heard her laugh, and I felt joy and freedom and more alive than I had ever been before.

I knew I loved her.

I knew that I wanted to be with her and that I needed this more than air.

I also knew I could never be with her. And I felt pain, like a limb had just been cut off.

As realization set in, I took a step back. Horrified by what all of this meant for her and for me. I would learn to know everything about her, but she would never know me and I would have to make sure of that.

By the time the old security guard had located me again, I was already getting the keys to my car back from the valet. I drove away from the Sheppards', dreaming of the next time I would be able to see my Emmy while she remained completely oblivious to me.

Today was Emmy's birthday ... and I wasn't there to celebrate it with her. She would have many more birthdays because I wasn't there. And I had to be thankful for this.

****

Spider threw a newspaper on the desk in front of me, sending my coffee flying into the graph charts that Carly had put together. We were holed up in one of our safe houses in Callister.

I did a once-over of the front page. A picture of Shield cuddling up to the drugs he had confiscated from a ship.

I used the paper to soak up my coffee.

Spider ripped the front page from my hands before my coffee took it over. "Shield just made the front page seizing our drug shipment in Los Angeles, and you have nothing to say?"

Tiny came through the door and gave me a signal. I nodded and got up. "It's not ours," I said to Spider.

"What do you mean it's not ours? I was there when we arranged for the shipment. Are you trying to tell me that a drug cargo came in on the same day, same port that ours was supposed to come in, and yet this cargo got seized and not ours?"

"Ours is actually coming in tomorrow in San Francisco."

I could tell that Spider was trying to make sense of all this.

"While the feds are congratulating themselves with this seizure and spending their precious government dollars on the investigation and determining who's going to get promoted, our cargo will be quietly coming into the port of San Francisco," I explained, even though I didn't have to.

"You set up a dummy shipment just to throw off the feds?" There was a sharp edge to his voice.

I shrugged, feigning nonchalance. I could tell that this hurt Spider, as I knew it would, but it had to happen this way.

"Look at how much was seized, Cameron. How can we even afford this?"

I took another look at the article. The amount that was declared seized wasn't even half of what I had actually shipped. Someone was keeping a commission for himself or herself. Shield was so predictable.

I slapped Spider's shoulder. "Don't worry about it."

I met Tiny at the door, and we headed outside to the waiting vehicle.

"Our guy got arrested," Spider said, keeping pace with us.

"And he'll be handsomely rewarded for his service and his confidentiality. We have a new guy now."

I shut the door, and we drove away, leaving Spider in the parking lot of our Callister apartment.

"I couldn't find Norestrom," Tiny immediately confessed to me. "Nobody knows where he is. Shield kicked him out of his clan."

"Jesus Christ!"

I wanted to get Norestrom so bad I could taste it ... almost as much as I wanted Shield dead. Though I wasn't surprised. I hadn't hidden my desire to torture and kill the man who ordered the kill on my little brother, and Shield wouldn't want to keep a liability like that around him. I had to remind myself that smashing my fist through the window would not have changed anything.

"So, where are we going?" I asked, trying to disguise my disappointment. Tiny had been putting in a lot of hours trying to get me intel on Shield's men while keeping everything hidden from Spider and the rest of the underworld. I didn't want Spider involved in any of this because he wouldn't approve of me doing all this dirty work with my own hands. And because things could go wrong very quickly, and I didn't want him to get caught up in my mess—the sort of mess one doesn't walk away from alive. Spider was one of my only two best friends He and Carly were like family. I needed to know that they would survive me. The shit I was getting myself involved in had to stay hidden from them for their own protection.

Spider didn't know that I had met with Shield a few weeks ago and told him about a shipment that I had coming in to Los Angeles. I had offered to split it with him in exchange for truce—letting bygones be bygones. Or so he thought. He had had my brother killed, he had kidnapped, almost killed Emmy, but what the underworld saw was that I was the loose cannon. Victor knew this, and he was using this to plot against me. But when he saw the amount of dope that he would be stealing from me, he was blinded by the possibilities, temporarily forgetting his scheming, not realizing how badly I wanted to rip the esophagus out of his throat. He had lost a big chunk of his own money when I stole it from him and pinned it on Breland. He was desperate to make up the lost funds.

I knew full well that he would betray me and use some of the shipment to position himself in the media, though I hadn't expected him to sock away such a large chunk of the shipment for himself. He was becoming more brazen—or stupid.

All this money and media attention, I hoped, would keep him distracted and away from Emmy. While we had taken every step possible to ensure that everyone in the underworld believed that I had left her and didn't care what happened to her, I needed to keep Shield away, even if it cost me everything I had.

We had to enlist a new shipment guy anyway. The other one was getting sloppy and reckless with his money.

On the day I headed to the port of San Francisco, I had already done research on one of the cargo supervisors, but I needed to see him for myself before I approached him with an offer he couldn't refuse. He wasn't the type of inside guy we normally worked with. He was a family man, married twenty-five years, with two daughters in high school and two more away at college. Expensive.

I had followed him in his beat-up minivan. We drove for almost two hours in traffic until we came to a quiet little town. Nice place to raise four daughters.

As soon as he got out of the van, one of his teenage girls skipped out of the house, kissed him, and drove off in the minivan.

He spent the next few hours cutting the grass and doing chores around the house, after he had just gotten off a night shift at the shipyard.

This was definitely my guy—one who needed the money and had everything to lose if he got caught or tried to go to the cops when I started blackmailing him.

My era of dark and deadly deeds was continuing to pile up as Tiny stopped in front of a decrepit duplex apartment building that was in the same neighborhood as my mother's. This was not what I had been expecting, but if Tiny said this was the place, then this was the place.

I had known Tiny for a long time. His uncle, Henry Grimes, was our accountant. A few years back, Henry had begged us to give Tiny some work, get him off the streets and out of trouble. It turned out that he did us a favor more than we did him. Tiny was a great addition. He wasn't much of a talker, but I trusted him.

I climbed up the holey carpeted stairs and let myself into the upstairs apartment, which was pretty easy given that the door was practically falling off its hinges.

I checked out the one-bedroom apartment. It was empty and cold, except for an old mattress that had been thrown on the living-room floor, with a phone next to it. The windows shook in the wind, and the heat was on just enough to keep the pipes from freezing. It wasn't what I had expected a guy making extra cash on the side to be living in.

I found myself a spot against a wall and sank down to the floor, expecting a long wait. Before I had time to even fully stretch my legs out, I heard someone coming in through the fire escape. I got my gun out and waited in the hallway that led through the kitchen. A figure came around the wall, and I jammed my gun against his skull.

I swore and pulled the gun away.

It was Spider. He was unmoved by the fact that I had almost shot him.

"What the hell are you doing here?" I asked him with a hiss to my voice.

He looked around the apartment. "Question is ... what the hell are *you* doing here? What have you and Tiny been up to?"

I put my gun away and went to find my spot on the floor. He sank against the opposite wall.

"This doesn't concern you," I said to him.

"There seems to be a lot of stuff that doesn't concern me these days."

We both watched the wall across from us for a while.

"How did you find me?" I wondered finally.

"You and Tiny have been going off on your own lately. I figured I'd follow you to see what you were up to." He clasped his hands behind his head and stretched out. "So, who are we waiting for?"

"One of Shield's ballbusters." I figured he'd have found this out eventually.

"Business or pleasure?"

"It's personal."

"Ah," he said, barking a dark laugh, "I should have known all this had to do with Emmy. Only she would melt your brain into thinking that this was a good idea."

"What would you have me do? Ignore the fact that the people who murdered Rocco and did that to Emmy get to walk this earth?"

"No. But you and I both know there are ways to get your revenge without you risking yourself. We have people who can take care of that for you."

"Like I said, it's personal."

"What if the captains find out that you've been personally doling out judgment? That you're on some sort of killing rampage? Do you think that they'd feel confident in you handling all the business affairs?"

"They won't find out about this. I've been very careful."

"You could have asked me for my help, you know."

"Would you have agreed to help me?"

"I would have definitely tried to talk you out of it. But I wouldn't have let you take all the risk on your own." There was pain in his voice.

"I didn't want you involved."

"In case something goes wrong?"

"Nothing will go wrong. You and Carly are not to get caught up in all this."

Spider's expression flickered. "We've always worked as a team, Cam. If I don't know what you're up to, how can I have your back?"

I didn't have an answer for him. He was right. Spider and I had had each other's back from the first day we met. The more I tried to hide things from him and Carly, the faster the darkness was spreading through. I could feel it.

"Is that why you set up the dummy shipment with Shield without telling me? Because of Emmy?" he wondered. "You know the captains will find out about the shipment and worry."

I should have known that Spider would eventually put two and two together when he saw that newspaper article about Shield's drug seizure. "The captains' shipment will be coming in safe and sound. All they'll see is the money rolling in and the cops too busy to notice the new shipment hitting the streets."

"And you don't think they'll want to know who was trying to bring in dope on their turf?"

"I'll confess it was me. That we were getting too much heat and needed to distract the feds. Besides, they won't appreciate seeing Shield with all that free dope."

"And they won't wonder who actually paid for the shipment?"

I also should have known that it wouldn't take Carly long to rat me out to Spider. I realized then how clouded my judgment was becoming. Dark clouds.

"We'll call it an early Christmas present. A freebie for all the other fuckups this year." My voice had faded. Somebody was climbing up the stairs outside the door. Spider and I eyed each other. We pulled our guns out. He got up to wait behind the door, and I just stood as the welcoming committee. When the door opened, Mike Westfall had a gun to his shaved head and was shoved into the living room by Spider.

"Officer Westfall," I exclaimed, clasping my hands together with elation. I was going to enjoy this.

"Sit," Spider ordered him.

Westfall took a seat on his dirty old mattress and waited, his expression oddly solemn.

"You know why I'm here?" I asked him.

"Yes," he answered and looked up at me. "I knew I would eventually have to pay for what happened to that girl."

I was taken aback by his response. I had expected him to deny everything and try to talk his way out, but Mike actually looked like he felt guilty. This made me curious.

I glanced at the bare room. "Quite the shithole you have here."

"I don't need much."

"You're a junkie?" I hadn't found any dope or drug

paraphernalia, but that was the only explanation as to the decrepit state of his apartment.

"Never touched the stuff," the officer replied candidly in passing.

Then he glanced up; he looked at my gun, and then he looked at me. "Have you ever had to choose between your family and doing the right thing?"

He waited, like he was actually looking for an answer.

Spider cleared his throat and signaled me with his gun.

Mike was the guard who had been stationed at Emmy's door after Shield had kidnapped her. Mike sat and did nothing while Emmy got beaten up. He could have protected her. He could have helped her escape before she was forced to go through all that. There was no doubt that I was going to kill him, but not just yet. I was suddenly interested in what he had to say.

Officer Westfall let his hands fall between his knees and dropped his head. "There was a moment. When the girl was behind the door and pleaded with me to let her out. There was a moment when I thought I was hearing my own daught—" He stopped and took a breath. "When I thought I was going to unlock the door and let her escape before that pig came back for her."

"And yet, you did nothing," I hissed.

He looked up at me. "You loved her, didn't you?"

I glared at him and pulled out my gun.

"You wouldn't have come for me yourself if you didn't love her," he surmised in a whisper as he dropped his face again and closed his eyes. He reached into his shirt.

"Hey! Hands where I can see them," Spider ordered, but I shook my head.

Mike's gun was still in its holster on his hip. Whatever he was reaching for, it wasn't a gun.

He pulled out a piece of paper—a picture that he kissed. Then he made the sign of the cross.

"We get to decide when you're ready, pal," Spider snapped

and looked at me with a question. "What are you waiting for?" he mouthed.

Mike was holding the picture in his palm, eerily calm.

"Who's in the picture, Mike?"

He looked up but did not respond.

"Give it to me," I demanded.

But he held my eyes.

Spider brought his gun to Mike's temple.

Mike got the message and finally conceded, handing me the picture.

It was a picture of a woman and a child sitting on a bed, smiling, arms interlocked. They both had shaved heads. They were in a hospital somewhere. The little girl was in a pink bathrobe. Her skin was gray, and she had tubes sticking out everywhere.

"Who is this?"

"That's my wife and my daughter," he answered, his eyes fixed on the picture as if he were right there with them, interlocked on the bed. "My daughter got really sick when she was five years old. She's been sick ever since. Leukemia."

I knew this could have been a ruse, a way to get sympathy so that I wouldn't kill him. But when he looked up at me as I held the picture in my hands, I could see it in his eyes—the hate. Just the thought of having some scum like me so close to his wife and child was enough to make him want to gut me and use my intestines as a speed bump. Only a man who was truly in love would have that kind of reaction. I would know.

I gave him back the picture, and he started to breathe again, putting the picture back inside his shirt so that I couldn't get to it again.

"The shaved heads?"

He brushed his hand to his naked skull, and a sad smile came to his lips. "She was pretty upset when she started losing her hair. She used to have long brown hair. It was so thick and curly you couldn't put a brush through it. We let her shave all our heads. It helped a little bit."

I leaned against the wall and crossed my hands over my chest, tucking my gun under. "Why the hell would you risk all that just to work for Shield?"

"Do you think I want to work for that asshole?" he growled. "I have no choice. My salary isn't enough to cover our medical bills. By working for Shield, I can afford to pay for her medical care, and my wife can stay at our daughter's bedside. Every penny I have goes to keep my girl alive."

I kept my composure, but something was rising within me. Something that I had been trying my whole life to quash, kill off.

"I had someone do research on you. None of this ever came up."

"My wife and I got married in Jamaica but never filed the paperwork here. My wife is extremely stubborn and didn't want to change her name when we got married."

"And no one has ever wondered, asked you about them?"

"No one here knows they even exist. Since I started working for Shield, I've been staying away from them." Then he looked me in the eye. "Wouldn't you?"

I stood by with my gun, knowing what needed to be done.

Mike continued, "I'm sorry for what happened to your girl. But if I would have let her go, then Shield would have killed me or looked into my past and then killed me. I chose my family."

We were done pretending that Emmy was just another girl. I believed that everything Mike had said was the truth. But now he knew how deep my love for Emmy ran, and he now knew that I was going against the will of the Coalition, that I was out for the blood of every man who had had any contact with Emmy. Mike was armed with information that would get me and everyone I ever cared for killed.

But Mike had his own reasons for being there, for having made really bad decisions. A deathly ill daughter. Mounting hospital bills. A family that was everything to him.

All of a sudden, Mike and I had a lot in common. And killing him would be the demise of his family.

"I'm letting you go," I told him. Spider and Mike just stared at me as though I were speaking Klingon. "Make the arrangements you need to safely get yourself out of Shield's grasp. Go back to your family. And if you tell *anyone* about *anything*, know that I will come after you and your wife and your kid. You'll wish I would have killed you today."

Mike's eyes were round, mirrored only by Spider's eyes.

\*\*\*\*

"What the hell was that?" Spider grunted as we walked down the block.

"It was my decision. I stand by it."

"It was that picture, wasn't it? Sick little girl. Devoted parents who shaved their heads to make their daughter feel better about losing her own hair. You believed that classic sob story about a kid dying of cancer. It could have all been a bunch of bullshit. He could have printed that picture off the Internet and kept it on him for the sympathy vote."

I remembered Mike's reaction as I held the picture. "He was telling the truth." Of this, I had no doubt.

"What if he wasn't?"

"He was. And if he wasn't, then he'll suffer an even worse death."

I found Tiny waiting for me at the meeting point.

"This is exactly why you should have never been doing all this yourself. Now you've given him enough time to warn Shield before disappearing."

"No one can ever disappear forever," I reminded him. "And he won't do anything to jeopardize his kid's life."

"That is, if he even has a kid," Spider mumbled as I got into the car.

"If he dies, so does the money that pays for the kid's medical bills."

Spider held on to the door so that I couldn't close it. "So we kill him and send his family more money than they know what to do with. They can pay bills or whatever the hell they want. Who the fuck cares what happens to them? Since when do *you* care? We don't leave liabilities, Cameron."

"My decision is final. Mike is to remain unharmed unless I order otherwise."

"Emmy's messed with your head too much. You're not thinking straight anymore. She's not even around, and she still manages to fuck you up."

"Let's go," I ordered Tiny.

As soon as Tiny pressed on the gas, Spider let go of the door and I shut it, leaving Spider to talk to himself on the sidewalk. We were immediately going to the closest airfield—initially part of my escape plan in case things with Mike went wrong.

Spider was initially supposed to meet me there, so I suppose I could have just offered him a ride to the airfield. But he had gotten himself to Mike's place, and he could get himself back. Besides, he needed time to cool off.

When we drove up to the tarmac, I was surprised to see Carly waiting by the plane.

I was going to ask her how she was feeling. But by the stern look on her face, I knew this attempt at compassion would be met with a grimace.

"Manny's been chomping to meet with you," she said, practically spitting out the words. Carly had never hidden her utter disdain for Manny.

"What about?"

"Probably wants to have your babies," she snapped. All of a sudden, her face twitched and went pale as the immensity of her words hit home. She quickly shook it off. "Obviously she wouldn't tell little ole me about her earth-shattering topic."

Manny. She had been born into the business of the underworld, literally. Her father, leader of the Latin Mafia, had been captain before her, before he was assassinated in broad daylight by a sniper bullet. Everyone knew she had masterminded the assassination.

But no one could prove it. And no one dared to bring it up. She hopped into his spot as though he had just been keeping it warm for her. Her beauty, her ruthlessness, her hunger for money had made her popular around the captains' table and in my bed.

"I'll talk to her before the big meeting," I said to Carly as my eyes followed Spider's car as he drove onto the tarmac.

I went up the stairs, and Carly followed me into our private plane. While I was pouring myself a drink, Spider came in and found himself a seat as far away from us as possible. Unfortunately for him, it was one of our smaller planes.

"I need you to look into something for me," I said to Carly, loud enough for Spider to hear. "There's a guy named Mike Westfall. I need you to look into him."

She shrugged. "What am I looking for?"

I could feel Spider glaring at me.

"He's got a wife and kid somewhere. You might have a bit of trouble finding them. He's been trying to hide them."

"And what am I supposed to do when I find them?"

"Find out what they need and give it to them." I pushed my seat back and threw a T-shirt over my face.

"That's completely unclear as usual," she grumbled.

****

When we landed in Houston, my first meeting was with Kostya, leader of the Russian Mafia in the United States. With saggy cheeks and a fat nose that looked like it had been punched one too many times, Kostya was the ugliest man I had ever met. He still had the marking of the bullet that had slid across his forehead in an assassination attempt ... the first time. There were two more attempts after that. He lost his wife over ten years ago to cancer. It seemed that with each isolated year that passed, his eyes sank a little deeper into the sagging skin of his face.

At first glance, Kostya looked like an undereducated thug. But in reality, he was well-spoken and thoughtful.

Nothing was ever as it seemed in the underworld.

In addition to managing his own turf on the East Coast, Kostya was responsible for pharmaceutical requisitions. Each captain was accountable for one aspect of our activities, whether it was product or police reports.

Kostya's car was waiting for us on the tarmac. Spider and I climbed in, leaving Carly to take care of everything else. Our one-on-one meetings were always in a moving vehicle. All of the captains had their idiosyncrasies. This one was his. After three assassination attempts, he was a little jittery.

"We need to drop our Chappelle de Marseille shares," he announced after offering me a drink that I refused.

This wasn't news to me. Chappelle de Marseille was the largest distributor of pharmaceuticals to the United States. For years, because of Bill, we'd had an inside into their distribution. Skimming their shipments. Arranging for truck deliveries to go missing. Dropping our shares also meant that we would be taking our business elsewhere.

For the last few months, Kostya had been trying to push me to agree to sell and get out. He had good reason: Chappelle de Marseille was about to undergo extreme government scrutiny following the seizure of its parent corporation. My problem was that the parent corporation was Sheppard Enterprises.

So far, the seizure was just a rumor. Everything had been hushed up by the government to give them a chance to quietly dig into the Sheppard funds before they totally disappeared.

Pulling our shares from Chappelle de Marseille wouldn't just bankrupt this small company; it would also set off a media frenzy, an avalanche that would bankrupt all of Sheppard Enterprises, Emmy's family. Emmy had refused to take my money after Carly had given it to her. I feared that if her parents were bankrupt, she would have absolutely nothing to fall back on if things got really bad for her.

I had been trying to stall the inevitable. "What's our

alternative?" I asked him, expecting no answer as had been the case the last few times we had met to discuss this topic.

"Advantis."

My expression remained uniform. "A little small for our demands, don't you think?"

"Not for long. My sources just confirmed that they are going to be merging with Chemfree. They're just waiting for funding … from us."

"Two small American firms that will corner the pharmaceuticals market," I mused. "That's all well, but we will need an inside guy before we move the business over."

"Already done," he said, a look of satisfaction flooding his ugly face. There was no trace of doubt in his voice.

When I hesitated, Spider eyed me to see what I would do. If we didn't make a move soon, we would lose millions. This was for the best of the Coalition, and that was why we were here.

"Sell our shares," I settled. "As soon as possible."

The Sheppard family, I knew, wouldn't survive this. But I comforted myself in knowing that Bill would have made the same decision.

## Chapter Seven: Emmy

## Smile. Though Your Heart Is Breaking

I was smiling. Because that was what the Charlie Chaplin song said to do, with promises that the sun would come shining through. So I hid my sorrow behind a smile. But the clouds never parted.

Time heals all wounds. At least, that's what people say. Yet I still found myself dreaming of Cameron and Rocco every night, each dream becoming more vivid as the pregnancy progressed. Each dream leaving me sweaty and heartbroken. I couldn't stop dreaming about them, even if I'd wanted to.

Griff had kept his promise and never left my side. At school and at work, he walked me to the door and was waiting for me when I was done. If I found myself wandering about the house in the middle of the night, he would come find me.

I'd smile. He'd smile. But we barely spoke. Well, Griff tried to talk to me, reason with me, plead with me initially. I had started talking to him in monosyllables.

It was weird how lonely you could feel even when you were never alone. Having Griff there was better than not having Griff there. So I smiled. Griff mostly smiled too. But I noticed his gaze wandering off into nothingness. I knew that I was breaking his heart, and as much as this killed me, I was incapable of giving him what he wanted: for us to move on.

If my roommates ever wondered why Griff kept so close to me, they never asked. Too mesmerized, I supposed. Griff had become somewhat of a celebrity around our house. Hunter had dragged everybody he knew to the house just so they could see Griffin the Grappler Connan with their own eyes. Everything about Griff was infectious. His laugh, his self-assuredness, the way his mouth crinkled at the side when he smiled. Hunter had quickly learned to not bring any girls around to meet Griff; otherwise, he'd be ignored the rest of the night as the girls swooned over Griff.

I knew that everybody was tolerating Meatball and me because of Griff.

Griff was a little put off by the attention, especially when we finally happened to find ourselves alone only to be immediately interrupted again. But he was polite enough and signed autographs when requested. He even eventually signed Hunter's poster after Hunter agreed to take it off their bedroom wall. All the attention Griff was getting made me feel even more alienated. The only time anybody ever really talked to me was to ask me questions about Griff—and then I hid behind a smile.

I hadn't realized how bad things had gotten, how bad *I* had gotten, until Griff was walking Cassie and me to school one morning.

"You changed your hair color," I remarked, making small talk with Cassie. Her hair had gone from kettle-black to blonde, and she had removed her pale-face makeup to reveal her blonde eyebrows. It seemed she had given up her vampire ways for sun-kissed.

Griff and Cassie simply looked at me as though I were talking to them from the moon.

"I changed it two weeks ago," she said with a smirk.

I had taken a liking to doing my homework in the school library. Because it was quiet; because Griff couldn't talk and I could be alone with my thoughts. While Griff picked a nearby table and read a book, I sat at a computer to write my criminology paper. The fact that I had decided to write on the topic of white-collar crime wasn't coincidence. Every day I scoured the news, looking for anything relating to my father. It had become an obsession, a release, a drug. I couldn't walk by someone's discarded newspaper without grabbing it. I couldn't sit at a computer without seeing what new information there was on my father. For the first time in my life, I was getting to know my father; unfortunately, it had to be through the eyes of various reporters. I just wished someone had something nice to say about him, other than his great ability to make money. At least I was double-dipping on my time and using the information I collected on my father's crimes to write my criminology paper.

Griff and I found ourselves having fewer and fewer things to discuss, that is, argue about. Everything had been said. He wanted to move forward, and I couldn't. We were at an immovable, focal impasse, and trying to make small talk was rendered pointless when there was such a huge boulder hanging over our heads. Sometimes we would walk all the way to school and back without ever saying one word to each other. Sometimes I would go to bed at night realizing that I hadn't uttered one word to anyone all day. I had already given up hope that Griff would come around, and I could feel that Griff was giving up hope that I would come around. But the more sedentary I became, the worse the dreams of Cameron and Rocco became. To the point that I barely slept or ate anymore. There was a lot of wandering around the house in the middle of the night.

The obsession with my father hadn't replaced my obsession with Victor and Spider. In fact, it had fueled it. On one of my news-hunting exercises, I had come across a picture of Victor in the *Callister City Standard*. He was standing next to a mound of paper-wrapped bricks of cocaine. Another glorious moment for the local hero. I wanted to punch a hole through his papered face. Instead, I cut out his picture and stuck it on my bedroom wall, hiding it under one of my Van Gogh posters so that Griff wouldn't see it. When I realized that this art project was half-finished, I drew a picture of a red ugly spider and stuck this next to Victor's picture. I had gone from staring at the glow-in-the-dark stars on my ceiling to glaring at a replica of *Wheatfield with Crows*.

I didn't just want revenge—I needed it. But with Griff following my every move, I couldn't do anything to obtain it. And this was slowly killing me, like a long drawn-out fever.

\*\*\*\*

"I made pancakes," Griff announced one Friday evening when we were alone in the house—a rare moment. I was lying on my bed doing homework—trying to do homework. My mind was always elsewhere nowadays.

I smiled. Of course I smiled. "Not hungry. Thanks."

But Griff had stopped smiling as of late. "C'mon," he ordered with that infectious voice of his.

This was something that Griff had started doing instead of smiling: insisting on food, for me. His cooking skills were my least favorite of his attributes. He would try to sneak healthy stuff in my food, like replacing sugar with protein powder. (*Who does that?*) I could barely keep anything down; eating pancakes that would probably taste like flaxseed oil was a new form of torture.

My eyes had found their way back to Plato's *Symposium*. I was already two weeks behind on the required readings for ethics.

Griff kept standing there. I kept ignoring him.

He sighed a sigh that came from deep within. As though it were his last breath. "How long are you going to keep this up for?"

"I'm not hungry," I insisted, with a smile that I really had to work hard on.

I saw Griff's body turn rigid, like something was rising inside of him. He lifted his fist, held it up like he was about to hit something. He took another breath through clenched teeth and let his fist slightly bump the doorframe. I could see it was taking all his resolve to not explode.

"Goddamn it, Emily. What is so wrong about wanting to move on from the bad into something good?"

I let go of the stupid smile. "I can't move on, Griff. Maybe you can forgive and forget so easily, but I can't. If I don't do something, I'll die."

"Because they're going to come and kill you?" he said, mocking me darkly. "You still haven't given me any good reason as to why they would ever come after you again. Why did they grab you in the first place?"

I stared blankly at him. This was more information that I wasn't letting go of.

His eyes were on fire. "So you're going to kill two drug lords. Have you ever even killed someone, Ms. Sheppard?"

"No," I said, wincing. "But there's a first time for everything."

"Do you know how ridiculous you sound?"

"I sound ridiculous?" I slammed my book shut and got up. "Rocco, a fourteen-year-old kid, a kid who looked up to you, gets killed for no reason. And I'm the ridiculous one? At least I have a sense of loyalty."

"He's dead," he shouted, his arms extended. "The kid was a really great kid, and something like that should never have happened to him. Or to you. But he's dead now, and we're alive. We have a chance to be happy. Karma will get those bastards back, and maybe someday we'll be able to settle the score ourselves. But for now, we need to stay out of their way and out of their world."

"I already told you, Griff. I'm not asking for your permission, and I sure as hell don't need you."

He was silent.

I turned sideways to avoid bumping into him as I left my room.

Griff pulled his arms around me, in a sort of hug, pinning my own arms against my body, my back held against his chest.

"What are you doing?" I demanded when I realized it wasn't a hug. I struggled to get out of his enfold.

"How are you going to get out of this, Em? If someone comes up and just grabs you like this. What are you going to do?" he asked me, on the edge of hysteria.

I wiggled around, tried to jump, tried to kick from behind, but nothing changed the fact that I was stuck. Meatball had come flying out from under my bed and tried to nudge us apart. Since he spent most of his days with Griff while I was at school or work, they had come to some kind of understanding. Now he was confused as to what he ought to do.

Griff was trying to make a point, and he had a point. I couldn't move.

Anger bubbled inside me. "Let go of me."

"These men that you want to go after, these men that you want to kill, they all have guns. You want to kill them when you can't even get out of my arms. What are you going to do when you come face-to-face with someone who'd love nothing better than to have you wedged against him like that?"

Furious tears came gurgling out.

Griff turned me around and held me at arm's length. "The hurt, the pain, the hate. You have to let go. If you don't, you'll become just like them, and you *will* die."

Pain shadowed the boyish features of his face.

And this made me so angry. Because I didn't want to be the one to cause him all this pain. And yet I was.

"You're an asshole," I hissed before he could say anything else.

I went through the closest door and locked it behind me. I bent over, putting my hands to my knees. I took several breaths and wiped the furious tears that Griff had managed to squeeze out of me.

Funny enough, I was in Joseph, Hunter, and, now, Griff's room. The room that anyone would usually avoid. But I remembered it being far messier than this. There was no food or dirty dishes lying around, and I could actually see the carpet. Griff had made a valiant effort at making his bed, which was difficult given that all he had was a mattress on the floor made snug between Hunter's and Joseph's beds.

I had no idea that Griff was so responsible in this world.

When we were at the Farm, in the underworld, Griff slacked off as often as possible.

At the Farm, I was the responsible one. The one who hoped for the best, the one who lay mostly passive, waiting for someone else's decision. Now the tables had turned. Griff was the responsible one. The one who made his bed and didn't go running after drug dealers.

I could hear Griff pacing outside the door, so I was in no hurry to get out. I just couldn't deal with his reality, which was probably pretty close to the rest of the world's reality. But it wasn't mine.

By grabbing me like that, Griff had basically told me that I was just a stupid little rich girl who was looking at life through her murky rose-colored glasses. It was worse than a slap in the face.

When I saw that Joseph's computer was on, I sat down and got on the Internet. Though I was scouring the news again, it wasn't for my father. I was looking for something, an article I recently read in the *Callister City Standard*.

While I was waiting for the archived search to load, a message bubble popped up in the screen's corner. It was a message from someone named Bubbalicious.

"Need help."

I snickered. I couldn't resist. "Don't we all?"

"Serious. I'm failing three of my classes."

"That really sucks," I wrote back. I knew what that felt like. I was lucky if I made it through class without drooling on my notebook while I slept.

"My boyfriend told me you hacked the school's system to delete the electronic library. Genius. Can you go in and change my grade too?"

I yanked my fingers off the keyboard as if it had just caught fire. So Joseph had been the reason why I had lost my job at the library.

The search engine returned with a list of articles matching my keywords.

"Hello?" Bubbalicious wrote back. I printed the article I had been looking for and had the good sense to print the conversation that Joe didn't know he'd had with Bubbalicious before I erased it.

Apart from the fact that he looked barely past puberty and spent a lot of time in front of his computer, I realized how very little I knew of Joseph. We had been living under the same leaky roof for over a year, and I didn't even know his last name. Then again, he probably didn't care to know my last name either.

When I was growing up, I wasn't allowed to watch TV. While Bill was in the next room allowed to poison his brain with whatever kept him quiet, I was sitting with another adult. Music lessons, science and math, French, German, Mandarin. It was never enough for my mother. If she suspected that one of her friends—acquaintances really—had smarter, more thriving, better children, then I could expect to have a brand-new teacher the next day. Everything I saw, everything I heard was being controlled by my mother and her paid minions.

When I was eight years old, my mother saw a little girl wearing the same dress as me at a party. My eight-year-old self must have looked fat because I had a nutritionist the next day and was put on a diet. I ate a whole cheesecake that night. My mother thought it was my way of rebelling against her, that my brother was a bad influence on me. I just really liked dessert.

I was eventually sent away to school because that was what parents did to rebels like me: they sent them to overpriced prep schools. My mother made special arrangements for me to get my own room, with no TV allowed of course. I just had to be the weird homeschooled carrot-haired kid who had no idea who Elmo was. Making friends was super-easy from then on. I hung out in the bathroom a lot.

I did full-out rebel when I left my mother's clutch and moved to Callister. But moving into small quarters with a bunch of other people had been a bit of a stretch for a social idiot like me. Now I wished I would have taken the time to get to know Joseph a little more. He seemed like the kind of guy a desperate girl like me might need.

Griff eventually gave up pacing outside the door. I heard him go down the stairs and back into the kitchen. Cold pancakes on his plate.

I was about to go back to my room when I spotted boxes under Joseph's bed. Reclusive, secretive Joseph. I couldn't resist. I quickly fell on my knees and started snooping. There were a lot of computer parts and wires and a serious lack of condoms. At least he wasn't so delusional as to think that he was going to get lucky sometime soon. There was also a can of red spray-paint. I imagined him a graffiti artist. Who was this kid? Whoever Joseph was, I liked him.

Griff had made his point—I couldn't fight a grown man with my bare hands. But he had also hit a nerve when making his point. All my life, others had been making decisions for me, deciding the person I was going to be. Griff's reality check had had the same effect on me as my mother's nutritionist. I needed to show them that they were wrong about me, about what this spoiled little rich girl could accomplish. Eating a whole cake did not kill me, and neither would Victor.

I folded my printouts and stuffed them in my pocket. Then I took the can of spray-paint and hid it under my shirt. I snuck back into my room to drop off my stolen goods and went downstairs with a smile so that Griff and I could go back to not speaking over cold pancakes.

****

Griff was right. I was not an assassin, and I did not own any weapons. But I wasn't totally helpless either. I had options, and I had a brain. I just needed to work through it all.

When I left for work on Monday morning, I was dressed in a gray hooded sweater and a pair of old navy-blue sweatpants. It hadn't escaped my attention that my clothes were floating on me lately, when they ought to have been fitting snug at around six months pregnant. I tried to put this out of my mind as I hid the newspaper article and can of spray-paint in my book bag.

Griff barely looked at me the whole way to work. When I reached for the door to the admissions office, he turned around and walked away. A small seam ripped inside of me even though I was grateful that he didn't decide to sit in the waiting area all morning until I was done working—something that he often did.

I knew it wasn't going to be too difficult faking illness to get out of work. I wasn't exactly a picture of health these days. After I struggled to put one foot in front of the other and had had to hold on to a desk when a dizzy spell came, Betty came to my rescue and had me sent home, even though I hadn't really spoken to her much in the past weeks. The worst part was that I hadn't even started faking my illness yet.

I hopped on a bus headed downtown and closed my eyes, waking up at every stop to ensure that I wasn't going to miss mine.

\*\*\*\*

The wind blowing through the buildings was vicious and cold. It took my breath away and practically knocked me over when I stepped off the bus. I strained, pushing to take every step as I walked up the two blocks to City Hall.

The city square was abuzz with camera crews and reporters. There were people looking over bridges; a few had climbed up lampposts. All hoped to catch a glimpse of Victor Orozo as he valiantly accepted the key to the city. They must have all read the same announcement I had in the *Callister City Standard*, though I doubted that they had the same plan I did. To be honest, I wasn't sure what my plan was. Not exactly.

Spider and Victor. One wanted to be lost; the other wanted to be everywhere.

How do you hurt two criminals who have only darkness in their hearts? How do you get your revenge and kill them when you're just one girl, as Griff had made me realize?

You go after the only thing they both cherish more than anything: supremacy. Their desperation to be king, I surmised, was their biggest weakness. They were hungry for power, and they were not good sharers. Only one could be on top, and any threat to his reign could send the other over the edge.

But neither could kill the other without approval from the captains of the underworld, something that wasn't going to happen. Not without a little encouragement. Cameron had told me that the one thing the underworld avoided at all costs was publicity, and nothing attracts the media more than a good old-fashioned gang war.

Spider and Victor were going to war … they just didn't know this yet.

As a white Cadillac drove up, the crowd soared, and so did my energy. I felt as though I had just been shot straight to the heart with adrenaline. I got close to the car, keeping my book bag close and my face hidden under my hood. Victor stepped out into the sunlight, and I stopped. I was remembering what he had almost done to me in that tiny room with the swinging lightbulb, remembering that he was the reason that Cameron had decided to leave me forever by choosing his death.

Victor walked to the podium, where the clueless mayor was waiting while the clueless crowd cheered and applauded. And I wanted to scream, expose him for the murderer that he was. His driver got back in the car and slowly drove away, avoiding the mob as it crossed the street to get a closer glimpse of the hometown hero.

I smiled and followed the car from the sidewalk, hidden among Victor's fans.

The driver parked the car around the block and got out, locking it before walking to the square. I waited in the shadow of one of the buildings. When he was out of sight, I marched ahead, pulling the spray can out of my bag and shaking it so that it was ready to go by the time I was by the car.

I didn't waste any time. I leaned over the hood and drew a

large red ugly spider on Victor's beautiful white Cadillac. Then I moved to the passenger-side door and repeated the same message. I was about to move around to the back of the car when three men dressed in black suits came through the crowd, smiling, quietly chatting with each other.

They hadn't seen me yet, so I pulled my hood down and started backing away from the car.

Then one of them stopped, midconversation. He saw the art I had left on Victor's car. And then he saw me.

He started running, and when the other two realized what was going on, they followed his lead. My legs unfroze, and I turned around, tearing down the sidewalk. I ran through traffic to the other side of the street, dodging shoppers and slamming into a few shopping bags. I ran around a truck that was pulling out of a delivery zone, got clipped in the hip in the process, and ducked into an alleyway when I was out of their sight line. My heart pumping, my breath gone, I sank behind a garbage bin and peered around its corner. A bunch of black suits ran by, more than the initial three who had seen me in action. I let my head fall back against the cold metal bin and waited for my breath to find its way back to my lungs.

It was only when I got up again that I realized how badly my hip was hurt. Keeping out of sight from the street, I kept to the brick wall and went to the first door. It was locked. But there were four doors in the other building that led into the alley.

Before crossing the short way to the other building, I held on to the bin and peered around its corner. I was tackled to the ground by a mass in a black suit.

We wrestled on the cement wet from the leaking garbage bin. His sunglasses went flying. He got hold of my arms and sat on my legs.

I kept struggling, to no avail. I wasn't going anywhere. The only thing that was going through my head was that Griff had been right.

The man dragged me up, pushed me against the brick wall,

and yanked the hood of my gray sweater off my head. My hair popped out like a jack-in-the-box. Victor's minion gasped.

I looked up, face-to-face with the man in the black suit.

It was Mike. The same Mike who'd stood outside the room where Victor was keeping me captive. The same Mike who had refused to help me get away from whatever Victor had planned for me.

Mike let go of my arms. "You," he said, incredulous.

I spit in his face. "Me."

I clenched my teeth, readying myself for the blow. But it never came. Mike wiped my spit off his face and just kept staring at me.

He glanced down at the spray can that had come loose during our struggle. His eyes made their way up my hands, which were stained with the evidence of red paint, and back up to my face.

His own face was crumpled in disbelief. A herd of dress shoes ran and stopped outside the entrance to the alley. We were still hidden behind the garbage bin, against the brick wall where he had shoved me.

Mike stood still for a second, as though he were deciding.

Then he put his finger to his lips before stepping out from behind the bin.

"Nothing in here," he reported as he walked the alley and tried the first door across the way. It was also locked. The men walked on, and Mike came back. "What the hell were you doing?" he demanded.

I furrowed my brow. "Sending a message."

He stood again, watching me. He looked at my sweater, and it was also splattered with paint. I obviously needed spray-painting lessons.

Mike grabbed the can of spray-paint from the ground and flung it into the garbage bin. Then he took off his jacket and pulled his T-shirt off.

"Take your sweater off," he ordered, handing me his T-shirt.

There was no way that Victor's minion was actually going to help me. Especially after he had refused to so many months ago.

And yet, I did what I was told and pulled my sweater over my head.

While I put Mike's black T-shirt on, he buttoned up his jacket so that you could hardly tell he was shirtless. He crossed the alley and checked the other doors. All locked. No exit.

He considered this, came back, and threw my painting sweater into the bin.

"Do you have a watch?" he asked me.

I didn't. He sighed and gave me his.

I was beyond trying to comprehend why he was doing this.

He sat me down against the bin and pointed his finger at me. "Don't move from here for the next two hours."

I nodded.

He left.

I had no idea what had just happened.

But I listened to Mike and did not move from my spot, keeping my eyes on the watch.

Within half an hour, I was shivering so hard my body was making the garbage bin rattle. Once the adrenaline wore out and the cold seeped in, I couldn't move without shots of pain up and down the side of my body.

Then the cramps came. In my stomach. It was unlike anything I had ever felt. It was the sort of pain that ran through every vein and lit coals in my belly. For once, my heart and my mind were on the same track. Something was happening; something was wrong with the baby.

As I crouched over, retching, panic rose and I rose with it, holding on to whatever I could. Oblivious to time and space. Indifferent to Victor or his security. I managed to grab a bus back to school and found myself at the clinic, feeling the wetness of blood in my underwear.

The nurse behind the counter was closing the plate glass as I walked through the automatic doors. Elevator music played in the background.

"We're closed," she told me, but I held the plate glass open. I caught a glimpse of my reflection. My hair was half in, half out of a ponytail, I had mud all over me from my scuffle with Mike, and my hands were covered in red paint.

There was a doctor behind her, his back turned as he put files away. He was the medical student who had somewhat patched up my broken fingers.

"Hey," I shouted like the madwoman I resembled.

He jumped and spun on his heels. It seemed to take him a minute to figure out who the hell I was.

I didn't have a minute. "I'm pregnant."

The nurse's eyes rounded and jumped from me to the med student. She likely assumed I was accusing him of getting me pregnant.

"I'm bleeding. I think the baby is hurt." I was shivering in the T-shirt that Mike had given me. This was not T-shirt weather.

The doctor in training bade the nurse good night and led me through the building into the basement offices.

"How far along are you?" he asked softly.

I wanted to cry, but I didn't. "I don't know. I'm not really sure."

He unlocked a door, and we walked through an empty waiting room to the back. He brought me to a small dimly lit room and made me lie down, pulling my shirt up. Cold gel was squirted onto my belly, and a lever hooked up to an ultrasound machine followed.

"This is the second time I've seen you, and you're coming in even more banged up than the first time," he observed, keeping his eyes trained on the screen.

I tried to look at the screen, but he had turned it away from me. He stopped and turned sternly my way.

"You need to relax. It's hard to see anything if you don't relax."

He went quiet again, one hand on the keyboard, the other swaying with the lever on my stomach. I could hear him breathe and tried to match his pattern to calm myself.

Breathe, Emily, breathe. One breath in. One breath out. One breath in. One breath out.

The swaying on my belly slowed down, and he started clicking on the lever.

I closed my eyes. Oh God. Breathe in. Breathe out. Don't cry. Breathe in. Breathe out.

There was no more clicking, no more swaying.

I stopped breathing.

The doctor kept the lever on me and clicked one last time on the keyboard, turning the sound on.

Boum-buh-boum. Boum-buh-boum. My eyes flew open. I knew exactly what that sound was. As if I had heard it all my life. As if I had been waiting all my life to hear it again.

The doctor had turned the screen so that I could see it. There was a tiny blinking light in the middle of a wiggly squash.

The doctor pointed to the screen. "That's the heart. The head. The arms. The legs."

It had arms and legs. It had a head. It had a beating heart.

"The baby is fine. Based on the measurements, you're about four months pregnant," he continued and sighed. "You, however, don't look well. Have you been taking any vitamins?"

I smiled at the screen. "Can't keep anything down lately."

He wrote something on a pad of paper and handed it to me. "These will help. But more than anything, you need to rest … and take better care of yourself. You need regular medical attention, from a doctor."

I could tell from the sound of his voice that there was something else he wanted to say. But I couldn't take my eyes away from the screen, and I couldn't stop smiling.

Eventually, he pulled the lever off my belly. And remained quiet as he put the equipment away. I pulled my shirt down, letting my fingers flutter over the skin of my stomach.

He helped me up and excused himself for a minute. I looked at the empty screen again, wanting more. Then my eyes went to the corner next to the bed, where a visitor chair had been placed close for excited family members, for expectant fathers.

I stared long and hard at the chair, imagining Cameron sitting there. But there was no one sitting there for us.

The doctor walked me out of the darkened building and hesitated. It was raining the kind of cold rain that gets sucked through your skin all the way to your bones.

"Do you need a ride?" he asked me.

I stepped out into the rain. "No, I'm fine." I would be fine. We would be fine. But I needed to be more careful from now on. I couldn't risk us.

He nodded and handed me a pamphlet before running out into the rain.

I looked down at the pamphlet. "Domestic Violence & Pregnancy."

I crumpled it and threw it in the nearby garbage before heading back home.

****

The wind and the rain blew the door open for me as I came through it.

Hunter was sitting on the stairs, with his phone in hand. He shot up when he saw me.

"Griffin has been looking everywhere for you. He's out with Meatball, walking through the school."

I ran past him up the stairs and into my room. I grabbed papers I had hidden under my mattress and went searching for my ethics notebook.

When I finally found it, Griff and Meatball came jumping through the doorway. Both were gasping for breath.

Griff had me in the fold of his arms before I could apologize and tell him he was right. That I couldn't fight two men who wanted to rule the underworld.

"Okay," he said in my ear.

I pulled away enough so that I could see his face. "Okay?"

"I'll help you with whatever you need," he said in a voice that was scared and defeated. "But you have to tell me everything, Em. I just can't do this anymore."

I threw my arms around his neck and let myself get scooped up closer to him.

"I'm so sorry I scared you, Griff. I'll never do that again," I said to him as we were cheek-to-cheek.

He chuckled a bit. "Never ever say never."

I dropped back down to the floor and took his hand. Then I dragged him out of my room and opened the door to his room without knocking.

"Uh, Em, what are you doing?"

Joseph was sitting at his computer and swiveled his chair, surprised by our brazen entry.

"Telling you everything," I said to Griff.

I marched us up to Joseph.

He took one look at me. "Why are you soaking wet?"

I handed him the printout from his computer. "I lost my job at the library because of you."

He took a moment to read the lines on the page. His expression went blank, his face pallid.

Then I handed him the sodden business card that Carly had given me. It had once contained the information of an accountant for the underworld who was to help me get Cameron's money.

"I need to find this person," I told Joseph.

It took a moment for him to register that I was blackmailing him.

He took another look at the card. "But there's barely anything on here. How am I supposed to find this person?"

I slit my eyes. "You seem to have a way of getting the information that no one else has access to."

Griff stood by me, watching.

# Chapter Eight: Cameron

# Crack

We were gathered in an old tin mill in Chicago when Manny walked in. And there were three things I noticed. First, her bra strap was peeking out from under her shirt, which looked big enough to fit a toddler (this was the second thing I noticed). Third, she was stalking toward me with a look that I could only compare to a lioness during mating season. She was stunning, and she knew it.

Carly growled from the second Manny had made a beeline for me until she was within earshot. And then she growled a little bit more before giving Manny and me some privacy. Manny kept a smirk on her face as she watched Carly leave.

"You need better help," she sneered.

"I was told that you wanted to talk to me about something?"

"What I said was that I needed to see you. But I'll settle for talking to you."

She was inching forward, her chest pulling her in, trying to close the space between us. "That's close enough," I told her, keeping a stern tone.

She glanced around the room as a few of the captains had filtered in. It was early still, and those of them who were being tailed by the feds took a bit longer to safely get to meetings.

The captains weren't oblivious to the fact that Manny was attracted to me or to the fact that we'd had a meaningless fling some time ago. (Secretly, they all wished they'd had the same chance.) But that was all over, and I wasn't about to risk any further distraction.

Manny was all about distractions. She rocked back on her heels and laced her hands behind her back, making every seam of her tiny T-shirt exert. A pigeon in heat.

"Been seeing anyone lately?" This was the question she would ask me every time we saw each other lately.

I knew what she was really asking me: Have you seen *her* lately? A question I had already answered and was done answering.

"Oh, there have been a couple broads here and there." I gave her my most arrogant smirk. "But you know me. I like to string them along for a while. I've never met anyone who was worth keeping around."

She winced. This had, of course, been for her detriment. Though I had always been clear to her that what we had was just another fling and that I would never have feelings for her, she wasn't getting it. I hoped this last punch would be enough to quiet her questions.

I started to walk away until she held me back.

"I still need to talk to you," she said, having regained her business edge.

I arched my brows and waited, my patience running thin.

"I've been able to make a deal with Mexico. The biggest deal we've ever had. Unlimited drugs, unlimited weapons. We could be running everything we want through their borders, and they won't stop us."

Manny had been responsible for keeping the peace with the Mexican cartel while ensuring our treaty was respected, a job that her father before her had excelled at. Manny had bigger plans than her father.

I stared at her. "Did you have this conversation with the

cartel before or after they started distributing beyond the agreed borders?"

"I didn't discuss this with the cartel," she said with a defensive tone and took a moment. "I've been talking directly with Julièn."

Manny knew she wasn't authorized to make these kinds of dealings on her own. If it was for the benefit of the Coalition, she had to come to me first. If it was for her own benefit, she had no business being there in the first place.

There were three Mexican cartel families: the Munoz, the Vasquez, and the Castillos. All three were extremely explosive, to each other and to outsiders like us. Because of their volatility and their constant struggle for power within Mexico, we had never been able to get them into the Coalition. So we had come to a treaty with the families, allowing them each a section of the States to deal in, in exchange for keeping their drug war from spreading too far.

I crossed my arms. "You're on a first-name basis with the Mexican president?"

She slit her eyes and smiled. "No one else would have ever been able to make that kind of a deal."

This gibe had been against me. It had always been clear that Manny didn't just have feelings for me; she had feelings for my power. She wanted both of us so badly she was willing to do anything.

"You're walking a very thin line," I warned her quietly. "While you were busy making backroom deals with the president, the cartel has been making themselves comfortable on our turf. You need to do your job and ensure that our treaty is being followed, without setting off a war."

"This deal would make everything easier for us—"

"Nothing's ever easy," I hissed.

Manny's jaw tightened. "You just wish you were the one who had been able to make this kind of deal."

I took her aside and glanced around the room. "If the captains get wind of the fact that you're making dealings on the side without authorization … you're putting yourself in serious danger."

Her lips thinned.

The rest of the captains filtered in.

She nodded and stepped away.

We sat around the table, and I started the meeting.

As we went through the day's agenda, I kept Manny in my peripheral vision. She fidgeted in her seat and spun her pen between her fingers, feigning the slightest of interests in the conversation topics.

Kostya ended the agenda with our decision to sell our shares in Chappelle de Marseille and fund Advantis. Apart from the regular grunted response, this garnered very little interest from anyone around the table. Anyone but me.

I took a quick glance at the faces around the table and asked if anyone had anything else they wanted to add, as I always did. Then I waited, my peripheral vision still on Manny.

The leader of the Southern West Coast street gangs piped up, looking slightly uncomfortable. "Wasn't sure when this was going to be addressed," he said, and he had a paper sent around to me. It was a printout from the front page of the *Callister City Standard*. It was dated with today's date, with a caption of "Vandals Put Damper on a Hero's Welcome" and a picture of a red spider spray-painted on a white sedan—Shield's sedan.

I passed the paper to Spider, who was sitting behind me. He glanced over the picture and placed the paper next to him, his expression stoic. All eyes were on Spider and me. Manny smirked.

"I meant to bring this to you before the meeting," Viper said respectfully and eyed Manny. "But you were busy."

*Yes*, I thought, *Manny was busy distracting me so that this would have to be seen and heard by all the captains, before I could kill and bury it.* Manny was working all angles today—first by trying to disrespect my authority, then trying to attack my most trusted man.

"Obviously, Spider didn't do that," I said, chuckling darkly at the picture of the pretty spray-painted spider. "He isn't that artistic."

"Still," Viper said, "the coincidence of someone else painting a spider on Shield's vehicle ... is kind of crazy. Especially after the hot vote—at your demand—to dispose of Shield."

I wished Viper would have had time to bring this to my attention so that I could think about the best way to deal with this. Even though Spider had had nothing to do with this, the coincidence was certainly uncanny. And it would be used as fuel to Shield's assertions to the captains that Spider and I were planning to kill him (which of course I was), which were found to be groundless. Until now.

As far as I knew, Shield had painted this spider on his car himself in order to swing the captains' vote his way, to show that I was brewing up a war that the captains had already declined.

I analyzed the faces at the table and made a quick decision.

"Well," I sighed, "I think that for the time being, until we can determine the meaning of all this and how this so-called coincidence occurred, Spider will remain out of sight and away from all of our business. Agreed?"

Grunts of approval went around the room.

I did not hear a peep from Spider, but I knew he would be fuming by the time the meeting ended.

"Anything else?" I asked the table before we exited.

Some of the captains had already started gathering their things and mumbling with their neighbors.

Manny placed her pen on the table, leaned forward, and cleared her throat. "I have something to bring to the table," she announced, her voice firm. A look of surprise flitted around the captains' faces. With most of them having been in the Coalition from the very beginning, Manny was still fairly new to the table, and with the still-questionable demise of Manny's father, this move came as unexpected.

She had their attention.

Manny went through the plans for manufacturing *and*

distributing our own products. Dope. Weapons. Cutting the cost of the middleman. Ensuring that she dropped Julièn's name as many times as possible. When she was done, she leaned back in her chair with a satisfied sneer on her face.

I watched as the old boys, the ones who had been with the Coalition from the beginning, eyed each other.

There was total silence around the table. But not for long.

The leader of the biker gangs was the first to break the silence with a bellow. His nickname was Slobber because of his lack of hair on top and his overgrown moustache, which fell at the corner of his mouth like he was drooling hair.

"Let me guess," Slobber said, not even attempting to hide his smirk. "In exchange for this deal of a lifetime, the Mexican president wants his cut?"

Manny stared back at him, trying to keep her composure as the old boys quietly cackled. The only ones who remained stagnant were two of the newly inducted street-gang captains.

"Julièn's at it again," Kostya mumbled.

I let this go, just for a little while, before bringing order back. Then I gave Manny a condescending smile. "Julièn," I explained, "has been trying to get in on the action for years, but the cartel wants nothing to do with him. He can't even control the drug wars in his own country and wants to partner with us, making all these promises he'll never be able to keep. Tell me, what does he want out of this deal? Because, we all know, nothing comes without a price."

Silence from Manny.

"Exclusivity? Am I right? He wants us to single-source through Mexico?" I looked Manny in the eye. "We haven't worked a long time just to build up reputable sources. If we drop all of them, they *will* find another way to bring the merchandise in. Not only would we be doing business with Julièn—someone who can't deliver on his promises—but we'd be at war with our partners."

Manny looked blankly ahead.

"Anything else?" I asked one more time at the table.

Some of the captains were chuckling among themselves as they pushed their chairs back.

"Manny, a word," I called as the rest of the captains filtered out. I passed some of the remaining paperwork back to Spider and waited for him to close the door behind him.

Manny stood erect behind her chair and watched me move around the table.

I grabbed her by the hips and brought my lips close to her ear. "If you ever disrespect me, try to upstage me like that again, I will have your throat slit."

She placed her hands on top of mine, pushing them deeper into her hips. She closed her eyes, leaned in, and kissed me hard on the lips. A rattlesnake's venomous bite.

When Manny and I walked out of the meeting room, Spider and Carly were already gone.

One of the guards took me back to our place in Houston. We had an apartment in a high-rise. From the outside, the building looked like a roach motel. Inside, it was worse.

The smell of cigarettes and sweat and mixed spices hit my nostrils as soon as I walked into the atrium. There were fliers and muddy floors over by the area designated for the post boxes, though most of these were being held shut by wires or other contraptions. There was miscellaneous garbage piled next to perfectly empty bins.

Five elevators would take residents anywhere between the building's twenty-eight floors—though only two of them were actually working. An old lady dragged herself onto the same elevator, wheeling her grocery cart of various junk and empty, stolen garbage bags behind her. This explained why all the garbage cans were sitting empty.

A kid had attempted to spray-paint a gang sign on one of the elevator walls. This made me chuckle, given that I had just sat at a table with the captain who led this street gang ... as well as the other two rival street gangs in this state. Kids needed to feel like they were fighting for something, feel like they belonged somewhere. Too bad they were fighting each other to make money for the same organization. Ours.

"This place is going to hell," the old lady mumbled to me, or to herself.

Little did she know that we—or rather, our company—owned the whole building and that we were the slumlords of this hellhole. It made for a great cover. There was no such thing as a nosy neighbor in these types of places.

The old lady got off on the second floor, and I went all the way to the top. The hallway to our apartment looked exactly like all the other hallways in this building. It was dimly lit, with a dozen brown doors on each side of the elevator and a carpet that might have once been of a purple shade. The smell was the only thing that was slightly better.

But once I unlocked the door, gone was the decrepit. Our apartment took up the whole top floor. It was clean and bright, draped in a lavishness that the people living in our building would never know in their lifetimes.

Carly was sitting on the arm of the couch, and Spider was leaning against the back of it. They were waiting for me, ignoring each other. The weird thing about Spider and Carly was that, even when they were fighting (or whatever *this* was), they couldn't stand to be more than a few feet apart.

When I saw Carly's face, I realized that she was waiting for me more as a warning than a welcome.

I barely had time to shut the door behind me before Spider exploded.

"*That* was your answer!" Spider shouted. "To kick me out of the business because some idiot painted a spider on a car? We both know only Shield would be stupid enough to do something like that."

"I agree," I said, slumping into an armchair. "But until we can prove that, I have to show the captains that their business is safe, that the Coalition is safe. This spider painting could push the feds to start looking for someone who calls himself spider. Who knows what that could lead to?"

Carly found a seat on a couch cushion. I waved my hand at Spider so that he would do the same. A quiet, rational caucus was better than wherever he was heading. Spider sat on the edge of the coffee table not too far from Carly.

"And what exactly am I supposed to do in the meantime?"

"For the time being, for the good of the business," I said, "I need you to work from a remote location."

"How remote?"

I arched my eyebrows.

"Nowhere near you or any of the captains," he answered himself. "You know this puts you in a dangerous spot. You can't just go out on your own."

When it came to business, Spider was never without me, and I was never without Spider. We had each other's back, always. At least, we used to. Our work together had been slowly dwindling as I had been going after Shield and his men.

"I'll have guards with me," I said.

Spider eyed me. "You know that's not enough. You need someone who's on the inside with you. Someone who's your eyes and ears while you make money."

"That's all we can do right now. You'll have to do what you can without actually being there."

"I'll go with you," Carly volunteered. Her tone suggested that she was actually serious.

Spider looked at her in horror. I tried to not start laughing, because I imagined that Spider's insides had just detonated.

"Pardon?" Spider asked her.

"I can be your number two, Cameron," she said to me.

Carly was tough and smart. She could handle pretty much anything. She had seen more in her childhood than most men would ever see in their lifetime. But doing what Spider did would take years of creating relationships and building a sixth sense, being able to sniff out trouble.

Even on her best day, Carly wouldn't be able to simply waltz into meetings with me because people were too paranoid for that. And I had to admit that Carly hadn't been at her best since the miscarriage.

Carly kept her eyes on me. I had seen that look a lot lately; it was wild, like a madness that was growing inside of her. What she had lost in the miscarriage was being filled by this blackness.

"I know you can do it, Carly," I started, and Spider shot up like a rocket.

"Absolutely not!"

Carly shot up too and faced Spider. "It's not up to you, Spider! You can't make that decision for me. I'm just as capable as any of you."

"But," I added, raising my voice to interrupt them before they got too deep into another shouting match, "this may not be the best time for you to take on that kind of role."

I had garnered the attention of both of them.

"Not the right *time*?" Carly questioned, her arms crossed over her chest.

I knew I was treading on unsteady waters, so I took my time trying to explain myself. "Well, with everything that's been going on, with the Coalition … and with you and Spider, I just don't think that it would be a good time for you to take on something new like this."

Spider's eyes were round. He was standing behind Carly, shaking his head at me. Begging me to stop.

"What do you mean?"

I was going to no-man's-land. "I'm just saying that with your emotional state—"

"My emotional state?" she barked.

Spider winced. I had always wondered how Carly, a five-foot-nothing girl, could all of a sudden look monstrous enough to spit fire. She stared me down with all her emotions.

In the end, I had managed to alienate both Spider and Carly.

At least they stormed off together.

I hoped that they would use the time to figure things out.

Of course, Manny was the real instigator of their departure. Viper's performance at the table had been laughable at best. He was new to the Coalition, easily tagged by Manny's beautiful venom. Manny had been trying to find a way to get Carly and Spider out so that she would have direct access to me. What she didn't know was that she had done me a favor. I had also been trying to find a way to get them away from me, albeit for different reasons.

The Coalition was fractured. I had felt cracks forming for some time, even before Emmy got swept into the underworld, causing such a stir. I noticed the small things at first, like Johnny, captain for the Italian Mafia, and Dorio, captain for the Asian triad, sitting next to each other at the table. A long history of violence, of family members getting sent back in pieces, would have made these two leaders undying enemies. Bringing them into the Coalition and having them in the same room without killing each other had been one of Bill's greatest feats. And now they were rubbing elbows. My suspicions were further raised when, together, they had convinced the captains that Ignazio and Seetoo, their counterparts in Canada, be brought forward as candidates for underworld leadership in Canada. They wouldn't have been my first or my second choice. One was too flamboyant, the other too sadistic. But all the captains had agreed that they were the only two in the running, and I hadn't insisted because I wanted to test out my theory.

Johnny and Ignazio were second cousins; their great-grandfather had a town named after him in Sicily. The American captains were not in Canada and didn't know what had gone down until I told them after the fact. One would have expected that when I advised them that I had killed Ignazio in favor of Seetoo, Johnny would have at least put up a fuss.

He barely blinked at the news.

Apparently, as long as either of their kinfolk was at the Canadian helm, they wouldn't bat an eye. Though I was pretty sure that Ignazio and Seetoo didn't know that their American brethren had had big plans for them. Not yet, anyway.

As far as I knew, they were the only two who were colluding. But it would be enough to overthrow the Coalition, and I knew who was behind it.

Shield had the so-called real world wrapped around his dirty little finger, but that wasn't enough for him. He wanted both worlds to himself. If his power were allowed to grow, if he were allowed to rule the underworld, I shuddered to think what that would mean for the rest of the world. War. Chaos. Destruction. Shield wouldn't stop until he was king of all, and he would kill anyone who stepped on his highway to total domination. The real world, the world where my Emmy lived and breathed, would become one with the underworld.

But I wouldn't be there to see it. I would be dead before I ever let that happen. Emmy's world would remain beautiful and safe for as long as possible, for as long as I was alive.

What Manny didn't realize was, in entertaining discussions with the Mexican president and estranging the three families of the Mexican cartel, she had set off an earthquake the size of the San Andreas Fault. One that would eventually divide the Coalition. The minute Manny had told me of her discussions with the Mexican president, I knew that the stage for change had been set.

The captains wouldn't let me kill Shield, and my suspicions, I knew, wouldn't be enough to change their minds—and going against the Coalition was a suicide that I wasn't ready for, yet. In the end, it would be a North versus South type of showdown, underworld style. Shield had already allied the Canadians and two of the biggest crime families to him. I would have to ally myself to Mexico and anyone else who followed. But this decision would have to come from the captains, something that Manny was probably already working on.

This was why I wanted Carly and Spider to leave. They were my biggest allies. They were the people who would always have my back when I needed them. But like Emmy, they were my family. Things were about to get volatile, and I didn't want them—any of them—to be around when the Coalition finally broke apart.

How long did I have before this happened?

I could only hope that, like Emmy, Spider and Carly would be out of the picture long enough for the other captains to be too busy fighting each other to try to go after them. Eventually they would go after them—no loose ends get left behind. But by then, I would have them safely hidden, somewhere, with Emmy. Hopefully.

Every move I made from hereon had to be precise and not appear to be of my own design.

## Chapter Nine: Emmy

## Can't Beat Them

Griff was teaching me how to fight. Nix that. Griff was teaching me how to defend myself, as he kept reminding me.

He had insisted upon it after I came back from spray-painting Victor's car. I was pretty scraped up and bruised and limped for a week. We never talked about what happened to me. I knew he wanted to ask me, but he didn't. And I appreciated that.

We tried out a few tactics back at the house, but after I almost went flying down the stairs, I asked Hunter to find us a safer spot to train. Because in my mind, that was what I was doing. Training. I was being as careful as I possibly could be.

Hunter got the school gym to lend us their workout room. It came with lots of padding on the floor.

Unfortunately, it meant that Hunter and his friends got to come too.

What Griff tried on me, Hunter and his friends practiced on each other. It wasn't every day that a prizefighter was showing off his stuff for free. Though I doubted that Hunter and his buddies were as careful with each other as Griff was with me. Of course, the first thing I asked him to show me was how to get out of the body hug he had done to me to prove his point that I couldn't defend myself. He still had no idea that his antics had almost sent me running right into Victor's lap.

My spray-painting exercise had merited me front-page news in the *Callister City Standard*. But all the reporters referred to me as the thug kid, and Victor was quoted as saying that the incident simply showed how much Callister's street kids were in need of guidance. It made bile creep up my throat. The story quickly died after that, and I never heard from Mike again. Why he had let me go, I didn't know. But I kept his watch on me just in case he ever came back for it. It was cheap, but at least it worked.

Griff and I were walking back from the gym, our arms rubbing between strides. His eyes darted every which way, from the face of a passerby to a car across the street. Ever since my secret escapade, I had seen a weariness grow on him, one that pulled bags under his eyes and left his shoulders tensed to his ears. He was rarely off his guard.

I could feel the darkness in my life spreading to him, and this made me ache all over. I needed Griff, but I didn't want him to feel the way I felt.

I tugged at the sleeve of his shirt to get his attention and smiled when he turned to me. His eyes searched my face for a second, then he chuckled. In a sweeping movement that had come so naturally, he grabbed my hand in his and squeezed it.

"Did Joseph find anything yet?"

"I don't think so," I said, not even attempting to hide the disappointment in my voice.

"What are you planning to do with all that money when you get it?"

"Use it."

When Griff asked me why I needed Joseph to find that accountant, in one breath I had confessed that I had a brother who had died and left me money and that the guy on the business card was the only one who could get it for me. I could see the question marks in Griff's eyes. What? Why? When? What? *What!* "Okay," was all he said, very calmly, as though he knew how difficult it had been for me to reveal this momentous information to him. I had spent most of my life doing everything I could to hide myself; or rather, trying to hide who my parents were. Coming from money was one thing, but coming from stinking-rich Sheppard money was a whole other ball game. Add two well-to-do Sheppard kids entangled in the underworld, and you had enough material to support all gossip magazines worldwide for three years.

Griff and I crossed the street. "You have a plan for it," he said matter-of-factly.

"Kind of."

"What does that mean?"

"It means I don't know *exactly* what I'm going to do with the money."

Griff slowed our pace. "But …"

"But until Joseph can find the guy I'm looking for, I need to keep moving." I swallowed hard. "There's someone else I need to find."

"I'm not going to like this, am I?" he wondered aloud as we rounded the corner to our street.

"How much do you know about the people you were working for when I saw you last time, in the barn?"

Griff looked to the sky in exasperation. "Enough to know that I never want to see them again."

We got back to the house, and Griff led me to the front porch. It was late November and freezing out, but he scooted me close to him to keep us warm.

"As far as I knew, I was guarding a heap of hay." He turned to me. "You know me, Em. I don't ask questions if I won't like the answer."

"Do you think you would be able to take me to the barn?"

"I have no idea where the barn is. I was taken to and from it blindfolded. The only people I talked to were the guy who came around to blindfold me, the other guards back at the bunker, and the creep who ordered me to open the trapdoor."

I knew that remark had been at Cameron's expense. Griff had

never concealed his dislike of Cameron, but he had been more careful lately to keep his feelings to himself.

I kicked at the frosted ground.

"Why do you need to go back to the barn?"

"Because I need to talk to the people I met when I was underground. Actually, one person in particular. His name was Pops." I propped my head up. "Do you know him?"

"Never heard of him."

"I think he's a significant drug dealer ... distributor," I corrected, as Cameron had once corrected me. "He'll be able to help me."

"Why on earth would a brute who puts drugs on the streets just to make a couple bucks want to help us?"

It hadn't escaped my attention that Griff had changed the "me" to "us." He was doing a lot of that too, as though it were second nature now, and I kept testing him, sometimes not on purpose.

"He's not like the others," I said. I knew this would sound ridiculous to Griff, so I took a moment before divulging another major piece of information I hadn't told him before. "He hates Spider ... and he knew my brother when he was alive."

Griff's eyes rounded. "*Your* brother?"

"Before he died, my brother was one of those brutes you dislike so much. Actually, he wasn't just a brute; he was *the* brute."

While we looked over the street, I told Griff everything I knew about my brother's business, everything that Cameron had told me about him.

"You've already seen my brother. A picture of him, anyway. In the car garage, back at the Farm. My brother's fake ID was in the plastic bag, and you called him a thug."

Griff reddened. "I'm sorry. I didn't know. Why didn't you say anything?"

"It was a pretty big revelation, even to me."

"And you didn't know if you could trust me," he accepted.

"So, this Pops person hates Spider. I like him already. What is he going to do to help us?"

"It was something that you said. You told me that I couldn't fight the whole underworld."

He grinned. "Yes, I did say that, didn't I?"

"And you were right."

He grinned even harder. "Say that again."

"You were right. I can't fight the whole underworld." I gulped. "But I can join them."

Griff winced as though I had just hit him with a stick behind the head. A small stick.

As the idea settled in his brain, I felt his arm go rigid against mine. "So you're telling me I'm responsible for this ... this ..." He couldn't find the word.

"This madness?" I found it for him because I knew this was what he was thinking. And he was right—if it hadn't been for him pushing me to prove my point (and almost getting myself killed in the process), I wouldn't have realized that I needed a better plan. "Have you ever had a feeling that you need to do something even if you don't know why?"

He chuckled very lightly. "I'm still here with you, aren't I?"

"I can't just walk into a room and kill Spider and Shield, not yet, even if that's what they deserve. But I can make them pay. I can make them crawl. I can take away what they love most."

"Which is?"

"Money. Power," I said, clamping my fists.

"And this Pops the drug dealer will somehow help us achieve all of this?"

There was that "us" again. I wanted to kiss Griff a million times over.

"How?" he added.

This was where my plan went a little murky. "He liked, respected my brother, and I think he liked me too. I'm not sure exactly how he's going to help us, but my gut tells me that he's the one who can make it all happen."

Griff remained quiet. I knew he wasn't in love with the idea. Far from it. But he hadn't walked away either.

"You've made a lot of contacts in the underworld. Do you have anyone who would know how to get to the barn or how to find Pops?" I asked him.

Griff thought about it and shook his head. "You can't ask those kinds of questions without more questions being raised. Whatever we decide to do, I don't want it advertised to hell before we even get there."

"Do you have any *friends* who would be able to tell us how to find Pops ... without asking more questions?"

Griff scratched the back of his neck as his mouth stretched thin. I could see it in his eyes. I had seen this look before whenever someone asked him for an autograph, asked him to talk about fighting.

"Nobody is ever really a friend in that world," he said. "The type of *friends* who would know anything would want something in return."

This I understood. What Griff didn't know was that it was in every world—under, over, and whatever illusory world my parents lived in.

We both took a breath, huddled on the porch. The deadness of a forthcoming winter left a silence on the streets of Callister's slums that was tantamount to being buried in cold mud. Ergo, there was nothing to kill the insatiable sound of my growling stomach. I tried to ignore it initially. We both did. But it only got louder, to the point that neither Griff nor I could even hear ourselves think anymore.

Griff bellowed a laugh. There was still some joy left in him. This made me laugh too.

"Let me guess. Hungry? Again?"

I hadn't stopped eating since the doctor had prescribed me those magic pills. I had even put on weight, so much so that my pants were getting a little tight. Finally. My energy levels were incredible. I couldn't stop moving until I fell into a deep coma at night. Truly magic pills.

Griff and I left the porch. While I headed up the stairs, he went straight to the kitchen to make us something nutritious. Of course I would eat whatever he would make, but honestly, I just really wanted a Big Mac and a dozen ninety-nine-cent tacos.

I still hadn't told Griff that I was pregnant. I was gearing up for it because if I didn't do it, nature would. I just hadn't found the right time. Was there ever going to be a right time for releasing that kind of bombshell? There had been a few moments when I had thought about telling him. Moments when we were silent. Moments when we were … just together. But then he would look at me and smile his Griff-smile, as though I were the first human he'd seen in the months after the apocalypse, and I would chicken out. I wanted him to keep looking at me in that way.

The look that he would afford me after he learned that I was carrying Cameron's offspring, I wouldn't be able to bear. To say that Griff didn't like Cameron was like saying that Cujo was a bad dog.

While I outgrew my jeans and opted for frumpy sweaters and elastic pants, I was left with restless butterflies in my swelling belly. Butterflies that were becoming more anxious with every opportune moment that passed between Griff and me.

I was scared. I couldn't bear to lose anyone else, especially not Griff.

When I got to the top of the stairs, I poked my head in Joseph's room. He was at his computer, as usual. But his hair looked like the skin of a dragon fruit, and he was mashing the keyboard as opposed to his habitual quick-rat clicks. I was holding a wrecking ball over his head, and it was getting to him.

I took a chair to his desk and sat down. Meatball had followed me in and sat between Joseph and me.

I had assumed that Joseph hadn't seen me come in because his eyes never left his computer. But his hand found its way to Meatball's head and behind his ears. Meatball's eyes rolled to the back of his head, and his tongue hung limp. I had noticed Meatball come in here on his own lately. Now I knew why.

"It's like this guy doesn't even exist," Joseph said, his voice winded, eyes still on the screen.

"It's okay. I know you tried your best." I unfolded the piece of paper that I had been keeping in my pocket. It was the wrecking ball of evidence that I had been holding against him. "I haven't told anyone or made any copies. You can have it back."

Joseph peeled his eyes away from the screen for exactly two seconds before continuing his obsession.

"I can find anything, anyone, anytime. I just don't understand why I can't find this guy. Don't you have any other information on him? Like just one extra phone digit or letter of the alphabet?"

"Don't worry about it. I'll find another way."

"I've looked in about a million databases. Tried a million different scenarios. Looked in deleted files. Nothing."

"You mean, you've hacked a million databases."

Joseph grimaced. Apparently the word *hacking* was taboo among hackers.

"I hope you got paid well for hack … getting into the library's system," I teased as I lifted from my chair.

Joseph reached into a bag of candy corn and threw it in the air for Meatball to catch. This also explained Meatball's budding love handles and the hint of caramel on his dog breath at the end of the night.

"I do a lot of stuff for extra cash," Joseph admitted. "But that one I did for pleasure. My mom works part-time at the library. She rolls one of those carts around and puts books away. The electronic library was going to put her out of a job."

This immediately made me feel like a jerk for having wallowed about losing my meaningless job … and for having used the hacking evidence to blackmail him.

"Your mom lives nearby then?" My voice had started out normal, but ended with a squeak, as though I had just hit puberty.

"She lives in the Projects not too far away from here."

I knew the Projects well. A memory of Cameron sitting on a picnic table waiting for me flitted across my brain. "That's really close by. You don't live with her?"

"There are two ways to live in the Projects. You either get recruited by one of the gangs, or you get shot and killed because you're not in a gang. Sometimes both. My mom doesn't want me anywhere near all that stuff, especially since my brother's already a gangbanger and wants me to join. I'm the first one in my family to even graduate from high school, let alone go to college. My mom works three jobs just to keep me in college."

I was past feeling like a jerk and heading into Cruella de Vil land.

"If she loses her job at the library, then she'll also lose the tuition discount the university gives to employees and their family. Even if my mom worked ten jobs, she wouldn't be able to pay for my tuition without that employee discount," Joseph finished.

Okay, I was the devil. "It must be hard not being able to go home when they're so close."

"I get to take my mom out to lunch every once in a while. When she'll let me. Plus she brings me home-cooked meals a couple times a week. Meatball really likes her meatballs."

I hated the fact that Joseph and I had been living under the same leaky roof for over a year and that because of my ... issues, I didn't know any of this. I could feel red leopard spots creeping up my neck.

While Meatball waited on the tiptoes of his paws for another treat, Joseph dug into his drawer, pulling out a small stack of printouts.

The first was an article on my father's bail hearing. The second was from the *Callister City Standard*'s gleeful announcement of Victor's key-to-the-city ceremony.

He pointed to my father's article first. "So you're *that* Emily Sheppard."

My breath was shallow. "How did you get this?"

"You left your Internet search history all over my computer."

He said this as though I had just asked him what color his blue shirt was. "Can't say I understand why you're broke all the time or why you even live in this shithole. But what really interested me at first was why you had printed this article." He pointed to Victor's article. "That is, until I saw this."

Joseph pulled out a third piece of paper—the article on the bum who had spray-painted Victor's car. "I recognized the color of the spray paint. Ruby Red. My signature graffiti color, which has mysteriously gone missing."

So he was a regular Sherlock Holmes, or I was the worst lawbreaker in the world.

The heat that had been creeping up my neck a few seconds ago was pushed down as the blood left my face. I simply stared at Joseph blank-faced, knowing that he had everything to destroy me.

Joseph laughed, leaning back in his chair. "It's funny how little you can know about someone you've been living with for over a year."

My exact sentiment. "What do you want?"

"What do you mean?"

"In exchange for the information. What do you want to keep your mouth shut?"

"Not everyone is an extortionist. Are you always this paranoid?" he wondered, crinkling his forehead. "I might not understand it, but I think what you did was really awesome. I hate that guy. When my brother was nine, he got caught by this same cop when he was trying to sell allergy pills he stole from the pharmacy. This Victor guy beat him up so bad that my mom didn't even recognize him when his friends dragged him back to our apartment."

The feeling of relief was quickly replaced with an inflow of anger. "And you didn't report him?"

"Report him to whom? Who would believe a street kid from the Projects over a hero asshole cop?"

I knew the feeling. Victor was untouchable. Almost untouchable.

"Why'd you do it?" Joseph asked me.

My mouth stretched thin, and my brows arched.

He shrugged, accepting my nonanswer. "I also guess that Griff doesn't know anything about it?"

I bit the inside of my cheek. Griff had only seen me coming home soaking wet. If he knew what I had actually been up …

Joseph continued, "It's probably best that you didn't tell him. He hardly sleeps as it is. His head shoots up from the pillow if you even move your big toe."

"Thanks" was all I could tell Joseph. He had done for me what I hadn't done for him: not use the information as blackmail.

"I'll keep looking for that guy," he told me when I was leaving his room, as if I didn't feel bad enough. "That kind of stuff bugs the hell out of me. Nobody should be able to hide from me like that."

He was taking my search as his own personal treasure hunt, sudoku for hackers.

\*\*\*\*

It turned out that I knew more about Pops than Griff did, even though I had only been there once. I knew it was likely near a reservation. Pops had mentioned to me something about tribal legends, though I couldn't remember which tribe. I also knew it was within a day's drive of Cameron's cottage. And there was that little hotdog stand we had eaten at—the one with the waterfall, the one where I had offered to Cameron that I join him in the *business*. He would be rolling around in his grave if he knew what I was up to.

The bad part was that there were at least ten different reservations that were within a drivable distance for my station wagon, and while our search had turned up over three hundred hotdog stands, none of them were located near a waterfall. In fact, we couldn't find the waterfall anywhere. I was sure, almost sure, I hadn't just imagined the waterfall.

It was exciting to be sitting at a computer with Griff, planning our weekends around road trips to the country. His mood had picked up, and so had mine. Because I was in the midst of exam season, there wasn't much free time. I studied all week and should have been spending my weekends studying ... but I didn't. I was pretty sure I had aced my constitutional law exam, but my ethics exam had definitely been a bust. I supposed this was evidence of my skewed morals as of late.

Our first weekend out had been a bust, but only in the sense that we didn't find Pops or the hidden barn. We had packed a really good lunch. But Meatball ate the sandwiches and the crackers when we failed to notice that the bag had fallen open on the backseat. So we settled for the leftover soup and hot chocolate that Meatball couldn't get to.

Everything was different now in the countryside. The land had gone cold and hard. Sunlit hours were few. This made playing *I Spy* really easy since everything was white or brown or pitch-black, but it made it difficult for me to recognize any landmarks that Cameron and I would have crossed.

On our way back, we bought a Christmas tree from a shady guy on the side of the road who had just a few firs in the back of his pickup truck. The tree trunks had been cut in many odd angles, with splinters coming out the sides. Wherever he had (illegally) acquired these trees, they had been hastily cut. We got home, dragged the tree in, and found a corner for it. And as Griff put his arm around me and we watched the black-market tree, I realized what this meant. That Griff and I were going to spend the holidays together. That this was going to be a happy Christmas. That I was starting to feel happy again.

I felt stronger with Griff at my side. Stronger than I did before he came to find me, and definitely stronger now that he was looped into my world. *Most* of my world. It was as though I had grown two inches, or perhaps I was just walking with my head held higher, my spine straighter.

We didn't make much more progress the following weekend

either. This time we had headed northeast, but the drive was slow because of the thick snowflakes and because the Roadmaster was starting to protest winter. When it took what seemed like its last breath for the Roadmaster to climb a slight hill, Griff and I decided to pull over to give the old girl a break before she gave up on life and left us out in the middle of nowhere.

We got out of the car and found a tree to sit where we could keep an eye on Meatball while he burrowed his nose into the snow like a drunken groundhog.

We both leaned against the wood and sighed at the same time. There was a part of me that wanted this moment to last. The other part knew that it couldn't, for so many reasons.

"This won't last forever, you know," I said. "Eventually we'll find what we're looking for."

"And then what?"

"I don't know. Things will change."

He shrugged. "Things always change. You just have to roll with the punches, I guess. Whatever happens, we'll figure it out together."

I watched Meatball throw himself into the snow, legs flailing skyward. I wished I was him.

"You've got a snowflake on your nose, Ginger." Griff took his thumb and wiped the snow off my nose.

I hadn't heard him call me Ginger in a long time.

"When we first met," I said, crossing my arms over my chest to keep warm, "you told me that you were planning to get back to fighting as soon as you could get yourself out of debt. You're out of debt now."

"Didn't you hear me earlier when I said that things always change?"

"I don't want to be the one who makes you give that up, Griff."

"Nah," he said, "that part of my life is good and over."

"You're a hero to a lot of people. Hunter wets his pants when you say hi to him. You were really good at it, and you seemed to enjoy it."

"Seemed. Past tense. I'm not going back to that, Em. I realize now that fighting had taken me to a dark place. I don't ever want to go back to being that guy in that world."

I knew I was being hypocritical. Because I was the one who was forcing Griff to stay, who was forcing Griff to give up something that he had clearly once loved. The guilt was starting to eat through my skin.

"Is it so bad that I just want to be normal … with you?" he said to me.

"Okay," I said in a tone that was sarcasm-heavy. He obviously had absolutely no idea what normal was.

Then Griff did something that I hadn't seen coming. He leaned in and kissed me on the mouth.

And I did something I hadn't seen coming. I kissed him back.

It was a soft, freeing kind of kiss. The kind of kiss that makes you want to spread your wings and fly up high and over mountains and above the sea and into the breeze.

But as Griff's hands came to my face as naturally as they would come to hold my hand, I pushed him back and shook my head, daring the tears that wanted to rear their ugly head to stand down.

I called Meatball over and walked back to the car. Griff followed a few minutes later, and we drove off.

His eyes flickered from me to the road as we sat in a silence that was so thick, so pressured, it could explode us. At least half an hour had gone by before any words had been uttered, until Griff piped up in the clearest voice I had ever heard, "I love you."

Boom! The detonation I had been waiting for.

I could see it even in the farthest corner of his eyes. The hope, the desperation. He wanted me to say it back. He needed me to love him as much as he loved me. I knew this. I had known this for a while. But I had chosen to overlook it.

Something was climbing up my throat. I put my hand to my

mouth, thinking I was going to be sick. Griff drove off the road, stopped the car, and watched me turn olive.

He reached out, but I stopped him. I wasn't going to be sick—what was climbing up my throat was words. Words that would be powerful enough to break him and me. To break *us*.

The words had reached the inside of my mouth, and swished around like Listerine. And then my lips parted. "Griff, I'm pregnant."

Griff didn't move. He didn't blink. His chest did not take in any air.

"Did you hear what I said?"

He took another minute and a breath.

"How far along are you?" he asked me, keeping his eyes ahead.

"About six months."

I could see him make a very quick calculation in his brain as he figured out whose child I was carrying. "How long have you known about this?"

I couldn't lie to him. Not anymore. "A while."

He stoically put the car in drive, hit the turn signal, and veered us back onto the road. Then he turned the music up and took us home without one more word being spoken.

When we got home, I grabbed Meatball's leash, but Griff took it from me.

"I'll take him," he said without looking at me. His lips were tight and white as he headed out the door.

I had expected to feel some kind of relief after finally telling Griff the truth about the baby. But all I felt was ache. The truth hadn't set me free. It had blown a suffocating bubble around me.

I needed to talk to Griff, even though I had no idea what else to say to him. Hadn't I said enough?

I went up to my room, sat on my bed, and stared at my leaky walls, waiting for him to come back, wondering if he would come back.

\*\*\*\*

Griff did come back a couple of hours later. He went into the kitchen, and I heard the cling of dog chow against Meatball's salad bowl, before hearing the front door close as Griff left. It only took Meatball a minute to scarf down his meal before climbing up the crate stairs I had built for him so that he could get onto my stilted bed. He burped in my face, then let me wrap my arms around his thick neck and stuff my face in his fur while I continued to wait for Griff.

It was total darkness when I woke up. Meatball was crowding all the space on the bed. I was about to push him over so that I could get a bit of breathing space when I noticed Griff sitting at the end of the bed. I leaned over Meatball and switched the lamp on.

Griff had already hopped off and leaned over the side, leaned over Meatball to take me into his arms.

He said, "I'm an idiot. Jesus, I'm such a bloody idiot."

Meatball grumbled and pushed us apart long enough to get off the bed and go find a new spot to sleep on the floor.

I had switched from burying my face in Meatball's fur to burying my face in Griff's neck. I let out a sigh that lightened the weight pushing against my heart.

"I should have told you," I mumbled through the crook of his neck. "I should have told sooner, but I didn't know how."

Griff pushed me to arm's length so that he could see me.

"Of course you didn't tell me. With everything that happened." He looked ill, as though he were the one who had been afflicted with morning sickness. "I'm sorry, so sorry all this happened. I understand now why you seemed like you had changed so much. How are you doing?"

I smiled, and my eyes watered at the corners as relief settled in. "I'm fine, Griff. The baby's fine. I saw a doctor a few weeks ago."

"You need more than just one doctor," he said, worry encasing his voice. "When I took Meatball for a walk, I was so angry. But my head cleared, and I realized what an asshole I was, Em. I've been in that world. I've seen these pricks in action. I felt sick when I understood what you were trying to tell me while I was too self-absorbed to listen." He fished a piece of paper out of his pocket, struggling to unfold it. "I went to the library, and then to the school crisis center."

I looked at the piece of paper, and my heart sank. Griff did not understand at all.

"I don't know how to help you, but there are people who can," he said. "And I'll be there with you, every step of the way."

There was a moment, a fleeting moment, after I read the piece of paper and realized that Griff thought I had gotten pregnant after being raped, that I considered letting him believe this because this would keep him with me.

But as soon as this glimpse of a thought flashed through, I felt sick to my stomach. Because Cameron and his memory didn't deserve that, even if he had chosen death instead of fighting for us. And because I was done lying to Griff for my own selfish reasons just so he wouldn't leave me.

Griff waited for me to speak, hope and desperation finding their way back to his eyes.

I gulped and took a few long breaths. "It's not what you think, Griff." I couldn't do it. I couldn't tell him. But I had to. "This baby was made out of love."

I told Griff about Cameron and me. About Cameron falling in love with me. About me falling in love with Cameron.

I had expected this to hurt him, but he instead kept a sympathetic eye. "Your mind was playing tricks on you to help you survive the ordeal. I know you think you loved him, Em, but you didn't. And believe me, he never loved you."

"I did love him. And he did too," I said, my voice calm.

"You knew the guy what? A few weeks? It doesn't make sense for you to have fallen in love so quickly with someone you barely knew."

"I know it doesn't make sense, Griff. I don't know why I fell in love with Cameron ..." I had asked myself that question many times. I didn't understand it, but I accepted it.

"You know, there's one thing I don't understand," he said. "When I saw you that day in the barn, he barely acknowledged you. He treated you as though you were his property. How can you love someone who treats you like that? Is that what chicks are into nowadays? Being with a guy who treats them like crap?"

I could hear the frustration in his tone. Cameron had been forced to ignore me, rebuff his feelings for my own protection. "It's complicated, Griff."

But this wasn't enough to satisfy him.

"How can you have loved someone who left you? Pregnant nonetheless!"

"Cameron didn't know that I was pregnant when …" I sighed, realizing I had never told him that Cameron was dead. "He didn't leave me, Griff. He was killed. By Spider. That's why I need to kill Spider and Victor—because they will eventually find out that I'm having Cameron's baby. And there's no way they are going to let that happen."

"What did you say?"

"That I need to kill—"

"No, not that. Cameron. You said that he's dead?"

I told Griff about being taken by Shield. About being locked in a little room. About what had almost happened. About Cameron using his last breath to save me before being shot by Spider.

A dark look took over Griff's features. When he didn't speak, I finished with what I needed him to understand most. "I love Cameron, and Cameron loved me. While I wish he would have fought for us, I can't change that. But I will fight for the child we created together." That was it. I had now told him everything.

Griff looked pensive for a second, but something inside him triggered. "You mean, you *did* love him. You said that you love him, but what you really meant to say is that you used to love him."

I knew this would hurt him. "There'll always be a part of me that will love him." I touched his arm. "But it doesn't change anything else. I love you, Griff. But I don't know if I love you in that way. Things are just too complicated and confusing right now. Nothing makes sense anymore."

Griff shrugged his arm from my grasp. "As long as you love him, you'll never be able to love me."

I didn't know what to tell him. But I felt as though I had just put a bullet through his heart.

He stood and paced. "So if that son of a bitch walked through the door right now, you would take off into the sunset with him? After everything?"

"There's no sense in hashing out hypotheses, Griff. Cameron isn't coming back. This is my life now."

Griff stopped pacing long enough to look at me. Watching me. Deciding what he was going to do. But I already knew what his decision would be. I could see it in the vacancy of his eyes. There was so much I needed to tell him. How much I needed him. How much his light made my life tolerable. How I could see myself being happy someday. But there was no point. It was too late. I had hurt him too much for that.

While Griff's body was still there, standing in front of me, he was already elsewhere.

Griff turned around and went to bed. Right before dawn burst, I heard him shuffling next door. He tiptoed past my curtain and down the stairs. When I got up in the morning, I went to his room. His bed was made. His duffel bag was gone.

Griff had left me.

The fact that I had fallen in love with his nemesis was killing Griff, like a bullet that lingered near his heart. The fact that I was pregnant with the child of his archenemy, the fact that I was bearing the seed of everything he hated, the fact that I still loved Cameron was enough to thrust the bullet to its final target.

# Chapter Ten: Cameron

## Fiction

There was no rewriting of this story.

There were times when I would lie awake at night with my eyes closed, imagining a different story. One that started with me choosing to take that scholarship to MIT, instead of taking over the drug world with Bill. I would meet Emmy on the street. I would smile. She would smile back, immediately taking my breath away. I would take her out to dinner, to an intimate but expensive place. I would make her laugh all night. We would stroll through the streets hand in hand, stay out until the sun came out.

Fall in love, unafraid, carelessly.

I would ask her father for her hand in marriage. He would slap me on the back, offer me a cigar. I would marry Emmy in a huge wedding, one with as many guests as my old high school had students. We would have children. As many as she wanted. They would grow up being able to play in the front yard in the thickest, greenest grass known to man, without having to live in fear of who might be lurking in the bushes. Emmy would live happy. With me.

I was lying on the couch with my eyes closed. She came into my brain. I pushed her out. She tried to inch her way back in. I opened my eyes and got up because there was just no changing the ending to my story. Mine would end badly. Not Emmy's.

I went to meet Manny at a Thai restaurant on the outskirts of Houston. It was as hot in there as it was outside, and it smelled like dead fish left in the heat. At least the place was deserted, as it ought to be. Manny and I grabbed a booth, and our guards found seats at tables nearby.

Manny took the water pitcher that had been left on the table by the owner before he left the premises. She poured us each a glass. I didn't touch it. As far as I knew, she had already laced it with toxin or some kind of roofie.

She took a big gulp from her glass as if she were answering my thoughts, proving me wrong. Then she ran her index finger along the side of her glass, picking up the condensation and bringing it to her exposed collarbone. While she pretended I wasn't watching her do this, I wondered if she had chosen this heated location just so she could wear the least amount of clothes possible and water herself.

Sunlight was poking in through the drawn plastic shades and hitting Manny's mane. But all I could think about was how lovely Emmy's skin would have looked in this light. And how that dress would make her eyes shine. Everything reminded me of Emmy these days. The less I saw her, the more I thought of her. It was becoming an obsession, one that I used to be able to control. Like steam caught under a lid, I used to be able to lessen the fixation just by seeing her, releasing the steam caught under. Then I could concentrate, go back to business. I didn't have that outlet anymore, so the steam pressurized under my skin. A pressure cooker.

"I didn't kill my father," Manny announced, forcing me out of my daydream.

I wasn't paying attention to her, so she had to get my attention somehow.

"I know everyone thinks I'm the one who ordered my father killed. But I didn't."

"Hm," I said as I checked my phone. There were fifteen missed calls from Spider—something was up. I put the phone back in my pocket.

"You believe me, don't you?"

I glanced up and examined her face. "Is it important to you that I believe you?"

She shrugged and looked out the window.

Manny and I had been spending a lot of time together lately as we tried to fix the mess she had made with the three cartel families. We were meeting with the Castillos, one of the three Mexican cartel families. It was a last-resort kind of meeting. The families were no longer pitted just against each other. Now they were pitted against us as well because they knew Manny had been meeting with Julièn. She had been cavalier about her dealings with the Mexican president, and the cartel saw this as a betrayal from the whole Coalition.

I suspected that she had been purposefully careless to get her way and force the Coalition to work with Julièn. To her dismay, the Coalition had still ruled in favor of mending our broken relations with the families. The current was, however, changing. I had already been quietly approached by three of the younger captains who voiced a sudden change of heart. Suddenly they wanted to work with Julièn.

Manny was apparently working hard behind the scenes. Which meant she was bribing them or blackmailing them or sleeping with them. Possibly all of the above. It had nothing to do with Julièn and everything to do with her being the one to bring Julièn into the fold. She wanted the captains to see that she could broker the big moneymakers; that when the time came for them to replace me, she would be first in line.

In the meantime, we still planned for a peace treaty. But Manny saw our time together more as an opportunity to get back into my favor and my pants. The more I rebuffed her affections, the more desperate she became. Knees swiping mine, shoulders close together, lingering looks. She reminded me of an orphaned baby raccoon. You see one lingering by your garbage—lost, motherless, needy, broken—cute enough to take home. Oh, she'll cuddle up to you, climb up on your lap, make you feel warm inside and out. But try to get too close, try to domesticate her, and she'll chew your face off when you're sleeping.

Carly called her evil. But evil was inaccurate. Manny was just a beautiful, intelligent, impulsive, total sociopath. Soft and cuddly on the outside; rabies-spreading creature on the inside.

I glanced around the restaurant at the men I had brought with me, the men who were being paid to protect me. I barely knew any of them. Not my best guys. But Manny's men were her very best men. Vicious, loyal murderers. Half of them were sitting inside, ready. The other half were outside on rooftops, ready to fire. This was supposed to be a friendly meeting.

Spider was still being kept out of the picture. Tiny was out looking for Norestrom. I had no friends in this room, and that was just fine by me—though part of me wondered how bad things were about to get for Spider to have called my phone so many times.

I looked at my watch.

"Looks like they're running late," Manny told me, preempting my question.

This was her meeting. She was responsible for scheduling it and mending fences. I was there as a show of support from the Coalition and to make sure Manny didn't make any promises we couldn't keep.

"Maybe they got stuck in traffic," I said, smirking. The cartel was never late. They came charging and prepared.

Manny tried to grin, but her talent for drama wasn't good enough to hide the anxiety that mounted in her. I wasn't the only one who had noticed how very quiet it was outside.

I took a sip of my drink, keeping my eyes on Manny. She had lost her easy manner as her gaze stayed on the door.

She reached for her cell phone too late. Our answer came bursting through the door in a torrent of bullets. I dashed under the table just as a bullet found the water jug and glass and water exploded everywhere.

Then I pulled a stunned Manny under with me, almost ripping her arm out of its socket in the process.

While our guards—whichever ones were still alive—answered the masked men's bullets with theirs, I took cover, dragging Manny with me, and made for the restaurant's kitchen.

"No. This way," she yelled at me, heading toward the patron bathrooms. There was a blast in the kitchen as the rest of the Munoz family unearthed a way in, blocking our only exit. I had recognized the Munoz group by their choice in weapons: AK-47-style rifle with a dot of pink paint on the handle.

Manny and I found ourselves in the women's bathroom. It smelled nicer than any men's room could ever smell, and it had three stalls and not a damn window in sight. A cul-de-sac, or a pretty-smelling coffin? Manny locked the paper-thin door and drew me to the back wall. There was an old-fashioned heat radiator, the kind that made walls seem as though they were playing the accordion. Manny pulled the radiator from the wall. It was a dummy, a fake. It wasn't at all attached to the wall that was pretending to play it. Behind it, a hole the size of the hood of a pickup truck had been dug out of the bricks, and a metal floorboard had been placed on the floor, filling the space between the subway tiles of the bathroom floor and the cement wall. Inside the hole, there was a small gray screen and a lever, which looked like the arm of a slot machine. When Manny pulled the lever, the metal floor fell open—a trapdoor—and the screen lit up with the number thirty. And then the number twenty-nine.

"We have thirty seconds to jump in," she yelled. Bullets were fired through the bathroom door. Manny shrieked, grabbed her thigh, and fell crouched to the floor.

I yanked the dummy radiator in front of us as a shield and gladly shoved Manny into the black hole. She rolled in like a garbage bag going down a hill, hitting her head on the back wall before disappearing. I fired my gun at the door to delay the cartel's entry, tucked my gun into the back of my jeans, and backed myself into the hole. I was hanging by my hands, darkness engulfing my free-flying limbs, and glanced up to see five seconds on the countdown. The men had burst through the door now. I could hear their bullets hitting the empty stalls as they searched for us. It was now or never.

I let go.

I slid, down deep, through a swinging hatch just as a ball of fire exploded above and was shut out as the hatch slammed back. I landed on a stack of foam, next to Manny, who was grabbing hold of her wounded leg.

I instantly recognized the expression on her face. It was a look of shock that it hurt, badly, but not as bad as you thought it would, mixed with a look of wonder as to where exactly the bullet was. Was it stuck in a muscle, like a pencil through a potato? Did it fragment? Did it go all the way through? Did it hit anything vital? Manny's gunshot cherry had just been popped.

I was in a metal room barely big enough to contain the two of us. I could hear more things exploding over and around us and it was blistering inside, but wherever we were, we were safe from the flames that were burning the cartel and our own men.

"Things didn't go as you planned." I pulled the hem of her dress up and checked her wound. The bullet was still lodged in her thigh, but she would live. I ripped a piece of her dress and tied it around her leg, placing her hand over the bullet wound.

Then I laced my fingers behind my head and rested against the metal wall. "Let me guess. You got a message to the Munoz family that we were meeting with the Castillos, so that they could get their opportunity to kill the Castillos. You told them that if they killed the Castillos and eventually the Vasquez family, we would give them some kind of exclusivity over all Mexican trades?"

"They were supposed to get the Castillos outside the restaurant," she admitted through clenched teeth.

"Outside the restaurant. So that you would know when they got there. So that your sharpshooters would have enough time to kill both groups. So that you and I would have time to escape. So that you would have time to burn all the evidence of your deceit."

"I just saved you, didn't I?"

"This is pretty cozy. Kind of perfect, actually. Though I supposed that's why you picked this place."

I held her eyes and grinned at the murderous wench. She smiled back sweetly.

Manny was the most dangerous kind of woman. A woman in love, a woman rebuked, a woman who would stop at nothing to get what she wanted—me.

She was willing to put us and her best men in danger; she was willing to get everyone—including me and including herself—killed, just so that she could have me, even if it were only in death.

"And you honestly thought that the Munoz family was going to let you decide their fate? That they didn't know what you were up to?" It felt good to see Manny humbled. "You realize that your sharpshooters were killed before they ever had a chance to feel a breeze? You just killed off all of your men."

I glanced over her face. I could tell she was trying to save face, but there was a hint of vulnerability in her expression. "I really fucked up," she admitted.

"Yeah, you did."

She crawled up on my lap as we waited for the fire to burn out and for the reinforcements that Spider had probably already sent flying in. He knew where I was meeting the cartel because it was his job to know. He just wasn't allowed to come with me, this time and from now on. Through his substantial contacts, Spider had undoubtedly found out about the ambush even before we had entered the restaurant. This was why he had called me so many times. This was why I had ignored his calls so many times. I knew that, had he been with me, or had I at least brought men that he knew and knew how to reach, we would have been out before the cartel had ever even loaded their guns. But that wasn't how it was supposed to go down.

In the end, Manny got what she wanted. Sure, she got a

dozen innocent men killed—hers and mine. Sure, she almost got us killed. Sure, she started a war—the last crack to break up the Coalition. But she got me. Stuck with her in a hot little room in the process.

It was too bad that she had gotten shot in the leg. Her legs were the best part about her.

****

"What the fuck were you thinking?" Carly yelled as though I weren't standing right next to her. "Spider tried to call you to warn you about what was going down, and you ignored his calls. We thought you were dead."

Spider stood next to her, watching my expression but remaining silent.

Manny and I had been found alive in the basement of the Thai restaurant once the fire burned out, almost twelve hours later. I had gotten on a plane and landed on a small tarmac outside Albany.

"Some things just need to happen the way they were meant to," was all I said.

Spider let a sad smile come over his lips before walking away. Carly guffawed at me and at him.

With the explosion and dozens of cartel men dead, things were going to be moving swiftly now. I didn't have any time to waste. I marched to my car. Carly ran behind me.

"This was all Manny's doing, wasn't it? She was the one who masterminded this huge fiasco."

"You said you needed to speak with me. You said it was urgent," I said, opening up my car door.

Carly held on to the door and watched me buckle up.

"It's Frances. She wants money, and she says she'll go to the cops with what she knows if we don't give it to her."

Frances. The woman Bill had cheated on Carly with. The woman Bill had cheated on Carly with and had gotten pregnant.

"Give it to her."

"I thought we had decided that we were done giving her money until we knew for sure what she was doing with all the money we've been giving her."

In reality, Spider had decided this, and I had simply gone along with it because I had bigger fish to fry than worry about Frances. But apparently, they were going to keep dragging me into this soap opera. "What difference does it make what she does with it? If she needs money, just give it to her. Hopefully she'll use some of it for Daniel."

I already knew what she was going to ask me, because this always seemed to come up.

"Why don't we just give the money directly to Daniel?"

"Daniel lives with Frances's mother, and Frances keeps them pretty well-hidden from everyone. You might be able to find them and give them money, but if Frances finds out, it might be enough to either snitch to the cops or betray us to someone else. Then we'd have to make the decision we've been avoiding."

Carly took a second before saying what she really wanted to say.

"Spider thinks that she's up to something already."

"And you?"

There was silence.

Being the other woman would have normally warranted Frances an ass kicking from Carly and death if we had even the slightest indication of treachery. Daniel was an innocent party to his parents' affair, and Carly had always tried to remain objective about the whole Frances situation for Daniel's sake. So had I—for Bill's sake. Even with all the time that had passed, it hadn't gotten any easier on her, and Spider wasn't helping.

"Spider always thinks that she's up to something," I said, my tone sympathetic. "I haven't seen anything concrete that would tell me that she's up to no good. Just give her the money, Carly."

Carly stood, as though there were something else she wanted

to talk to me about. I had an idea of what that might be, but now was not the time.

I closed the door and drove away.

I was on my way to the reservation to see Pops and Hawk, unannounced. It would have been faster to land in Callister, but I couldn't trust myself with Emmy so near. Now more than ever, I had to stay away from her. I didn't just have Shield's eyes on my back anymore; with Manny's doing, I also had the cartel's, and they were a lot smarter and more dangerous than Shield. Once word of a broken Coalition spread, once it was known that we were no longer an army, we were going to be attacked.

When I got to Pops's place, he was already outside, cutting wood in his rubber boots.

He wasn't surprised to see me. He was *never* surprised to see me.

Pops stopped what he was doing and wiped the sweat off his brow. He glanced at me, though I wasn't sure if he ever actually saw me, and then his eyes turned to the treetops.

"The wind is changing," he said to the air or the earth or any of the elements he worshiped.

Hawk came out of the house holding some kind of meat on a stick, eating it as though it were cotton candy. His mother looked after her overgrown baby from the window.

"What's this about?" he asked me with a mouthful.

As gruff as Hawk was, I still preferred to do business with him. He, at least, was in it for the money. Something I understood. Something I could work with. His father, on the other hand, had always had his head in the clouds, talking in prose and long-winded legends instead of getting to the point. This only got worse with his advancing age. I liked him. Of course, I liked him. He had been there for Bill and for me in the worst of times, when no one wanted to deal with us. Despite his deteriorating state, I owed him.

They grew the best marijuana in North America and had one of the few remaining safe drug entries that were left completely unguarded. They were small, yet influential, and no one owned them, not even us. One of the few last-standing independents.

"I want to offer you a chance to join the Coalition," I said.

"Let's walk," Pops said. Despite the freezing temperature, we headed into the woods on a path beaten by his soles. Hawk followed closely behind his father.

"You already offered this to us. Many years ago. This offer was refused."

"This is the last time I will be making this offer."

Pops smiled.

"We've been fine without your Coalition. We answer to no one," Hawk answered.

"Things are changing. If you don't join the Coalition, you will lose our business."

It was a matter of weeks, possibly days. Once we joined forces with the Mexican president, once the Coalition broke apart, it would quickly ensue that all known independents would have to pick a side or see their work, their family, everything they had ever known and loved burned to dust. If the tribesmen joined our side—joined me—I could protect them. If they joined Shield, they were the enemy. I didn't want to see this happen.

Pops stopped at a tree and examined a lone wisp that was growing out of the trunk.

"What will happen to you if you lose our business?" I wondered, my voice low.

"We will go elsewhere," Hawk grunted.

"What if there is nowhere else to go? What if the only other place to go is worse than us?"

"We've always found our way. With or without your Coalition."

I wish I could tell them, tell Pops, about what was about to go down. How bad it was going to get.

But Pops was too busy looking at sticks and trees. "This twig is nothing more than a cumbersome piece of wood," he said. "It sticks out as though it was a mistake. Some would see it as something that needs to be broken off, because it whips them in the face every time they pass by, because it doesn't fit with the rest of the tree. Look at this tree. It is beautiful, tall, and thick. But inside, it is dying, and this misplaced little wisp is its only hope. Disease has already spread though the veins of this tree, and what was meant to die, will. There's no changing that. But this tree will grow strong again because of this insignificant piece of wood. In the end, this twig will become its strongest branch."

I knew not to expect an explanation, and I really didn't have time for one anyway. "I won't be able to protect you anymore. If you don't join, this will be the end of our affiliation."

Pops turned and made his way back down the path. Hawk and I followed him all the way to my car. Apparently I was being escorted out.

Pops took a serious tone as I opened my car door.

"As planned, we have arranged for a full shipment to come through in two weeks, and the plants that you have requested us to produce are almost ready for cultivation. If you honor your covenant, so will we."

He walked away. They were on their own from now on.

# Chapter 11: Emily

## Hate to Love

As my roommates finished their last exams, the house slowly emptied. Everyone was going home for the Christmas holidays. Joseph and I were the only ones still left. And Meatball, of course.

I wasn't exactly sad to see everyone go. No one had really talked about the fact that Griff was gone overnight, but there were the uncomfortable stares. I knew what they were thinking: *it should be you who left, not him, not* our *Griff.* Except that he wasn't *their* Griff—he was mine. And I was the one who had sent him running.

It wasn't like I wasn't used to people leaving—eventually, everybody did in some way or another. My brother, Bill ... Rocco ... Cameron ... and now Griff. If Cameron had, or had had my heart, then Griff had my soul. But there are only so many pieces people could take from you before you disappeared altogether. I could feel myself sinking, as though I had plunged through thin ice and gotten pushed down by the undercurrent, hands skating under the cold hard ice, unable to come up for air.

And then there were all the nightmares. At least one every night since Griff had left. Spiders falling, dangling from my ceiling. Trying to run away from Victor with my feet stuck in quicksand; him holding an olive branch, watching me go under.

My dreams of Cameron and Rocco had been replaced by my own eventual, definitive demise. My prophesy.

After Bill died, I came to loathe the holidays. All holidays. Because my brother wasn't there with me and because I was forced to be with my parents, wherever they were in the world, without my brother as a buffer. When Griff bought that Christmas tree and we started making plans to spend the quiet Christmas holidays together, I had started looking forward to this, like a prisoner looks forward to a day pass. I was imagining carolers coming to the door while we sipped hot cocoa ... I didn't really have much experience with *happy* holidays.

In the end, the holidays would still be quiet ... very quiet. At least there were still Meatball and Joseph, I thought.

But when I came out of my room and Joseph was loitering by my curtain, I realized that I wouldn't even have that. He was swaying, as though he had been deciding something and been caught trying to escape. When he saw me, he held off and forced a smile. I was embarrassed for putting him in that position. Of course, he wouldn't be there to spend the holidays with me or with Meatball. He had a family. A mother who loved him, who worked three jobs to keep him in school, who sent home-cooked meals because she was worried he wasn't eating enough.

I felt my stomach flutter in a way that comes only when you come to terms with the fact that you're a total loser.

"Oh, hi, Joseph," I said, adding the element of surprise to my tone. I quickly turned to my bins that were stacked against the wall outside my room and pulled off the lid. "I thought you had left already."

"Yeah, I'm, uh, heading home. For, you know, Christmas. And all that family stuff." He stood for a second, watching while I started digging through the top bin. "Did you, uh, wantta come?"

I could almost hear what he was thinking. *Pleasesaynoplease-saynopleasesayno.*

"Thanks. That's really nice of you to offer. But," I quickly added before regret could settle his features, "I really should go through these bins before Hunter calls the fire captain on me."

Joseph flipped his backpack over one shoulder and rushed to the stairs before it was too late. "Okay. Happy holidays."

Meatball followed him down and waited by the door. Unfortunately, he was stuck with me. We were each other's only family.

Even though Joseph was gone and I really didn't need to keep up the charade, I kept plunging through my bins. I hadn't really gotten around to it since Carly and her cronies brought them back to me. More than anything, I needed to keep busy. The house was just too quiet, and the sound of work underway made it slightly less monstrous.

I remembered running through the house as a little girl, looking for Maria. Whether I was upset or scared or needed to be with someone who wasn't trying to mold me, I would run through every room until I found the one Maria was cleaning. Then I would pick up a rag or a mop and try to help; she would hum, and I would talk about nothing, and she would listen anyway.

For me, cleaning was tantamount to a hug.

Though we always had to keep an ear out for Mother. Catching me fraternizing with the staff (cleaning no less) would get Maria fired and earn me a disappointed scowl like the mother duck gave to her ugly duckling.

I went through the Rubbermaid bins rather aimlessly. Searching for clothes that would fit my growing state, knowing that I had barely enough clothes at the most skeleton of times. I made a small, very small pile of things I could probably toss, which included miscellaneous class notes, inkless pens, a key chain, and a sock without a partner. I put the single sock back in the keep pile. As less than an hour had gone by when I popped the lid off the last bin, I worried. Now what? I immediately comforted myself with the remembrance that I lived in a student dump. A million hugs awaited.

While I worried about keeping myself busy, I ought to have

been worried about what I would find in the last bin. Part of me had initially, briefly wondered where these had gone, while the other part stopped me from really searching for them, hoping that I would never see these again. There, under the scarf and mitts that I had been looking for a few days ago when the really cold weather started poking through my jacket, was *Rumble Fish*—the book and the movie. The book I had been reading when Bill died, and the movie Cameron had gotten me to help me deal with Bill's death. More reminders of love and loss, reminders that I didn't need and could hardly bear.

I carefully placed the lid back on the bin, my hands trembling. Then I stacked the rest of the bins back on, burying the find, putting its contents back to forcefully forgotten places. I walked down the stairs slowly, mechanically. Meatball was still waiting at the door as I passed him on my way to the kitchen. In my peripheral vision, I saw the lone tree sitting in the corner. Griff and I had bought a box of secondhand ornaments that we had placed next to it, ready for some happy time around the tree. Would there have been Christmas music in the background? And then the carolers would come knocking, and we would turn the music off and go sip our hot cocoa on the front stoop.

It hit me. It really hit me. I was alone, completely, totally alone. I had a dog who wished he were somewhere else, and a child growing inside me who would soon wish the same.

I grabbed my car keys and Meatball's leash, and we headed out.

For the past couple years, my mom had been spending the holidays holed up in a Belize spa, which was code word for the plastic surgeon's office, where she worked on looking rested. She had gotten nipped, tucked, and filled so many times that she was starting to look like a balloon animal: a little twist here, a little air there, and voila, you're a poodle!

As for my dad, he was wherever work took him.

As a kid, my parents would plunk me in some hotel or in one of our houses—Hamptons, Aspen, Paris—where the staff were paid to ensure that I had a merry Christmas. One year, my mom had even paid some of the staff's kids to come over and play with me on Christmas Day. I ended up hiding in a corner, watching them as they jumped on my bed and complained about my lack of toys. I had no idea how to play with kids or toys.

Eventually, I made Isabelle and Burt's life easier and cheaper by finding something better to do over the holidays. Last year I'd found a professor who was looking for an assistant to do free grueling research over the holidays. He never thought he'd actually find someone desperate enough to do it.

When Meatball and I pulled up to the gates, it was already dark. With my parents gone, I had expected the Hamptons estate to be sparsely staffed and no more than dimly lit. Instead, it was fully decked out for the holidays. Large Christmas wreaths hung on each of the iron gate egress panels, and little white lights had been spiraled around the stone pillars. This was as Christmassy as the Sheppards had ever gotten. I didn't know they had it in them.

"It's Emily," I yelled to the freestanding speaker pole.

"Who?"

It was a new voice on the other end. A new head of security. I sighed. Lansing had been head of security for as long as I could remember. I think he was already ninety years old when I was born. I knew he would have to retire eventually, though sorrow filled me as I realized I hadn't been there to see him off.

"*Sheppard*. Emily Sheppard. I ..." While I struggled between *I live here* or *my parents live here* or *I'm selling Girl Scout cookies*, there was a scuffle over the speaker.

"*Tesoro*! Is that you?"

Maria had come on the line. Her voice had aged into a scratchy coo, but I would have recognized it anywhere. She had called me *tesoro*, Spanish for treasure, since I was a kid. It was a comforting pet name, though I had always wished she had chosen a different one. Treasure reminded me of something buried, something that could be looked at but not touched, which I suppose was true.

The gate swung open, and we drove ahead. Meatball sat erect next to me. Even he could feel the impending doom. But this was still better than spending the holidays alone, cooped up in decrepit student housing. At least, he'd have room to run around here.

The cobblestone driveway led into the trees and was lit up by lampposts, each adorned with chic flags that hung down like icicles. Artsy snowflake, tasteful snowman, artsy snowflake, tasteful snowman. It was like driving on the main street of small European towns. My mother's personal touch?

The end of the tree line disclosed a surging four-tier water fountain and a mansion that was lit like it was goading landing airplanes—no carbon credits were being saved here. Good-bye, Amazon forest!

I wasn't sure if my parents were "home," though it sure looked like they were. I went straight for the service entrance, which was where I really wanted to be. My parents would find out soon enough that I was there.

Maria was waiting for me hands on hips, devilish smile, when I pulled up to the side. The service entrance was barely lit, and once I turned off my headlights, Maria would have disappeared in the darkness had it not been for her blotted white apron. I had to use the weight of my whole body to drag Meatball out by the leash. He was resolute on spending Christmas in my car. I didn't blame him.

Maria ushered me into the kitchen, not knowing that I was accompanied by a beast. When there was light, the look Maria gave me spoke loudly: *your mother is going to have a heart attack when she sees that.* I smiled her devilish smile and shrugged my shoulders in response.

The kitchen was not what I remembered it to be. Darlene, our head cook, used to have the kitchen running like she was in the midst of a magazine shoot: smiling over steaming pots, a little stir here, a little jiggle there, sipping on a glass of Cab-Sauv. Everything amazing always. And she had a full staff bouncing at her commands. Now there was a staff of three, steaming over enough food to feed the queen's jubilee. Saucepans overflowing, dishes falling over in the sink. More new faces—young faces—stress closing their faces. I felt as though I had just entered a university dive that served caviar and risotto.

"Where's Darlene? Where's everyone else?" I asked Maria, eying the kid security guard sitting on a bar stool by the speakerphone and playing a game on his phone.

When I turned to her, I saw strain reflected off Maria's features. There was only a twenty-year difference between the two of us. And yet Maria looked as though she had aged an extra fifteen on top of that. Her hair was graying, and I could swear that she used to be taller than that. But more so, Maria never—I mean, *never*—had a dirty apron. Even if my mother had her scrubbing the cobblestone around the pool, Maria always reappeared looking untouched.

"Darlene found something else," she said, using her apron to wipe off fish guts. I noticed a half of salmon left bloodied on a plank.

"And Lansing?"

She gave me a sympathetic smile. "He found something else too. Are you hungry? I can make you something, if you like."

"How long have they been gone?"

She brushed my shoulder. This was as much touching as she could get away with without getting fired. "Just a few months. I don't remember your mother advising me that you would be coming home for Christmas. How's school? We've really missed you, you know. Darlene was just saying the other day—"

"You mean, before she left?" My jaw was so tight I thought my teeth were going to pop out of my gums. Darlene and Maria were best friends. My childhood was filled with memories of their inside jokes that I never understood but giggled at with them. Neither had ever gotten married; neither had ever had children. Maria's family was in Mexico, and Darlene never talked about any family. All they had was each other.

"Don't worry, niña. Everyone's okay. But it looks like that one might be hungry." She pointed at Meatball, who was salivating a puddle on the kitchen floor.

"He's always hungry." We had that in common lately.

When I went to find a paper towel to wipe the saliva off the floor, I received nasty glares from the young staff. They were sweating over stoves; I was in their way, and I was distracting Maria, their fish gutter.

"I'll go find my mother," I suggested with a bit of a growl to my voice.

Maria smiled without argument and rushed back to her station. I wasn't dumb enough to think that Lansing and Darlene, two loyal employees, had left voluntarily. They were either fired or forced out for whatever reason.

I pulled Meatball away and headed through the halls into the main house. It appeared as though the Christmas spirit had oozed into the house. My mom had had the place professionally staged to make it feel warm, happy, and un-Sheppard-like. Clearly, she was planning a big party.

Meatball stayed close as we checked the rooms, looking for my parents, who I feared might have been eaten up by all this happiness. In the dining room, a tuxedoed waiter was setting up a table for eight, even though there was enough food in the kitchen to feed all of New York State. Economy had never been in my parents' vocabulary.

It wasn't too hard figuring out where in the house my parents were. Their screaming voices were enough to wake all four seasons at once.

I thought about turning around and heading back to my very quiet Christmas with Meatball. But I was curious, so I treaded into my parents' quarters.

They had their part of the house.

And I had a whole other part that I used to share with Bill. This part was on the opposite side of the house—as far away as possible from the adult area, like a contagion antechamber. Though I wasn't sure which side was more diseased.

As I approached the master suite, the reproachful words were sharp, each one enough to leave a mark. I was about to knock on the door, holding my knuckle an inch away from the wood. Then I caught a glimpse of Meatball. His ears were so flat against his skull that they almost disappeared into the fur. He was right. Going into the war zone would be like two hyenas fighting over a pig carcass, until a buffalo with a broken leg limps in between them. They would eat me alive.

I slid to the bench in the vestibule and Meatball crawled under, his head popping between my legs.

"I don't know how much more I can take of these evenings. It's one thing to be forced to stay put and play hostess to these never-ending evenings. It's another to have to beg and plead these people to help us. It's degrading."

My mother was screaming in French, but my father responded in English. He never needed to scream—even at its coolest, his officious tone was enough to change the earth's rotation.

"You need to get off your French high horse and start pulling your weight. We need their support, and we'll do whatever is necessary to ensure that this happens."

"How far? How far will this have to go before you realize that it's enough? Last night, Mr. Greyson dropped a shrimp in my cleavage and used his fat fingers to fish it out. And you watched. And you laughed. And you offered him another drink. What else do I have to do, Burt? Pull my dress up so that he can stuff money in my undergarments?"

"That would be rather helpful," my father said without any trace of hilarity in his voice. "He's our largest financier, dear. If he wants to pinch your ass, dress you up as a French maid, and make you clean his lavatory, then you do it."

"Lavatory," I sneered to myself using my father's self-important tone. Only my parents could snob up something as simple as a bathroom.

"Is that what I've been reduced to? Prostitution?" my mother wondered shrilly.

"I didn't marry you for your ability to think, dear."

"And I didn't marry a man who is willing to do anything for a buck."

"Ah, but you did, my love. Who pays for the mansions, the cars, the trips, the extravagant lifestyle you love so dearly? Just smile and look pretty. You'll be fine."

"What lifestyle? I'm stuck here, with you, playing little miss hostess to people who would like nothing better than to see us sink. We have to pretend that everything is all sunshine and rainbows when I've had to let almost all of our staff go and I'm running to my family for money when they're barely keeping afloat as it is."

"This reminds me," he said. "Have you called your brother, as I asked you to do yesterday?"

"Henri just had a heart attack, Burt. Because of all the stress that you've been causing him. If I bother him with any more of this ugly business, it might just be enough to kill him."

"*Bother* him?" my father said as though he had swallowed a handful of sand. "If you don't *bother* your mindless, spineless brother, we will lose everything. If they decide to sell Chappelle de Marseille, it will send our backers running, with their money."

"But if my family doesn't pull out, they will lose what little they have left."

"Tonight. Call him tonight."

My mother paused, her voice hushed. "I've already asked them for so much. They're barely taking my calls anymore. This will be the last straw. I'll never be able to convince my brother, and my family will disown me."

"You could convince the pope to lend you his dirtiest underwear. You can convince your dimwitted brother."

"I can't. Burt, I just can't."

There was a long, dramatic sigh. "I knew I ought to have never married into your dirty family money."

"My *dirty* family money saved your perfect, old, bankrupt family. Do you even realize the mess you made? Do you see what people are saying about you in the papers? Cheat. Fraudster. Thief. No one wants to get anywhere near you, and you call *my* family *dirty?*"

I had never spent much time with my mother's family. A vague memory of a cousin in France with leaves stuck in her hair and muddy feet was all I knew of my mother's family. As for my father's family, they hadn't hidden their disapproval of my mother and me. Mostly me (my mother had apparently proven to be a little useful). It seemed I didn't turn out the way anyone thought I would or should.

Growing up, I was taught to keep quiet and listen to what I was told to hear. Apart from Bill, I knew almost nothing of my family members, even my own parents. There was never a time when I was lying in front of a sparkling fire, chin cupped in hands, listening with my heart open as my parents told the story of the day they met and fell in love. Perhaps they had been in love, once upon a time. But I had never seen this. I was rarely in the same vicinity with either of my parents for longer than a few minutes at a time, let alone with both of them together in one place. And certainly not long enough to hear a When Harry Met Sally story.

It wasn't until my father's face started appearing in the news that I really got to know my parents. The Sheppards had come to hard times in the eighties, when my father quickly divorced Bill's mom and miraculously fell for breathtaking Isabelle Tremblay, heir to the Chappelle de Marseille empire. It was a bit of so-called luck given that my mother's company had recently bloomed and was ripe for a Sheppard takeover.

I remember sitting around a table the size of a soccer field as my grandmother, the first Emily Sheppard, called the Tremblay family a bunch of hippies whenever she could, whenever my mother was within earshot. My father, her one and only precious child, would chortle. My mother would keep smiling and order me to sit up straight.

When my father strolled out of the quarters he shared with my mother, he saw me sitting on the bench a few feet away from him. There was barely a pause before he kept his pace all the way out into the hall until he disappeared.

Sometimes I wondered if my father would recognize me if we happened to be passing each other on the street. Probably not.

When I found my mother in her room, she was sitting in front of her mirror, dabbing at the tear stream that had dug a path through her foundation, one straight line down each cheek. Even her tears were calculated—enough to get a point across, not enough to completely ruin her makeup. Her eyes unflappably peered to my appearance in her mirror before going back to her own reflection. She had her lilac silk bathrobe on over a midnight-blue evening gown that went to her elfin shoeless feet. Her hair was pulled back into a tight bun, with a waterfall of curls gushing through the middle of the knot.

I waited behind her, waited like a soldier would for a dormitory inspection. I was suddenly conscious of my to-be-deemed disagreeable appearance. I was wearing the only oversize cotton sweatshirt that fit me, under which an unbuttoned pair of jeans was hidden. My hair was in what had once been a ponytail. Now it was just an elastic band hanging on edge.

When my mother finally finished working on herself, she turned around to examine what had become of me. The smirk that spread thin on her lips warned me that she wasn't thrilled. She let her silk robe slide over her bare shoulders and fall to the back of her chair. She pulled her chin up and glided off the chair toward me.

I stood still, too spellbound to be scared. She stood in front of me and cupped my chin under her long fingers. And then she pinched the skin under my chin, hard enough that I let out a yelp.

"Is this what they call the college weight gain?" she sneered in a heavily French-accented English before releasing her pinch but not her stare.

It was actually called the freshman fifteen, but I didn't correct her because there was no point. It always seemed that she purposefully blundered English expressions, in a mocking sort of tone. Her undertone mutiny against my father's heritage, I guessed.

I wanted to say something, perhaps defend myself and come back with something witty to insult her with. We hadn't seen each other in over a year, which should have been enough time for me to at least have some one-liners ready and waiting. But I was still too entranced to say anything. Being under my parents' roof, in my mother's snare, I felt like I was back to being the little girl whose pigtails had to be tight enough to withstand tornado winds.

My mother's gaze left my fattened face and my double chin to find Meatball. I pulled him close, as though I could protect him from her.

I could hear her teeth grinding. "This is new," she said. "Yours?"

"Mine," I said resolutely, feeling as though my feet had just steadied to the ground.

"Well, you can tie him up in the garage while you're here."

"Yeah, that's not going to happen. He goes where I go."

My mother's eyes jumped back to my face, clearly taken aback. I rested my hand on Meatball's head, and he pressed against it as a show of unified strength.

Isabelle glided back to her mirror and picked out a pair of diamond earrings.

"Why are you here?" I asked her before she could demand the same from me.

"Your father can't leave the country." She said this with triumph, as though my father heard her, as though her words could embarrass a man like him. "And now I get to play good wife while your father talks his way into getting favors."

She pricked an earring into her lobe and stretched a smile into the mirror. "If I'd thought you would come, I would have let you know that we would be here."

I smiled back. We both knew what she was really saying and what I was really thinking: sorry to ruin your Christmas alone.

The young security guard came in to announce the guests' arrival.

My mother glanced at him, thanked him, and smiled until he left.

"We have a long week of guests coming here and events to attend," she told me.

"You don't need to change your plans," I said. "We'll only be here for a few days."

She stood erect, taking one last disapproving look at my frumpy disposition and my hairy dog.

I understood. I was to stay hidden.

"You'll hardly know I'm even here," I reassured her.

My mother stepped into her heels and walked out.

When the chatter noise from the guests downstairs dissipated out from the foyer into somewhere out back, I felt secure enough to walk across the mezzanine without being seen. The last thing I wanted was to embarrass my poor distraught mother.

As ornate as the main-floor rooms were, the east wing—the children's wing—was undressed. Plastic-wrapped furniture, paintings leaning against the marble walls, bubble-wrapped statues, boxes stacked up. This wing was being cleared out and was certainly not to be seen by the important guests. My parents' reality was sinking in. They were broke, selling their possessions and perhaps eventually the Hamptons estate. I didn't know how to feel about this. I never really thought about any place as my home, but if I had, this was the closest place I had to it. This was where I had been cooped up most of my childhood.

I headed into my quarters and straight into Bill's room, afraid of what I would find. His bed had disappeared, as had everything else. His books, his clothes, his posters, all of what I had left of him—gone. I made it to the center of the room before sinking to the carpet. It didn't even smell of him anymore—just fresh paint and carpet cleaner. Meatball left my side and sniffed around the room. He found a clean spot against a built-in bookcase that my mother could sell off, lifted a leg, and left a new scent.

I laughed so hard I cried.

We left Meatball's self-appointed room and headed to the opposite side of the sitting room, where my room was.

Though empty boxes waited in a corner, my room had been mostly untouched. A few packed boxes were on the floor marked "For Emily" in black Magic Marker. I wouldn't have cared what was inside had I not recognized Maria's handwriting. I grabbed a side, pulled, and grinned. It was Bill's stuff. Of course Maria would never let my mother get rid of all of Bill's stuff without saving the stuff that mattered for me: pictures, yearbooks, old maps, notebooks filled with stupid car drawings.

\*\*\*\*

When I woke up, it was to a blinding spotlight in my eyes. I had forgotten what it was like to sleep in a room with windows. I would have gotten up to close the curtains, but these had already been removed.

My king-size bed was littered with Bill's stuff. At the time Bill died, people had real books and shoeboxes filled with pictures and were still using maps—*paper* maps—to find their way. My heart tightened. Bill never got to grow old and see the world change.

Meatball was sleeping next to me, so closely that I was about to fall over the edge. It was as though the dog were afraid of space.

I rolled over the side, stretched, and went to wash up in the bathroom—the "lavatory." While I waited for the shower water to warm up, I stood over the sink. It was in these lavish surroundings that I realized how much I looked like my mother, or at least, what my mother looked like somewhere under all the plastic. The freckles over the cheeks and nose that reminded me of the Milky Way. The eyes a shade lighter than seaweed. The nose that curved at the base. The bony parts around my neck that stuck out under another cluster of freckles.

This would have normally made me cringe and turn away

from the mirror's reflection. But as I started to undress, letting my clothes fall to my feet, I smiled.

My face was rounder now and I had a second chin, as my mother had so subtly pinched out last night. I let my hands fall to my expanding waist, resting over the little bump that was pushing out. If it were a girl, would she look like me? If it were a boy, would he look like Cameron?

All of a sudden, I could picture a little girl running with a full head of red hair splashing behind her. Beautiful freckles dotting little hands, feet wiggling. I turned my green eyes back to my own reflection, a reflection that would be mirrored in my child. And I realized how beautiful I was.

It didn't take long for Meatball to come find me in the shower. It was one of those open, privacy-lacking showers. Meatball lapped at the water pooling on the floor, but stood far enough away so that he wouldn't have to get wet. I flicked water off my fingertips into his face to make sure he got wet. This was enough to make him hop back and around like a bunny.

I put my bathing suit on under a large terrycloth robe and took him over to the indoor pool. At least one of us should have fun while we were here. I was about to pull my robe off when I saw my mother lounging in the corner in her evening dress, dozing off as she held a glass of orange juice precariously over her chest. While Meatball sniffed around the edge of the pool, I went over to grab the glass before it smashed to the ground.

My mother's eyes snapped open as soon as my fingers touched the glass.

"Rough night?" I wondered, though the distinct smell of alcohol that came off her breath and through her pores and over the rim of her glass told me it was also a rough morning.

I took a seat on the chair next to her as she steadied herself and tightened back up her drowsy features. She glared as Meatball paced around the pool. "I don't want that thing anywhere near the pool or around my house."

"Don't worry; he's scared of the water." Lying was second

nature to me under the Sheppards' roof. So was hostility. "What happened to Darlene and Lansing?"

"Who?"

"The chef. The security guard. The people who had been working for you for twenty years."

"I had to fire them. Things had been going missing around the house." She pressed a finger into her temple as though a headache were throbbing, one that started with an E and ended with Emily. "How they could rob us after we have been so good to them over the years? With everything that your father and I have been going through? It's inhumane." My mother's view on inhumanity was viciously skewed. First-world problems skewed.

"You mean you fired them on a so-called suspicion of theft so that you wouldn't have to give them the exit package they deserved?"

Isabelle chortled a laugh. "Did you learn those big words at your half-rate college?"

"I learned enough to know that what you did was wrong. If you and Dad have fallen on hard times, it's your fault, not theirs. You should give them the money you owe them."

"Your father and I are not on hard times. Please don't state such things." She took a sip of her screwdriver.

"Oh? Is that why you're emptying the east wing? Bill's room, my room? Or are those part of the things that have mysteriously gone missing?"

"Those rooms have been empty for a very long time. I decided it was time to clean house. You're never here, and William will certainly never be coming back."

*William*—Bill—*will never be coming back*. She had said this with an edge of humor in her voice. My fists clenched so hard I actually thought I was going to punch my drunken mother.

Instead, I decided to fight back the only way she knew—with words. "Well, it's good to know that you and Dad are doing fine because I need money."

"Am I to understand that because you want money now, our money is no longer beneath you?"

"I didn't say that I *want* your money, Mother. I said I need money. I believe I still have a trust fund."

There was a sadistic twinkle in her eye. I had just given her enough ammo to bring down the barriers I had spent years building to keep her out. But there were things that needed to be said on both sides.

My mother said, "I *need* to get out of this house. I *need* to get out of this country. Your father *needs* his legal problems to go away. Everybody needs something, dearest. It does not mean they will get it."

Meatball had been inching his way closer to the edge of the pool, trying to see how far he could stretch out his neck without falling in. He fell in. My mother swore like a French sailor.

It was in the shallow end, so his head popped back up right away. He stood on his hind legs, paddling with his front paws just enough to keep him upright. He stared at me, shock washed into the fur of his face. It was as though he had forgotten he could swim. Less than twenty-four hours in my parents' clasp, and he had already forgotten what he could normally accomplish on his own.

I got up and pulled my robe off, revealing a crescent moon bump under my bathing suit. "I'm expecting, Mother," I announced calmly and walked over to the pool, jumping in.

I swam over to Meatball, who all of a sudden saw great fun in the fact that I was in the water with him. I could tell his little tail was wagging by the tremble that went up his body and made his head shake from side to side.

"You're expecting?" my mom said, in a whisper loud enough that I could hear but not loud enough that the staff could hear. "A baby?"

"No, I'm expecting a kayak from Amazon." But the joke was lost on my mother. "Yes, I'm pregnant. I'm going to have a baby."

I tried to lure Meatball out of the pool, but he didn't want to come out anymore. I started to dog paddle around him to show him what he used to be able to do. But he only saw this as an invitation to try to pounce on me. He reminded me of a string-puppet, swaying from one side to the other, with just his front paws sticking out and daintily flapping in the water.

My mother sat up. "Anyone I would know?"

I couldn't help but snort a laugh at the last hope casing my mother's voice. Did the father come from a prominent family? Would I be the one to save the Sheppards, as she had once done by getting pregnant with me? "No one you know, Mother."

Like that last bit of soda at the bottom of a cup, my response had sucked every last smidgeon of hope out of her. She got up, her face turning to stone.

"I need access to the money in my trust fund," I told her before she could escape. I did need the money. Badly. But more so, I wanted her to admit that things were not what they seemed. It wasn't that I wanted to thrive on her misery, as she would mine. I needed her to admit that she was human—that shit happened, even to her and the prominent Sheppards.

My mother stopped, took a sip, and looked over the rim of her glass but did not look at me. "You have no trust fund. There is no money. I have nothing for you."

And there it was. My parents, who once had more money than anyone should ever be allowed to have to themselves, were broke.

My mother walked to the doors and stopped, keeping her back to me. "It would be best if you left the house and stayed away. Your father is under enough scrutiny as is. If the papers get news of this, it will cause irreparable damage to your father's already precarious situation."

The chill of her rejection trickled down from the top of my head, down my neck to the back of my knees. Meatball must have felt the chill because he stopped the game and balanced his way to the steps, where he waited, water dripping.

It wasn't as though I had expected my mother to be pleased about becoming a grandmother. In her synthetic mind, she was still in her twenties, not her fifties. And I certainly hadn't expected her to welcome the news of an heirless child with open arms. But this form of rebuff, disownment of her only child's child, one who had done nothing wrong but be born to me, Emily of the Sheppard clan, was a new low for my mother.

I never wanted to hurt her more than I did at this very moment. "Why does Father call your family dirty?" I wondered with a hiss in my voice before she could fully disappear into the house.

She stood gracefully erect, ready to spit fire. "Your father forgets that all money is dirty. If your father were to look at the story of anyone who has made a fortune in history, he would find that none have clean hands. The promise of money makes humans do awful things to each other. My family may have made a quick fortune from the rise of cocaine and heroin in the seventies, but at least it wasn't off the backs of slaves in America."

She left the pool, deserting me.

I got out of the pool and towel-dried Meatball and me.

My mother was a thief of any joy that could possibly come to me. As a child, I prayed to a God that I didn't know, hoping that she would change. Hoping that she would see me. I never understood why she hated me so much.

The screwed-up thing was that I loved my mother. I knew I loved her because her unbroken rejections took small pieces of me every time. Whoever said that it is better to have loved and lost than to never have loved at all didn't know my mother.

****

When I got to my room, I went to my bed and started gathering up Bill's treasures. The pain that was twisting inside me should have been enough to make me cry. But I didn't let myself give in to tears that had already soaked my girlhood pillow.

Maria came in, carrying a breakfast tray. She smiled in a way that reaches over and strokes your cheek.

I cleared my throat and stretched a brave smile.

"Don't be so hard on your mother," she told me softly, putting the tray down at the foot of the bed. "She's been going through a very difficult time."

"You overheard us talking?" I had my back to her, putting my brother's things back in the box.

"I guessed as much when I saw you yesterday. Pregnancy gives women a youthful glow that no wrinkle cream in the world will ever be able to match."

Maria kneeled next to me and put her hands over mine, stopping my progress. "You're about six months along, yes?"

I couldn't look at her, so I nodded over the box.

There was no hesitation in Maria's movement. She pulled my shoulders toward her body and wrapped her arms around me. I was taller and bigger than her (definitely rounder), but in that moment I felt tiny. I felt like the little girl who used to occupy this room and wished for the very same thing that was happening to me.

"Congratulations, sweetheart," she whispered in my ear.

When I realized what she was doing, I jumped back. "Maria, you'll get fired if my mother catches you."

She flapped a hand in the air. "Bah."

I watched her. And I knew. "She's firing you too, isn't she?"

She kept an unaffected smile and shrugged her shoulders. "I'm just here to help her through the holidays."

"Why? She doesn't deserve that. She doesn't deserve you. You've been here for her, for us, all these years, and this is how she repays you."

"She hasn't always been like this, you know. When I first started working here, when your mother and father were just married, your mother was, well, a lot like you. But your father's family, they're not easy people. My mother used to say that a woman can only love an ogre so much for so long before it starts to change her."

*Was my father supposed to be the ogre?*

"Your mother thought she was marrying for love, and she continued to love your father, despite him, despite who he really was."

There was a moment of silence as we realized what Maria was really saying. That my mother loved my father more than she loved me. That she had been molding me—trying to mold me—into the perfect Sheppard, so that my father would love her back.

"So, you're having a baby," Maria exclaimed, clapping her hands together. "Let me guess. The father's tall, dark, and handsome?"

"Am I that predictable?"

"For years we saw that boy coming around, driving around the property, checking on you. Lansing caught him sneaking into the house on your sixteenth birthday. Darlene always said he would be the young man who would come to take your heart."

Maria had no idea the bomb she had set off inside of me. On the outside, I kept blank-faced, but inside, it was a nuclear holocaust.

"Where's the father now?"

I bent my head.

I knew that Cameron had been watching over me for many years, because Bill had asked him to. But Cameron, near my house, under my parents' roof, on my birthday … I hated my birthdays without Bill. But my sixteenth birthday was the worst of all. My mother had put together a huge bash of people I didn't know. I had been introduced—over and over again—to the families of potential suitors. Placed on a pedestal, ready to be auctioned off to the highest bidding family. My father off to the side, talking business, not even noticing when I had blown out the sixteen candles on my cake. My mother constantly rearranging me between meetings. The best part of the night was being able to scarf down some cake with Maria and Darlene in the kitchen.

Maria had been watching me a little while as I pushed items around Bill's box so that I could fit more in.

"Do you remember when you were a little girl and Darlene

told you not to touch the stove because it was hot?" she reminisced. "You touched it anyway and got a nasty, nasty burn? You didn't even cry. You walked to the sink and doused your hand under cold water. It was as though you knew it was going to happen but tried it anyway to make sure, ready to deal with the consequences after."

I did remember doing that. My hand hurt like hell for days.

Maria tittered. "You were the most stubborn, challenging little person I had ever met. I never knew what trouble you were going to get yourself into next, but I always knew that, no matter what, you were going to find a way."

Tired of waiting for someone to offer him some of my breakfast, Meatball had helped himself to a piece of bacon. Then he waited to see if he were going to get into trouble. When nothing happened, he cleaned the plate.

"Where are you going to go?" Maria asked me while I struggled to slide the flaps of the overflowing box closed.

"I don't know. But I have to get out of here." Because my mother had thrown me out, because I couldn't breathe when she was too close. It was amazing how claustrophobic one could feel in so much space.

"But it's Christmas Eve. You shouldn't be alone on Christmas."

Maria put her hand on my shoulder. "Stay. Your mother and father are leaving for the city today. They'll be gone for a few days. We can spend the holidays together."

I hadn't realized it was Christmas Eve. I really didn't want to be alone on Christmas. But that didn't mean that I was ready to ruin Maria's Christmas either. No one wants to spend Christmas with their deadbeat boss's kid. No matter how much Maria loved me, I would always be Isabelle Sheppard's spawn.

Maria chimed in before I could find a good enough excuse. "I've already told Darlene that you're here. She'll be here as soon as your parents leave. We'll get drunk and plug in the karaoke machine in the party room. Well, Darlene and I can get drunk. You can watch."

She was genuinely excited.

I leaped over my box and into her arms.

I couldn't wait for my parents to get out. In the meantime, Meatball and I spent most of the day walking the property. He dug into every flowerbed he could find, and when I ordered him to stop digging, he dug more fervently. So I let him destroy the yard.

When my parents finally left, Darlene drove in right away, as though she had been waiting by the gates.

There were lots of hugs and rubbings of my belly. Darlene sent the young kitchen staff packing and took over the kitchen—*her* kitchen. Darlene and Maria kept their promise. They got good and drunk, digging out the best booze. I got the virgin versions.

It was as though nothing had changed. Even though everything had changed. Or maybe I had just never really paid attention before.

I had always assumed that Darlene and Maria were best friends. There was friendship there. But there was also love. I watched them as they watched each other. Giggled at things I did not get. By the end of the night, they were dancing together, and I was smiling so hard my face was going to split in two. I was happy that I had gotten the chance to see this before they disappeared from my life.

I excused myself, citing fatigue, which was true. Really, I just wanted them to get to spend Christmas together without having to babysit me for once in their lives.

****

In the middle of the night, there was a knock at my door. Maria opened it before I had time to say anything.

"Look who I found lurking by the gates."

Out of the shadows, he walked into my bedroom. Maria gave me a knowing, slightly drunken smile before closing the door behind her.

"I just keep fucking up, don't I?" Griff told me.

Yes, he did.

I sat up in bed and turned on my bedside lamp. "How did you know I was here?"

"You left your cell phone on your bed. When I found the house empty and all your stuff left behind, I was going to try calling the number that said 'home.' And if that didn't work, I was going to call the cops. Some lady picked up when I called. She confessed that you were here. She sounded like the same lady who just brought me in here."

"Her name is Maria."

"It cost me a fortune to cab it all the way here from Callister."

"You were gone awhile. Where did you go?"

"I got drunk and flew home to England."

I sighed. "Your mom and brothers must have been happy to see you."

"Never made it out of Heathrow. I realized as soon as the plane took off that I was making an idiot's mistake. As soon as the plane landed in London, I went searching for a flight back. It took me a while. Everything was booked up for the holidays."

Meatball dragged himself out of a deep sleep to let his heavy head fall on Griff's lap.

"Can you forgive me? Again?" Griff wondered.

As much as his leaving had hurt me badly, I knew I wasn't innocent in the spreading of pain. "Only if you can forgive me for lying, for keeping the pregnancy from you. For not telling you about Cameron and me."

Griff watched me. I could swear there was pity in his eyes.

"Have you changed your mind?" he asked me.

"About?"

"About going to the barn and talking to the drug guy?"

I stared back at Griff. My resolve had only fortified. Pops was my last hope, and I now had a plan. I knew how he could help me.

"That's what I thought." He took my hand and placed a piece of paper in it. "Happy Christmas."

## Chapter 12: Cameron

## The End Is Just the Beginning

"Aye," Slobber announced.

"Nay," Kostya answered.

The time had come for the Coalition to take a stand, one way or another. We were joining forces with Julièn, or we were letting the cartel slowly take over our drug trade. Every captain had his or her reasons for voting one way or another. What they didn't realize was that with each vote, their Coalition was breaking. The underworld was about to detonate. The question was: how much of this would seep into the real world, where Emmy lived?

"Nay," Johnny said.

"Nay," Dorio said.

The Italian and Asian Mafia. Double-crossing bastards. How much were they snitching to Shield about what was going on in the Coalition? I had been waiting to see which way they were going to vote, because it would give me a glimpse into Shield's demented brain.

*Nay.* It seemed Shield didn't want us to move in with the Mexican president, even though it would be the death of me. He wanted to pick the captains off, one at a time, from the shadows, like the underhanded little twerp he was. He wanted to take the Coalition from me, see me lose everything, then kill me. I would die, but not at his will and not before I chopped his hands off and watched him bleed to death.

"Aye," Manny said.

I hadn't told the captains that Manny had been the one to screw up the meeting with the cartel, permanently severing relations. Telling them would have signed her death warrant—they would have fed her to the cartel, like beef stew, with the tiniest of hopes that this would be enough to get the cartel back to the table. The cartel had remained mum about the incident because they had no proof that one of our captains, Manny, had orchestrated the assault—any witnesses to our presence at the Thai restaurant were dead, and it was hard to imagine that anyone could have ever survived the blast. The fact that Manny and I had survived would have been suspicious. But even if they had found out that we had been there all along, even if one of their men had survived and told them we were there, having an escape plan "just in case" was not abnormal. And Manny did have a brand-new bullet hole in her thigh—proof that we hadn't been immune. As far as they knew, the Vasquez group—the only family that remained untouched in this debacle—was behind the whole thing. For now, the Munoz and Castillos stood down, watched, and waited.

I had never hidden anything from the captains, except perhaps the real story behind Emmy's snatching. Because of Shield, the Coalition was on the verge of collapse no matter what I did. For the good of the underworld and the other world, I needed to fortify whatever was left of the Coalition before Shield could have control over all of it. Neither of the worlds would survive that.

"Aye," said Viper, eying Manny. He was the last to vote, and with that, we had a tie. The Coalition was split right down the middle.

All heads turned to me as the deciding vote.

"Aye," I said.

I had sealed my fate.

****

Carly slapped a piece of paper in front of me and started pacing back and forth. She had insisted on meeting with me after the Coalition vote and stormed into the meeting room as soon as everyone had vanished.

"You meant for me to find this," she accused.

I should have known Carly would go snooping before it was time. I knew she had found it a while ago and wanted to talk to me about it when I was on my way to visit Pops. But she didn't really know what to make of it. She had finally put two and two together. This argument had been meant for her to have with my corpse.

"Now I understand what you've been doing with all of your money. This must have cost you a fortune. What else have you been hiding from Spider and me? How long did it take you to cover your tracks so that it couldn't be traced back to you?"

"A while," I admitted, avoiding her first question and glancing over the aerial pictures of the property—a small island in the South Pacific. I had purchased it, sold it, purchased it again through various corporations and charitable organizations, some fake, some legit. It had cost me a whole lot more than it was worth. And yet it was priceless.

"The vote today," Carly said, her tone still biting. "You're going to be doing exactly what you said you were never going to do. Work with Julièn when you know what he's going to do. What he's going to get *you* to do. Assassinate the cartel so that you can take over the Mexican trade with him at your side. He knows only you can get it started for him. And then you'll die when all of Mexico's drug world goes after your top job."

"Is that what you think?"

"'*You kill the heads of the cartel families, and a hundred more are born.*' That's what you told me once."

Damn Carly's impeccable memory.

"It is a beautiful place," I told her, pointing at a picture of the sandy beach. "Completely uninhabited, and you can watch humpback whales go by from your backyard. Though you'll need to take good notes. You're supposed to be there to study their migration. That's your cover."

I had slowly been making plans, trying to find a safe place for them, somewhere where they could disappear until the dust settled. I had to move very slowly and keep under everyone's radar, with the hope that I would have everything in place before the war erupted and my life came to an end.

"This is for us. This island," she said matter-of-factly.

"And Emmy. I trust you to get her out when the time is right, when no one is watching."

Carly looked me in the eye. "But you're not going to be there."

I wished I would be there with them. I had even let myself imagine what it would be like, living free on a little island north of Fiji. Emmy sitting on a beach in her bikini; or better yet, Emmy on a beach without her bikini. But that would never happen. I would be hunted down with all the manpower the underworld had to offer. Emmy, Carly, and Spider would be nowhere near me when this happened. They would be studying the migration patterns of the humpback whale for the Society for Cetacea, the bogus foundation I had set up as a cover.

Carly held on to the back of the chair with both hands and narrowed her eyes. "So how exactly am I supposed to do this? I wait until you're dead. Until you're *really* dead. Then I knock on Emmy's door. *'Hey, how have you been? I know you've been grieving for Cameron for months. It turns out he wasn't actually dead. But, yeah, now he really is, so you should be crying over him now. On the flip side, he bought you an island.'* And then I kidnap her again and force her to go to this place without you there? So that she can grieve you *for realsies* since you are genuinely dead this time?"

"Emmy will get over it eventually. This island is gorgeous. She'll forget me, and she'll forget about this mess I put her in. The important part will be to get all of you out of here and in a safe place before I'm gone. You'll be able to leave it someday, when the heat is off."

"You've lost too many people, Cameron. You've forgotten what it's like to bury someone you love."

Carly glared as she shoved herself away from the back of the chair.

"You don't '*forget*,'" she said, fingering quotation marks in the air. "You don't '*get over it*.' You just find a way to stuff the pain in a pocket somewhere inside. But every once in a while, something—some stupid, insignificant little thing—triggers it. The worst pain you have ever felt. And you have to start all over. Feel that same jerking agony that only comes when you realize, when you remember that you'll never see his face again, that you'll never be able to share that stupid thing that reminded you of him in the first place. The pain never goes away. It only dulls, waiting for another trigger."

Carly snatched the paper from my hands.

"Emmy won't get over you. No matter how hard you try or how much money you spend, you're going to kill her." She turned on her heels. "You're a fucking idiot if you think otherwise."

## Chapter 13: Emily

## A New Chapter

On Christmas Day, Griff had given me a gift. A location. It wasn't what I had expected. Not the barn, where Pop's secret underground drug lair was. Because, as he explained it, we would have been shot down before we had even come within a mile of the place.

What Griff had given me was Pop's actual home address on the reservation.

But it had come at a cost. I didn't know what he had had to give to get the information, but by the withdrawn look in his eyes, it wasn't good.

We left my parents' house as quickly as I could get out of there, after many concerned hugs from Maria and Darlene. My brother's boxes were loaded on the backseat, leaving Meatball just enough room to sit and glare at me.

Griff pulled my hand from my lap and squeezed it. "What's the plan?"

"You'll see."

"Won't your parents be upset that you left on Christmas Day, before they had a chance to say good-bye?"

I tried to not burst into laughter.

With every mile that we drove, I grew more nervous. Preparing different versions of my speech in my head. What Pops would say, how I would respond. I realized it was Christmas Day and that his entire family would probably be there. I would have to be prepared for that too. Above all, hiding the pregnancy was key—not just for our safety but for business's sake. Which drug baron would want to team up with a pregnant girl?

While I silently rehearsed my lines, Griff interrupted my thoughts.

"I want to marry you," he announced, glancing back at me.

It took a second to focus on what he said to me.

"Like, right now?"

"If you want."

"Why do you want to marry me? Because I'm pregnant? I'm not going to marry you just because it's convenient. That's what my parents did. I won't do that."

"Fine. Then marry me because you love me."

I held my breath and shook my head, never breaking eye contact. And I could see the fissures cracking through him.

"I understand," he said.

I squeezed his hand. "I do love you, Griff. I love you so much, but—"

"But you don't love me like that, I get it."

"I don't love you like you deserve to be loved."

He took a breath. "Will you ever love me? Like that?"

"I don't know," I confessed.

"Do you *want* to love me? Like that?"

"I do," I answered with no hesitation.

He forced a smile through the mask of pain. "Then that's enough for me."

We didn't speak for the rest of the ride. Griff's announcement had been enough to distract me from the leap ahead.

For some stupid reason, I had expected that the landscape would change as soon as we drove into the reservation. But there were no teepees or men walking around in moccasins. Mostly, the landscape was as cold and barren as it had been outside the reservation. The only change I noticed was the poverty. Tiny wooden shacks sitting on patches of mud, crumbling tin roofs, windows blocked with newspaper to keep winter out. Each with a satellite dish sticking out the side.

It took Griff and me a while to find Pops's house. The roads were not clearly delineated, and neither were the address numbers on people's homes. It was as though they all wanted to be shut in and forgotten. Griff and I actually drove past Pops's house twice because we were looking for a drug lord's mansion. But his house was only slightly better than his tribesmen's.

My old car took a beating as we drove down the potholed driveway. The windows were curtained, as opposed to newspapered. There was no visible satellite dish and only two cars in the driveway. I leaned over the seat and took a map out of Bill's boxes, reassuring Meatball with a rub of the ears before getting out of the car.

The old woman who opened the door looked a little shocked to see Griff and me standing at her doorstep on Christmas Day. A waft of turkey roasting and carrots boiling on the stove came to the door with her.

"Hi. My name is Emily," I announced. "I'm sorry to disrupt your Christmas dinner, but I need to speak with Pops. Please."

The woman's hair was gray and pulled back in a bun. Under her apron, she was wearing a blue polyester suit and polka-dot blouse. Her Christmas best.

She glanced at us, unsure.

My heart was beating bongo drums. I had to stuff my hand in my jacket pockets so that she couldn't see how badly my hands were shaking. Griff put his arm around my shoulder, which helped to calm me but it wasn't enough to stop my teeth from chattering. The cold, the nerves were getting under my skin.

Probably realizing that a girl who looked more scared than a turkey on Christmas wouldn't be much of a threat to her, the old lady grinned and moved aside to let us in.

With a wave of her hand, the woman brought us to a living

room of sky-blue couches and navy-blue lampshades that matched the color of her suit. So she really liked the color blue.

She left us sitting on the couch. The minutes that passed seemed to turn into hours. My apprehension was overwhelming, pushing against my skin like the devil trying to escape. I just couldn't sit still anymore, so I got up and walked around the room. There were a few framed pictures on the walls. One of Pops outside in rubber boots. Next to that one was a yellowed one of a kid who looked like a mini-version of his son, Hawk. And then there was a more recent one with Pops and Hawk, each with an arm around the old lady who liked blue.

I walked to the corner, where a black woodstove was blazing. There was a black and white framed poster near it. I stood, warming my shaky hands over the stove, my eyes on the poster. It was a picture of wrinkled old hands open on the bottom corner, with a white dove flying out of the other corner.

"Do you like it?" someone asked from behind.

I spun around. Pops was standing by the door in his rubber boots. His son, Hawk, towered behind him with a load of chopped wood in his arms.

"What does it mean?"

He removed his boots and stuck his socked feet into burgundy slippers. "Have you ever heard of the expression, 'If you love something, let it go'?"

Of course I had heard it before. "If it comes back to you, it's yours forever."

"And if it doesn't, it was never yours to begin with," he finished.

I hated that expression. Did anyone ever bother to ask the bird how it felt about this little experiment?

"So, do you like the picture?" Pops asked me again.

"Not anymore."

"Neither do I," he said. "But until I have pictures of my grandchildren to put up, it fills the empty space."

I turned to him. "You're not surprised to see me?" What I was really wondering was whether he was upset that I had found him, in his own home. And whether he was in a killing mood.

He touched my arm and motioned for me to sit back on the couch next to Griff, who sat tranquilly but motionless, examining.

"Surprised? No. Happy? Yes. Though I am surprised to see your change in company."

"This is Griff," I told him.

Pops scanned Griff's face and smiled, extending his hand to shake Griff's. Then he backed up to sit in the powder-blue La-Z-Boy on the opposite wall, letting his slippered feet flip up.

"My son, Hawk," Pops said to Griff, nodding toward his son, who had come to stand next to his father's chair after stacking the wood by the stove.

"How many grandchildren do you have?" I asked Pops, making small talk.

"None. That's the problem."

Hawk eyed me dangerously. "What is this about? Who sent you here?"

"No one. I'm here of my own accord." I cleared my throat.

A quizzical look came over both their expressions.

"Well?" Hawk pressed.

"I'm here because," I stammered, "I'm here because I have a business proposition for you."

Hawk let a laugh without a smile escape him. "You? You have a business proposition? For us?"

I was losing my nerve.

Griff gently knocked his knees against mine to urge me forward.

I inhaled and kept my eyes on Pops. He hadn't laughed but had kept a questioning watch over Griff and me. Was he wondering where Cameron was? Did he even know about Cameron's death? Had he been dealing directly with Spider now? Could I really trust him? Was I an absolute idiot for thinking that I could?

If Pops had questions, he remained silent.

"A few years ago, my brother, Bill, came to you with

a proposition. You took a chance on him, and he didn't disappoint you."

"And now you are coming to offer us the same thing your brother offered us years ago? Something we already have?" Hawk's tone was debasing.

I held his stare for an extra second before answering. "I'm here to offer you something better."

I pulled out a marker and the map I had taken from Bill's box and spread it on the coffee table.

"The country is about to undergo a major pharmaceuticals shortage. Which means that there will be a very high black-market demand for all prescription drugs."

"And how do you know this?" Hawk inquired.

I uncapped the red marker. My hands were steady. "Because my family is about to create the shortage. Chappelle de Marseille is the biggest pharmaceuticals company in the United States, and it's about to close its doors." My parents were in too deep. They would not be able to save the Sheppards, and the Tremblays were going to go down with them, unless they got a better deal—from me.

I drew large circles on the map. New York. California. Arizona. Nevada. And then I moved to Canada. Ontario. Quebec. "These places all have protected lands that are occupied by Native American tribes."

Hawk guffawed. "Only a white girl would bunch all Native Americans into one big group. The territories you're pointing out belong to different tribes. Siouan, Shawnee, Lumbee, Chippewa …"

Pops placed a hand over his son's chest, silencing him.

"I realize that," I continued, realizing how ignorant that first remark had sounded. But I wasn't done. "Because you all do have something in common: oppression, thievery, lies, evictions. The kidnapping and reeducating of your children. And now, an epidemic of drug and alcohol abuse among them. Extreme poverty. You may be of different tribes, but your pain is mirrored.

All of your tribes are dwindling in numbers, and the government is taking more from you every day until eventually your children will die too young, be assimilated, or be forced to leave the land for good."

Pops managed to sluggishly cross one foot over the other. The soles of his slippers were only hanging by a few threads. "And yet we are still here. We don't wallow in our plight, young Emily. We have fought and won many wars. This fight we will win too."

I put the cap back on the marker and leaned back into the sofa. "For years, millions of dollars have been allocated by North American governments to Native American tribes as so-called reparation for the wrongs committed in the past. How much of this money have you and your tribesmen actually seen?"

"I am reminded of an old Cree proverb," Pops said stoically. "*'Only when the last tree has died and the last river has been poisoned and the last fish has been caught will we realize that we can't eat money.'* I am not a political soul, Emily. Any money from a government is of no use to us. No wrongs can ever be righted with money."

He was a proud man. He was a generous man. A man who made millions but wouldn't keep enough for himself to buy a decent pair of slippers.

"But you realize that, right now, your people need money and purpose to thrive, to fight, and that the money you're making from the drug shipments and the marijuana will never be enough to help all of your tribesmen."

I could tell by the look of dismay in his expression that I had hit a deep nerve. "What is it you're proposing?"

My voice hit a deeper, stronger octave. "I'm proposing that we become partners. I have the family contacts to make the best pharmaceuticals money can buy, and you have the ability to get these into the country. We could team up with all tribes across North America and supply the people with cheap drugs."

Pops folded his arms over his extended belly. "We did hear of Chappelle de Marseille moving its business out of the country.

But you may not be aware that Advantis and Chemfree have just announced a merger. This will make up for Chappelle de Marseille closing its doors."

"Yes. I'm aware of that. But Advantis and Chemfree are two small companies that only have very few factories, all of which are in the United States. It will take them years to be big enough to supply enough for the whole of North America. In the meantime, they will have monopoly over the pharmaceuticals market, and they will jack up the price of the drugs that people need to survive. People will be looking for a cheaper, better alternative, and this will be us."

"And once Advantis and Chemfree are able to reach demand and sell drugs at a cheaper rate, we will either have to sell pharmaceuticals at little to no profit or go broke?" Pops argued.

"Advantis and Chemfree will be too greedy for that. Besides, they will have a hard time ever getting enough steam to ever get any bigger, what with the cyber hackings and the major fire that will burn down their main factory."

Hawk was grinning now. "The fire?"

"With the unification of Native American tribes, we will have significant resources and manpower across the land. We will have the ability to make things happen quickly and efficiently and most of all, quietly. Native lands are virtually untouchable, at least by local police. And if the feds want in, they can't do so without creating a political nightmare. At least, without us ensuring a political nightmare."

While Hawk had been growing more excited with every word I uttered, Pops's frown deepened. He had watched every movement Griff and I were making. Swing of the hand. Itch of the nose. A cough. A shift of the body. If I hadn't been wearing an oversize sweatshirt, I could have sworn he had noticed my swelled stomach.

"What do you think, Pops?" Hawk asked his father. He was foaming at the mouth. I thought he might jump up and hug me. Or at least give me a high five.

Public speaking had never been my forte, to say the least. Stepping up—on purpose—in front of a crowd, your every word to be judged, like some new form of sadistic self-sacrifice. To me, it was tantamount to a virgin climbing the steps of the Mayan temple and offering her neck for Aztec examination.

But the more I spoke in this small room with Pops, Griff, and Hawk listening to my every word, the more confidence I gained. I knew what I was talking about, and I knew that my idea was, well, a total work of genius. It all felt right.

"Our life's path is not always the one that is illuminated by the morning sun," Pops answered as his wife came in carrying a tray of cookies and tea. He got up and pulled my map away so that she could rest the tea on the coffee table. He gave her a kiss on the forehead before she exited the room.

While Griff stuffed his face with cookies, Pops poured the tea. I looked at Hawk. He looked at me. Neither of us had any inkling as to what on earth Pops meant.

"I don't understand," I admitted.

"Tea?" the old man asked me.

I didn't want tea. I wanted an answer I could understand.

Pops sat back down in his chair, holding his saucer with a shaky hand, before enlightening me. "No. This business venture is not right for us."

While Pops's words repeated in my head and I tried to determine if he had really just flat-out turned me down, Hawk was about to protest his father's decision before being shushed with the raise of his father's wrinkled index finger.

"Is it me or is it the business idea that has you unwilling?" I asked him, anger sharpening my tone.

"You will find your way, young Emily. Of this, I have no doubt. But this path is not your own."

"I'll cover the first shipment. You won't have to risk any of your own money. And I'll still split the profits."

"I'm sorry."

"You're sorry," I echoed. "So that's it then?"

He smiled a pitying smile.

I tried again. "I thought you of all people would understand my plight. You're the only one who can help me."

"Not every path is lit by the morning sun," he repeated in different words, as though it would make more sense, and took a sip of tea, keeping his eyes on the wall behind me.

"Let's go," I told Griff, pulling him up before he had time to lick the empty plate of cookies. I stormed out to the driveway, where Meatball was patiently waiting for us in the car.

"There's an old Cherokee saying," Pops called out from the doorway of his tiny house. I stood by the car, my hands gripping the edge of the door, my hair catching the winter wind. "'Don't let yesterday use up too much of today.'"

I snorted and shook my head in disbelief before getting in the car.

"Now what?" Griff asked me once we were back on the road.

"Now nothing. This was it. Pops was my last hope. I'm about to have a baby, and I have no way of defending us."

"You're not alone. We fight together. We'll find our way, Em. Like Pops said, this wasn't right for us, but something else will be."

I sighed. "Griff, I have no money and no way to make money. I'm not going to be able to work at the admissions office much longer, and your money will run out eventually."

"It already has," he confessed, keeping his eyes on the road.

I had known that the information on Pops would have cost him. I just hadn't realized that it had cost him all the money he had left. "I'm sorry, Griff. I bankrupted you for nothing. Getting information on Pops turned out to be completely pointless."

"It wasn't just the information on Pops that was expensive. It was all the other stuff too. The debts plus interest, the rent, the plane ticket to England. It all added up in the end. I barely had any money left by the time I went looking for information on Pops."

Griff gripped the wheel.

"You had to give something else up, didn't you?" I knew what it was. Something he swore he would never go back to.

He sighed. "The good thing is that I'll be able to make money. Good money. For us."

"And give up your freedom."

"Let's face it, Em. There isn't much else a guy like me can do. I've been fighting my whole life. It's all I know."

I grabbed his arm. "I'll be right there with you."

He smiled bravely and let me pull our hands together over the console.

When we got home, Griff pulled the mattress out of Hunter's and Joseph's room and dragged it into mine. He jammed half of it under my bed, and the other half came up to the doorway, taking up the rest of the floor space.

He hadn't asked my permission to do this. Because he didn't need to. It was how I wanted it as well. I needed him with me.

We slipped under the covers and eventually closed our eyes. Before I knew it, I was standing in the bathroom under a cloud of steam. I brought my hand to the mirror and wiped the steam, standing still as it clawed its way back up the mirror. I wiped it again and started pulling my hair back into a ponytail. Cameron came behind me, pulling my hands down, watching my reflection. He tucked my wet hair behind one ear and then the other. Watching me in the mirror, stroking my ruddy cheek with the back of his hand. He leaned in and kissed my shoulder, holding my reflected eyes. He pushed my hair over and ran his lips down the nape of my neck. His hands came around and pulled my towel off, letting it fall to our naked feet. He watched me in the mirror as his hand slid down my back. I wiggled and tried to keep my composure until I just couldn't stand it anymore and laughed. He chuckled triumphantly, his face lighting up. I loved when his face lit up like that. His smiles were an endangered species.

As our eyes locked in our reflection, we became serious again. Cameron's hands looped to my chest, pressing against my breast.

And he watched me.

He always watched me.

He brought his hands to my waist and spun me around to face him. He lifted me up onto the bathroom counter, pressing me against him, pressing his face against mine, pressing his lips to mine. I ran my fingers up his neck and up through his hair, wishing that this moment would last forever. But it ended, as did the dream.

My eyes flickered open to a room that was solely lit by the glow-in-the-dark stars on my ceiling. I turned my head to find Griff sitting against the wall, arms on his knees, head leaning over his solid arms.

"You're not sleeping," I murmured. It had come more as a question because I couldn't be sure. He hadn't moved.

His head finally looked up, and he stared at me for a minute until he finally spoke. "You were talking in your sleep." His features were emptied.

My dreams, my memories were draining him.

Something bumped against the inside of my skin, and I nearly fell off the bed.

I brought my hand to my belly, which sent Griff springing off his mattress onto my bed. There were three more knocks from the baby—one against Griff's hand and the others against mine.

I wished that Cameron had been there to feel his child's life for the first time. But he wasn't there.

Griff was.

I may have had doubts as to whether Pops had actually figured out that I was pregnant, but in the end, it didn't matter. I finally understood what he had meant about letting the past, missed opportunities, take up the good things that lay now and in the future.

"For what it's worth," Griff said in a half whisper, keeping his hand on my stomach even though the baby had settled again, "I was proud of you today. The way you spoke about your idea to the old guy. Brilliant. I know you would have been able to pull it all off and make it work. With everything that's happened, with everything that's been done to you, you still always find a way to survive. You're a really amazing woman, Em."

He slid back and laced his fingers under his head. Together, we watched the fluorescent stars on my ceiling.

****

As soon as the sun was up, I was out the door with Meatball. Griff insisted on keeping watch over us. It was freezing out but we walked quickly, keeping warm with purpose. It didn't take as long as I had expected to get to the cemetery.

I asked Griff to wait for me as I went to find Bill's grave and knelt.

It took me a while to get started. I had to say something. To Cameron. To Bill. To Rocco. To all these men who had come into my life, leaving their mark, and left.

"I just can't do it anymore," I whispered to them. "The dreams. The pain. Holding on to all your memories with a pointless hope, as if something will change. As if you were going to come back. It's not fair to Griff." I took a breath of cold air into my lungs. "It's not fair to me."

I started digging my fingernails into the ground, but it was frozen solid.

"Meatball, dig," I ordered him, pointing to a spot on the grass.

Meatball sniffed it and wagged his tail.

Ugh. "Meatball, don't dig," I properly ordered.

So he dug. I let him go until the hole was big enough. I took the *Rumble Fish* book and the *Rumble Fish* movie and placed them in the hole. I hadn't had anything of Rocco's, so I had stolen a dry lasagna noodle from Hunter's cupboard to memorialize Rocco's love of food. I placed this on top of the other two other items.

Bill. My parents had forsaken him. Pushed him aside so that he had no choice but to leave.

Rocco. His life cut short before he ever had a chance to really live it.

"Cameron ..." I had to gulp down the tears that were working their way up my throat. "You had all of me, and you chose to end it. I gave you everything I had. I wanted to fight for us, even after you were gone. You broke my heart. It hurts so much, sometimes I think the pain will explode me."

I pushed the loose dirt over the lot. I patted the earth and let my hands rest over the bump for a little while. Nothing I did would ever bring any of them back.

"There will come a time when I will get revenge. I promise you that I will not let your death go unnoticed. I will not let you be forgotten ever again." This I knew for sure. "But ... for now ... I have to let go." I closed my eyes and leaned closer to the earth.

I let them go. I let them rest in peace so that I could live to do the same, so that I could heal, so that I could survive, so that I could learn to love again.

Someday, there would be revenge.

But not right now.

## Chapter 14: Cameron

## Ghosts

*"Emmy won't get over you. No matter how hard you try."* Carly's words were still echoing inside my head.

I was in the back of a bulletproof limousine outside Mexico City in the midst of a motorcade. Manny was crashed out next to me. Her legs were curled under her, and her head bounced against the window with every bump on the road. She didn't look so evil when she slept.

I rolled up my jacket and stuffed it under her head so that she'd have a softer landing.

We had been up all night, traveling, trying to lose the tail that the Mexican cartel had sent us. For them to get wind that the leader of the Coalition was officially meeting with the Mexican president was a declaration of war. At my insistence, not even the captains knew exactly when we were meeting.

We finally managed to burn our cartel shadow in Arizona.

I had a book in my hands that I had picked up off a bench at a small airport somewhere in California. I had opened it and read it before our plane had even taken off, but would keep it until I found or stole another one. Then I would replace the book I would steal with the book I had already read. It was a habit, though some people might have called it an eccentricity or an oddity. Then again, a normal person wouldn't have chosen a life of drugs and murder over a scholarship to MIT.

For as long as I could remember, I had a book within arm's reach. As a kid, I used to sneak into waiting rooms around Callister—dentists, doctors, lawyers—they almost always had some book or magazine left behind. Eventually, receptionists would start recognizing me and shoo me away. Then I was stuck going to the library, though there wasn't much fun in stealing books that they wanted you to take.

My first vivid memory was of me sitting in someone's bathroom, waiting for my father to come get me. I must have been maybe five years old. The bathroom had little blue and white tiles on the floor and gold faucets attached to gold double sinks. There was a toilet and a matching bidet that I thought was a water fountain for dogs. Everything was covered with a layer of grime that only comes from abuse and neglect of oneself. Hopelessness. My dad had recently realized that I could read any brick of a book within twenty minutes, and he started to bring me along to these grimy places—his coke parties. I was the entertainment.

"Pick a book, any book," he would call out to the party hosts. And then the adults would go running around the house, looking for the biggest, most boring books they could find. They would lock me in a bathroom with a stack of books, and I had an hour to read them all.

Then they were supposed to come find me and test me to see if I really was the prodigy my father had made me out to be. But they almost always forgot to come back (or they were too high to care), and I would end up falling asleep in someone's bathtub. At least I had access to a toilet.

One of the adults once brought the New York State penal law for me to read. It was supposed to be a joke, but it turned out to be the best book I had ever read. It was fraught with inconsistencies, gray areas, incomplete definitions. I was ten years old, and I thought I was going to become a lawyer. This makes me laugh now.

In the end, someone would unlock the bathroom door sometime the next day when he or she came searching for any leftover blow. I would go find a bus stop and make my way home.

My mom may have been a drunk and totally oblivious to me, but at least she didn't know how to use me when I was a pathetic kid. That would come later, when she went looking for a cigarette in my Transformers backpack and found stacks of cash instead. She bought herself a case of gin and a membership to Costco and brought a new boyfriend home. If I'd had a backyard, I would have buried the money there.

Manny stirred just as we were going through the gates of Julièn's estate. When she popped her head up, she glanced at my bundled jacket and put it on her lap. She still had the marks of the zipper of my jacket imprinted against her cheek.

We were in the desert, yet there was lushness on Julièn's land that made it almost hallucinogenic, like a mirage to the gates of hell. There were so many flowers that they seemed to have rained down from the sky. The smell of vivacity was just inharmonious with the death that surrounded it.

We were escorted in by Julièn's wife. She was dressed in a one-shouldered, almost see-through white blouse and white trousers. She was a tall, slim, statuesque woman—a model turned one-hit-wonder pop star during the nineties—who had gotten ensnared in Julièn's flashy lifestyle. Her walk reminded me of a white elephant's: slow, but every step deliberate and resilient.

"My husband is still away," she told us, her voice monotone. She eyed Manny from head to toe. "Make yourselves at home."

She left us standing in the middle of the villa.

Manny showed me around, outlining intimate details with every step. She had clearly been there before, and based on the reception we had just received, Julièn's wife had been absent then—though she clearly knew of Manny.

In the main living quarters, full-grown palm trees grew through holes in the porcelain floor. There was a fishpond that half mooned around the spiral staircase.

"This is the indoor garden," Manny explained. "The fish in the pond are Mangarahara cichlid. Very rare."

I glanced over the edge at the captive fish. I had read about these; they were from the Mangarahara River in Madagascar. And they were extinct. Thought to be extinct.

The sunken living room overlooked the infinity pool, where three boys were splashing about as their model mother watched them from the sideline. I knew Julièn had three boys, though I was surprised that he had brought them here. I would not have wanted them anywhere near the likes of us.

From my peripheral vision, I saw something move at the back of the property. Manny slipped her hand into mine as a chill ran down my spine. When I brought my gaze to that place where I had seen that something, it was gone.

I took my hand back from Manny's grasp, despite the softness of her skin. Despite the hollowness at the pit of my stomach that only fills with a woman's touch.

We moved through the rest of the house.

Every room had a view of the garden outside. And every time, I went to the window and looked back to that place in the back. There was simply nothing there.

The heat, the lack of sleep, this place of hell were already getting to my brain.

It wasn't until the evening that Julièn finally made his appearance. And an appearance was exactly what he made. A convoy of at least fifteen cars. Enough bodyguards to protect the Tower of London. And a truck just for his luggage.

Mariella, Julièn's wife, came to greet him at the door without the children. He held her at arm's length and gave her a quick peck on the cheek, before his suit could wrinkle. She disappeared as soon as he released her. His children would be brought to him a little later at his request while we were in the middle of discussions. The children stood erect, as though they were in the principal's office, as he patted each of them on the head and sent them off.

Trying to talk business with Julièn was like talking to a toddler. He changed the subject if he didn't like what you were talking about. He threw tantrums at the staff if his meal were too hot, if his wine were too cold, if it rained outside. He had even planned playdates for us.

"I have a few friends I would like to introduce you to," he said on the second day we were there. We were only supposed to be there two nights, and yet we still hadn't gotten to the crux of the business. It was going to take a lot longer than two nights.

I wasn't surprised by this. That morning, I had noticed a dinner table that had been set for at least twenty people. "Cancel," I ordered Julièn. He listened, begrudgingly, but would never gain any concept of keeping things quiet.

"You know, I came from nothing," he reminded me every time the subject of money came up, which it always did as often as he could possibly bring it up. He would wave his hands around, pointing at a piece of crappy, overpriced artwork on the wall or some mahogany serving tray he had acquired from wherever. "Some tiny little village," he would add, as though this would create some kind of kinship between us. As though I were one of his constituents and I didn't know that he had actually been raised in the States in a middle-class suburb of Phoenix. Hardly outdoor plumbing.

What he did have, however, was intel on the comings and goings of the three cartel families within Mexico. Where they lived; where their wives, children, and mothers lived. Where they shopped for groceries. The Christmas presents they had purchased for their children last year. Julièn was concentrating his efforts on finding and killing the cartel, creating a name for himself across Mexico and the world as a leader who was tough on drugs, while making money hand over fist on his own drug production. He was the Mexican version of Shield.

But I had still heard nothing of how he was going to manufacture and distribute the promised goods. He either had no plan or he wasn't sharing this information. This was worrisome.

And his obnoxious personality was wearing me down. I just wanted to put a bullet through his fashionable brain and be done with it. I couldn't. Not yet. But when the cartel came for revenge, I promised myself to do his children a service and be the one to end his miserable life.

The more I watched his interaction with his children, the more I understood his reasoning for having them there at the same time as us. Julièn liked to flaunt his power, whether it was over an entire country or over his three young children. And perhaps he hoped that I wouldn't blow his brains out and paint his walls with them while his wife and boys were there. I was tempted, more than once.

Manny had observed as much of Julièn's behavior as I had, but she had a different perspective.

"My father never wanted a daughter," she told me one evening. "He wanted an heir. Not a girl." We were hunched over a blueprint of the Munoz compound. Julièn had just made his eldest son spend two hours standing in front of us with a whole steak sitting in his mouth after he had refused to eat it at dinner. Julièn had left us to go after his wife, after Mariella had grabbed her son and walked out of the room.

"My mother had four pregnancies before me. All girls, based on the ultrasounds. My father would make her get abortions as soon as he'd find out. When she got pregnant with me, she hid it from him. Until she had me. She had to get all the wives of the underlings involved so that he wouldn't kill me. When the men threatened defection, he promised to keep me, but he left my mother and kept me away from her. She killed herself when I was five. My father married the nanny after she gave him his first son."

I went to bed that night with no doubt in my mind that Manny had killed her father. And that one of Julièn's sons would do the same to him someday if I didn't get to him first. People like us shouldn't have children. This was clear.

\*\*\*\*

I had kept the air-conditioning off in my room because I couldn't hear anything over the hum. I needed to be able to listen for anything out of the ordinary. An ambush in the night.

It was like sleeping in a BBQ.

I went to open the window a little wider, as though this would make a difference, and saw something, a shadow, moving in the grass.

It was there. I could see it. The figure of the woman in a flowing dress, red hair that seemed to glow in the darkness like its own October moon and flew behind her. I wasn't imagining it, and I obviously wasn't sleeping.

I ran out of the house and headed in the direction I had seen the woman go. I looped around the staff kitchen and toward the garbage bins, where I could see smoke rising over one of the spotlights.

I did find a lady. But her hair was darker than the night.

Mariella was sitting in a lawn chair, sucking on a cigarette and staring at me. She still had her evening dress on and a bottle of wine next to her.

I was in my boxer briefs.

I nodded hello. She took a puff of her smoke and glanced away. She saw me as one of her husband's confrères. If only she knew how badly I wanted to spoon his eyeballs out.

I headed back where I had come from, feeling sickly and disoriented.

Manny was walking down the staircase in a black silk baby-doll. "Cameron? Are you okay?"

I went to find her in the darkness. "Fine. Can't sleep?"

"I hate this place," she told me in a whisper. "I hate the smell. I hate the heat. I hate how quiet it is. I feel like I'm going crazy here."

The shimmer of the pond water was reflecting over her face. Her hair was up in a messy ponytail, and she had a pendant that fell into her cleavage.

I let the back of my hand come to her neck and make its way

down to the silver pendant, pulling its weight between my fingers. It looked like three leaves intertwined over a circle.

"It's a *triquetra*," she explained. "My grandfather gave it to my grandmother as a wedding present."

I didn't want to ask if she'd had to yank it from her grandmother's cold dead hands.

While I held on to the pendant, Manny pressed my hand on her chest.

Manny's gaze went from eye to eye. Large, dark pupils stared back at me.

"Stay with me," she pleaded, pulling at my hand.

"Good night," I told Manny in a low voice.

The vulnerable softness of her face disappeared and was replaced by her stern self. She turned on her heels and went back upstairs.

On my way back to my suite, I let myself glance outside. It was as black as the inside of a coffin. There was no way I would have ever seen anything outside, let alone at the back of the estate.

Haunted. That's what I was. And it was destroying me. I needed to refocus.

I tried something that night when I closed my eyes in bed. I forgot where I was. I took a deep breath and imagined I was somewhere else. That place I would never forget, that was forged in my brain, that was part of my DNA. It was the only time I had truly slept.

I was at ease. With Emmy. I could forget; I could let things go. Even for just a few moments in her arms, I was liberated from myself.

I could breathe again and remember.

She was alone most of the time. Surrounded, but alone. Alone, but not lonely. Alone by choice. We had this in common. This need to be self-sustained. And this was what had drawn me to her initially. I had seen myself in her. She was me, the other, better version of me—the one that could have existed in another dimension.

Then she matured. She became a beauty—the kind of beauty that one can't help but stare at, as though it were absolutely not possible, and yet it was. I watched her, from afar. I got to know Emily Sheppard ... the way she moved, the sound of her laugh, her habits, the people who surrounded her. This, I had thought, must be love.

How can someone who has never been loved be able to love? Jesus, I had no idea what love was.

The person I was watching was a fictional character. Someone I had made up in my mind. I had given her a personality, feelings, thoughts that were not her own, because I didn't actually know her.

I could have spent my lifetime being in love with this beautiful girl I thought I knew. If that day in the cemetery had never come and if Emmy and I had never met, that would have been just fine with me. I wouldn't have known any better. She would have lived her beautiful life, and I would have watched her do it.

She would have been ignorant of me (I had reproached Emmy for this), but I would have also been ignorant of her. I would have loved her. But not really her.

Emmy, it turned out, was real. She was hotheaded and emotional and overdramatic. And she was kind. She could make your heart start beating again. She could bring life to the darkest place, to the darkest man. With one tear, she could make you feel like the shittiest asshole in the world. But with one smile, you were invincible.

That thing that was tearing me apart—the visions of the lady in the garden, barefoot, red hair flowing behind her in a nonexistent wind—was the knowledge of what I was missing.

Being alone but not lonely together. Being each other's counterparts, each other's best part.

There would never be another. For her or for me.

After having had a taste, I knew what I was missing, and I couldn't continue life if she weren't next to me. I had been sending myself to an early grave because I couldn't be Cameron without her.

I knew this.

So what the hell was I supposed to do now?

****

In the morning, after a good night's sleep next to the spirit of Emmy, I met Julièn and Manny at the breakfast table.

"The Coalition will not be single sourcing to you," I announced as I took a seat.

Manny choked on her orange juice.

Julièn readjusted the napkin on his lap. "We had a deal. Measures have been taken based on our agreement."

By measures, he meant that he had already made promises, taken bribes, and spent the money he would have made after the deal went through.

"I would be doing the Coalition a disservice if I didn't test the proposal before fully investing all of our efforts." I looked Julièn in the eye. "I am not satisfied that you will be able to deliver on your promises."

Manny sat erect. "Cameron, it's all going down in a couple of days. We've already spent so much time planning—"

"The Coalition is committed to building a business relationship with you," I continued, cutting Manny off. "As a show of our loyalty, we will offer you exclusivity over all marijuana being distributed throughout the United States. This will be at a considerable peril for the Coalition. We will be severing relations with all of our current growers, who have proved themselves efficient and trustworthy for many years." I needed to keep the peace with the cartel for as long as possible, until I could bring Emmy back to me.

Julièn leaned back in his chair and crossed one leg over the other, showing off his leather shoes. "I suppose this could be temporarily achieved—"

"I will, of course, need detailed and complete intelligence on your current grow-ops. As an equal show of good faith," I added.

He kept his gaze locked on me. "Of course."

Most of our growers were partners of the Coalition. While there would be some rumblings of the decision to single source all marijuana through Mexico, the captains would find ways to make amends and keep the peace.

But there was also one independent grower. And he would not be happy to know—following an anonymous tip—that his license to grow had just been revoked.

## Chapter 15: Emily

## Trigger

The bright side of hitting rock bottom, of having exhausted all options, was that my eyes had been opened to new possibilities. It was like getting lost in the desert carrying an empty jug of orange juice, collapsing with dehydration, and on my last breath being handed a jug of apple juice and a map sending me in a totally new direction.

It was March already. I was sitting cross-legged on the floor in some seedy gym in south Callister, my homework splayed in front of me. But I was focusing on Griff, who was punching out a balloon bag in the corner. He had been training hard to get back into fighting shape and had already won a few bouts, held in shady backroom fighting rings. Everyone we encountered was excited to see him back in fighting shape. Griff wasn't just a good fighter. He was gifted. And with every day that passed, I noticed his confidence growing. While he wouldn't admit it to me, I could tell that he was happy to be back in the ring. He was home.

I envied him. I knew how it felt—to do what you were always meant to do. I had caught a glimpse of this when I was with Pops. The glimpse had croaked the second Pops had turned me down.

At least the dreams and the nightmares had stopped so that Griff could get some shut-eye.

I hadn't forgotten that there was a whole world of bad people who wanted me and who would want my child. But for now, I had pushed this aside—because I had no other choice.

A few days after Griff and I had come back from our fruitless meeting with Pops, a large cardboard box was delivered to our door. It was the kind of box that my roommates usually got from their moms. Boxes with clean Spider-Man sheets and Kraft dinners. Except that this box was for me. It had a bunch of clothes of a bigger size to accommodate my growing self. XL shirts and stretchy pants. A brown and red woven poncho. And a large terrycloth bathrobe that, quite magically, had a thousand dollars stuffed in one of its pockets.

As soon as possible after Christmas, my loving, doting mother had my medical benefits canceled so that I now had to pay cash for my nausea medicine. I guess this was her way of rejecting me and rejecting my child again (in case it wasn't clear to me that she had already done so on Christmas Eve). So the care box obviously wasn't from my mother, but from two people who were as close to a mom as I would ever get: Maria and Darlene. I knew that a thousand dollars was a lot of money for them. And I knew that if I tried to send it back, they would be really hurt.

Since Griff wouldn't let me out of his sight, I'd had to stop working because my schedule was getting in the way of Griff's training. And honestly, I was too exhausted to work. I could barely manage going to class and keeping up with my homework. Some days I felt as though my neck were holding up a bowling ball. But I kept this from Griff.

Griff's fights were quite small (compared to what he had once been used to) and paid little, so the money that Darlene and Maria had sent me came in handy, keeping us fed. And the box of clothes helped me continue to conceal my pregnancy. As far as I knew, no one knew that I was pregnant. Griff and I planned to keep it that way.

Griff and I, we wedged together as though we had always been meant to. Before I knew it, spring was trying to claw its way out of the irrepressible snow.

Griff had finished training for the day, and I was taking yet another trip to the washroom while he went to get the car. I had learned to be speedy. The last time I had (apparently) spent too much time in the women's washroom, he had a handgun placed in my purse the next day, and I got a two-hour refresher course on self-defense from one of his assistant trainers.

When I pulled my pants down in the stall, my insides twisted when I found that I was bleeding again. This had been happening on and off for weeks. The nausea, the fatigue, the bleeding, the fear for the baby's health, the fear of what was going to happen next—it was all weighing on me like a metal jumpsuit. But with my mother having pulled my medical insurance and having no alone time to stalk the student doctor, I had to take comfort in the fact the baby was still kicking my insides to a pulp.

I rushed outside to find Griff parked with a wheel on the sidewalk, the passenger-side door open for me and Griff on his phone. He hung up as soon as he saw me.

"Everything okay?"

"Sure," I said. I had been hiding my health issues from Griff because he didn't need the added anxiety. Some days he was so wound up from the stress of fighting, of money, of watching out for me that I thought he might actually unstitch. "Who was on the phone?"

"My promoter."

He drove out of the parking lot, nearly colliding with an oncoming vehicle. Something was up.

"And?" I wondered when we were safely stopped at a red light.

"There's a fight in two weeks. At the Bolster Coliseum."

There were posters all over Callister, and his gym mates had been yakking about it for weeks. The first time Callister City hosted a mixed martial arts fight in its largest arena was big news, but it was no longer *new* news.

"And?" I asked again.

"One of the fighters just got injured in training." He turned to me before I could repeat the same question. "They want me to fight his fight."

This was big and new news. "That's good, isn't it? It's what you've been hoping for, training for."

But Griff didn't seem as excited as I thought he should have been. "This is a title fight, Em. It's the main event. I'm not ready for that."

"Then you will be ready. Two weeks is enough time to get ready for it. Right?"

"If I train twenty-four hours a day for the next two weeks."

"So do it."

"It's not that simple."

"What's not so simple? You train hard. You win. Done. If anyone can do it, you can."

He chuckled. "I want you there. You're my lucky charm."

"Of course I'll be there." I had been to every one of his fights, watching from the back, where no one could see me. Staying out of sight as much as possible was the best way to keep the baby and me safe.

"No," he said. "I want you there. In the stands. I need to be able to see you when I'm in the ring."

"Griff—" I started.

"Please, Em. You're the reason I've been winning all this time. I can't do it without you."

I laughed. I found that hard to believe. He had been winning all those years before he even met me. "This event will be televised, and I'm as big as a whale. How exactly am I supposed to keep this pregnancy secret with millions of people watching?"

"Emmy, you're barely showing. If I didn't know you were pregnant, I would have sworn you just had a really big dinner." His eyebrows jumped up and down, and he grinned. "Besides, they won't be watching you. They'll be watching Griff the Grappler Connan."

He had a point. When Griff entered a room, nobody could take their eyes off him, including most of my roommates.

****

Two weeks later, it was mid-March and the day of Griff's fight. My belly was still quite small for being eight months pregnant, but finding something nice—nice enough to wear—was a major challenge. I was combing through my bins, trying to figure out what to wear to the arena when I got accosted in the hall by Hunter and Cassie. I had noticed them spending a lot of time together lately. Cassie had kept her hair blonde, though the rest of her still screamed bloodsucker. Vampire girl and frat boy was a weird combination, but they both had something in common: their love of seeing someone pummeled by all means necessary in an escape-proof ring.

Griff had gotten everyone tickets to the fight so that I wouldn't be sitting by myself ... so that Griff could take his eyes off of me long enough to beat up the guy they put in front of him. He was the hero. I was the hero's sidekick.

Griff came up behind them and stood snickering as they handed me a plastic bag.

I narrowed my eyes at Griff while I opened the package. There was a lot of deep purple in there. I unfolded the material to find that it was a cotton sweatshirt with a life-size picture of Griff, when he was a kid. He looked to be about ten years old, smiling proudly, with one of his front teeth missing.

"They asked me for pictures," Griff told me. "I asked that this one be made especially for you. My brother had knocked out my tooth after I peed in his morning cereal. Classic."

I was at a loss for words. "Thanks. It's ..."

"Really ugly."

Cassie and Hunter both unzipped their hooded jackets, revealing similar ugly sweatshirts. This sweatshirt would bring way too much attention to me, but I couldn't remind Griff of this while Cassie and Hunter were within hearing distance. And Griff was just too preoccupied with the fight for me to remind him of all the other stuff we had to be worried about.

I looked at the tag: extra large. I sighed. Well, at least they had accounted for my college weight gain, and this would indeed hide my belly. When the rest of the roommates came out of their rooms proudly wearing their ugly sweaters, I knew I had to make a decision, even though I had no choice really.

At least I wasn't going to be on my own.

I threw my shirt over my clothes. "I love it."

We all left the house together—Griff and his ugly-shirt army.

My roommates went to find their seats in the arena while Griff and I went to a changing room in the back. The camera crews were already there, as was Griff's fight team. I found a corner to hide in away from the limelight while Griff got ready and got filmed getting ready.

Every time an undercard bout would end in the arena, the camera lit up and came back to Griff: Griff punching the air, Griff wrestling one of his teammates to the ground. Soon, it was Griff's turn to go out. The camera crews left the room to film his exit and entrance into the stadium. Griff and I had a few moments alone.

I jumped in his arms as soon as everyone had left the room. We stayed like this for a while, cheek to cheek, listening to the noise outside.

"Even if I lose—"

"You won't."

"Even if I lose," he said again, "the second prize is still more than I would make winning in a hundred of the other fights. This money will give us the ability to hide for a bit, at least until the baby comes."

My heart tore a bit. This was the biggest night of his life, and he was still worried about our next meal. I wished he would focus on himself for once.

I didn't want to let Griff go. But when a light knock came at the door, our arms fell to our sides, and I was ushered out before we even had a chance to say good-bye, before I could wish him the good luck he didn't need.

As soon as I was out the door, the noise was deafening and only getting louder with each step. The baby was doing gator-sized rolls against the skin of my belly as I came out through the gateway. Stands went all the way to the ceiling and all seats were filled, though no one was sitting in their assigned chairs. Screaming from spectators took up any air left in the arena. I felt as though I was crawling deep into the bowels of an anthill.

It was easy enough to find my seat: I just looked for the ugliest sweaters in the crowd. My roommates' seats were just a few rows back from the front. Griff had planned it so that I would be close enough for him to see me in the crowd but not so close that the cameras would point my way. Griff's anthem came over the loudspeakers, and none of my roommates even noticed that I had arrived and found my seat (even though I had to step over a couple of them to get there). I stretched my neck, but I didn't see Griff make his entrance into the arena. As soon as he was in the ring, he turned his head my way, and our eyes connected.

Another song came on the speakers, and I looked at one of the mega-screens hung around the stadium. Griff was fighting a Brazilian fighter named Batte Gomez. He had apparently held the middleweight title for almost three years, which was unheard of according to the gossip at Griff's gym. Until that moment, I had no real idea what this guy looked like, other than the picture that was on the millions of posters posted everywhere in town.

The posters did not do this beast justice.

His hands and his forehead were big enough to crush a school bus like a beer can. He was less human, more buffalo.

My eyes immediately went looking for Griff. I was shaking my head. He needed to get out of there.

Griff was standing at one corner, hidden by his fight team standing behind him. The monster entered the ring, and I was foolishly yelling at Griff, my voice lost in the anthill.

Griff was doing this for me, because of me. He would die doing this for me.

The referee was introduced to the jeering crowd, the fighters bumped fists, and just as the fighters were parted, Griff glanced back. He was looking for me, and one last time our eyes locked before he got kicked in the face. He had just enough time to shake off the pain of his opponent's foot against his cheek before the buffalo's fist found his jaw. There was a gasp from my row of roommates as Griff staggered back. He moved away from the Brazilian while he once again tried to shake it off.

Using his gloved hand, he dabbed at the blood that was leaking out of the corner of his mouth, and then he glanced at the blood on the glove. All of a sudden, I saw something change in Griff as he wiped the blood against his shorts. He smiled and waved at the crowd. He rolled his shoulders back and went after Batte Gomez.

I watched him take on the buffalo swiftly and powerfully. He was careful, methodical, relentless, and a lot faster than his heavier counterpart. Griff grappled Gomez to the ground, and when the first round ended, he was sitting on Batte's chest trying to find a hole under his arms so that he could get to his face.

The second round came as quickly as the first round ended. Griff charged as soon as the bell rang, his fist ahead of him leading the charge. It found a space under Batte's jaw, and Batte fell back, his head hitting the rubber mat.

Griff stood with his fists held ready in suspension. His opponent put an elbow under himself in an effort to get up, but it buckled under his weight. He fell flat again, and the crowd almost went quiet, or perhaps my ears had tuned them out. As Griff was about to take advantage of his opponent's incapacitation, the referee jumped in front of him, fell over Batte, and waved his arms.

The whole world went still, along with Griff.

I could feel the wave of disbelief rise as everyone, including

Griff, realized what had just happened. Griffin the Grappler Connan had won. Against all odds.

Griff's team were jumping up and down around him while Griff turned, trying to find me in the crowd, but he was being blocked by the crowd that followed the golden belt. As Griff's team parted to let the belt come through, Griff took off running. He flew down the stairs, flew between the rows of fans.

I knew where he was going. I was about to step over Joseph to meet him halfway and drag him to the back, to where the cameras couldn't catch us, but Griff was already there. He lifted me up and kept me in his grasp while everyone nearby tried to jump into our row to get their hands on the victor, stepping on my roommates, on Griff and me, in the process.

Security had to fish all of us out, and we were shepherded back into Griff's changing room. Hunter had a bloody nose, and one of the twins' shirts had been torn. They never looked happier. I hoped that the stampede of people would have kept us hidden from the cameras. I made a quick decision to just let it go. For the first time in several months, I stopped worrying about what could happen and celebrated with everyone else. I enjoyed the now.

Griff still had me in his arms when I pressed my hands against his face. "You didn't think you would win."

"No," he admitted.

"You should have told me, explained to me what you were walking into. I would have never ... we would have found another way. I thought you were going to die."

"No one would have let me die. I promise you that I won't leave you, in life or in death."

The door burst open as the rest of Griff's fight team came through carrying champagne and the belt he had left behind.

After the mind-blowing win, Griff was immediately booked for a press conference, interviews with the media, and meetings with sponsors and promoters. I ended up driving home with Joseph, while the rest of the lot stayed to follow Griff around, drunk on his refound celebrity.

"You didn't want to stay with everyone else?" I asked Joseph while we were in the car.

"I'm not much of a drinker."

I rolled my eyes. "How much did Griff pay you?"

"Enough to make it worth my while."

\*\*\*\*

I was going down the stairs for my regular 3:00 a.m. snack of peanut butter and apples when I heard the door jiggle. One of my drunken roommates, rolling in after partying with the fighters. After the roommates had gotten back from Christmas break, Griff had ordered them to lock the door from now on. And no more parties! The order was well-received, because it came from their beloved Griff. But at least once every weekend, someone, usually a drunk someone, got locked outside after forgetting or losing his or her key. There must have been twenty keys to our house floating around in bars across campus.

I let the drunk someone on the other side of the door suffer before I went to let him or her in.

There was someone standing under the broken porch light, still holding the two paper clips he had been using to try to jimmy the lock. When he took a step forward into the light of the hallway, Meatball came charging down the stairs. I had time to loop an arm out and latch onto his collar before he attacked the man under the cloak.

This man looked filthy, like he had been sleeping under a leaky bridge, and smelled like he had been eating out of a garbage bin. I didn't immediately recognize him. But when he pulled his hood off, when my eyes met his, I knew exactly who he was. In this instant, I also realized that he was pointing a gun at me.

Norestrom.

The bastard who had killed Rocco.

If he hadn't had a gun pointed at me, I would have let Meatball rip the arteries out of his neck.

"I was starting to think I was never going to get you alone."

I wasn't alone. Joseph was sleeping upstairs. But I didn't tell him this. Clearly he had been watching me, and clearly he had lost touch with reality.

"I am alone. What do you want?"

He was jittery, moving in quick sequences. Like his brain was moving faster than the rest of the world. Meatball was snarling, foaming at the mouth. I was having trouble keeping him close to me. When Norestrom took a gentle step forward, Meatball lunged up, almost yanking my arm out of its socket. So Norestrom went back to his original spot.

"I won't hurt you," he told me. "I just need money."

I tried not to laugh.

"How much?"

"Just enough to disappear."

I really wanted to punch him in the face. But I was also enjoying seeing him so squirmy. I couldn't tell if he was high or frightened out of his mind.

There was a noise upstairs. Norestrom pointed his gun quickly at the stairs and quickly came back to me. "I thought you said you were alone?"

"Don't you have connections? People who have enough money to buy you your own island?" I wanted to keep him calm and talking.

But his arms had started shaking, and the wildness in his eyes was mounting like his time was about to run out.

"Not anymore," he answered. "Because of you."

He had been forsaken by Victor, by his own kind. I was loving this newfound fact.

"I'll give you all the money you need," I said to him. "Just come back tomorrow, and I'll give you everything I have."

"I need it now. Tomorrow will be too late."

"Well, I don't carry that kind of cash with me."

Back and forth his eyes went from my face to my guard dog. Until something else caught his attention. In my struggle to keep

Meatball at my side, my bathrobe had come undone, and my belly poked out from my too-small T-shirt.

While the wildness of his eyes remained, a smile crept over his face. I recognized that smile. It was demonic. It was the same smile he'd had on his foul face before he had ordered his men to kill Rocco.

"Okay," he said, backing away. "I'll see you tomorrow."

He would see me tomorrow. With Victor or with whoever else was willing to pay the price of knowing that Cameron's baby was hiding inside of me. With whoever was willing to pay the price of being able to use my child as leverage in the underworld.

While Norestrom was lowering his gun and I was trying to figure out how to get to the revolver that was in my purse on my bed so that I could shoot his head off his shoulders, Joseph had sleepwalked down the stairs.

"What's with all the barking?" he muttered. Norestrom jumped and I jumped and Meatball got free of my clasp of his collar. A shot rang out. Before Norestrom had time to pull the trigger again, Meatball had bounded, slamming him to the ground and sending the revolver flying into the pile of shoes stacked by the door.

Norestrom was kicking and screaming, using his free arm to punch Meatball in the head. I tried to pull Meatball away before Norestrom could really hurt him, but his jaw was firmly set into Norestrom's puny arm.

Joseph rushed to help me, and together we finally managed to get Meatball off him. Joseph held his collar, while I rushed to grab the gun on the floor.

Norestrom was already on his feet, getting ready to pounce on me until I raised the gun. He was brought to a halt, his gaze jumping from my face to the gun that I was pointing at his head.

Rocco.

All I could see was Rocco. How much he loved to goof around. How much he loved to eat. How his teenage body had matured before his brain had had a chance to catch up. Standing in this hallway entrance with a gun in my hands, I could hear the echo of his laugh—a child's giggle stuck in a man's body. He was the funniest kid. He was a brother and a confidant. He was sunshine in darkness. And the piece of shit who had taken this child's life, the one who had robbed the world of Rocco, was standing in front of me.

I steadied my stance and felt every muscle of my arms tighten around the gun. The blood left Norestrom's face.

He stood erect, a step away from the front door, and fished something out of his front shirt pocket.

"Hands up," I growled.

He had already pulled out a shiny badge and held it in front of him—a shield to my gun. "I'm a cop. You can't shoot me."

Norestrom kept his shield in the air and took one step back. He was right; I couldn't shoot him. He turned around and grabbed the door handle.

I pulled the trigger.

I pulled the trigger.

I pulled the trigger.

With each pull, his body pulsed forward like he was getting hit by lightning bolts.

I kept pulling the trigger until nothing but air came out and Norestrom was lying with his cheek squeezed against the door and his limp body in a pool of his blood.

When the smoke cleared, a whimper from Meatball made me spin around. His front legs gave out, and he fell to the floor.

*No. No. Nonononononono.* I ran to my dog's side. I grabbed his head, feeling warmth under my fingers. When I pulled my hand away, I saw red.

Meatball's head went limp in my arms. My pajama bottoms were already saturated with his blood.

"No," I screamed. "Meatball. Not you. I won't, I can't lose you."

Meatball was looking blankly at my face, and his eyes started to close. I could feel his breath leaving him. I started trying to pull him up, but his deadweight was too much for me.

"Please, Meatball. I need you. You can't leave me here. Not like this."

Meatball let one long sigh escape him and forced his eyes open. "I won't make it without you." The top of his head was soaked with my tears. He managed to wag his thumb-sized tail. Then he dragged his head up to my face to lick my nose.

I glared up through my tears and yelled at a dumbfound Joseph, "Help me!"

Joseph roused from his daze and helped me carry Meatball to my car. While Joseph drove, I had my big monster of a dog lying on my lap while I whispered urgently. I promised Meatball all the popcorn he could eat. I promised him that I would pay Joseph's mom so that she brought him her famous meatballs every day of his life. I promised him that I would never leave him as long as he never left me.

With every breath, Meatball's body weakened against my legs, sinking deeper into obscurity. I knew he couldn't see me anymore because he just looked vacantly at the seat ahead. But I knew he could hear me. So I didn't shut up. Not for one second until I was finally pried from his side at the twenty-four-hour veterinary clinic.

\*\*\*\*

I didn't know how long I'd been pacing outside the surgery door in my blood-soaked pajamas before the doctor came walking out. He took his time. Removing his mask, removing his scrubs, taking a breather.

He bade me to sit, but I refused. I was ready to wring his neck for information.

"The bullet missed his heart, but made a mess of his humerus." He put his hand on my shoulder, as though he could sense I was about to fall. "I was able to eventually dig the bullet out, but he's lost a lot of blood. He's weak. Very weak. But I think he'll be okay."

I kept my eyes on his expression, while his words clumsily processed in my mind. When the doctor smiled tiredly, I flung myself into his arms and hugged this perfect stranger as though he were the father I never had.

Joseph and I were brought into the back room, where Meatball was sleeping on a metal gurney. The vet let him wake up just long enough for me to see him. When his eyes flickered opened and he saw me, he tried to get up, but I soothed him back down. I hopped onto the bed, gently pushed his big head onto my lap, and rubbed his ears until he fell back asleep.

Joseph pulled cash out of his torn wallet and handed it to the vet. It would take me a while to pay him back, but I would. Every penny and more.

The vet left us so that we could visit with Meatball.

While my dog lay sleeping on me, I left one hand on his chest so that I could feel him breathing in and out, feel the pulse of his beating heart under my fingers. And then I remembered what was waiting on the floor at the house. "What am I going to do with the body?" was the murmur that came out of my mouth. I wasn't worried about the fact that I had just killed someone. I was worried about how I was going to get rid of that excuse of a human being that was lying in a puddle of blood on the carpet. Former human being.

"It's already been taken care of," Joseph said, his voice completely calm, as though we were talking about picking up a pint of milk.

"How?"

"I called my brother. He took care of it."

My breath was cut short. "You shouldn't have involved your brother in all of this. You've just made him an accessory to murder. A cop's murder."

Joseph laughed. "Are you serious? My brother couldn't wait to take credit for the kill. The guy you killed has apparently been wanted by some big bad drug guy, and there was a huge reward for whoever managed to find him. My brother's going to soar up the gang ranks with this one." He put a reassuring hand on my shoulder. "No one will ever know you had anything to do with it."

I tried to breathe through the disquiet that was building in my stomach.

"I need a favor from you. Don't tell Griff about this."

Joseph's shoulders sank. I knew he liked and respected Griff. But it had been a long time since I had seen Griff that happy. Norestrom might have been dead, but more like him would come.

"Won't he wonder what happened to Meatball?" Joseph wondered.

"I'll make something up. I'll tell him he got neutered."

Joseph winced and looked at Meatball sympathetically. "Meatball will be happy he only got shot."

I knew that I would have to think up a better story because the white patch over Meatball's chest wouldn't match the story. But Meatball was going to stay at the vet's clinic for a few more days until his wound healed. I didn't want to leave his side, but the vet wouldn't let me spend the night by his cage. To get me out the door, the vet assured me that Meatball would be in a drugged coma so that he couldn't scratch at his stitches and that he wouldn't even know that I wasn't there.

When we got back to the house, the sun was about to poke its head over the horizon. The hallway carpet had been ripped out, exposing sparkling clean parquet flooring. My cell phone was ringing in my bedroom. I had expected it to be Griff, but I didn't recognize the number.

"Hello?"

"My father has asked me to tell you that we have accepted your offer. We will be in touch," said a voice over the phone. The man hung up.

It only took me an extra second to figure out that Hawk had just called me.

And that I was about to become a drug lord.

I let my body fall into the mattress. It was no longer a matter of *if* I were going to do this. The deal was done. I was doing this.

I turned my head and saw one of Bill's boxes at the foot of my bed. I had been going through his things slowly, methodically, hoping I would find him somewhere in there.

If he saw me now, about to embark on a major drug deal, he would have locked me up in a tower and swallowed the key. But he was gone. And I needed to do what I needed to do to protect myself. All of a sudden, I thought of something.

I went searching through the box that contained Bill's high school stuff and pulled out his last yearbook. I flipped through the pages until I found what I was looking for. Frances wasn't hard to find. She was on every other page. I burst into Joseph's room and jumped on his bed.

"I need you to find someone for me."

He pulled the blanket over his face. "I still haven't found the last guy you wanted me to find."

I yanked the blanket back and threw my brother's high school yearbook on his chest. "I have a first and a last name. I even have pictures."

Joseph grinned devilishly and jumped out of bed.

"This is it," I told myself while he was clicking away. "This is how I am going to make this right."

## Chapter 16: Cameron

## Faith or Fate?

"Cameron." My eyelids flipped open. It was Emmy's voice. She was in my head again.

She had as much room as she wanted in there now.

I threw a T-shirt on and marched out of my room into the guest suite I was now sharing with Carly and Tiny. They had arrived late last night with news. I had dragged both of them to the waterfall outside so that our voices would be drowned out by the crash of water.

Tiny stood waiting. He wanted to tell me something but watched Carly from the corner of his eye. I knew it had to do with his secret task of finding Norestrom.

Carly huffed at Tiny. "If you needed to come here without me, then it's obviously something you guys don't want me to know. So I obviously need to know what this is about. I didn't come all the way here to be kept in the dark. Spill it, Tiny."

I didn't care anymore if Carly knew what I had been up to. I just wanted to get to Norestrom.

"Go on," I ordered Tiny.

"Norestrom is dead."

"How sure are you?"

Tiny glanced around and pulled out his phone. A video came

on. Gangsters hidden under neck scarves, waltzing around a body. Norestrom's dead, useless corpse.

"He was shot in the back."

"Who shot him?" Carly wondered. She wasn't surprised as to what I had been up to.

"The Finch Street boys. They heard about the reward that was being offered, and they found him hiding in one of their neighborhoods. They killed him when he tried to run."

The Finch Street boys ... their neighborhood was close to Emmy's neighborhood. Norestrom had been close to Emmy. Too close.

"Give them the reward," I told Tiny, even though the reward had been for Norestrom to be delivered alive. They had saved Emmy without knowing it. As much as I wanted my revenge on that bastard, Emmy was more important. Shield would just have to suffer my revenge for Norestrom as well as himself.

I had spent a lot of time working with Julièn and Manny. Visiting the pot fields. Meeting growers who had no idea what they were doing. Julièn was good at making deals, but he was not a businessman. He took no care in the product he delivered. As long as there was product and he got paid, the rest was immaterial. He had a lot to learn from Pops.

Yes, I had put in a lot of hours with Julièn, but I still had a lot of work to do. I had to make amends with all three cartel families. I had to make amends with Pops. I had to kill Shield. I had to fix the Coalition. It wasn't too late. I could fix anything.

First, I had to get Emmy back, if she would have me back. Yes, I could fix anything.

Tiny was watching yesterday's sports highlights from the designer couch that doubled as his bed. The television was small in terms of the kind of system Tiny was used to. It was hidden behind a fake Rembrandt because it didn't fit into Julien's European décor. As though Europeans didn't watch TV.

Carly was sitting by the window with a cold cup of coffee in her hands. I was in a hurry, energized for the first time in months.

I couldn't wait to loop her in. But there was something that slowed me down. Her eyes were moving, but she was absent. Body. Mind. Spirit. All disjointed.

She had never been so far away for so long from Spider. This was no accident.

Julièn's boys were playing soccer on the grass outside. Carly was watching them.

I sat across from her and poured myself a coffee.

"What are you doing here, Carly?" I asked her. We both knew Tiny didn't need to be escorted here to give me the news about Norestrom.

"Apparently you have a death wish. I came here to make sure you didn't get yourself killed. Or get Manny pregnant. Same difference."

One of the boys, the youngest one, ran for the soccer ball but forgot to stop when he got to it. He rolled over the ball and went soaring into the soft grass, making his brothers and his mother cackle. I thought of Emmy and chuckled. Carly remained detached.

"We both know you're not here for me," I said.

She turned her robotic gaze to me. "He got a vasectomy."

I remembered what Spider had said to me after Carly had miscarried—the last time Carly had miscarried. "I can't let her do this to herself anymore," was what he had said. I guess he had found a way.

"The funny thing is," Carly continued in thought, "he isn't the only one who can get me pregnant."

She said this as though Spider weren't the only one for her. I sighed.

"Not everybody is meant to have children." *Definitely not us,* I thought but didn't say.

"Julièn has kids. And he is the worst."

I couldn't deny that. But the boys—the three successors— were Julièn's trophies. He had provided the seed; this was the extent of his attachment. I was trying to find a way to explain this to Carly, but the usually subdued Tiny interrupted us.

"It's that guy. The ginger who used to work for us."

He leaned over his fat belly to get a better look at the screen.

I wouldn't have bothered to get up had it not been for Carly. She stared at me, wide-eyed, like she had surprised a bear in the bushes and was deciding whether she should run or scare him off.

I saw the screen just as that guard, whatshisname, came out through the archway under the stands. He bounced his way down to the ring.

I would have spotted her anywhere, even in an arena of thirty thousand screaming heads. And I had. I stopped moving, hypnotized by the small screen that was out of place in this European design. I sat on the uncomfortable couch and leaned over like Tiny.

The sports anchors talked about his knockout win. About Griffin the Grappler Connan. That was his name. Griff. The one who'd had his eye on Emmy. The one whose face I had wanted to kick in. Still wanted to.

The Grappler's triumphant return to the ring wasn't the real news, though. What he had done afterward was. He had run out of the ring. Before shaking his dumbfounded opponent's hand as a show of respect for the sport. Before the referee had raised his hand and officially declared him the winner. Before the belt had been looped around his waist.

Before Griffin the Grappler Connan had had a chance to celebrate his win, he had run out on all of them and into the crowd. Stepping over fans, to get to this unknown girl. The camera honed in on them—she was in his arms.

The picture stilled and diminished to a floating image between the heads of the two jocks reporting sports. *The real knockout*, the caption read under Emmy's face as the anchors giggled craftily. They moved on to the next highlight. They could do that—move on. As though this were just another day in the office.

Tiny had already quietly disappeared from the suite. Only Carly and I remained.

"This?" I shouted, grabbing my head in both hands. "This was your plan to keep Emmy safe? Send her into the arms of that … of that …" I was shaking my head, trying to erase the image of Emmy's arms around that bastard's neck.

Not him. Not him and her. He wasn't good enough for her. Those arms, that skin of hers, smooth, silky, around him.

Carly cocked her head and fought back angry tears. When she spoke, I realized it was me she was angry with. "This was what you wanted, wasn't it? For her to be safe? For her to move on without you? She's moved on. I did what you asked me to."

"She deserves better than him." She deserved … me. The better version of me. The one who had gone to MIT. The one she had met on the street and fallen in love with over a candlelit dinner.

"You left her. She deserves to love. *And* be loved back. And he loves her, Cameron. I saw it. The first time I spotted them together at the Farm. So did you. That was why you were in such a big hurry to get rid of him."

I was about to tell Carly about getting Emmy back, like she had wanted me to do, asked me to do, but she beat me to the punch.

"This life … no one wants this life. I miss her too, Cameron. But did you see? How good Emmy looked? She's happy. Griff makes her happy. He's a good man. He'll protect her. He'll put her first."

I never thought I would want to punch a girl so much, let alone one of my best friends.

I had to breathe. I had to focus on every breath.

Carly was right. He was a good man. And I was scum. Emmy. She was smiling, beaming. When he had come to her. She looked more beautiful than I had ever seen her. It was as though she were shining. Glowing under the camera lights.

Happy? Emmy was happy? Emmy had moved on?

She had found someone else, someone of her own kind, almost.

She had done exactly what I had asked her to do. For once in her beautiful life, she had done exactly what I wanted ...

She wasn't coming back.

And I wasn't bringing her back.

She didn't belong with me. I was an idiot to think, to have thought that we were meant to be. I was an idiot to have hoped.

As I turned to Carly, I had solidified and my heart had deadened. "It would be best if you left immediately."

"What?" she asked, even though she had clearly heard what I said.

"Go with Tiny. That's an order."

She kept a steely gaze on me. Then she nodded once.

I grabbed the doorknob, left the room, and went to knock on another door.

Manny was still in her nightie when she appeared through her doorway. She placed her hand on my chest, and I pushed my way inside.

Broken hearts are for fucking saps.

## Chapter 17: Emily

## Broken Promises

Frances and I pulled up to a gray skyscraper in the core of downtown. It was a busy street, with no parking in sight. We were blocking traffic, and cars were honking behind us. I rushed out of the car, and Frances took off in search of parking.

Joseph had found Frances pretty quickly for me. Like half an hour quickly. I'd waited for Griff to come back from his celebrations and sneaked out as soon as he had conked out on his mattress, which was about two minutes after he had come through the door with the rest of the drunken clan.

Frances lived in a ritzy apartment building downtown. The doorman looked at me a little strangely as I walked to the stairs—then again, my walk was more of a waddle these days. After several unanswered knocks on Frances's door, I sank to the ground and rested against her door, ready to wait as long as it took.

When her door opened, I rolled back like a beach ball, my head hitting her welcome mat, my legs splayed in the air, like Humpty Dumpty falling off his wall.

I peered up at Frances, who was in a silk kimono.

"Emily?"

I rolled back up and brushed myself off while Frances recovered from the shock. There was an old man in a suit standing behind her. If disease had a face, it was his; he was ugly but looked harmless enough.

"My sister," she stammered to him.

He kissed her on the cheek, keeping his eye on me, or rather on my nonblonde sisterly hair color. As soon as he was out of sight down the hall, her charmed grin left her lips, and she dragged me into her apartment, slamming the door.

"Did anyone see you come here?"

"I need your help."

I pulled my poncho aside, revealing my secret belly.

Frances brought her hand to her mouth.

After I handed her the mostly erased business card that Carly had given me and asking for her help in finding the underworld accountant, she had hesitated.

"Emily," she started, "the baby. Is it—"

"It's mine," I said sternly. "All mine. Are you going to help me or not?"

As the blood left her face, she sat down on the arm of her ivory chaise and grabbed one of the whisky glasses sitting on the coffee table.

"You really shouldn't be here," she said over the rim of her glass.

I took a chance sitting on the fragile glass coffee table and reached for her arm.

"Do you remember asking me if Bill had left me any money? Well, it turns out he has left me all of it. This accountant can help me get the money."

She was still shaking her head and looked at my face and at my stomach until her gaze turned to empty space.

****

Twenty-four hours later, I had a name, an address, and a ride downtown.

A northern gust was blowing people away, but I was steady

on my feet. I held my poncho tight to my body and ran into the building. There was a manned information kiosk in the middle of the lobby that I ignored. I walked up to the golden plaque on the wall and looked for the name I had been searching for so long: Henry Grimes. He was on the eighth floor.

I spun on my heels and waited for Frances. She had insisted on coming in with me. "Emmy," she had said, "this man that you are going to see manages money for the biggest drug dealers, murderers in the country. You are pregnant, and you are not going in there by yourself."

And so I was waiting. People in business suits were filtering by me and cramming into the elevators. I was wringing my hands, feeling how close I was to retribution and to my freedom.

I took another look around. No Frances.

There was a large clock on the wall. I watched as the seconds ticked away, each one feeling like a lifetime. I started to tread toward the elevators like a mosquito to a porch light.

I couldn't wait for Frances to get there. I couldn't wait for anyone else, for anything else.

I got stuffed into the elevator with the rest of the traffic and was luckily the first to get off.

Goose bumps ran up and down my arms; I wasn't sure if it was because of the excitement or because the eighth floor reminded me of a school hallway. The plastered walls, the wooden arches, brought back memories of getting run over by girls who were prettier, smarter, more popular than me. Part of me wanted to scurry through and find an empty bathroom stall, any spot to hide. But that part of me had been slowly getting snuffed out in these last few months. And now it was gone. I wasn't that nervous, insulated target anymore. My name was Emily Sheppard. My brother had been Bill Sheppard, once king of the underworld. I was going to be a mother. I was carrying Cameron's child—Cameron, who had also been king of the underworld. Now I was going to take a piece of the world for myself and my child.

While office workers shuffled through the hallway, I advanced to door 10E without fear and with my head held high.

There was no name on the door, but I didn't doubt myself. I had read correctly on the golden plaque downstairs.

I turned the knob and let myself into what looked like a small waiting room, except that there were no chairs, no front desk or assistant. I made my way across the blood-red carpet and opened the next door.

A beast of a man sat behind a small cheap oak desk. He was wearing a suit that looked like it had fit him three sizes ago. His hair was buzz-cut into a lopsided geometric form, something that would have been all the rage in the eighties. Clearly, this accountant for the underworld was still living in the past.

Although Henry Grimes hadn't seemed surprised to see the door open without a knock, his expression turned quizzical as he peered over his paperwork and saw that I was the one who had opened it.

I took a seat in front of him. "My name is Emily Sheppard," I announced, having practiced this meeting so many times in my head. "I was sent here by someone named Carly."

Henry Grimes leaned back in his chair, lacing his sausage fingers over a well-fed belly.

This reminded me of my own basketball belly, and I tugged at the edge of my poncho to ensure that my own belly remained hidden. I felt as though Henry and I had met before, as if I had seen him somewhere. There was definitely something familiar about him, though I couldn't figure it out.

"Bill Sheppard's sister," he said, as though he were trying to convince himself of this. "Carly did mention that you would be coming to see me. But that was a long time ago. A few months at least."

I took the angel pendant off my neck and placed it in front of him. "I need access to the money my brother left me."

He immediately flipped the angel over and looked at the code under it, and then he smiled, a genuine, wholehearted smile. He had obviously seen this pendant before.

"When Bill told me about his plan to inscribe your inheritance onto this cheap piece of hardware, I honestly thought it would never come back. He must have known you well enough to know that you would hold on to it without knowing what its true meaning was."

Of course I had held on to it. It was the last thing Bill had given me before he died. I held on to it as though Bill were trapped somewhere in it, like a genie in a bottle.

This man had met, had conversed, and had laughed with Bill ... I had to tighten every muscle of my face to keep my emotions at bay.

Henry wrote numbers down on a piece of paper. "I can't get the money for you." He gave me back the angel pendant and held his other hand up before I could start shouting all the vicious names that were bouncing around my head. I couldn't handle any more spikes in the road.

"The codes that your brother had inscribed on your necklace are mine. He made sure that, as an additional safeguard, you would have to come through me in order to get the bank account numbers." He handed me the piece of paper. The numbers on it looked like the account numbers the bank manager had shown me some time ago.

"You wouldn't be able to get the money without these numbers," Henry explained, though I had already figured this out.

I took a calming breath and considered the information. "You said that this was an additional safeguard. Meaning there is more than one safeguard?"

"There was always the risk that someone else would try to have your money moved without your knowledge. You do realize how much money is at stake here?"

"Sure, sure."

"Bill set up the account so that you and only you would be able to have it unlocked."

He waited.

I looked up at the sky. "I have to go to the Cayman Islands myself, don't I?"

"If you want your money." He laughed, not knowing what a spectacular inconvenience it would be for this pregnant lady to board a plane to the tropics.

I sighed.

"Your brother was very fond of you, Emily. And I was very fond of your brother. If there were any other way, I would have found it for you. Consider this a vacation."

"A vacation," I whispered to myself, unsure if I was going to cry or laugh.

I got up from my chair in a daze, but as I grabbed the door handle, I realized that I had forgotten something crucial. While I had practiced this moment many times in my head, this part I hadn't really figured out yet. But having met Henry Grimes, my next move was clear. I turned around and opened my mouth.

"I won't tell anyone you were ever here," he said before I could ask him.

I closed the door and said a little prayer as I walked across the carpet through the empty waiting room. If everything he had said was true and he had cared for my brother, then I had to trust him. But if he had lied, then I had very little time to act.

I waited for the elevator and saw two men—the shady clients Henry must have actually been waiting for—go into his office.

When the elevator doors opened, Frances jumped out with a crazed expression. I dragged her by the arm back into the elevator. Unfortunately, I dragged us into an elevator that was going up instead of down.

"Did you already meet the accountant?" she asked me when we were finally alone and on our way down.

"He couldn't get the money," I whispered, which seemed appropriate even if there was no one else who could hear us. "But there's still a way for me to get it."

As the doors opened and more people got on, she watched me, taking this in.

Frances left me outside to go fetch the car, sprinting. She'd had to park two blocks down.

I stood in the cold, rubbing my hands together under my poncho and jumping from one foot to the other. The frigid Callister weather was inhumane. Maybe a trip to the islands wouldn't be so bad after all. When the baby kicked me as I was thinking this, I took it as a sign that we needed to go.

I was trying to keep warm by getting my mind working, figuring out how I was going to pay for this trip and how I was going to tell Griff about what I had been up to. He had left me this morning for a day of interviews with the media and potential sponsors. I had to pretend I was too sick to go with him. It took me a while to convince him to go without me.

I turned to face the building, afraid that I was going to see Henry having changed his mind and coming after me. I also didn't know how much time I had if he broke his so-called promise and alerted Carly and Spider to my calling. I didn't know if Spider would even care, given that Carly had tried to give me all of Cameron's money anyway, which was probably ten times more than what Bill had achieved in his short life.

While I was busy working my brain, I hadn't noticed that someone had been watching me from the entrance of Henry's building. She was holding on to the door as people shoved past her, her eyes fixed on me. I was in a trance as I saw her, unable to move. At first her expression was that of disbelief, as was mine. Could it really be her, or was I imagining this?

She broke the spell and moved toward me. This wasn't just happening in slow motion ... Carly was moving slowly, every step seeking validation.

A gust of wind twirled around us, grabbing my poncho with it. Her eyes went down to my rounded and now exposed belly, and she stopped. I managed to pull my poncho back down, but the damage was already done.

I had expected the anger, the hate, the murderous glare at this new revelation. But what I saw scared me even more. Carly's eyes were hungry, as if she had been starved, deprived from birth. And the blood rushed from my face.

I took one small step back, as if I were trying to charm a cobra out of a bite. Carly just stared back.

I turned around and walked away, desperately seeking Frances's car.

Carly came to grab me by the shoulder.

"Is this true? Are you pregnant?"

I glared back and held my head high because I was Emily Sheppard.

She reached her hand over. "And it's Cameron's."

"Stay away from me," I hollered over the wind and took a step back.

Carly's expression was one of surprise, and she pulled her hand away as if getting burned.

I started walking as fast as my belly would allow in the direction I thought I had seen Frances go. I turned onto the first street, realizing it was just an alleyway where garbage collected, a dead end. After a few seconds of freedom, Carly came running after me. I could have screamed bloody murder, but there was no one left around to hear me over the wind. So I spun around to face her.

"Don't you think you've done enough to me? You, Spider, don't you think I've suffered enough?"

I could tell that Carly wanted to say something. Yet nothing came out of her mouth.

"Just let me be, Carly. I've moved on. Let *us* be. You'll never have to worry about us again." I clenched my teeth as a tear unwillingly escaped. I immediately swiped at it, as though it too had betrayed me.

Carly grabbed her forehead with two fingers as if I were giving her a migraine, and her eyes went from my covered stomach to my face.

"Please," I begged.

Then she took a piece of paper from her pocket and gave it to me. "This is my number. We need to talk, but not here. Not like this."

I had no answer.

She grabbed my hand. "Promise me you'll call me the minute you get home!"

My eyes were round. "Okay."

I started to peddle back, keeping my eyes on her until I reached the main street again.

Frances's car pulled up, and I hopped in before she had even fully stopped.

"Go. Go! Now!" I shouted before Carly could see who was in the car with me. The less she knew, the better.

Frances stepped on the gas, and we peeled.

"Was that who I think it was?" she asked me.

I cracked the window and let Carly's number fly in the wind. "Can you lend me some money?"

"Sure," she said, too slowly. "What's going on?"

"To answer your first question, yes, that was Carly. And what's going on is that I need to go to the Cayman Islands. That's where the money is, and it won't be released unless I go there myself. In person."

"Does Carly know that—"

"She knows now. And soon enough, the rest of her world will also know that I'm pregnant."

While Frances considered this information, I wished she would drive faster. "I don't have a lot of time before they all come for me."

"Of course, I'll lend you the money, but I need a bit of time to make arrangements," she said, gripping the wheel.

"What kind of arrangements do you need to make?"

"I think I'm coming with you," she said with hesitation. Then she turned to me and smiled. "I'm not going to let a pregnant lady fly by herself."

While I really didn't want or need any company, there was no time for disagreements. Plus Frances was lending me the money. How could I refuse her company?

"How much time do you need?" I wondered.

She considered this and shot a glance at the phone on the console before answering. "A couple hours?"

I sighed. "Okay. Drop me off at home, and I'll meet you at the airport."

After Frances left me on the curb, I shot into the house and went digging for my passport. Griff was still out, and I was extremely grateful for this. What I was about to do, I knew he wouldn't just disapprove; he would try to stop me from moving forward. But I just couldn't stop.

I ripped a page from my notebook and stared at it for a while. I put the tip of the pen to the paper.

*"I'm going to the Cayman Islands to seek the fortune that my brother left me so that I can start a pharmaceuticals black-market business, take over the underworld, and make everyone who ever hurt me pay. And this after I promised you that I was over all of this revenge stuff. Oh, and Spider now knows that I'm pregnant and will now be coming after me with everything he's got."*

This was the truth. This was what I had promised Griff I would always tell him. The truth.

But the truth wasn't what I wrote.

*"My Mom is really sick."* (True, in a sense.) *"She's in the hospital."* (Not true, even though it should be.) *"I have to go see her."* (Definitely not true.) *"I'll call you as soon as I get there."* (If by *there*, I meant Cayman Islands, then yes, this was true. Though I wasn't looking forward to that phone call.)

I placed the note on his pillow.

Before heading back out the door, I left Joseph a quick, simple note to take care of Meatball and grabbed the envelope of cash Maria and Darlene had left me. Two hundred bucks was all that was left.

I had a few precious minutes before meeting Frances at the

airport. I used them to go see my big ball of meat. Meatball was still under heavy drugs, snoring in a corner of the veterinary clinic. I had brought the yellow comforter from my bed so that he'd have something that smelled like us when he awoke.

Even though he had no idea, I hugged him as though it were the last time I would ever see him. I rubbed under his chin. I rubbed behind his ears. Even though he had no idea.

I was distracted. And driving through an airport when distracted was a really bad idea. The million one-way lanes that led in circles, the million parking lots—green P, red P, blue P—for each and every damn terminal! After going around in circles, expending a ridiculous amount of the fuel I couldn't afford, and now running very late, I finally pulled up to a lot only to realize I was in the airport staff parking lot.

Frances had booked us on a flight at noon. It was already eleven o'clock, and I hadn't even checked in or gone through security.

A car pulled up behind me, so that I couldn't back out. I got out of the car, smiled, and waddled over. After a sob story of forgetting my parking pass and being very late for work, I got into the parking lot using the card of the maintenance guy behind me and scored a quick ride on his buggy to Terminal 3. Frances practically lifted me off my feet to drag me to the Cayman Airways' check-in desk.

"Make sure you hide your belly," she whispered to me as I was pulling my passport out. "They won't let you on if they know how far along your pregnancy is."

After a suspicious glance from security at my bulge, we barely made our flight.

While I sighed with relief as the plane took off, Frances was digging her fingernails into the arms of her seat. Apparently, self-assured Frances was a nervous flier. There were a lot of things that I had learned about Frances in the short time we had spent together.

"That man who came out of your apartment, was he your boyfriend?" I wondered in a whisper.

"I guess."

"He seems a little old for you."

"He's been kind to me."

"Do you have many of these *kind* boyfriends?"

She had no response.

When I had gone into Frances's apartment, one thing had struck me: how very lovely and impersonal it was. It looked like a hotel suite. There were no pictures of her. And no pictures of her child. The fact that Daniel didn't live with her was not because she didn't care for him; it was because she didn't want him in her world.

"You're too beautiful to be doing what you're doing," I told her.

With wistful eyes, Frances watched the stewardess pass us with a drink cart. "What else am I going to do, Emily? I barely graduated from high school. All I have to offer is something nice to look at."

"Is that all you do? Give them something nice to look at? Or is it more than that?" The term *escort with benefits* seemed a little more appropriate for the circumstances.

"The kind of guys whom I have to hang around with are not interested in playing house with me. At least I get paid for doing something I'm good at. Whatever money I get, I send to Daniel. For a time when I will have absolutely nothing else to offer."

"Or for a time when you come back to your son in a body bag."

"You play the cards that have been handed to you. Daniel's better off without me in his life. At least he'll never have to worry about money like I have."

It was hard for me to imagine that a beautiful girl like Frances could think so little of herself.

"What happened to the money my brother left you?"

Her lips stretched thin. "Gone."

"How?"

The second flight attendant came up with a drink cart. Frances ordered a double vodka.

"What happened to the money?" I asked her again.

"I suppose one can call it a business deal gone bad."

"You mean someone took the money from you. One of your *kind* boyfriends?" I regretted saying this as soon as the words came out of my mouth.

Frances took one small sip of her drink as though testing it, and then brought the plastic glass back to her lips, downing the rest of her double vodka in one gulp. It didn't matter how she had lost the money. The fact was that it was gone and that she needed to prostitute herself to keep food on the table. I was a self-righteous rich girl.

The flight was only about four hours. As the plane prepared for landing, I turned to Frances. "This money. It should be yours and Daniel's. Not mine. You know I would give it all to you if I could. Right?"

Frances smirked as she straightened her back and pulled on her blouse to get the travel wrinkles out. "Of course. I understand—"

"I'm not finished. I can't give you all of the money *right now*. But I can split it with you and with Daniel. You can each have a third of whatever money Bill left behind. I'll take the other third. I don't know how much that will be, but whatever I do take, I will pay you back as soon as I possibly can." I knew Bill would have probably wanted me to keep at least some of the money, but I knew I could make my own. I wouldn't need it forever. Frances would.

She frowned. "Why would you ever do that? You barely know me or my son."

I waited for her to look at me before answering. "I don't know what it's like to have a real family. I lost it all when Bill died. But Daniel is Bill's son; he has some of Bill in him. That makes us family." While Frances went quiet, I chuckled. "Don't worry. I won't show up uninvited to your Christmas dinner or Easter-egg hunt. But I just want you to know that as far as I'm concerned, you're part of my family."

Until the plane landed, Frances hadn't said a word to me, but kept glancing my way. I glanced back every time, looking her in the eyes.

"You're serious, aren't you?" she finally said as passengers grabbed their carry-ons from the overhead compartments. "You would actually give us all that money. No strings attached."

"Not would. *Will*. What's mine is yours."

She looked at me for a while, though it felt more as though she were looking through me.

We had two hours to get out of the airport and to the bank before it closed, and Frances was walking so slowly she was practically going backward. You'd think I'd never offered her all of Bill's money. I thought I was going to scream when she said she needed to use the washroom, but she looked like she was going to be sick so I resisted.

When she finally returned from the washroom, I expected her to be in full Oscar attire, but she actually looked worse than when she had walked in.

"You're looking a little green," I noted.

She winced. "Last night's pizza is coming back to haunt me."

Luckily, Caribbean taxi drivers are as crazy as they are in the States. We got dropped off in George Town in front of the bank with time to spare.

Cayman International Bank seemed small on the outside, but as soon as you walked in, you could smell the money. The floor was of white and burgundy marble tiles, each big enough to fit an entire car; gold-sprayed columns adorned the sides, and the Caribbean sun came reaching through the domed ceiling. It reminded me of St. Peter's Basilica in the Vatican, though perhaps the god being worshiped here (money) was a little different. Perhaps not.

At the end of the church of money, where the pope would have sat, was a gray marble counter with clerks standing behind it. And there was an over-the-hill security guard practically falling asleep at a small desk posted by the entrance. I could see a couple of younger guards having a smoke in the small storage room behind him. Maybe what I smelled wasn't money, but tobacco and arsenic.

When Frances and I walked to one of the clerks at the counter, I handed him my passport and the piece of paper that Henry Grimes had written on. The clerk had what seemed like fourteen extra letters after his name—bachelors, masters, doctorate—and I could have sworn all the clerks were wearing matching gray Armani suits. These clerks were not the minimum-wage, cleavage-busting clerks of Callister City Bank. Still, they looked just as bored.

"There's a password on the account, Miss," the clerk told me, trying to withhold a yawn.

"What do you mean?"

"There's a password on the account," he repeated, because saying exactly the same thing twice was enough explanation.

"You need me to tell you the password?"

He arched his brows and forced a smile, as though I shouldn't have been let outside my padded room.

"How many tries do I get?"

He looked at me strangely.

I stepped away and found an empty seat so that I could think.

Frances scanned around and sat next to me, grabbing my elbow. "What's the password, Emily?"

It was hard to think when she was pressing me like that. "Give me a minute."

I put my face into my hands, closed my eyes, and let the images flash through my brain. My childhood. My unorganized, immature, fart-jokes big brother. The feeling of isolation, of abandonment after Bill died. The feeling of having that last bit of laughter stolen from me with his last breath. Being angry at him for leaving me (for dying). Being angry at him for leaving me a stupid pendant, as though it was supposed to be enough to replace him. Feeling guilty for feeling all that I was feeling and for not having been there to hold him, to comfort him when he died.

I went back to that day—that last day, that last hour, that last minute—Bill trying to smile as he handed me the stupid angel pendant. Bill telling me, telling me, telling ... What the hell did he tell me again? I searched my brain, trying to find a small needle hidden in a stack of painful memories. "Hold on to this and don't ever forget about it," he had said. I took the pendant into my hand and pressed it in until it left an imprint in the skin of my palm. But that wasn't what he had meant. We were sitting on my bed, and he had brought something else of his from his room. Something else that was totally valueless. A stinky, disheveled bear. It only had one eye. And my brother had named it Booger.

My eyes shot open.

I sprang from my seat and got to the desk of the excessively educated clerk just as he was pulling out his closing sign. "Booger. The password is booger."

The guy at the counter scoffed, swung his head to the screen, and typed in the word he had probably not said aloud since he was five years old.

I could see that the screen had changed color from the reflection that bounced off his face.

He cocked his head to the side. He looked at me, he looked at the screen, he looked at me again.

"Please excuse me for a minute." He hopped away and into an office, where he took a seat and spoke to a man in an even more expensive suit. They both glanced back at me simultaneously.

"You got it wrong," Frances whispered feverishly to me, as though I hadn't already figured this out myself.

"What's going to happen now?" I wondered.

Frances glanced around her, her eyes stopping at the front entrance. Two men were on alert, watching us. They were dressed in jeans and suit jackets, as though this was supposed to make them look like regular Joes who were supposed to blend in with us, the other regular Joes. They reminded me of mystery shoppers or undercover rent-a-cops.

"Miss Sheppard?" a voice disrupted our worst thoughts. The

man from the office had come out to the desk. With an open palm, he bade me to follow him. Frances and I marched ahead.

"I'm sorry. We only allow the account holders in the safe room."

Frances held on to my arm protectively. But I couldn't turn back now. It was like driving for months to get to the Grand Canyon and keeping your eyes closed when you got there. My eyes were wide-open.

"It's okay. I'll be okay," I told her. After all, a room that was dubbed "safe" couldn't be too dangerous—could it?

She held on to me for a second longer, then let me go.

The so-called safe room consisted of a beige-walled room with a table and a chair. I was left alone for a few minutes until the man came back with a metal box.

He placed it in front of me and opened it to reveal a container made of some kind of foam.

"The box is sealed. Once the seal is broken, all contents must be removed. We are not responsible for any forgotten items." He said this mechanically. A speech prepared by overpaid lawyers. "Do you recognize the signature, Miss Sheppard?"

I smiled as he pointed to the signature on the seal. "I do." It was Bill's.

He cracked the foam as though splitting open a thoracic cage. He left, closing the door behind him.

Inside, there were two envelopes. I ripped open the first one—the thicker one. I would have deemed myself a rich woman had it not been filled with pieces of paper. Parking receipts, movie tickets, a bubble-gum wrapper, a piece of paper with a telephone number and the name Brandi with a heart over the "i" written on it. I pulled each piece out, one by one, until I came to a letter-sized, sealed envelope. It was addressed to Carly.

I gritted my teeth and opened the second envelope. Two more sealed, skinny envelopes lay inside. One was addressed to me, the other to Cameron. I immediately opened mine.

It wasn't money. It was a letter. In Bill's messy, half-illegible handwriting.

"*Emmy*," it started.

I hungrily started drinking in his words, knowing that the bank was about to close. Each word, each revelation sank me deeper into my brother's mind and into his screwed-up world.

I didn't even hear Frances come in until she grabbed my arm and shook me awake.

"How did you get in?" I asked, stuffing the letter back in the envelope.

"I snuck in while they were busy with a rush of customers. Looked like all the local business owners wanted to do their ridiculous insignificant money deposits before the weekend," she said with a smirk. "Did you get our money?"

I saw her. For the first time, I saw her. The wench. The goddamn greedy, deceitful, murderous bitch.

"There is no money. Just letters. Sentimental stuff."

The man who had let me into the room appeared in the doorway, throwing annoyed glances in Frances's direction. "Only the account holder is permitted in this room. I'm calling security to have you escorted out."

"We're leaving," I snapped.

"Please ensure you have collected all your belongings before exiting the room. We are not responsible for forgotten items."

I left nothing behind.

"My cell phone died while I was talking to my mom. Can I borrow yours?" Frances asked me as we made our way back to the front of the bank. The face of an angel. A wolf in lamb's clothing—designer clothing.

She glanced at the two envelopes in my hand. I gave her my cell phone, knowing that she would be grabbing for the envelopes next.

I could have screamed. I could have yelled, "*There are bad people after me!*" The police would have been called. People would have been questioned. I would have been questioned. More time would have been wasted. In the meantime, the underworld would be looking for me, and the first place they would go searching would be the last place the whole world had seen me: on television, hugging Griff the Grappler Connan. After Griff had hopped out of the ring, it had made headlines across sports news networks the next day—our faces splashed everywhere as the joke of the day.

The more time I spent answering questions, the less time I had to get back to Griff before they did. And I definitely didn't want the police involved in my and my big brother's nefarious affairs.

"How could you?" I asked Frances as I held my hand over the baby inside me. I wasn't crying. I was steaming, raging mad. Like an angry sea ready to swallow an entire ship.

I looked Frances in the eye. She glanced longingly at my belly and let her hand slip down to her own empty womb while she gripped my wrist even harder with her other hand. She said, "Imagine having one of your limbs ripped from you and watching it, *feeling it* grow on someone else like it was never yours in the first place. Then imagine being handed the opportunity to get it back."

"You mean, buy it back. With Bill's money. With me and my child."

Her mouth stretched thin. "You don't know what it's like to have your child taken from you. Love for your child being used against you, making you do the very worst just on the promise of being able to see your baby for a few minutes every week. Years go by, and your child doesn't even know you're his mother."

"Victor did that to you. And now you're making it happen to me? Is this some kind of retribution?"

"You'll do anything for your child. I'm no different than you."

"I don't deserve this, Frances. My baby doesn't deserve this."

She sneered. "Have you ever even had a cavity, Emily Sheppard?"

It always came down to that, didn't it? My so-called charmed life. The life that would make me deserve misery for the rest of my days. And now make my unborn child deserve this same misery.

I followed Frances's gaze to the front of the lobby.

The two jeaned mystery shoppers I had seen earlier had their eyes fixed on me. They didn't work for the bank, I realized. They worked for Frances; rather, they worked for Victor. I noticed the hint of a gun peeking through one of the men's suit jackets.

The bank was about to close. Most of the doors of the bank had been locked, except for the one in the middle where the old guard stood, ensuring that no one else came in. Outside, past the windows and doors, traffic went to and fro, as though everything were fine. I stopped and turned to face Frances. Her features were cold and determined.

"How many men are with you?" I asked her.

"I had no other choice, Emmy. Someday, you'll understand that."

As she called me Emmy, I wanted to spit in her face. "How many?"

"Other than the two waiting for us at the door, there are two more waiting by the car outside. There's nowhere for you to go."

"And Victor?"

"He was in Canada when you came around and couldn't make it back on time. He was afraid you were going to disappear with the money if we didn't stay close. Besides, there are too many cameras in the bank and at the airport. He couldn't risk being seen when this happened. But he's waiting for you in Callister."

"He likes to get pretty girls to do his dirty work. That man is all bravery," I said with an indignant smirk.

The same knowing smirk came to Frances's lips.

"At least you'll have a good alibi," I told her.

A quizzical look came over her face, right before I yanked my upturned hand to her expensive nose, feeling it break under the pressure of my palm. I followed this by twisting my whole body, the way that Griff had showed me, to get my wrist out of her grasp.

While Frances tried to recover, I ran toward the sole exit, directly in the path of the two men. They took a few steps forward and smiled apathetically at me.

"Oh my God! Those men have guns! Everybody get down," I shouted at the top of my lungs, pointing my dainty finger at the men out front. There were screams from the patrons in the back.

My voice was so loud that the old security guard was already running on his slow feet, pointing his gun at the two men before he had even fully woken. An alarm went off just as I got to the door that was being held open by a customer—who had probably been happy to see the guard leave so that he could sneak in and get his banking done before the bank closed but was now standing in a stupor at the action unfolding in front of his eyes. From my peripheral vision, I could see that two more guards had come to take down my intended abductors. Once I was on the street, I did a quick glance to my left and right. A woman was stepping out of a taxi a few feet away. Two men were running toward me, and I was already winded from my run out of the bank. But I ran, mustering up every inch of breath I possibly could. I was within the men's grasp as I reached the taxi, barreling onto the backseat.

"I'm out of service," the driver tried to tell me. But I had already thrown my last two hundred dollars at him after locking the passenger door.

"Airport. Quickly. Please," I said, holding my pregnant stomach.

Our gazes met in his rearview mirror, and he sped forward, leaving two angry men on the sidewalk.

It should have taken us an hour and a half to get to the airport. But forty-five minutes later, I was in the terminal and threw my passport at the airport attendant. "Next flight to Callister, New York."

Pain shot down my back and into my legs, making my knees buckle. I had to hold on to the edge of the counter.

The woman behind the counter got on her tiptoes and looked over.

"How far along are you?"

"I'm desperate," I told her, trying not to cry. I felt as though the world were watching. Every passerby who happened to look in my general direction was the face of an impending enemy. Trying to lie to her while keeping an eye out for the world was too much.

The woman watched me. She had a ring on her finger, her hair was pushed back in a tight bun, and she was of my mother's age. My heart sank.

She kept my passport in hand. "You're already booked for a flight in three hours, Miss Sheppard."

"It's Emily," I snarled. If one more person addressed me as Miss, I was going to tip over the edge. "And I know. I'm asking you for your earliest flight. When is that?"

"They have already boarded." She arched her brow. "Does your mother know where you are, dear?"

I laughed, and a tear escaped the edge of my eye. I was exhausted, physically, emotionally. My head fell into my hands while she kept on working, typing, picking up the phone, muttering as though my life didn't depend on her.

It was only a few minutes later when I heard, "Ma'am?" This time it was a male voice. I couldn't raise my head, but a tap on the shoulder forced me to. An airport usher was standing next to a cart. "We can get you through security immediately. The plane is waiting on the tarmac for you."

I turned to the attendant behind the desk.

She smiled. Like a mother would, should. "Have a nice flight, Emily."

Despite my waddle, I was afforded several nasty glares on my way to find my seat on the plane. I was sitting between two old ladies. While they bickered over me, loud enough so that their hearing aids could pick their voices out of the crowded plane, I opened Bill's letter to me once again, savoring every blotch of ink.

*Emmy,*

*How do you start writing a letter when you know your words will be your last, be the final voice, the final time your little sister will hear from you? I can tell you that there are not enough words in this world when you know they are your last.*

*I hated you. I never told you this, but when you were born, I hated* you and wished you would die. Your mom pranced you around—this thing that was covered in pink frills—as though you were the Second Coming. My mom had just died, and nobody cared; they came to see you and celebrated. They wouldn't let me anywhere near you, which was fine with me because all you did was cry and cry and cry. Anytime anyone picked you up, anytime visitors came around, you cried.

Eventually, they all got sick of you crying and disappeared. You were alone in your room. You were screaming as usual. It was the middle of the night. I went up to your crib with Booger. I dragged a chair and peered over your bassinette. I put Booger next to your face, not sure if I was going to put him over your face. You stopped crying. You looked at me and stared. I put my finger in, and you grabbed it and shook it. I never left you after that. You cried with everyone else. Never with me. You had my heart the minute you looked up at me. No one has ever looked at me the way you did. The way you still do.

That's why I wish that you never see this letter. Because it means that you know. About me. About what your dumb brother has done, has become. And this, above all the other shit, makes me feel sick. I never wanted you anywhere near this life that I've created for myself.

Too little, too late, I guess.

I suppose there is one silver lining: Cameron. He was the only one who could have led you here. He's a good kid. Trust him. I left an envelope for him. Please make sure he gets it.

You have likely come here looking for money. There is lots. I hope you can find something good to do with it. I never could. Unfortunately, the money is not here, as you likely expected it to be. Bad people will be looking for this money, and I will get to that in a minute, but I have placed one more obstacle for you. The reason I have done this is obviously to keep your money as safe as possible, and because I want you to find someone who has grown to take the other piece of my heart. Her name is Carlita Fernandes ... but don't ever call her that to her face, and please don't tell her I told you her real name or she'll hunt me down and kill me again. Her name is Carly. I know it's a dumb thing to say, but I really hope the two of you will like each other. Carly has so much to teach you, and she has so much love to give even though she has a strange way of showing it. If you think she hates you, then she probably loves you more than you know.

Now, about the money. You probably already opened the bigger of the two envelopes (you obviously haven't changed) and were probably disappointed to find scraps of paper. Do not throw these away! They are worth a lot of money. Take them to Carly. She will know what to do with them.

You will have a lot of questions as to my death. I won't be able to answer all of them because I simply don't know how I am going to die. I don't even know if they will leave a body behind for fear of discovery, of retaliation.

But there are things I need you to know so that you can keep yourself safe now that you have been exposed to my world.

You have likely heard from our dear parents of the trouble I have been in (since birth apparently), and you know that I was sent to live with my police-officer uncle, Victor. What you don't know is that Uncle Victor is no honorable soldier. He is deceitful and a sadistic criminal. He has dual personalities—the one he wants everyone to see and calls Victor, and the real one, named Shield. He had big plans about becoming lord of the underworld while keeping a grasp on the rest of the world. When I went to live with him, he immediately put me to work as his drug lackey and talked to me as though I were some dimwitted kid who had no idea how the underworld worked. Little did he know, I knew more about it than he did. He did have some good ideas, though, so I stood back and listened.

In the meantime, I was still going to high school, and I met this girl. Frances. She was hot. I won't gross you out with any further description. I'll just tell you that we dated for a while. It was nothing serious. I took her around with me. She met Uncle Victor, and his eyes practically popped out of his head when he saw her.

And then came Carly. There was no one else, I knew, after that. Unfortunately, she was tied to this guy named Spider. I tolerated him as long as she loved me. I immediately broke it off with Frances, and she disappeared. It wasn't like we were in love, but I was fond of her. She was a nice girl, and I wished her well.

*When the time came and with my best friends at my side, I reinvented the underworld. I had the worst of enemies sit at the same table with me at the helm and for one common goal: money. By getting the underworld to work together as one, we were making more money than ever. Sure, it was initially Victor's idea; I was the only one smart enough to make it happen, though.*

*However, Victor was not prepared to let me take over the spot he claimed as his. He went to the captains. He used his police authority to try to blackmail the lords of the underworld to have me dethroned. This backfired, and he was lucky they didn't sever his head from his shoulders.*

*I thought that was the end of Victor, until Frances came knocking at my door. Her face was beaten to a pulp. She was covered with bruises. And she was pregnant, with Victor's baby. While I had been busy taking over the underworld, Victor had used this time to woo Frances, blinding her with presents and money.*

*If I hadn't introduced them, if I hadn't been in Frances's life, none of this would have happened to her.*

*No one in my world knows that I am related to Victor, and I have kept it this way because I don't ever want to be associated with that bastard. We may look similar and have some of the same rotten blood in our veins, but as far as I'm concerned, we are not related. You, Carly, and Cameron are my only family. (Don't worry. Cameron will ensure that Victor never goes anywhere near you. I have asked him to watch over you; though, given that you know about our world, he didn't do a very good job. I may have to roll over in my grave and haunt his ass.)*

*At first, I thought I could hide Frances. I got her an apartment; I bought her groceries. I gave her money. But that wasn't what Frances wanted. She wanted what every mother-to-be wanted: for the father to love his child. I had had my suspicions. Frances wasn't a very good actress, and bruises kept appearing on her skin. When I saw the bruises on her belly, I knew this was going to end badly for her. I confronted her about Victor. She didn't deny that she'd been seeing him.*

*I never told anyone about Frances. I never told Carly about her, because I was ashamed of what I had done to Frances and because I wanted to keep my family ties with Victor a secret. Keeping such* huge secrets from the people you admire the most is like jumping out of an airplane without a parachute. You free-fall until you hit the ground. I was getting skittish and making decisions without really thinking. Everyone was suspicious; Spider, the idiot, even accused me of cheating on Carly in front of her.

Now I am on my way to meet Frances. She called me this morning, frantic, crying. She said that Victor had dragged her to a seedy motel in Callister and wanted her to work in his escort business. Apparently some of Victor's slum-of-the-earth clients like pregnant women.

My gut tells me that it's a trap and Victor will be waiting for me when I get there. He has been wooing some of the captains and must actually believe that if he takes me down, the captains will choose him as their leader.

They won't.

Cameron is and has always been my successor, even if he doesn't want it. He is brilliant.

My beautiful, smart little sister. As I'm writing this letter, I'm incredibly sad. Not because I know what's about to happen to me, but because I won't be there to watch you grow up to be the strong (stubborn) woman I know you will be. The fact that you're reading this letter means that, once again, you didn't listen to me, that you went looking for trouble and found it. I wish you would be more cautious, but that was never you. I love you so much, kid. Not a day goes by when I don't think about you or talk about you.

By the time this letter reaches the bank's coffers, I will have likely left this earth. If there is one thing I can impart to you before I am gone, it is to believe in yourself. You, more than anyone else I have ever known, can achieve anything you put your mind to. If only you could see yourself through my eyes, through the eyes of everyone who has ever encountered you, you would understand the effect you have on people.

*I love you. Be safe. B.*

P.S. I really wish I would have locked you in a tower before I died. Please make sure Cameron gets his envelope.

\*\*\*\*

The two old women flanking me on the plane were actually sisters, named Georgia and Beatrice. They were bachelorettes who had lived together their whole lives but couldn't stand sitting next to each other on a plane. They were off to visit their younger sister—who had been married (twice) and had a flock of kids and now grandkids. All ungrateful, all impolite, all of whom were coming to pick them up at the airport.

"I would love to meet them," I found myself saying.

They grinned.

I spent the next hour complimenting Georgia on her knitting. It looked like a blanket, but it was a shawl. The sisters enjoyed bonbons—these they did not share.

By the time the plane disembarked, I had a green scarf blanket on my red head and Georgia and Beatrice's arms scooped into each of mine. As they had promised, their sister's entire family immediately jumped for them, with flowers and banners. As all ungrateful, impolite family do.

We were surrounded as soon as we came into sight and led to the carousel in a tornado of hugs and chatter.

While I was introduced, I kept an eye out for Victor's men. There were a lot of people in the airport, many of whom wandered around looking for someone. Any of them or all of them could have worked for Victor. But no one seemed to have eyes on me. As far as the world was concerned, I was just another one of the fat old ladies. The third bachelorette.

I snuck away from the sisters' circle as we got to the parking lot, when I was sure we weren't being followed. Then I went to get my car, remembering that I had left it in the staff parking lot and that I had no way of getting out of there without a pass.

Once I got to the car, I sat behind the wheel for a second or two. Then I turned the ignition on, reversed and sped up to the parking arm without stopping. I watched the bits of wood and car fly in the air from my rearview mirror.

Despite being low on gas, I drove as fast as the Roadmaster would let me, but as I neared the corner of our street, something told me to slow down. A sixth sense that had been growing on me from the day I had met Cameron.

I immediately saw a police car parked in front of our house. I turned on the opposite side and parked close enough to see the house but far enough to keep out of sight.

There was a Callister City police officer at our door, talking to one of my roommates. It looked like it was Hunter. The officer looked agitated, swinging his arms, gesturing in time with his words. Hunter kept shaking his head in response, with a look mixed of fear and concern.

I was glad that Griff wasn't the one at the door. He probably wasn't home from his interviews yet. God only knows what he would have done if he had been confronted by these defectors.

Once upon a time, I swore that when given the opportunity to fight for love, I would. I swore that I would not disappear just to keep someone I loved, someone who loved me, safe. I swore I would never hurt someone the way Cameron had hurt me.

As I watched the officer leave the front porch, thwarted because he hadn't found me, and go back to his car to wait for me to come home, I did exactly what I swore I would never do.

I put the car in drive, and I left.

For Griff. For Meatball. Because they would be safe as long as they didn't try to fight Victor for me. Victor would leave them alone as long as I stayed away.

Penniless, running low on gas, I headed for the freeway.

I didn't have any time to waste. I had to keep driving.

I took one deep breath, then another. But each breath became shallower, getting pushed out by a devastation so deep I couldn't swim out of it. I pulled over to the side of the road and let my head fall against the steering wheel. I wanted to cry, so badly that my insides were hurting from my defiance. Every part of me was contorting.

In my peripheral vision, I caught sight of an envelope sitting peacefully on the passenger seat. It was clearly labeled "Cameron" in my brother's clumsy handwriting. I grabbed it and ripped the seal. (It wasn't like Cameron was ever going to read it.)

*Hey, Buddy,*
  *Stay the fuck away from my sister.*
*Sincerely, B.*

*P.S. Thanks for watching over her. Thanks for everything. But seriously, don't even think about it.*

I stared at the ink on the page. A snort escaped my throat. I smiled, and then I grinned. Then I was laughing so hard, cool gushers came strolling down my cheeks.

I put the car in drive and rolled away.

The car practically coasted to Cameron's cottage, as though it was hooked to a fishing line, getting reeled in. But halfway down the driveway, the Roadmaster officially ran out of gas. I got out and abandoned my car. I had forgotten how the blackness of night could consume everything out here. There was no moon and no stars to light my way, so I kicked at the pebbles to ensure that I was sticking to the driveway.

Eventually the trees cleared and my eyes adjusted enough to the darkness so that I could make it to the door.

I had gotten so used to the feeling of bleeding that I had stopped noticing the wetness. The problem was that when I turned the light to the kitchen on, I saw that this blood had already soaked my underwear and my pants. I was exhausted, but I was in no pain. I changed into some of Cameron's old clothes that he had left in a corner cabinet and went to lie down.

The agony did come. It was still dark when I was awoken by the excruciating pain in my back and pressure at the bottom of my abdomen. It felt as though my body were building up to explode. Or implode. I forced myself up and brought my hands to my stomach. I didn't need to have the light on to know that my blood had soaked the mattress.

As dynamite detonated inside me, I let out a scream, one that came from deep beneath, before falling back into the pillow.

Into the darkness.

****

I woke up again. My arms and legs were numb. I rolled over onto the floor and stretched one arm in front of me and then another, dragging myself to the stairs in an army crawl. I lifted my arm, trying to grab the rail.

Before rolling back into the darkness.

## Chapter 18: Cameron

## Lifeless

"A toast." Julièn raised his champagne glass, and the rest of the table followed his command. Mine was already empty. Manny refilled it, and I chugged it down while Julièn spoke.

"The great Winston Churchill once said that '*War must be, while we defend our lives against a destroyer who would devour all.*'" Julièn nodded at all of us, so that we could fully absorb the power of his words. The idiot had actually just quoted a passage from Tolkien's *Two Towers* novel. I poured myself another glass of champagne.

"Ladies. Gentlemen," he started again once the moment had passed. "Tonight, we have freed Mexico from the tyrants who have killed and stolen from us, filling their pockets with the people's money. Today is a day that will be marked in history as the day Mexico was returned to its people. May God have mercy upon our enemies, because I won't." He chuckled at his clever comment, which was actually a quote he had stolen from General Patton.

"Cheers!" I said, raising my empty glass, and glasses clinked around the table.

From the pout on Julièn's face, he wasn't done with his speech.

He took a sip and thankfully sat back down so that we could eat our damn meal.

My end had come after I had seen Emily with Griff, after I had gone to Manny's room and told her that I'd had a change of heart, in many respects. We were back on track—suicide mission. At exactly 4:00 a.m., tactical teams would be marching into bedrooms and assassinating the leadership for all three cartel families.

Julièn, Manny, and I would soon have control over all of Mexico's drug trade. But as far as "the people" were concerned, we had just cleaned house and ridded an entire country of its drug problem.

I could already feel the storm surging, like clouds darkening, billowing, merging above. As news of the change in command spread, the remaining cartel members would plan revenge, and a hundred others would see the fall of the leaders as their opportunity to appoint themselves as drug kingpins, each trying to out-shock the other. Murder, torture, theft ... this was nothing compared to the violence that was to come.

We had unleashed a torrent of power struggles. But we would never live long enough to see it happen.

While we were celebrating ourselves in San Luis Potosi, I wondered who would be first to come for us. The remaining cartel members—the ones who were loyal, who believed in the old tradition of an eye for an eye—or the wannabe kingpins?

It didn't matter. The end would come all the same.

The plates for the main course had finally started circulating around. Mine came in the form of a cell phone. I looked up cockeyed. There was a waitress. Young. Hot. Then there were three of her.

"You have a phone call," she yelled, as though she had told me this already. She came back to being only one of herself.

"You're like an accordion."

"The person on the line said it was urgent. Very urgent."

"What's your name?" was what I tried to ask her, though the words sounded more like "wazunayme."

The waitress gave me the phone and left.

Amused, I put the phone to my ear while I watched her tight ass leave the room.

"It's Carly," Carly announced on the line. "I've been calling your cell phone for hours. You haven't been picking up."

"There was champagne—"

"It's about Emily."

Like a punch in the face, I immediately sobered up.

\*\*\*\*

"I think she was with Frances," Carly murmured, as though she were the one who was sitting in a bathroom, hoping no one was trying to listen in. I had quickly stepped away without an explanation and knew that Manny was probably standing with a glass between her ear and the door. I had called Carly back on my cell phone because I couldn't trust Julièn at the best of times, and certainly not with this.

"What do you mean?"

"I mean, she got into a car. I can't be sure. They left so quickly."

"Was it Frances, Carly?" I insisted. "If you had to bet your life and mine and hers, was it Frances?"

"Yes, it was Frances," she replied firmly.

I took a breath. This didn't mean Emmy was in trouble. We had our doubts about Frances, but maybe, just maybe—

"Cameron, there's something else." I could hear Carly breathing quick, stressed breaths over the line. "She's pregnant. She's very pregnant."

I hung up and got on a plane.

\*\*\*\*

"What do we know?" I was on the jet, flying over the Mexican border. I had left the party without excuse, without even announcing my departure.

Carly said, "I talked to Griff. He doesn't know where she is either. She left him a note. Something about her mom being in the hospital. Something totally bogus."

"He lost her," I said through gritted teeth.

"He lost her? You *abandoned* her. Emmy's been put aside and left behind more times than one human being is capable of handling. I'm surprised she's made it this far without falling apart," Carly snapped.

Then she took a breath. "He's hysterical, Cameron. Just like the rest of us. I'm just glad we got to him before anyone else."

"Has anyone seen Frances?"

"No one. We went through her apartment and talked to her mother. No one has seen her or heard from her. Spider has guards standing outside all her known hangouts. Nothing yet."

Emmy was with Frances. I could feel it. I had overlooked Frances because—because why? Because she was the mother of Bill's child, because I didn't want to think Bill had ever been wrong about her. Because I got lazy, stopped paying attention. I had forgotten—let myself forget—my role. Nobody was ever to be left without supervision, without consequences. My epic failure to do my job was going to cost me Emmy and the child she was carrying. *My* child.

"I don't know. I just don't know," Carly whimpered. I could tell that she was starting to fall apart herself. We didn't have time for that.

"Where was she when you saw her?"

"Downtown. I was on my way to see Henry. I've been working with him to get all your funds liquidated—"

"Did you see Henry?"

"No. Obviously not! You can't think that after I saw Emmy, pregnant, leaving with Frances, that I would be worried about your damn money!"

"That's not my question, Carly. You gave Emmy Henry's information some time ago. Did Emmy go see Henry? Has anyone talked to him?"

"I'm sure Henry would have called me if she had," she said, though it was more of a question to herself. She immediately hung up.

****

"Henry's dead," was the first thing Carly told me when she called me back. I was flying over Kansas, pacing back and forth between the empty seats. "We found him in his office. Two shots to the head."

Emmy had seen Henry. Someone knew she had gone there and had assassinated Henry before he could warn us.

"She went to the Cayman Islands. Check the airport," I ordered.

When I finally landed, I was trying to get the door open before they had even stopped the plane.

Once outside, I immediately saw Carly and Tiny, who were waiting for me at the bottom of the plane's stairs. Tiny was standing, stoically. Henry was a good man—a great man. He had been loyal to all of us, asking little in return. This was a rarity. And he had practically raised Tiny.

I nodded to Tiny, and he nodded back. Whoever had murdered his uncle would pay. But right now, we had to find Emmy.

"We had someone check the flight registry. She did go to the Cayman Islands with Frances. And then she came back. No one has seen or heard from her since the plane landed." Carly's hair sprang out of her ponytail, as though she had been trying to rip it out herself. I could tell that she had been crying and was trying not to start again. "Spider went to the airport as soon as you told us, but the flight had already disembarked its passengers. We weren't there when she came out. We missed her."

"And Frances?"

"She was on the flight after Emmy. She was grabbed by a bevy of Victor's men. There were too many of them. Spider couldn't grab her himself."

I closed my eyes and rubbed my forehead. Frances had been and still was Victor's pawn. Spider had been right all along. Frances was the mole. She was the one who told Victor about Emmy, about where he could find us. She was the one who got Rocco killed. And now, she had sent Emmy into Victor's grubby fingers. No, I had sent Emmy running into Frances's arms. Frances had just taken me up on the opportunity I had allowed her.

"They have her, Cameron. They have her and the baby."

Carly wasn't helping my concentration. I would get Emmy back, one way or another. Whatever it would take. I tried to block out the images of what would happen to her if I didn't get to her fast enough, if I didn't get to her before the baby came and they started sending her to me in pieces.

"Has Victor called yet?"

Carly knew what I was asking: had Victor called to gloat, to make his demands, to use Emmy and the baby to blackmail me?

"No. Not yet."

"And you're sure it was Victor's men who picked up Frances?"

"Positive. Spider followed them out to the car. Victor was waiting for her."

"Did Frances look like she was surprised to see him?"

"No. But Spider said it looked like she had been crying and Victor's men were pretty rough with her while they led her into the car."

I opened my eyes and looked into the darkness that went beyond the small airport beams of light.

"Did you check her car?"

"We couldn't find it. We checked all of the airport parking lots near her terminal. Nothing."

"And no one has seen or heard from Emmy?"

"No one."

My eyes turned back to my car, which Tiny had driven onto the tarmac for me. In the light of the airport, from a little less than two hundred feet away, I could see the purple jacket that I had stolen from Emmy, which was still draped over the passenger-side seat. I started running.

"Where are you going?" Carly asked, running after me.

"What about her roommates?"

"No. We already checked with—"

"And her parents?"

"No one, Cameron. What's going on?"

"Keep your phone on and call me if you have any news," I told her as I slammed my door shut and sped off.

However slim, there was still a chance …

An hour later, I curved onto the driveway to the cottage, barely taking my foot off the pedal. The sun was just about to explode over the horizon, but it was still dark under the shadow of the trees and I almost slammed into the back of Emmy's car. It was halfway between the road and the cottage, and the driver-side door had been left wide-open. I was out of my car and running, catching a heart-wrenching glimpse of the blotches of blood on the front seat. I started screaming her name before the cottage was even in sight.

I came crashing through the door, scrambling to find the switch. When the light came on, I saw her. At the top of the stairs, half of her hanging over the first steps. There was blood dripping over the side of the loft onto the floor below.

"Emmy," I said as I came to her, though I hadn't found my voice yet.

She was completely limp and ghostly.

"Wake up," I told her as I pushed the hair stuck to her forehead. She did not stir.

"Emily, wake up," I said more forcefully while I rubbed her cheek, felt her slight breaths.

I took my cell phone out of my pocket and made a call to Doctor Lorne.

He picked up on the first ring, as he always did. "I'm coming in hot. Emmy's pregnant and bleeding badly." He didn't need to ask any questions, and I didn't need to tell him to be ready because he was always ready.

"You have to keep fighting, Emmy," I pleaded with her as I ran back to my car with her in my arms.

I had her head lying on my thigh as I drove like a maniac, daring some idiot cop to even try to stop me. One hand was on the wheel; the other one was on her neck.

There was a pulse. There was a pulse. And then there wasn't.

## Chapter 19: Emily

## I Was

"Wake up."

There is that one, monumental question everyone has asked themselves at one point in their lives, whether they live until they're one hundred or until they're twenty years old.

*What happens when I die?*

"Emily, wake up," I could hear myself saying to myself.

"To what?" I answered in my snidest tone.

"You have to keep fighting."

I guffawed. "I'm done with that."

And the light came.

It wasn't what I was expecting.

It was not soft and peaceful. There were no angels singing or harps playing. The music was, at least, orchestrated, but it was hot—rather blazing. Like an ant burning under a magnifying glass.

Hell?

I shouldn't have laughed at this, but I did. The old Emily Sheppard would have never done anything interesting enough to get herself to hell.

As I brushed my hands against my clothes, readying myself for what came next, I was caught off guard by how smooth my clothes were. When I looked down, I saw that I was wearing a white ballroom dress that went all the way down to my knees. And I had a spotlight on me.

I looked to my side. My mother was holding a microphone to her lips. She was wearing a similar gown, though hers glistened under the bright lights, like a mermaid's tail.

I was at my sweet sixteen party. Or rather, I was at the sweet sixteen party my mother had thrown. I just happened to be turning sixteen that day.

"Oh dear God, I really am in hell," I said aloud, but no sound came.

If this were hell, then I really was being punished for my sins. I had taken a man's life, and this did not go unnoticed, no matter how evil that man had been.

All of a sudden, my mother's face disappeared, and the spotlight softened. The orchestra's music died, and a breeze picked up, cooling me off. I was able to see off the stage, see a blank-faced crowd of my parents' friends—acquaintances—standing in tuxedos and prom dresses. They swayed with the breeze. It felt as though I were standing before a cornfield of people waiting to be cultivated.

I took a step forward and got off my mother's stage. My feet were bare.

As soon as my toes touched the grass, the corn crowd parted with my every step, letting me walk by them without me having to touch them, without them having to touch me.

I got to the edge of the pool.

"Cameron," I called out.

Even if I couldn't see him, I knew he was there. He had always been there. I just didn't know how to look for him.

The swarm of faceless people on the other side of the pool parted, and Cameron walked through. He was wearing a gray hooded sweater and jeans. And a baseball cap that was pulled down to his eyebrows, shadowing his features. Like the first day we met. But with every step he took, he transformed. By the time he reached the other edge of the pool, he was dressed in a tuxedo, with his collar undone and his black bow hanging loose.

He smiled.

It was amazing to me how quickly he could take my breath away.

I had missed him.

I had missed seeing him—his face, his shoulders, his hands.

I reached out to him, even though there was a pool of water between us. I could feel him taking hold of me, cloaking me like a ray of sun.

I let him enfold me like that for a little while, knowing that something was wrong. Something was very wrong.

I put my hands against his chest, against his heart, and I pushed him away.

"We have a child," I whispered to him. But again, no sound came from my mouth.

I brought my hands to my stomach and found that it was flattened. Empty.

Suddenly, the pool was between us again.

I took a step back and stopped there, beaming at Cameron. He frowned.

I took another step back. He reached for me.

I shook my head.

"I'll see you later," I mouthed to him.

"Stay with me," he pleaded.

I smiled at my beautiful Cameron. "I'll be right back."

I turned into the darkness.

## Chapter 20: Cameron

## And Then I Wasn't

When you lose the person you've always lived for, do you die?
Do your lungs just stop taking in air?
Does the blood stop flowing to your brain?
Do you turn to dust and disappear as though you never were?

# Emily's Epilogue

## Billy

An eye for an eye, a life for a life. We'll all pay for the blood we spill. Ultimately.
But not yet.

****

It was the incessant sound of beeping that roused me.

When my eyes fluttered open, I found myself in a room, in an elevated bed, surrounded by the machines that had awoken me and that I was apparently plugged into. I couldn't feel my legs, and the parts of me that I could feel were numbed.

It occurred to me that I might be in a hospital, except that the room didn't have the coldness and sterility of a hospital room. And it smelled of manure.

The mattress was soft and not plastic-coated, and a crocheted blanket had been placed over me. My hand slowly pushed it down and stopped when it reached my stomach. I couldn't feel anything below my chest, but I could feel the hollowness of my insides. A scream rose up from my empty nest, but the noise that escaped my parched vocal chords was barely a mouse's whisper.

Something stirred next to me.

I forced my head to turn and nearly jumped out of my skin.

Spider was nestled in a comfy chair, surrounded by pillows, with his legs up on an ottoman. A plate of pastries lay on a table next to him, with a carton of chocolate milk. You'd think he was on vacation at a chalet by the sea. I tried to move quietly, not wanting to rouse Cameron's killer. Thinking I could actually escape before he caught me.

He turned his head slowly. Our stares met. His eyes were dull, and he was blanched. He looked as surprised to see me as I was to see him.

"My baby. Where's my baby?" I croaked at him. Spider was slightly panicked as I started to push my way out of the bed, simultaneously tugging at the wires that were sticking out of my arms. I was trying to roll myself over, making up for my numbed legs.

"Carly!" he called out, though his voice was faint.

White coats came rushing in, followed by Carly. She was carrying a roll in a blanket. A bundle that was not moving. I kept my eyes focused on the blanket while medical staff plugged me back in.

"Billy's here," I thought I heard Carly utter.

*My brother? Billy? It can't be.* "That's not possible," I heard myself growl, my eyes always on the immovable object in her arms.

Carly's face went pale, as though she hadn't expected me to hear her. "We didn't know what you wanted to name her. We just thought ... You can change her name to anything you want, of course. She just reminded me so much of Bill."

She took a step forward but was held back by one of the coats. "Not yet. She's simply not strong enough."

The back of my brain recognized this doctor. But the rest of me didn't give a damn.

"She?" I wondered.

Carly pushed the doctor aside and made her way to the side of the bed.

I immediately extended my feeble arms, yearning to get the bundle—my child ... my little girl—into my arms.

Carly resisted. "There's something I need to tell you."

My gaze reached hers. I could see the doctor—Doctor Lorne, I remembered—shaking his head in my peripheral vision, disapproving.

The darkness was creeping up on me, as though answering the question, giving me the answer I needed to know, giving me the answer I didn't want to know.

"Is she ..." I started to ask, but I couldn't finish the sentence.

Carly looked horrified. "Oh no, no. It's not that. No, Billy is just fine. She's sleeping like a rock."

She immediately forgot what she was going to tell me and placed my bundle on my chest. She folded my bloodless arms over so that I could keep hold of my baby girl.

The background noise disappeared.

Seeing Billy for the first time was like putting a face on all the love and the joy I had in me, I had ever felt, multiplied to infinity. I didn't know something so beautiful could even exist in this ugly world. She opened her striking green eyes—my striking green eyes—and for the first time, we saw each other. For the longest time, she had been hidden inside me, and now I could see myself in her.

She watched me as if deep in thought, finally putting a face to the voice she had been hearing for months. It was like her pink skin was magnetized so that I couldn't pull my eyes away from her, so that I had to touch her.

My hand found its way to her mouth, where it lingered, feeling the hotness of her tiny breaths. My thumb found its way to her nose, brushing the cluster of dry skin that was splashed across it, like the tail of a shooting star. I examined every inch of her face. I unfolded the blanket and found her miniature hands. Then I pushed the hat off her head, and a spring of black hair popped out—her father's hair.

I pushed myself up and put my cheek against hers.

"She's tiny but mighty," Carly murmured, smiling from one side of her face to the other. Smiling from some deep-rooted place. "She drank a whole bottle in almost one gulp. I've never seen anything like it."

"Billy," I called her. It was perfect.

Spider was up and standing by the bed, holding on to the rail with a bandaged arm. I could have sworn he'd grinned when he looked down at Billy. Then a hush spread around the room like an earthquake. Spider's eyes turned to the doorway, so I followed his gaze.

It took a few seconds for my brain to believe what my eyes were describing.

"Cameron," I exhaled. Cameron stared at me, unmoving, afraid to take a step. Bright-red blood covered his white tuxedo shirt and had crusted his pants.

Carly reached for Billy as my arms started shaking.

I heard Billy crying as she was pulled away. I was desperately trying to hold on to the light. but it was like trying to climb up a greased-up rope.

Then the light was gone.

\*\*\*\*

I was arched over, my hands gripping the wooden rail in front of me. That was the only way I could keep from falling over. The stitch along the bottom of my belly hurt so bad I could barely walk and couldn't stand fully erect. Like the Hunchback of Notre Dame.

I watched the horses in the patch over the cobblestone driveway. There were so many cars in the driveway you'd think they were lining up for a parade, with Cameron's black Audi at the head. But there was no parade. And it was very quiet.

Guards could be seen throughout the property, if you knew where to look for them. But I kept my eyes trained on the horses. Most of them were far out in the pasture, avoiding the fuss. But two stood guard at the fence, keeping an eye on Meatball, who was trying to go say hello but his big head wouldn't fit through the fence's levers. So he sat and whined instead.

The wind picked up, and I hugged the shawl Carly had insisted on putting over my shoulders before I escaped to the porch. The breeze was warm and I was standing in the sun, yet I was still shivering. I felt like I had already lived a thousand lives, so I supposed the old-lady shawl was appropriate. Carly had wanted me to stay in bed, but Doctor Lorne ordered me to get back on my feet, to get some fresh air and stretch out. I needed time alone, time to think. So I followed the doctor's orders.

When I heard the porch's whitewashed floorboards creak behind me, I diverted my attention from the horses and saw Cameron approaching, Billy nestled in his arms. He was skin and bones, as though he had really been dead.

"I picked her up when she woke, but she fell back asleep," he whispered, his eyes on Billy. She was mummy-wrapped in a million blankets. With only her chubby little face peeking through, she looked like a peapod. Carly's fussing, I guessed.

"I thought she might be cold, so I put another blanket around her," Cameron admitted, like he knew what I was thinking and needed to prove me wrong.

He looked up at me, but I kept my eyes on my beautiful baby girl, who was sleeping in her father's arms. She looked peaceful, like she was exactly where she was always supposed to be. The fact that she and I almost didn't make it, the fact that I had almost lost her, crossed my mind again. But I blocked this out before my imagination ran wild. She was here, with me, right now, and I would be forever grateful to Doctor Lorne. And forever grateful to Spider.

Cameron must have sensed I was itching to have her in my arms because he gently grabbed my elbow and helped me to the swing, handing me Billy as soon as I was seated. He then amassed the cushions from all the chairs. After building a fort of cushions around Billy and me, he sat down, swung my legs onto his, and swayed us back and forth on the swing.

Feeling his legs under mine made my heart twist in confusion. I could hardly bring myself to look at him. I longed to touch him, hold him tight, never let go. How many nights had I wished I could be with him just one more time?

But now, seeing him, being so near to him brought me so much pain. The pain of betrayal, of abandonment. I could hardly breathe. I never knew that I would be able to love and hate someone at the same time.

"You left us, Cameron," I said. It was barely a sigh.

"I had no idea. I should have, would have never ..." he started, then stopped. He swallowed hard and looked into my eyes, searching. "I didn't know you were pregnant, Emmy. I didn't know about Billy."

"Sorry," I snapped. "Let me rephrase that. You left *me*, Cameron. And I cried over you. Every night, for whole days at a time, for months after you died. After you supposedly died. How could you do that to a person you supposedly loved?"

"*Love*," he corrected me. "Never *loved*, never supposedly. Love in the past, the present, and the always." He kept his dark eyes on me. "To say I made the wrong choice, the wrong decision, is like saying the sun sets in the west. I'll never forgive myself."

We sat in silence, rocking slowly, Cameron's hands resting on my ankles, as though we had been doing this for years.

"What happens now?" I finally asked him.

"I don't know, Emmy," he said, keeping us on a swaying rhythm. "But whatever happens, we'll figure it out together."

Together. I wondered what the future would hold. I wondered whether I would ever be able to forgive him for the agony he caused me. The pain. It was still there. The knife had been pulled out, but the wound continued to gush.

But I loved him. Undoubtedly. Fully.

Carly and Spider joined us on the porch. Carly pulled a chair up, trying to sit as close to Billy and me as she possibly could, and

Spider leaned over the railing. He still had a bandage on his arm where Doctor Lorne had punctured his skin to get to the blood that was rare, the blood that was the same as mine.

I had died. When Cameron brought me to Doctor Lorne, I didn't have a pulse, or so Doctor Lorne had explained to me. I had just lost too much blood. They told Cameron that I was probably not going to make it. Doctor Lorne had saved Billy, though, and he had saved me. But most of all, Spider, his blood, had saved me from death, and it would run through my veins. In the end, Spider and I were going to be forever linked. Serendipity.

A car came tearing through the driveway, and Griff jumped out of the passenger side before Tiny even had a chance to fully stop. I couldn't even think about what I was going to say to him.

My eyes went back down to check on the hot bundle in my arms.

Meatball limped to Griff, and they made their way to the porch.

And Billy slept while the horses neighed in the pasture.

*Where do we go from here?* I wondered.

*Who the hell knows?* I answered myself.

But whatever happened, we were in this together.

For Billy.

## Cameron's Epilogue

## Billy

A woman in love with a man who only rejects her could just about be the most dangerous thing on the planet. I used to think this, foolishly. Until I had a daughter.

The love of a father for his little girl?

It's a weapon of mass destruction.

It's something you just don't fuck with.

# Acknowledgments

Thank you to my husband for being my Cameron inspiration, sans the drugs and violence and bloodshed. Okay, maybe not so much like Cameron—rather, my love inspiration.

Thank you to my kids for napping in the afternoon so that Mommy could finish this book, and to my mom and dad for being nothing like Isabelle and Burt Sheppard.

To Sophie Normand: if it weren't for all those fall-head-over-heels relationships and subsequent inevitable broken hearts, this book would have never come to be. We laughed, we cried, we cried some more, we laughed again. We grew up eventually.

A special thank you to Alan Bower. Alan has changed the lives (in a good way) of so many self-published authors out there (I know—I googled him). There aren't many people in the world who can look beyond the ugly words (mine) of a first-time author (me) and see the story. There are even fewer people who listen to the readers, appreciate the passion they have for a book. Alan, you have done so much for *Crow's Row*. You make me hope that someday, if I keep working at it, I won't cringe every time I reread something I wrote.

Thank you to my editors, Elizabeth Day and Cheri Madison, for using kid gloves in telling me that *Scare Crow* still needed a lot of work and for being the reader that nightmares are made of.

And thank you to iUniverse and Author Solutions: when everyone turned *Crow's Row* down, you were there to ensure that Cam and Emmy's story would be shared with the world and not just end up at the bottom of my closet with the rest of the things I don't know what to do with.

Now, to the fans of *Crow's Row*. Where do I start? You guys are crazy. You drive me crazy. I appreciate your offers to babysit my children so that I can write, though there were times when I thought that if I didn't finish *Scare Crow*, one of you was going to come to my house, hopefully make my kids dinner, and chain me to my computer until I was done. Let's face it: if it weren't for your constant hounding (in a loving and encouraging way, of course), I would have never finished *Scare Crow*. Cameron and Emily's story would have stopped after *Crow's Row*, and it would still be gnawing away at all of us. I hope that you liked *Scare Crow*. I hope that I did justice to Cam and Emmy's story. Otherwise, I'm afraid for my life.

Made in the USA
Middletown, DE
24 August 2015